Praise for Susan M

'Witty dialogue, plenty of rom
delicious charact
—*Publishers Weekly* on S

'A wonderfully fast-paced delight! You can never go wrong with Ms Mallery's fascinating storytelling.'
—*Romance Reviews Today* on *Sweet Success*

'When you think of passion, drama and heart-warming stories, think Susan Mallery. As always, she delivers a top-notch story.'
—*Romantic Times*

Praise for Jennifer Archer:

'Lighthearted, funny, a delight to read.'
—Jodi Thomas, *New York Times* bestselling author, on *Body and Soul*

'A fun, exciting, humorous, fast-moving story!'
—*Romantic Times* on *Once Upon a Dream*

'…well written and clever. It's an all around fun book to read.'
—*The Romance Reader* on *Shocking Behaviour*

A Mother's Day

THERE'S ALWAYS PLAN B

by
Susan Mallery

SANDWICHED

by
Jennifer Archer

M&B™ and M&B™ with the Rose Device are trademarks of the publisher.

First published in Great Britain 2007 by Harlequin Mills & Boon Limited, Eton House, 18-24 Paradise Road, Richmond, Surrey TW9 1SR

A MOTHER'S DAY © by Harlequin Books SA 2007

There's Always Plan B © Susan Macias-Redmond 2005
Sandwiched © Jennifer Archer 2005

ISBN 13: 978 0 263 85552 4
ISBN 10: 0 263 85552 X

24-0207

Printed in Great Britain by Clays Ltd, St Ives plc

THERE'S ALWAYS PLAN B

by
Susan Mallery

To Gail Chasan who said
this would be a great idea,
and who turned out to be right

Susan Mallery makes her home in Southern California, where the eccentricities of a writer are actually considered normal – what a relief! When she's not working on her latest novel, she can be found cruising the local boutiques in her quest for another pair of shoes. Susan would love to claim to be a fabulous gourmet chef, but she is not. She does, however, do fabulous take-away ordering and always serves said take-away on lovely china.

Don't miss Susan Mallery's latest novel,
The Sheikh and the Virgin Secretary,
which is available in March.

"I don't know why you always have to torture me," fifteen-year-old Tiffany Spencer said as she folded her arms over her chest and stared out the passenger-door window. "Some moms actually like their children. Some moms care about their happiness. Why can't you be like that?"

Carly Spencer tightened her grip on the steering wheel and tried to figure out why she'd ever complained about her daughter asking, "Are we there yet?" when she'd been younger. Given a choice between that question and the one currently on the table, "Are we there yet?" seemed amusingly simple to deal with.

"I care about your happiness," she said, even though she knew it was a huge mistake to engage her daughter. At this point it was obvious Tiffany simply wanted to be the martyr to all decisions parental.

"Ha! Oh, sure. Because dragging me away from all my friends and my school and Justin Beakly, who looks just like Matt Damon and who was probably going to ask me to the Spring Carnival dance, is going to make me faint with happiness. Here I am. Fainting."

Tiffany collapsed against the door. Carly hoped her daughter would stay mock-unconscious for at least ten minutes or until the headache remedy Carly had popped a few minutes before had a chance to kick in.

But it was not to be.

"And if we had to leave all that because you're so determined to ruin my life," Tiffany said seconds later, "you could have at least let me get my belly button pierced. I mean what's the big deal? It's *my* body. I bet I'll be the only high school girl here, too, without one. Although maybe not. Have they heard about piercing at the ends of the Earth?"

Her daughter was certainly bright enough, Carly thought, as she desperately searched for a silver lining in what felt like the world's largest dark cloud. Eventually Tiffany would learn to use her highly developed verbal skills for good instead of mother abuse.

"I don't know what they've heard," Carly said cheerfully. "It's possible they're still existing with horse-drawn carriages and cooking on an open fire. Maybe we'll be so modern, they'll think we're aliens from another planet and they can worship us like goddesses."

Tiffany rolled her eyes. "You're not helping."

"Ditto."

"What do you mean by that?"

"You're not helping, either," Carly said. "This move is tough on me, too."

"But it's your fault we have to go." Tiffany sounded outraged. She turned in her seat and glared. "If you hadn't made Dad leave, we wouldn't be doing this."

Carly drew in a deep breath and counted to ten. When

that didn't work, she counted to twenty, then promised herself no matter what, she would go to the grocery store later, buy a pint of Ben & Jerry's cookie dough ice cream and eat the entire thing by herself.

Tiffany was a still a child, she reminded herself. Under the carefully curled blond hair, the formfitting clothes and too much makeup lurked a young teenager not yet prepared to deal with the realities of the world.

"Your father and I divorced by mutual decision," she said slowly, going for an "I'm so calm" voice instead of the shrill tone that lurked just beneath the surface. "There were a lot of issues, some of which are private."

"He quit his job." Tiffany sounded both shocked and scared. "Just like that. He says he's sailing to Hawaii."

"I heard that, too." At times she thought her soon-to-be ex was a complete mystery. Other times she hoped he got lost at sea.

"I should have stayed in L.A. with Dad," Tiffany mumbled. "I could have moved into his apartment and not had to change schools."

Carly ignored that mostly because she didn't know what to say. In truth, Neil hadn't been interested in sharing custody of his daughter. It was as if once he'd decided to leave, his only child no longer existed for him. Carly couldn't understand that, but in the past few weeks she'd realized that Neil had become a stranger to her. Maybe he always had been. Maybe she'd been fooling herself throughout their marriage.

What she didn't know was how it was possible to live with a man for sixteen years, have his child, sleep with him, talk to him, plan a future with him and find out she'd been wrong about almost everything. Her mind spun every time she thought about it.

"Are we there yet?" Tiffany asked.

Carly chuckled. At last a question she could answer. "About another forty minutes."

Now that they were north of San Francisco, Carly found herself studying the changing landscape. The Northern California coastline was as rugged as it was beautiful. She remembered the narrow, rocky beaches, the high cliffs, the storms that would blow through. But mostly, she remembered the beautiful bed-and-breakfast/house where she'd grown up.

Chatsworth-by-the-Sea had once been an elegant English manor with a different name. Her great-great—however many greats—grandfather had made his fortune during the gold rush in the 1850s. Determined to leave a legacy, he'd bought a massive house in England and had it brought over stone by stone.

For Carly, Chatsworth-by-the-Sea had always been *home*. With everything going on in her life, she longed to return to the comfortable welcome she'd always found there. And yet she felt unsettled.

"I can't wait to see the old place again," she said. "You always liked it, too."

Tiffany shrugged. "To visit. I never thought we'd live there. Is Grandma going to make us do work and stuff?"

"You'll have a few chores, but nothing worse than you had before." Carly almost said "at home" but stopped herself in time. The last thing she needed was Tiffany in tears again. Her daughter's blue eyes were still swollen from that morning's crying jag.

Not that Tiffany was the only one upset about leaving behind their house in Santa Monica. Change was never easy. Given the choice, Carly would have stayed put. But she hadn't had a choice. The difference was she'd kept her pain and sadness to herself. After all, she was the mom and it was up to her to be the strong one. Carly didn't mind that so much. What made things really hard was the sense of being trapped by circumstances she couldn't control.

"Are you going to run the bed-and-breakfast for Grandma?" Tiffany asked.

"That's the plan. I'll learn the family business and take over responsibilities. In two years, Grandma will move to Las Vegas."

Carly's mother had already bought a town house in a complex she liked and was renting it out until she was ready to retire there. After Rhonda left for the wilds of Nevada, Carly would claim the wonderful B and B as her own. She would have a secure job, an income and an inheritance to leave her daughter. It was really the perfect solution for everyone.

Carly knew she should be grateful that everything had worked out so well. She had a job and a place for her and her daughter to live, while her mother would be able to move somewhere warm and go to bingo every day.

So why did she feel so lousy? Why did it seem that less than two months from turning forty, her life was already over?

"What would Grandma have done if you and Dad hadn't split up?" Tiffany asked. "Would we still have moved here to run things?"

"I don't know what would have happened," Carly said, which was both true and a lie. She and Neil had never discussed the fate of the B and B because he'd made it more than clear he wasn't interested. But there was no way Carly would have let her mother sell it. Not after it had been in the family nearly a hundred and fifty years.

"I still would rather live in Santa Monica," Tiffany said. "It was great there. This is going to be totally gross."

"'Gross' is harsh. I know moving to a small town is going to be different for you," Carly told her daughter. "But there's still a lot to do. The mall's not that far away. There are movie theaters and lots of after-school activities."

Tiffany wrinkled her nose, but didn't speak.

"I had a favorite place high in one of the towers," Carly continued. "I used to take a book up there and read on rainy afternoons."

"Oh, yeah, *that* sounds thrilling."

So much sarcasm dripped off the words that Carly half expected to see a puddle on the car mat.

"There's also the ghost," she reminded her daughter.

Tiffany only looked bored. "I never saw the ghost except for that stupid painting in the dining room. Are you sure it's real? I don't think anyone believes in ghosts anymore, Mom."

"I do. At least I did when I was your age." The ghost was one of Carly's favorite memories from growing up. Like the way the house looked at Christmas or on a stormy night.

In truth, she was willing to admit that while the ghost had been very real to her when she'd been Tiffany's age, now she had a little more trouble believing. But she wasn't willing to let the idea go completely.

"I used to read up in the tower room and sometimes I'd look up and see a pale, shimmering essence right there, next to me."

"I don't think a 'shimmering essence' counts as an actual ghost, Mom," Tiffany said. "Besides, Daddy always said it was bogus. Whoever heard of a ghost named Mary?"

"He never came to the B and B, so he wouldn't know. We're in all the ghost registries, including the national one. They're very fussy about who they register. Chatsworth-by-the-Sea is famous for our spectral phenomena. We've had scientists and ghostbusters visiting for as long as the house has been here. No one has ever been able to prove there *wasn't* a ghost."

Tiffany frowned. "But she's like nice, right?"

"Of course."

"I don't want her hanging around when I'm getting dressed and stuff."

Carly grinned. "I thought you didn't believe in ghosts."

"I don't. But maybe, I don't know, there's something." Tiffany glanced at Carly. "How did she die?"

"I don't know. We couldn't find out that information about her. I know your great-grandmother did a lot of research on Mary and never discovered much about her. The theory is she somehow came over with the house. The documentation about her says her clothes appear to be from the Regency era. That's around 1811. She's young—maybe twenty-two or so. She likes flowers."

"How do you know?"

"I saw her in the garden once." Or she'd seen something. It had been close to midnight, on a perfect summer evening. Carly had been around her daughter's age and hating life as much as Tiffany did when things didn't go her way. She'd been crying and there'd been some kind of...

"More shimmering essence?" Tiffany asked.

"Yeah." It could have been moonlight or shadows.

Tiffany shook her head. "She's not *real*."

"I know, but she's still entitled to her privacy."

Carly shrugged. Okay. Maybe it *was* a stretch to think there was a real ghost, but the possibility was there. To her mind Mary had always been a wary and benevolent presence. Almost a friend. After all she'd been through, Carly figured she needed all the friends she could get.

As soon as she and Neil had started telling people they were getting a divorce, Carly had been stunned by all the supposed friends who had disappeared from her life. It was as if she had a contagious disease they were desperate to avoid. Suddenly women she'd known for years weren't returning her calls and were too busy to have lunch. She'd felt more and more isolated. Then Neil had moved out and Tiffany had gotten even more difficult.

When Carly's mother had called to offer her the chance to take over the B and B, Carly had accepted. Moving north would give Tiffany a chance to finish her education in an excellent high school in a charming town. Carly could still work full-time while being around for her daughter. Both of them would have a chance to start over.

The only potentially troubling aspect of the plan was that Carly and her mother had never exactly been close. There was too much friction between them.

"I'll make it work," Carly murmured. She had to. There weren't a lot of other options.

"Are you talking to yourself?" her daughter asked.

"Yes. Does it make you nervous?"

"No. It's just weird."

"Which you expect from me," Carly said.

"Pretty much."

Carly nodded. Not a surprise. She'd always wanted to be one of those cool moms, but somehow she hadn't figured out how. If being cool meant letting her daughter get her belly button pierced or stay out until midnight or date older guys, then Carly was willing to be weird and difficult.

They exited the highway and turned toward the ocean. Chatsworth-by-the-Sea stood on the edge of a cliff over-looking the Pacific. Wooden steps led down to the beach below. There were beautiful grounds, a few hardy vineyards and some fruit trees, but for Carly, nothing compared with the wonder of being able to watch the ever-changing ocean. She liked storms best, although sunny days were great, too.

"This is going to be a lot of fun," she said to Tiffany. "You'll see."

"Fun for you, maybe. You're getting everything you want. I'm getting nothing and it's your fault I don't have my dad anymore. I hate you."

The unfairness of the accusation burned Carly down to her bones. As Tiffany began to cry softly into a tissue, Carly had to fight her own pain. Oh, yeah, this was everything she'd ever wanted. Running a bed-and-breakfast, living with her mother and daughter, trapped in a life that wasn't the one she'd chosen. She was making the best of a bad situation. She was doing most of this *for* Tiffany so her daughter could have a sense of place and belonging.

Carly considered several responses, and tossed them all away. Sometimes the better course of action was to suck it up and wait it out, which is what she decided to do. But once, just once, she would like someone to consider *her* feelings. She would like someone to take responsibility, to do the right thing and let her have the tantrum.

She drove down the familiar street and reminded herself that she would soon be back in the house where she grew up. At least she would have her mother to help. The burdens wouldn't be hers alone.

"We're nearly there," she told her daughter. "If you're crying, Grandma's going to have about fifty thousand questions."

"I know." Tiffany sniffed, then wiped her face. "I just wish you'd been a better wife."

As far as knife wounds went, this one cut right to Carly's heart. But before she could catch her breath, or think of a response, they'd pulled into the large gravel parking lot to the side of the massive four-story building that was Chatsworth-by-the-Sea.

Carly parked next to her mother's Jeep and turned off the engine. The pain faded as she studied the stone structure, the climbing ivy, the old and familiar trees. She could see the first of the towers.

"We're here," she said, as if Tiffany wouldn't notice the big house in front of them. "Let's go find Grandma."

Right now what Carly needed more than anything was a hug and a promise that everything would be all right. She wanted to drink cocoa and eat cookies and pretend she was Tiffany's age and the biggest problem she had was fitting in at school.

"Just leave the luggage for now," Carly said as she climbed out of the car. "We can get it later."

The crunch of her feet on the gravel made her smile. The sound was familiar, as was the scent of flowers and sea and something undefinable but old that had always made her think of home. Because it *was* home. It was simpler, easier times—when the world still made sense.

She led the way through the side yard where herbs and vegetables grew to a wooden door that led through the mudroom into the kitchen. At this time of day, her mother would be preparing the appetizers that were served from four-thirty to six.

"Hi, Mom, it's us," Carly called as she walked into the large, airy kitchen.

Rhonda Washington stood at the wide center island, cutting slices of cheese. She glanced up when her daughter and granddaughter entered, smiled and put down her knife.

"How was the drive? You made excellent time. Tiffany, you're growing up to be so beautiful. Did your mom feed you something decent or have you been living on junk food all day?"

"Hi, Grandma."

Tiffany stepped into the offered hug and didn't answer the question. Carly ignored the flash of irritation and told herself that her mother hadn't meant it as a criticism. Not really.

To distract herself, she studied the different generations of women, noting that Tiffany was a couple of inches taller, but that they shared both bone structure and eye color.

Rhonda had been born blond. Over time the color had darkened to a light brown, only to fade into gray. Tiffany's pale blond had yet to darken at all, although Carly suspected it would with time. But the similarities didn't end there. Both of them had the same smile and ability to speak their minds in a way that left her dodging bullets.

A small price to pay for sanctuary, Carly reminded herself.

Rhonda kissed her granddaughter on the cheek, then turned to Carly. "How's my baby girl?"

"Good, Mom. I'm doing okay."

"Are you sure?"

Eyes as blue as her own studied her face. Carly offered a smile she was pretty sure looked sincere and even normal, then stepped into her mother's embrace. Familiar scents and memories enveloped her. Her mother's insistence on wearing Chanel No. 5 perfume every single day of her life. The warmth in the hug.

"It's good to have you here," Rhonda said.

"It's good to *be* here."

They straightened. Carly noted there were a few more lines around her mother's eyes and mouth, a slight drooping at her shoulders, but otherwise she looked much as she always had. The Washington women seemed to have sturdy genes, a fact Carly appreciated as she stood less than two months from turning forty.

"Let's get you two settled," Rhonda said. "I'm so excited that we're going to be living together. Three generations in the same house. It will be like the Waltons."

"The who?" Tiffany asked as she snagged a slice of cheese.

"Some old show on TV," Carly told her. "A big family living in one house. They all said good-night to John-Boy. You sort of had to be there."

Tiffany didn't look convinced by the thrill of the experience. "So where do we sleep? I have my own room, right? I mean I have to. I'm fifteen, Grandma."

"I know. It's amazing how fast you're growing. Of course you have your own room. Two rooms, really. I picked them out especially for you. I think you'll really like them. They're in the tower."

Tiffany stiffened. "The one with the ghost?"

Her grandmother drew her eyebrows together. "No, dear. Not by the ghost. What a silly question. Carly, honey, you're on the third floor in one of the older rooms. You can pick something else if you'd like."

"I'm sure it will be fine," Carly said, knowing that "older room" wasn't a euphemism. No doubt the room her mother had picked for her hadn't been refurbished in close to a hundred years.

While the working section of the B and B had twenty-five bedrooms and five suites, the house had closer to forty. Some were too small to be used for guests. Others were in noisy areas, or didn't get any light. When the house had been converted from a private residence to a B and B in the 1930s, some bedrooms had been held back for family.

Carly followed her mother to the old-fashioned elevator that took them to the third floor. From there they had to walk to the tower staircase.

"Are you going to be comfortable here on your own?" Carly asked her daughter.

Tiffany's response was to roll her eyes and sigh heavily.

"She's not a child," Rhonda said crisply. "She's an independent young woman who needs her privacy."

"See," Tiffany said as she raised her chin. "Grandma doesn't think I'm a child."

Carly knew there was no point having *that* conversation. She went up the stairs to the narrow door that led to the tower rooms.

"Isn't this terrific?" Rhonda asked as she opened the door and stepped inside.

Originally three rooms had made up the tower. The smallest had been converted into a bathroom. The other two consisted of a small bedroom and a sitting room.

"I brought up a desk so you have a place to study," Rhonda said. "The bedspread is new and the wallpaper is only a few years old. Of course we can replace it all if you'd like."

Tiffany walked through the rooms. "They're great," she said, sounding delighted and surprised.

Carly agreed with both assessments. This tower faced south, so it got a lot of light. There were windows in both rooms, with the one in the sitting area looking out over the ocean.

The bright floral-print wallpaper provided a cheerful color palate played out in the rooms. The bedspread was lavender, the desk-chair cushion pink and the club chair and ottoman had been done in periwinkle. Thick carpeting covered what had been hardwood floors.

Instead of a closet, each room had an armoire. The bathroom was tiny but functional. There were bookcases, shelves and what signified true joy in any teenager's life—a phone.

"I love it!" her daughter said happily as she moved from one room to the other. "I love everything about it."

Carly winced. She was happy that Tiffany was pleased, but a little wounded that she couldn't be the one to provide the joy.

Rhonda pointed to the phone. "Your own line. I wrote the phone number down somewhere." She checked the pad on the desk and pointed to the top sheet. "Here it is. I got you a plan that gives you fifty dollars' worth of long distance a month so you can stay in touch with your old friends."

Tiffany's eyes filled with tears, but for once they were happy ones. "Oh, Grandma, you're the best." She hugged Rhonda.

Carly sighed with relief. She'd been afraid her daughter would hate everything about the house and the move, but finding such great digs at the end of the trip would go a long way to setting things right.

We may just survive this after all, she thought happily. Wouldn't that be great?

"Want to see your room?" her mother asked.

"Sure."

They went back the way they'd come, taking the stairs down a floor. A large set of double doors closed off the guest section of the floor from the private part of the house. Rhonda went through one of them and walked to the end of the corridor.

Here the house was much older and not nearly so shiny. There was dust in the corners and bits of backing showing through the carpet.

"I picked a corner room to give you more light," her mother said as she opened the last door on the right.

Carly stepped into a big room with windows on two

walls. The furniture was old—original Art Deco style—which she loved. The bedspread looked new and out of place with the gleaming wood, but she figured she could change that later. There was a big armoire, a desk in the corner and a chair pulled up in front of the window facing the ocean.

"It's great," she said.

"Are you sure?" Her mother sounded worried. "I know it's not new. Usually when you visit you stay in one of the guest rooms and they're much nicer."

"It's fine," Carly assured her. "I'll enjoy the quiet." She knew her mother kept a suite of rooms on the first floor.

"Good."

Tiffany glanced around. "Where's the bathroom?"

"Down the hall," Rhonda said. "But she doesn't have to share it."

"Cool. I'll go get my stuff and start taking it upstairs," Tiffany said as she bolted for the door. "When will the truck arrive?"

Most of their furniture had been sold, but they'd kept a few things.

"Tomorrow," Carly told her. "Think you can survive without your TV until then?"

"Oh, Mom. Of course I can. I'm not totally worthless."

Tiffany ran down the hallway toward the elevator. Carly walked to the window and stared out.

"It's the same view," she said, feeling the pain and uncertainty fade away. Coming back to the B and B had made sense. Of the very few choices open to her, this one had the most opportunity for success. If it wasn't the life she would have chosen, so what? At least she had a place to go and someone to help her get back on her feet.

"I'm glad you're here," her mother said.

"Me, too. The past couple of months have been a nightmare, but it's all behind us now. Tiffany and I can start over. I really appreciate the opportunity, Mom."

"Yes, well, this has always been your home. I'm just glad you wanted to come here so I didn't have to sell the place."

Carly turned to her mother. "You wouldn't really have done that, would you?"

"Oh, it's so big and a lot of work. I'm not getting any younger."

"But you have your staff. It's not as if you're cleaning rooms yourself."

"I know, but there are responsibilities." Her mother cleared her throat. "People aren't traveling the way they used to. In my day, travel was an adventure. Now most folks would rather sit home and watch cable." She shrugged. "But that's all right. Now that you're here, we'll get things on track."

Carly didn't like the sound of that. "What do you mean?"

"There have been a few lean years. I've wanted to make some repairs—needed to, really—but I couldn't. This is your legacy, Carly. It makes sense to invest in it."

The cold, dark panic of the past two months returned. Invest? What did she mean *invest?* "What are you talking about, Mom? Is the B and B in financial trouble?"

Rhonda avoided eye contact, instead giving the bedspread an unnecessary tug. "Just a little. But with your divorce settlement, we can get on our feet financially."

If Carly had been able to breathe, she would have laughed.

As it was she could only stare in disbelief. She'd come here seeking safety and security, but apparently that was not to be.

"You had all the equity in the house," Rhonda continued. "Neil had that great job for all those years. I know you probably don't want to tap into your savings, but you'll earn it back. Plus you have the alimony and child support. We'll be fine."

Carly's chest tightened. "Mom, there's no money. No savings, no house equity. I got half of everything, including half of the debts. I couldn't afford to stay in L.A. That's why I came here."

"You're wrong," her mother said. "There has to be money. You're just being ridiculous, and selfish." Disapproval tightened her face. "I expected you to be more mature about everything."

Carly opened her mouth, then closed it. She'd been home all of four minutes. Maybe she and her mother could put off fighting for at least an hour.

"Let's talk about this later," Carly said with a smile. "Right now I'm just happy to see you."

Rhonda didn't look mollified but she didn't speak, either. Probably because they could hear Tiffany heading toward them. The teenager clumped down the two back stairs and entered the bedroom.

"Mom, I brought one of your suitcases."

"Thanks."

Tiffany shrugged. "It was on top of mine. Anyway, there's tons more stuff."

They spent the next fifteen minutes unloading the car. Carly went up to Tiffany's room to make sure she had started unpacking, only to be told by her daughter that she wasn't a baby and could manage emptying a suitcase without supervision.

"Feel the love," Carly murmured as she walked down one floor to her room and stepped inside.

The view captured her attention instantly. She crossed to the window and stared out at the ocean. Living in Santa Monica had meant they were within a couple miles of the water, but nothing compared with living so close to the vastness. She loved how the colors changed with the variations in light and weather. The water could be dark blue one minute, then gray, then nearly black, then almost turquoise. As a teenager, when it had seemed her world would never be right, she could always count on the ocean.

After unpacking her clothes and putting them in the dresser and hanging a few things in the armoire, she walked downstairs and into the main rooms of the B and B. There was a parlor to the left of the big, open foyer. Sofas and chairs sat in groups in a semicircle around the big fireplace. She noted the furnishings were exactly as she remembered, although the hardwood floors looked as if they'd been refinished not that long ago.

On the other side of the foyer was the dining room. A long table that seated fourteen stood in the center of the space. Several smaller tables seating four or six were up against the walls. There were large windows that overlooked the grounds and the ocean beyond. A portrait of Mary hung opposite the window.

Carly ran her hand along the main table, liking the smooth feel of the wood and how the carvings reminded her of days spent doing her homework in this room. Three large chandeliers provided overhead light in the evening—the cut glass casting shadows that had made her think of foreign lands and battles with dragons and being a princess.

So many memories, she thought. Most of them happy. Had that changed?

She walked to the office area and checked on the board. Only four of the twenty-five rooms were occupied. Carly frowned. Sure, it was midweek, but it was spring break. Shouldn't the B and B be more busy?

She headed for the kitchen where her mother had put out two bottles of wine. With so few guests, they wouldn't need more than a couple.

Maybe she could sneak one upstairs into her room and drown her sorrows, she thought glumly. A nice cabernet sauvignon and some chocolate could go a long way to making her feel more perky about her life.

"All settled?" her mother asked.

"I'm unpacked," Carly said, not sure how long it would take to feel settled. Between Neil walking out, having to sell the house, moving and starting over with a life she wasn't sure she wanted, she didn't think "settled" was on the agenda.

"Something smells good," Carly said as she moved to the oven and pulled it open.

"Maribel made those this morning," her mother said. "They should be about done. Do the crusts look brown?"

As Carly checked out the mini quiches, her mouth began to water. "They look perfect." She reached for the hot pad on the counter and pulled the two trays out of the oven.

"I'm glad Maribel is still working here," she said, pleased to know there would be at least one friendly face in residence.

"I'd be lost without her," Rhonda said. "She knows it, too. She's always after me for a raise, and as badly as things are going here, I don't see how she has the nerve."

Carly took a step back. Okay, not a conversation she wanted to have her first day here. At least not the part about Maribel. But she was going to have to get the rest of it straightened out at some point, and why not now?

"When did things start going badly, Mom?" she asked as she slipped the mini quiches onto a cooling rack. "You never mentioned anything to me."

"I didn't want to worry you. I knew you had your hands full with Neil. Besides, what could you do from all the way down there?"

Technically there was nothing wrong with what her mother had said, Carly told herself. If she put those three sentences in front of an impartial jury, they would tell her that her mother was being sensitive and stating the obvious. Most likely Rhonda *hadn't* wanted to worry her daughter, and Carly had had her hands full with Neil. As for being far away, it was true, too.

However, this wasn't an impartial jury, and in the momspeak Carly knew so well, what Rhonda had just said was: "You're too busy for me, as always. Sure I could have told you what was going on, but you were always more interested in your husband, who left you, by the way. Of course being so far away meant I was totally on my own. But you're selfish and I'm used to that."

"You can tell me now," Carly said, proud of how calm she sounded. "What's up with the B and B? I would have thought it would be more full, what with it being spring break."

Her mother glared at her. "Oh, sure. Be critical of how I run things. What happened with you? What do you mean there isn't any money from the divorce? There has to be. Neil made a lot of money in his marketing job."

So they were going to talk about her failure, Carly thought. Might as well get it over with.

"Neil did well," she admitted. "My job didn't pay so much." The office manager position with a single-doctor practice didn't pull in the big bucks. "We were careful to put money aside for Tiffany's college, but after that, Neil lost interest. We took all those expensive vacations, then there were the cars."

Neil had liked to lease a new one every two years. The monthly payment for their last Mercedes had cost more than their food bill. She'd hated that and had protested, but Neil had pointed out that it was important for him to have a car that matched his position in the company. Carly had tried to argue the point with him, but he'd told her she couldn't possibly understand. That had felt so much like being patted on the head, that she'd yelled at him. Then they'd had a big fight. In the end, he'd gotten the car anyway.

"We put in the new landscaping last year," she said. "There were other things we bought. In hindsight I should have pushed back more on the budget. The bottom line is, by the time we split everything, I owned half of nothing."

"But the house," her mother protested. "That had to be worth a fortune."

"It was. And we owed nearly as much."

Carly didn't know how to explain that it had been easier to give in to Neil than to fight him all the time.

"You were raised better than that," her mother said.

"Not helpful," Carly told her.

"Don't you get alimony?"

"Yes, and no. Neil quit his job. Until he gets a new one, he doesn't have to pay. He owes child support, although that's on a sliding scale. Basically if he gets back into marketing at the level he was at, he's going to be passing about half his salary on to me for alimony and child support. That doesn't give him much incentive to start looking."

"I think this is all just wrong," her mother said as she set the serving trays on the counter. "In my day a man knew his responsibilities. Your father never left me. He wasn't that kind of man. You should have thought about that when you married Neil. I never liked him, you know."

"Mmm." Carly went for the noncommittal response. What was she going to say? That both her parents had adored Neil from the second she'd brought him home? That for the first two years of their marriage she'd joked that if she and Neil split up, her parents would want custody of *him?*

"You used to have a good job," her mother said. "What happened to that?"

"The events planning? That was a million years ago." She tested one of the quiches to see if it had cooled enough, then began sliding them onto a serving plate.

"You should never have given up your career," her mother said. "If you'd kept up with it, you wouldn't be in trouble now."

"Agreed, but it was too difficult to handle big parties and corporate events once I had Tiffany. I wanted to be home more."

"At least you got that right," her mother told her. "You needed to be there."

Carly felt as if she were in a fun house. Could her mother just pick a side and stay on it? Any side. At this point Carly didn't even care if it was one in which she was the villain.

She handed over the plate of quiche.

"I don't know what we're going to do," Rhonda said as she set the plate on the tray. "I thought you'd be able to put some money into the B and B. But if you can't…"

She stopped talking and pressed her lips together. Carly watched her. They were family, she thought sadly. Shouldn't they be able to pull together on this?

Obviously her fantasy of coming home and finding everything in her world put to rights wasn't going to happen.

"I suppose I could sell," her mother said as she walked to the cupboard and pulled down several wineglasses. "I still have a lot of equity in this place. We could use it to buy you something in Las Vegas. Or I could sell my town house and we could buy a larger place together."

Carly figured she would rather be tied naked to a fire-ant hill. She'd known moving back to the B and B would mean sharing relatively close quarters with her mother, but there had been a time limit. In two years, Rhonda would head off to her retirement. Carly would run the B and B and send her mother a monthly check for her share of the business. It wasn't a perfect solution or one she would have chosen, but it solved so many problems.

However, living with her mother on a permanent basis was something else entirely.

"This house has been in the family for nearly a hundred

and fifty years," Carly said. "You can't be serious about sell-ing it."

"I'm not sure there's a choice."

"There has to be another way," she said, not sure what it could be, but determined to find it. "This is a lot of infor-mation. I need to think about it all."

"Be my guest," her mother said. "I've been worrying for seven years."

Carly refused to translate *that* into momspeak.

"Of course you and Neil may work everything out and get back together," Rhonda added.

"Unlikely," Carly said. "Not only wouldn't I take him back, but I can't imagine anything making him want to go back to his old life."

"I'm so sorry, dear."

Her mother patted her arm.

Carly frowned. "Sorry about what?"

"That Neil left you for someone else. Is she much younger and prettier?"

Carly didn't know if she should laugh or cry. "No, Mom. Neil didn't leave me for anyone. There's no other woman. He just wanted to go find himself."

Carly escaped to her room after dinner. Tiffany was going to watch TV with her grandmother and Carly took the op-portunity to sneak away.

It wasn't that she didn't want to be with her family, it was that she needed time to think. Nothing had turned out the way she'd thought and that was going to take some getting used to.

At night the ocean was a blanket of darkness. She opened

the windows, and although she couldn't see waves or even whitecaps, the sound of the sea was audible and she could smell the salt air. At least *that* was as she remembered. But the rest of it—not so much.

Carly settled on the window seat and stared into the darkness. At what point had her life taken this unexpected turn? Had there been signs along the way? Had she simply not been paying attention? Sure, things with Neil hadn't been great for a while, but it hadn't occurred to her that divorce was an option. They had a child together; there had been vows. She'd chosen to spend her life with him and a few disappointments along the way hadn't been a reason to change her mind.

So why had he changed his? Had his experience been worse than hers, or had he not believed in the "forever" part of their marriage? Was she a fool for staying so long, or was he a jerk for leaving? Did the truth lie somewhere in the middle?

She wasn't sure it mattered. After all, they were divorcing now and both starting over. Neil had his dreams and she had… Carly sighed. She had no clue what she had. A teenage daughter who would rather live with her father, a mother who had kept the news of the failing business from her only child, and a future that looked far too uncertain.

Which meant Carly didn't have a lot of options. Either she stayed and fought for the B and B or she left and started over somewhere else. While she'd been working steadily for the past twenty years, she wasn't sure her recent job qualified her for much. Sure she'd run an office, but it had been small and the paycheck had matched.

Eighteen years ago things had been different. She'd been a successful events planner and she'd loved the work. In three years she'd risen to the top, with a list of clients that made her competition weep. But then she'd had Tiffany, and the sixty- to seventy-hour workweeks and constant late nights had been impossible with a baby.

In an effort to balance her love of event planning with having a husband and a baby, she'd turned to wedding planning. While the hours had been better, Neil had hated her being gone nearly every weekend. In truth, she'd never seen him. So she'd quit that, too, and had found the office manager job.

Could she go back to events planning? Unfortunately she hadn't kept in touch with many of her old friends from the business. Plus she wouldn't like the hours anymore now than she had when Tiffany had been a baby. One of the reasons she'd come to the B and B was so that she could be around for her daughter. These last three years before she went off to college were important and Carly didn't want to miss them.

But she also had a responsibility to put food on the table and a roof over their heads. If events planning wasn't an option and L.A. was too expensive and she wasn't staying here, then she would need to look at moving somewhere else. There had to be places with a less crazy cost of living.

If only she had—

A soft knock on her door brought her to her feet. Carly crossed the floor and pulled open the door. Tiffany stood in front of her. The teen wore teddy bear pajamas and carried a tattered stuffed dog in her arms.

"What's up?" Carly asked.

"Nothing." Tiffany shrugged as she stepped inside. "My room is great. It's just…" She shrugged. "You know."

"It's a little creepy up there?"

Tiffany dropped her chin. "Maybe a little. I'll be completely fine," she added quickly. "I love my room. I just thought, you know, for the first night."

Carly glanced at the large bed, then closed the door. "Sure, you can sleep with me."

"Good."

Tiffany ran and jumped on the bed. "I took the back stairs. It's really weird because the house is so quiet, but there are all these noises."

"Old places are known for that."

"It made me think of the ghost. Not that she's real."

Carly stretched out in the bed. Tiffany set her dog on the nightstand, then shimmied under the blankets. She snuggled close and rested her head on Carly's shoulder.

"Grandma was pretty cool tonight," the teenager said. "We watched HBO together."

"Nothing R-rated, right?"

"Oh, Mo-om. You're so old."

"Grandma's older than me."

"Yeah, but she's more fun."

Carly tried not to take the comment personally. As her daughter's mother, it was her job to be a parent, not a buddy. But just once she would like someone else to be the bad guy for a while. Neil was never willing to take on that task. Of course, he'd never bothered all that much with his daughter, despite the fact that Tiffany adored him.

She stretched up and turned off the light, then settled back on the bed. Tiffany sighed.

"Where do you think Daddy is?" she asked, almost as if she knew her mother had been thinking of Neil.

"I don't know. I thought he was going to stay in L.A. for a while. Until he bought his boat."

"Do you think he's really going to sail to Hawaii?"

"That's what he said."

"Wow. It's so far. And there aren't any, like, places to stop."

"I'm sure he'll take a good map."

Carly did her best to keep the bitterness out of her voice. Neil got to buy a boat and run off to Hawaii while she was left behind to be the grown-up. Again.

"Do you think…" Tiffany hesitated, then swallowed. "Do you think he misses me?"

"Of course he does. You're his best girl."

"I guess. It's just he never wanted to, you know, spend time with me, and he hasn't called since he left."

"He'll call," Carly said, then vowed she would find Neil and force him to call his daughter. Damn the man for being such an insensitive bastard, she thought grimly. How could he do this to Tiffany? She could try to forgive a lot of things, but never that.

She wrapped her arms around Tiffany and squeezed. "He's going through a lot right now. But he'll settle into his new life and you can be a part of it. That will be fun."

"Yeah. We can go sailing together."

"Good idea."

Tiffany sighed. "It's nice here. I kinda didn't want to come because I thought it would be way stupid, but I like the house. You're not going to make me clean rooms, are you?"

"We'll negotiate a chore list," Carly said. "The maids make pretty good money."

"How good?"

"Let's talk in the morning."

"Okay. Night."

"Night, baby. I love you."

"I love you, too, Mom."

Carly listened to her daughter's breathing. It didn't take very long for it to slow and get very deep. When Tiffany was asleep, Carly tried to memorize everything about this moment—how her daughter clung to her even in sleep, the way her hair smelled, the feel of her thin arms. There wouldn't be many more nights when Tiffany needed to sleep with her mom to feel safe, and Carly didn't want to miss a moment of what might be the last one.

"They grow up too fast," she whispered.

Carly woke up to a morning so beautiful, she couldn't help but feel optimistic about the day and her future. She left her daughter asleep and went downstairs to fire up her morning with a jumbo mug of coffee. Sunshine, the smell of the ocean and a jolt of caffeine. Did it get any better than that?

She took the back stairs instead of the elevator and enjoyed the play of light on the old paneling. Even the servants had had a view, she thought humorously as she walked across the landing and glanced out at the expanse of gardens below. When she reached the main floor, she headed for the kitchen. If she hadn't been sure of her destination, the mouthwatering scent of cinnamon and something baking would have drawn her in.

Anticipation quickened her steps. Not just for the yummy stuff, but also to see Maribel. Although they talked regularly by phone, she hadn't seen her friend in over a year.

"Hey, you," Carly said as she opened the kitchen door and stepped inside. "You're up early."

Maribel pulled something out of the oven, straightened, turned and grinned. "You made it!"

Carly waited until her friend put down the baking sheet, then approached. She opened her arms wide for a hug, only to come to a complete stop and stare.

"You're…you're…"

Maribel laughed, then smoothed the front of her white chef's coat over her belly. "Pregnant. I know."

"But… You can't be. You're…"

Carly didn't know what to say. "Too old," came to mind. As she and Maribel were practically the same age, her friend was also within weeks of turning forty.

"You didn't say anything," Carly told her instead.

"I know." Maribel moved close and hugged her. "When I found out about the baby, you and Neil had already started talking about the divorce. I didn't know if I should share my news or not. Then when you mentioned coming here, I figured I'd tell you in person. Don't be mad at me. I was seriously torn."

"I'm not mad. I couldn't be. I'll admit to being stunned. A baby. Wow."

Carly squeezed her, then stepped back. She studied her friend's bright, happy expression and the blush on her cheeks. Always petite and curvy, Maribel now defined lush. Her new shorter haircut emphasized her pretty features.

"You look amazing. Seriously, you're doing the glowing thing. But a baby? Are you excited?"

"I am now," Maribel admitted. "But at first it was a real shock. Only Dani's still in high school, the other three are in college. Pete and I figured we were finally going to buy that RV and see the world. Or at least the part we can drive to. Then this happened."

She touched her stomach. "I cried for three days when the doctor told me I didn't have the flu. Then I had a dream I wasn't pregnant and I woke myself up crying because I was so sad. That's when I figured I really *did* want the baby."

Carly nodded, even though she didn't understand. She and Maribel had gone different ways—Carly had attended college for a couple of years before starting in events planning and Maribel had married right out of high school. She'd had her first child on her twentieth birthday.

"Tiffany's fifteen," she said. "I can't imagine starting over with a newborn now."

"The kids are still getting over the shock," Maribel said as she walked to the island and began cutting up strawberries. "I suspect it's a whole lot more about Mom and Dad having sex than the actual idea of a baby."

"Pregnant," Carly said, still trying to take it in. Talk about a life change. "You're putting my divorce in perspective. When are you due?"

"Four more months."

Carly eyed her friend's large stomach. "Really?"

Maribel laughed. "Yeah, I know. I'm huge. I've always carried big, but this time I swear it's part elephant."

Carly walked over to the baking pan and stared at the cinnamon rolls. "Want me to take these out?"

"That would be great. So, enough about me and my surprise. How are you doing?"

"Okay. It's weird to be back."

Maribel dumped the cut strawberries into the fruit bowl. "Have you talked to your mom about anything?" she asked, sounding neutral.

Carly appreciated the sensitivity. "If you're asking if she's already mentioned that she wants me to use my divorce settlement to rescue the B and B, then yes. If it's something else, I'm not sure I could handle it."

"No, it's the money thing," Maribel said. "She's been really anxious for you to arrive. It's all she talks about."

Carly didn't consider that especially good news. "It's the week before Easter," she said. "Shouldn't we be busier?"

"Things have been slow for a while," Maribel admitted. "Bookings are dropping off. My food order is about half what it was this time last year."

"As bad as that," Carly said quietly. So much for hoping her mother had been exaggerating the situation.

A timer *dinged*. Maribel moved to the second oven and pulled out a pan of muffins. Carly drew in a deep breath.

"Those smell heavenly, too. Now I don't know which I want."

"Have one of each," Maribel urged.

"I'd love to, but I don't have the cash flow to replace my wardrobe with a larger size." One of the joys of getting older, Carly thought. She could no longer eat whatever she wanted and still fit into her clothes. Soon she was going to have to get serious about organized exercise, and how twisted was that?

"Do you have any big plans for the B and B?" Maribel asked. "Your mom thought you might."

Carly sensed her friend's interest was more than casual. No doubt she wanted to keep her job. The hours were perfect for someone with children and Maribel had always loved cooking.

"Not off the top of my head," Carly admitted. "I didn't

think I would have to jump in to rescue a failing business my first day back."

Actually she'd planned on relaxing a little, basking in the whole "moving back home" thing. But apparently not.

"It would be a shame to lose all this," Maribel said.

Carly agreed. Did she want to save it, and if she did, could she?

They both turned at the sound of footsteps in the hallway. Tiffany pushed open the swinging door and smiled shyly.

"Hi," she said. "You got up way early."

Carly glanced at the clock and raised her eyebrows. "So did you. You remember my friend Maribel, don't you?"

"Uh-huh. Hi." Tiffany inhaled. "I remember your muffins, too. You're the best cook."

"Aren't you sweet for saying so." Maribel grabbed a paper towel and pulled one of the muffins out of the pan. "Be careful," she said as she handed it to Tiffany. "They're still hot."

"Thanks. I'm going to walk around outside," Tiffany said.

"Have fun," Carly told her. She wanted to add something about not going too far, or staying away from the main road, but she held back. Her daughter was smart enough to know all that and right now Carly couldn't face another eye roll.

The back door slammed shut behind her. Maribel sighed.

"She's beautiful and she looks a whole lot more grown-up than fifteen."

"Tell me about it. Older guys are constantly asking her out and I'm stuck trying to explain why this isn't a good thing."

"It gets worse," Maribel said cheerfully. "But then it gets

better. Of course just when they settle down enough that you want to spend more time with them, they go off to college. Isn't that the way?"

"I don't remember being *that* much trouble," Carly grumbled.

"Me, either, but I'm guessing we were. Remember how we were going to change the world?" Maribel laughed. "I was going to live in Paris and become a world-class chef. You were going to marry a movie star and plan fabulous parties for all of Hollywood."

While Carly could remember talking endlessly about what she and Maribel had wanted to do with their lives, she had an odd feeling of being disconnected from the whole thing. As if it had been someone else dreaming those dreams.

Maribel picked up a kiwifruit and started peeling it. "That was a long time ago. Funny how now I don't want anything but what I have."

Carly envied her friend her contentment. If pressed, Carly wasn't sure she could say what *she* wanted. Not anymore. Maybe not in a long time.

Carly put off unpacking to go online on her laptop. If she and Tiffany didn't stay here to make a go of things, they were going to need an alternate plan. But what? Her most recent occupation wasn't about to excite anyone and she didn't have the start-up capital or the savings to try going out on her own as an events planner.

She went to a couple of different cost-of-living Web sites and found out that she could indeed support herself and Tiffany on a doctor's office manager's salary in, say, Bakersfield. Or if they left the state. There were a lot of places cheaper to live in than Los Angeles.

If she wasn't at the B and B she wouldn't want to stay here. It would be too hard to be close to the house but not a part of it.

Is that what she wanted? To move somewhere new and start over without friends or family nearby? Not that there were all that many friends since the divorce. But still, there was the whole pain of leaving the familiar.

She left the Internet and went into the word-processing program. Maybe a list of pros and cons, she thought. Reasons to stay in L.A., reasons to stay and make the B and B work and reasons to locate elsewhere.

In Los Angeles, she had contacts, even if she hadn't used them in years. She might be able to land a job working for an events planner. Of course, as she reflected again, the hours *were* hideously long and she would be home while Tiffany was in school and gone the rest of the time.

If she stayed here, she would have to bring the B and B back from wherever it was and make it successful again. Which meant she needed to know how bad things were. As her mother wasn't the most forthcoming of information givers, Carly wasn't looking forward to *that* conversation. But staying meant being able to hang out with her daughter, to attend school functions, to be a mom.

Carly leaned back in her chair and closed her eyes. There were a thousand details to consider under any scenario. Like medical insurance. Getting it for Tiffany wouldn't be that difficult, but what about herself? Was she going to be considered "hard to insure" because of her age? And what about the fact that she would soon turn forty and have to check a different box on all those forms that asked for age in groups? Perhaps not relevant for her job search, but still depressing.

She looked back at her list. Obviously staying here was the best solution, assuming she could find a way to make it work.

Carly remembered growing up here. The B and B had always been crammed with guests. They were sold out for all the major holidays months in advance. There had been a wedding every Saturday from May through September. The holidays had been magical, with period decorations covering every inch of the public rooms. And she'd felt safe and happy, secure in the knowledge that she knew where she came from and where she was going.

"We could make that happen again," Carly told herself. "*I* could make it happen."

She had determination, drive and a willingness to do the hard work. Surely that would be enough. Which meant first up, she had to get accurate information from her mother.

Conveniently, Carly heard Rhonda calling for her. Unfortunately, Tiffany was also yelling for her, and the teenager didn't sound happy.

Carly saved the information and closed the computer program. Then she began the shut-down process as she yelled, "In here. What's going on?"

Tiffany marched in first. Her daughter looked upset and defiant. Tears sparkled in her eyes.

"Grandma's being mean," she announced.

"Your daughter is very spoiled and uncooperative," Rhonda said from behind the teenager.

Tiffany turned on the older woman. "You can't be serious. It's totally illegal to make me work so much. There are child labor laws. I know—I read about them in school. You can't exploit young workers for your own financial gain."

Rhonda's eyes widened with indignation. "I would think you'd be more grateful that I took you in, young lady. You're spoiled."

"Am not."

Carly stared at her daughter. "Tiffany, you're speaking to your grandmother."

Tiffany opened her mouth, then closed it. "She started it."

Rhonda looked smug. "You should have your daughter help more around the house. If she's part of the family, she needs to have responsibilities."

Carly wanted to reprimand her mother, too, but knew it wouldn't go over well.

"I blame you for this," Rhonda said.

Of course she did, Carly thought. When in doubt…

"Tiffany has always had chores," she said calmly. "We'll have to work some out for her." She frowned. Tiffany was fairly typical in having to be reminded to do her work, but she never absolutely refused. Plus, the girl had always liked her grandmother and wanted to hang out with her.

"What happened?" she asked.

Tiffany sniffed. "She told me to fold sheets."

Carly wanted to do an eye roll of her own. "The way you were talking, I expected to hear she put you to work sweeping the roof. It's just sheets. What's the problem?"

"It's *all* of them."

Carly didn't understand. "Not just the ones for your room?"

"Of course not. I'd do *that*." Her tone indicated that it wasn't possible for Carly to be more stupid. "I've never seen a pile this big. There were hundreds."

"Twenty or thirty sets," Rhonda said with a sniff. "You shouldn't exaggerate, Tiffany. It makes people think you're lying. I'm surprised your mother hasn't taught you that."

Carly ignored that. "Why so many sheets?"

"I haven't gotten around to folding them from the weekend," Rhonda said as she walked to the window and stared out at the view. "I've been busy."

Her mother's activities were the least of Carly's concerns. The real issue was why the housekeeping staff wasn't doing the laundry.

"Don't the housekeepers take care of the sheets on Tuesday?" she asked, knowing the staff was usually busy Monday, cleaning up from the weekend.

"They wash and dry them. I've been doing the folding."

Not good, Carly thought. She had more questions but didn't want to get into it in front of Tiffany.

She turned to her daughter. "We'll talk later today and come up with a chore list."

"You let her decide that sort of thing?" Rhonda asked, obviously annoyed.

"I think her input is important," Carly said. "But she doesn't decide."

"I could," Tiffany said defiantly. "I'd do a great job."

Carly narrowed her gaze. "This would be a great time for you to keep quiet."

Tiffany opened her mouth, then closed it. "Fine," she muttered between clenched teeth.

"I still need help with all those sheets," Rhonda said. "I suppose if everyone is busy, I can just do them myself."

Like that was going to happen, Carly thought. "I'll help," she said. "Tiffany, why don't you write up a draft of what you think is a reasonable chore list and we'll talk about it later this afternoon? Aside from keeping your room clean, you'll need to help around the B and B, so think about what you'd like to do."

"I don't want to be a maid even if it pays good."

"You don't have to be. There are lots of other things. You could help Maribel in the kitchen, you could prepare the evening appetizers, be responsible for arranging the fresh flowers in the public rooms and the guest rooms."

Her daughter perked up. "I don't know how to arrange flowers."

"It's not that hard. I could teach you."

Tiffany's eyes widened. "You know how to do that for real? You were always putting flowers in the house, but I didn't think you really knew what you were doing."

"Gee, thanks for the vote of confidence. My point is there are a lot of ways to help and I don't mind if you pick one that's fun for you."

"Okay. I'll do that." Her expression cleared and she headed out of the room.

Rhonda watched her go. "You're spoiling her."

"Because I'm willing to let her have a say in what her chores are? I don't consider that spoiling, Mom. She's more likely to do the work if she has some input in the process. There's already plenty of friction with her being a teenager. I would like to avoid adding more to the situation."

Her mother shook her head. "I would never have let you pick your chores."

"I know."

Her mother glared at her. "Is that a criticism? Do you want to blame me for the problems in your life? Is it my fault you couldn't hold on to your husband?"

"None of the above," Carly said as she wondered if living in say, Iowa, would really be that bad. "Come on. I'll help you fold the sheets."

She would use the time with her mother to find out the real situation at the B and B and then make her decision about staying or leaving. If she was going to move again, she had to do it soon, before Tiffany got too settled. Plus there was her daughter's school to think of. Spring break was only a week. She didn't want to keep Tiffany out of school because they were moving yet again.

Ten minutes later Carly found herself in the basement laundry room. Despite the fact that it had probably once been a dungeon, the space was bright and airy. Several small windows up by the ceiling let in light while the sunny yellow paint added cheer. Three industrial-size washers lined one wall, and matching dryers lined another. There were long folding tables and cabinets with laundry supplies. A dumbwaiter in the corner allowed the clean laundry to be sent up to the guest floors.

Carly stared at the piles and piles of sheets. They were on top of the tables, on the machines themselves and in baskets. She could see why her daughter freaked.

"Were you full for the weekend?" she asked her mother as she reached down and pulled out a sheet.

"No. We're a little behind on the laundry."

No kidding, Carly thought. She would guess that laundry hadn't been done in a month.

"This has been hard for you, hasn't it?" Carly said, knowing the conversation would go better if she took her mother's side and was careful not to make anything sound like an accusation. "You've had to take on a lot of responsibility."

Her mother picked up a pillowcase. "It's been horrible. After your father died, I couldn't really function. You can't be married to a man for thirty-five years and just get over it."

"I agree," Carly said.

"At first this place ran itself. I liked being in the familiar surroundings and having all the guests come. The ones who had been returning for years were like old friends. Then business slowed. Just a little at first. But now…"

Her voice trailed off. Carly tried to think of a tactful way to ask how bad it was. Before she could, her mother continued.

"We're still getting the die-hard ghost fanatics. Being in all the registries helps, of course. We *are* the best documented haunted house."

"That's a big plus," Carly said. Without Mary, Chatsworth-by-the-Sea was nothing more than an old English manor in the middle of pretty much nowhere. "But overall, bookings seem to be down."

"I know." Her mother sighed. "People just don't travel the way they used to."

"What kind of advertising are you doing? There are so many specialty magazines and cable channels."

Her mother reached for another pillowcase. "Don't be ridiculous. We can't afford to spend that kind of money on something as silly as advertising."

"It's not silly," Carly told her. "If people don't know the B and B exists, how can they come stay here?"

"They know."

"How? Is there some kind of cosmic information booth that informs them?"

Rhonda pressed her lips together and closed her eyes. "I can't believe, with all I've been through, that you would be so mean to me right now."

Carly stared at her. What, exactly, was making her mother's life so difficult at this exact moment?

"I'm sorry you feel that way," she said, trying to keep her voice even. "I'm trying to point out that people won't know about our place if we don't tell them. Word of mouth is great, but it's a slow way to build up clientele."

She finished with the sheet and set it in a basket. "The thing is, Mom, I need to know how bad things are right now. If I'm going to stay and help you bring the B and B back to a profitable status, I have to know where we're starting from."

"You know we never discuss money in detail. It's rude."

"This is business, Mom. Our family business. I thought you wanted me to help."

"I do."

"Then I need to know what's going on."

Her mother snapped open the pillowcase. "Fine, but I don't want you talking about our personal finances with all your friends."

"I won't." As if she ever had. Ah, but secrets were important in this family.

"Then I'll show you the books. Although I can't imagine what you want with them. You'll never understand them."

Carly gaped at her. "Excuse me? This is what I do for a living. I was in charge of the finances at the doctor's office."

"You don't have to get huffy with me. I thought you had a bookkeeper."

"We did, and I'm the one who checked her work." So much for her mother paying attention when she'd talked about her job, Carly thought in amazement.

"Then I guess you can see them after we finish here," Rhonda said. "Whatever the problems are, they're not my fault."

"Of course not," Carly said automatically.

Whoever said coming home again was a good idea had obviously had a very different family, she thought. Could she do this? Could she work with her mother, live under the same roof, day after day for the next couple of years? Did she want to commit her life to the bed-and-breakfast?

There was still the possibility of a small town somewhere. She could walk away from all of this, let her mother simply sell the old place and get on with her life.

Which choice was better? Which would be the most beneficial for Tiffany? And wouldn't it be great if someone was making decisions with her, Carly's, best interest in mind?

Carly knew the news wasn't going to be good, but she hadn't expected things to be as bad as they were. It took her two hours to study spreadsheets, ledgers and the previous two years of tax returns. She didn't worry about things like payroll or food orders. Instead she focused on guest revenue and large expenditures.

The big surprise was that the B and B had been existing on a line of credit against the home for the past eighteen months. The business hadn't been profitable in nearly three years.

Declining bookings were the real problem. There had been a steady drop since Carly's father had died. The first couple of years after his death showed a slight decline, then the numbers plummeted. The B and B hadn't had a full night since Valentine's weekend, two years ago.

Carly flipped through different ledgers. There wasn't a single wedding or big party planned for the entire summer. No large groups had requested to take over the B and B, something she remembered happening all the time when she'd been growing up.

In addition to the loss of income, there were some interesting choices in the expense department. The dishes had been replaced to the tune of fifty thousand dollars. At the same time, contractors, including their local plumber, hadn't been paid. Based on the checkbook, she had a feeling the property taxes were two months overdue.

Carly leaned back in her chair and studied the pile of books, papers and the blinking cursor on the computer screen. Was it possible to make this work? Could she do it? Making the B and B profitable would mean changing a lot of things, and her mother wasn't a big fan of change. There were—

Her cell phone rang. She reached for it, flipped open the cover and stared at the unfamiliar number.

"Hello," she said after she'd pushed the talk button.

"Hey, Carly. How's it going?"

It wasn't that she didn't recognize the voice—she had lived with the man for over sixteen years. But she wasn't expecting to hear from her ex-husband, and it took a second for her to place him.

"Neil?"

"Hey. What's up?"

She frowned. "Why do you want to know?"

"I'm just being friendly. You know, regular phone chitchat."

The last two words made her wince. Was there another man on the planet who used "chitchat"?

"Okay. I'm fine, and yourself?"

"Great. I've been looking at boats. Man, there are some beauties out there. I can't really afford anything new, but I've narrowed my choices down to three older sailboats. I can really fix one of them up and then head off to Hawaii. The cost of the navigation system is going to kill me, but it's a pretty big ocean and I sure don't want to get lost."

Uh-huh. Did she get a vote on that? "How nice," she murmured. Was she missing something here? "Neil, why are you calling me?"

"What do you mean?" He sounded genuinely baffled.

"I mean, why are you calling? What is your purpose? Do you want to talk to Tiffany?"

"Naw. I'm just checking in. Saying hi. Hi."

Had she ever thought of the man as charming? "Neil, we're getting a divorce. You decided you didn't want to be with me anymore. So why are you checking in?"

"Because we're friends. Don't you want to be friends with me, Carly?"

Not even for money, she thought. Why didn't Neil get it? She could handle him being as much of a jerk as he wanted where she was concerned, but Tiffany was another matter.

"What I want is for you to stay in contact with your daughter. It's been over three weeks since you last spoke with her."

"I've been busy. This whole boat thing."

"Neil, she's your *daughter*. She has to matter."

"You know you're much better at the whole parenting thing than I am."

What he meant was she was willing to make the sacrifices that went with having a child and he wasn't. "I know she loves you and misses you. Just because you don't have to pay child support while you're not working doesn't mean you abdicate your responsibilities. You're supposed to see her every other weekend. She needs that and I think you need the time with her, too. She's growing up fast. You have to be a part of her life."

"Lighten up. You take things too seriously."

Carly held the phone out in front of her and stared at it. She replaced it against her ear. "You're kidding, right? We're talking about your *child*."

"I know."

His tone dismissed her in such a way that in less than three seconds she went from annoyed to wanting to maim him.

How did this always happen? They started out with her wanting him to change something and they ended up with her being the bad guy. She wanted to scream at him that it had never been her plan to take life so seriously, but no one had given her much of a choice. Someone had needed to be the grown-up and Neil sure as hell hadn't volunteered. It had all fallen on her.

"You know, Carly, if you're going to be like this, I'm not going to call you anymore."

"Amazingly enough, I can live with that. The person you need to be calling is Tiffany. You need to plan to spend a weekend with her and soon. I mean it, Neil. If you don't do this in the next two weeks, I'm contacting the judge. I'll make it a court order if I have to."

Tiffany adored her father and Carly was going to make sure the man didn't let her little girl down any more than he already had.

He grumbled something she couldn't hear but doubted was very flattering to her.

"Fine. But what about the plane ticket? Do I have to pay to fly her down?"

"Yes. Or you could come up here, but you're not staying at the B and B. You'll have to get two hotel rooms somewhere else. And before you ask, yes, Tiffany needs her own room. She's fifteen."

"But that's a lot of money."

"So sail up here on your boat. That will be free."

"What? Hey, Carly, that's a great idea. Maybe I'll do that."

"So there's no point in telling you I was being sarcastic about the sailing remark?"

"Naw. Okay. Gotta run. Have a good one."

He hung up.

She did a little grumbling herself, then pushed the end button on her cell phone.

What on earth made Neil think she wanted to be friends with him? Sure, she was more than willing to keep things civil between them. It was important for them to get along—for Tiffany's sake. But friends?

Maybe she would be a better person if she were willing to let Neil stay in her life, but that was *so* not her style. She'd moved past wanting to see him cut up into little pieces and fed to the carnivores at the L.A. zoo, but that didn't mean she wanted to "chitchat" about his hopes and dreams.

None of which mattered, she reminded herself. What was important was his relationship with his daughter. If he followed through on that, she would ignore the rest of it. If he didn't, she would make good on her threat to get in touch with the judge.

In the meantime, she had books to put in order and a profit-and-loss statement to work out.

But instead of reaching for the keyboard and entering

numbers on the spreadsheet, she turned her chair toward the office window and stared out over the side lawn.

What had happened to chase guests away? Or had they simply forgotten about the B and B? Was it the same with the groups and the weddings? Carly remembered attending large bridal fairs with her parents at least twice a year. Then there were a couple of big travel shows. There had been brochures and pictures and letters of recommendation by previous guests.

Without turning away from the window, she reached for a notepad and a pen.

"Contact previous guests by postcard, giving them a discount," she wrote. They still had the old registration information. Sure, the mailing would be expensive, but they would be reaching people who had wanted to come at one time.

What next? Weddings, parties of all kinds. They were coming into the busy season. If she spoke with some of the local hotels in town, told them they had availability, maybe they could get some spillover bookings.

They could run specials during the slow seasons and they weren't that far from San Francisco. What about advertising locally? Chatsworth-by-the-Sea was off the beaten path, but they did have a ghost. She would have to feature that prominently.

Okay, those ideas worked for the weekends, but what about during the week? Based on what she'd discovered, the place was mostly empty, even on holiday weeks. So what made people travel during the week, when most of them were working? What would make them give up their precious vacation time to come here? Or was she missing the point? What if they got to come here without giving up vacation time? What if their travel was about work?

Carly grinned as she put pen to paper and began to write as fast as she could form words.

"This is just stupid," Tiffany said from the passenger seat. "I don't want to go to school."

Carly resisted the urge to remind her daughter that she loved school. The classes were mildly interesting, but what really got Tiffany excited was the activities and hanging out with her friends. No doubt if she said that, she would be reminded that due to the move, Tiffany had no friends locally.

"Even if I wanted to let you stay home, which I don't," she said, "the state of California has a real thing about truancy. You gotta be there, kid."

"But I'll hate it. Besides, Grandma said she's not sure we're staying, so why don't I wait until you decide what you want to do about ruining my life even more?"

Carly stared at her daughter. "What?"

Tiffany sighed. "Grandma said we may not be staying with her. That you've mentioned going somewhere else. Not that you'd discuss it with me. I'm just the one with the broken life. Why should I know anything?"

Carly felt her temper rise and it had nothing to do with Tiffany's negative attitude. How dare her mother discuss moving with Tiffany? Carly hadn't decided what to do about staying or leaving, but she'd been determined not to worry Tiffany until she had a clearer plan. Tiffany was only fifteen— her life should be about classes and friends and boys and growing up. Not worrying about where they were going to live.

"I'm sorry Grandma said anything," Carly told her. "It's true I don't know if we're staying. I've been working on trying to figure out if I think I can make the bed-and-breakfast profitable. She and I are going to talk about my plan this afternoon. I've come up with some ideas and suggestions, but ultimately, it's her decision whether or not she wants to keep the place open. If she doesn't, then we'll be moving somewhere else. But until we know otherwise, we're assuming we're staying."

"Easy for you to say. Your life isn't destroyed."

Tiffany folded her arms over her chest and stared out the window. Hard to believe this was the same girl who had, only a few nights earlier, wanted to sleep in her mother's bed. She'd worried that Tiffany was growing up so fast. Maybe she should worry she wasn't growing up fast enough.

"I'm working through the last of the numbers this morning, then I have to talk to your grandmother. As soon as we know, you'll know."

Tiffany didn't say anything, but her folded arms and closed expression more than communicated her displeasure. Carly knew it was going to get a whole lot worse with her daughter before it got better. Tiffany had never changed schools before, and while Carly wanted to believe the transition would be smooth, she had her doubts.

Funny how knowing a situation had the potential to be difficult didn't make it any more pleasant when it occurred.

She pulled up in front of the high school and stared at the familiar building. Wings had been added on each end, nearly doubling it in size, but even with the addition and the two separate buildings behind the main one, it was still much smaller than the school Tiffany had attended in Santa Monica.

"This is it?" the teen asked in disbelief. "What are there, like twelve students?"

"I'm sure there are at least twenty," Carly said as she turned off the car and unfastened her seat belt. "Come on. Let's get you registered. I called last week and the office already had your transcripts, so that will help."

"Nothing's going to help," Tiffany muttered.

Carly ignored that and walked toward the main entrance. She remembered everything about this school—she'd attended it herself. More years ago than she could count, she'd been thrilled to finally be in high school. It had seemed so mature and exciting. Some of the seniors had been close to eighteen. The senior guys all had deep voices and a lot had beards or mustaches.

Carly smiled as she recalled clinging to Maribel as both of them had stared at all the older guys. It had been like waking up on a different planet—an exciting one filled with possibilities. She and her friend had spent that first lunch period walking around the campus, figuring out where things were. One of the seniors had actually smiled at them and said hi. Carly had a feeling she and Maribel had shrieked and run off in the opposite direction.

Hard to believe she'd ever been that innocent and silly. Good times, she thought wryly.

She led the way to the administration desk. None of the staff looked familiar, which made sense. She'd been out of high school nearly…

Carly did the math, redid it, then groaned. Nearly twenty-two years. Was that possible? No way. She wasn't *that* old, was she? Apparently she was. Talk about depressing.

"May I help you?" the young woman behind the desk asked as Carly leaned against the counter.

"I'm here to register my daughter. Her transcripts were sent ahead. I called last week to confirm."

The woman smiled. "Of course. Tiffany Spencer."

Tiffany shuffled up to the counter and gave the heavy sigh of a child being punished by horrible parents.

"I'm new," she said with as much cheerfulness as those facing certain death in the Spanish Inquisition.

"I know settling in to a new school can be difficult, but you'll do fine, honey," the woman said. "I'm Jenny. I work here in the office. Let me get your file and we'll figure out what classes you're taking. Oh, and you'll want to meet with Mrs. Beecham, the girls' vice principal. Just this one time," Jenny added with a wink. "You don't want to make a habit of hanging out with her."

Jenny bustled out of the front office and disappeared into a rear room. Carly looked at her daughter.

"She seems nice."

"Sure. And lame. We're not going to be friends. Why does she want to pretend any of this matters?"

"Can't she just be a nice person who wants to help?"

"Right. Plus it's totally weird that you went here. It was a really long time ago, but still. What if one of the teachers remembers you? I don't want anyone talking about that. Then I won't make any friends for sure."

Carly thought about pointing out that most of the kids

in the school were locals and most likely their parents had attended the school, as well, but she doubted Tiffany would find any comfort in that.

"A lot of my teachers were pretty old," she said instead. "I'm guessing many of them are retired."

There were a few exceptions. Her gym teacher had been in her twenties and Mr. Everwood, her math teacher, had just finished college. Carly almost mentioned that when she remembered how both she and Maribel had had huge crushes on the man. He'd been maybe twenty-five and very hunky, in an older man sort of way.

She and Maribel had sat together in his geometry and algebra classes, giggling softly at the wonder of being so close to the object of their affection. Mr. Everwood had broken their hearts their second year when he'd invited them to his wedding.

Maribel had been out of town that weekend, but Carly had bravely attended with a couple of other friends. She'd found her heart miraculously mended when a junior on the basketball team, also a student of Mr. Everwood's, had danced with her twice, then asked her out for the following Saturday.

"What's so funny?" Tiffany asked suspiciously. "You're smiling. It's because you're thinking of a new way to make me miserable, aren't you?"

Carly laughed. "Not even a little. I'll tell you a secret, Tiffany. Not everything in the world is about you."

"I know. Just the bad stuff is."

Thirty minutes later Tiffany had a class schedule, books, a locker and was being led away by the ever-cheerful and pleasant Jenny. Carly turned from the administration office and walked back toward the main entrance. As she reached for the door handle to head to her car, someone called her name.

"Carly? Carly Washington?"

Carly stopped, turned and blinked at the tall man walking toward her. He was familiar. Older, sure, with gray at his temples. He wore his dark hair shorter, and there were more lines than she remembered. The brightly printed shirts he'd favored had been replaced with solid-color ones, and he'd probably put on ten or fifteen pounds. Otherwise, he was exactly the same.

"Mr. Everwood," she said, feeling herself blush even though she knew there was no way he could have a clue that she'd been thinking about him a few minutes before. "Wow. You're still here."

He grinned as he approached. "I know. I should have gone on to bigger and better things, but I love teaching. I've tried not to, but I think it's too late for me to change now." He stared into her eyes. His were still dark brown.

"But that's great. We need good teachers and you were that. I'm sure you still are."

"I like to think so. You wouldn't recognize the old classroom. These days we do a lot with computers and programming. Every student has a computer station in nearly all the classes."

"That will make Tiffany happy. She's of that generation—the one that doesn't remember a world without computers."

Carly nearly groaned. Could this conversation be more lame? Could *she?*

"How old is your daughter?"

"Fifteen."

"She might be in my class."

"I hope not," Carly said, trying to relax. "She's deathly afraid of coming face-to-face with one of my old, um, former teachers and have him or her tell the class I used to go here. So if she is in your class I would appreciate you not saying anything. Lucky for me, I didn't mention I'd ever had Mr. Everwood for math."

He raised his eyebrows. "We're both adults, Carly. You can call me Steve now."

Steve? Steve? No. That wasn't going to happen. She'd been raised to call teachers by their last names and there was no way she could ever think of Mr. Everwood as anything but a teacher. Steve?

"Okay. Sure."

The humor faded from his eyes. "I sometimes speak with your mother," he said. "I'm sorry to hear about your divorce."

News sure spread fast, she thought, knowing she shouldn't be surprised. "Thanks. I'm okay with it."

"I'm glad to hear that. Of course your husband's stupidity is my gain."

Carly knew her mouth was open because she'd felt her jaw drop. Was Mr. Everwood coming on to her?

"Yes, well, at least we've managed to stay on speaking terms." She swallowed. "Me and my ex-husband. Not you and me. Of course we can speak, too."

"I'd like that."

He would? Why?

"Okay. Great. Look, I really have to get back to the B and B."

"Sure. Would you mind if I gave you a call sometime?"

Him? Call her? For what?

She wanted to run shrieking into the night, except it was day and shrieking would only make her look stupid.

"That would be fine," she said as she backed toward the door. "You probably have the number."

"Of course. Good to see you, Carly."

"You, too, Mr., um, Steve."

Carly drove directly to the B and B, then breathed a sigh of relief when she saw Maribel's car still parked in the side lot. She flew across the gravel and raced into the kitchen.

"Where's my mom?" she asked Maribel, who had just put a bowl into the refrigerator.

"Upstairs. Why? Is something wrong? Were you in an accident?"

"What? No. Oh, God." Carly pulled out a stool and sank down, then she looked at her friend and started to laugh. "I registered Carly for school," she said, between bursts of laughter.

"Sounds like it was a fun experience."

"It was fine, but afterward I ran into Mr. Everwood."

Maribel sat next to her and patted her arm. "We're all adults now, Carly. It's okay to call him Steve."

"That's what he said," Carly told her even as she lost control of another burst of giggles. "I think he asked me out. He said he was going to call. Mr. Everwood. Twenty-three years ago I would have been thrilled, but now it's just plain weird. Besides, isn't he married?"

"A widower, and something of a ladies' man. You be careful around him."

Carly held in another shriek. "Our former math teacher is a ladies' man? I can't grasp the concept. And you don't have to worry about me. I'm not going out with him. There's a huge *ick* factor. This guy used to be my teacher."

"Twenty years ago."

"I know, but still. I can barely call him Steve. I certainly can't date him."

Dating? Not in this lifetime. Or at least not for a very long time. She already had too much going on.

"I'm still trying to get settled here. Plus, I was married for nearly seventeen years. The last thing I'm looking for is another man."

"What about sex?" Maribel asked with a grin.

Carly stared at her. "You can't expect me to have sex with Mr. Everwood!"

"I guess not if you can't call him by his first name. He's actually pretty nice and not bad looking. I'm just saying be careful. He has a reputation for being a love 'em and leave 'em kind of guy."

"This is too surreal," Carly said. "Tell me it's five o'clock somewhere. I think I need wine."

Instead of drowning her sorrows in a glass of chardonnay, Carly chose to put her morning activities behind her and work on her plan. She'd decided to make a formal presentation to her mother, putting everything in writing so they were both clear on where they were going. Assuming this all came to pass.

After spending most of the past four days brainstorming ways to bring the inn back to profitable status, she found herself getting more and more excited about the possibilities. If her mother agreed with Carly's ideas, there was a better-than-even chance they could make a lot of money. Things had a chance of going badly, as well, but Carly didn't want to think about that.

She ran the numbers for the fourth time that afternoon, then made sure all her spreadsheets were in order. While she would have liked to do her presentation on the computer, she thought her mother would be more comfortable with actual paper in front of her.

She was so engrossed in what she was doing that she didn't notice the time, and was shocked when Tiffany stormed into her room.

"I'll never forgive you," the teen announced as tears spilled down her face. "Never, ever."

Carly glanced at the clock and was surprised to see it was nearly three-thirty. She was supposed to meet with her mother at four.

She put aside her paper and rose to face her daughter. Obviously her first day at a new high school hadn't been a success.

"Tell me what happened," Carly said quietly.

"Nothing. Exactly nothing. No one talked to me, no one even looked at me. It's like I was invisible. I sat by myself at lunch. That's *never* happened to me before. I'm the popular one. I'm the one who gets to say who's in and who isn't."

She wiped her face, then threw her books on the bed. "Plus you let Grandma come pick me up. Do you know how humiliating that was? She was standing outside the car! She called my name and waved."

Carly winced. When her mother had offered to pick up Tiffany, Carly had been grateful for the extra time to polish her work. She hadn't thought to warn her not to acknowledge Tiffany in any way until she was in the car and they were safely out of sight of her friends.

"I'm sorry about that," Carly told her. "I know this seems horrible now, but it will get better."

"How do you know?" Tiffany demanded. "You never changed schools when you were growing up. You never had your life destroyed. I hate you! This is all your f-fault." Her voice broke on a sob. "If you weren't such a bitch, Daddy never would have left us. We wouldn't have had to move here. *You* did this. You—"

Her eyes widened and her mouth opened, as if she'd just realized what she'd said.

Carly experienced her own brand of shock. Her daughter had gotten angry with her before—countless times—but she'd never sworn at her. Sympathy turned to annoyance and threatened to grow into something else.

She wanted a chance to have her own tantrum. When did she get to rage at the unfairness of it all? She wanted to give her daughter a few facts about where the blame lay, and point out that her precious father had only called under threat of a court order.

Then the anger grew and was joined by the sharp pain of raising a teenager and being the bad guy all the time. Eventually she and Tiffany would reconnect. Eventually her daughter would understand what was important, but that era of peace and unity was years away. Until then there was only this.

"I meant it," Tiffany said, raising her chin. "I don't care if you punish me. What does it matter if I'm grounded? I don't have anywhere to go or anyone to see."

Carly turned away. "Get out of here."

"What? Aren't you going to punish me?"

"Right now I don't even want to look at you. Go to your room and stay there."

"You can't tell me what to do."

Carly turned on her daughter. She didn't raise her voice, but for once she didn't hide her disappointment, anger and pain.

"Get out of my sight."

Tiffany gasped, grabbed her books and fled.

Carly did her best to clear Tiffany from her mind as she set out the papers in front of her mother. A couple of hours alone in her room might give the teen time to rethink her words and actions and come to the conclusion that she'd been rude and wrong. Given Tiffany's current hormone level and mental state, it seemed unlikely; but hey, a mom could dream.

"I'm interested in a three-pronged approach to growing our bottom line," Carly said after she'd set up an easel and put up the first graphic of three arrows pointing up. "First, individual bookings, second, group bookings and third, day visitors. The individual bookings are going to account for most of our weekend reservations, so the other two need to fill up our midweek slots. My marketing emphasis will be based on the haunted-house angle. It's the only way we'll get people to come out here. The decrease in visitors in recent years proves that without a hook, we're not going to make it."

She flipped to the second graphic, this one showing a couple in a car. "I want to use the existing database to send out a letter to all our previous customers. We can offer them a twenty-percent discount for their next stay. I'll also put together some packages—a cooking weekend, day trips to Napa, or an afternoon on a marine research vessel. I already have some contacts there."

Her mother didn't comment, nor could Carly read her expression. So she just kept on talking.

"We'll advertise in very specific magazines. I've listed them on page two, along with their rates."

Her mother flipped the page. "This is a lot of money," Rhonda told her.

Carly thought about pointing out it was way less than it had cost to replace perfectly good china and flatware, but didn't.

"I have more specifics on attracting couples and families, but right now I'd like to continue the overview," she said. "The group bookings would be small conferences. There are lots of groups looking for a unique place to come and have a two- or three-day session. I've had interest from some horror writers— obviously they're excited about the ghost angle. There are three culinary institutes who would like to book for three- and five- day sessions at a haunted house. Management off-sites are another opportunity. I'm still getting information on that."

"This is all very nice, Carly, but I don't want a bunch of strangers in my house."

Carly opened her mouth, then closed it. "Mom, this is a bed-and-breakfast. Strangers is what we do."

Her mother sighed. "You know what I mean. Nice married couples are one thing, but horror writers? And I don't want a bunch of business people here."

Carly had expected resistance, but not like this. "What do you have against business people?"

"For one thing, we only offer breakfast. I'm not interested in opening a restaurant."

"I agree. It's too expensive and too iffy. But we can offer boxed lunches with advance notice, and catering. I've spoken to several of the restaurants in town and they're more than willing to deliver out here. In fact, the boxed lunches tie in with my idea for day visitors. We could offer the larger, public rooms for meetings of local clubs. Civic groups, women's groups. We make a couple of bucks a head on their lunch and give them the parlors for free."

"How is that going to help anything?"

"If they like what they see then they'll think about holding their daughter's wedding here. Or a birthday party. Or putting up out-of-town guests. We need to remind the world we're still here. I've spoken with a few groups and they're very interested. They love the idea that we're haunted."

"Seems like you've been talking to the world."

"Just trying to get a handle on things. Everyone who has been here loves the place and those who haven't are really intrigued. Without the ghost angle, I couldn't get anyone to return calls. But Mary is a fabulous selling point. Who wouldn't want to stay at a haunted B and B? That's going to be our main selling point with the management off-sites. That, and the quiet."

Rhonda flipped through the pages. "I just don't know. It's all so much. Do we have to do this?"

Carly sat across from her. "No, we don't. But if you don't want to make changes then you need to sell right now. The B and B is losing between two and three thousand dollars a month just to stay running and that doesn't count the repairs or any replacement costs. Or property taxes. They're incredibly high. At the rate you're burning through the equity in this place, you have about three years left."

"What happens in three years?"

"You won't be able to get enough money out of the sale to live on the proceeds. You'll have to get a job."

Rhonda leaned back in her chair. "I don't want that. I'm ready to retire."

"I know, Mom. The thing is, I would really hate for you to sell this house after all this time. It's a part of our heritage. But I also want you to be financially secure. What I propose is that you give me one year to get the B and B back on its feet financially. If I can't do it, then you can still sell and have your nest egg. If I can, then we'll go back to what we'd always talked about—that I would take over the business and slowly buy you out."

"You want to make a lot of changes. I'm not comfortable with this. Why does it have to be different?"

"Because you're losing a lot of money."

Her mother closed her eyes. "I hate this. I wish your father hadn't died. He always took care of everything. This has been so hard for me."

Carly sat next to her and took her hand. "It has. It's been a long seven years and you've done a great job. But I don't want you to lose your retirement and I really don't want to lose the house."

Rhonda nodded, then looked at her daughter. "I just don't know if you can do it. What if you fail?"

Carly tried not to take the lack of confidence personally.

"I'm asking for a year. That's all. If things aren't going well at the end of that time, you can still sell and get out enough to live on for the rest of your life."

"All right. I'll think about it."

Carly held in a sigh. Her mother was notorious for thinking about things for weeks at a time and then still not deciding.

"I need to know by tomorrow."

"What?" Her mother glared at her. "I can't decide something this big that quickly. You're pressuring me. What does it matter if I take a few weeks?"

"It matters to me. I need Tiffany settled. If you're going to say no, I need to find a job somewhere else and get her into a new school. I don't want to have her start to make friends here only to uproot her again. It's not fair. I'm asking you to decide in a reasonable time frame. I have responsibilities to my daughter, and I take them as seriously as you took your responsibilities to me."

Her mother's eyes filled with tears. "This isn't fair. If your father were still alive…"

"But he isn't."

"You think I don't know that? I've had to deal with this all by myself. You haven't been any help. You've been running around having a good time while I suffered."

Carly stood and stepped back a couple of steps. "I've been raising my child."

"With that no-good man you married. I don't understand it. And now you come back here and want to order me around."

Carly knew that however this went, she was going to be the bad guy. "That's not my intent. I saw us as partners. I've offered my vision for what we can do to make the B and B successful again. I'm willing to work sixteen-hour days and devote myself to the project. All I ask in return is for you to either agree or disagree. But I won't wait forever. If you don't like what I want to do, then you'll need time to figure out what you want to do instead."

"Oh, sure. Put it all on me. You've always been difficult, but I don't remember you being so hard-hearted. When did that happen?"

"I have no idea," Carly told her, feeling both sad and resigned. Why couldn't her mother simply make a decision? Obviously she'd known changes would have to happen to make the business a success.

Of course Carly already knew the answer to that. If her mother decided anything, then she had to take responsibility—the one thing she hated to do. Life was better when whatever went wrong was someone else's fault.

"You're not giving me much choice," Rhonda said. "Either I agree or you walk away from me forever."

"That's not what I said. If the B and B is going to be closed, then I have to make a life for myself and my daughter. That's hardly abandoning you."

Rhonda didn't look convinced. "Fine. Have it your way. You'd probably do it without me."

Carly sank back into the chair. "You're saying yes? You're agreeing with my plan?"

"Yes. It's your idea and you're in charge."

Carly understood the momspeak. That she wasn't just in charge, she was responsible. If anything went wrong, she was to blame.

She was okay with that—in this case it was true.

"I suppose you'll be taking over everything," her mother said sadly. "I won't matter at all."

"That's not true. I'll need your help more than ever. With me getting all the advertising in place and coming up with different ideas, I'll be swamped. You're the heart and soul of this B and B, Mom. You always have been. Yes, I have a lot of things I want to get done, but none of it will happen without you."

She squeezed her mother's hand. "I mean that."

At that moment Rhonda looked old and small. Carly opened her mouth, then closed it.

Was that the *real* problem? That her mother didn't feel needed by anyone?

Rhonda sighed. "I just don't have the energy I used to, but if you need me, of course I'll be there."

"Thanks. I want to take the load off you and I will. But at first I'll need your help in the day-to-day running of things. At least until I'm up to speed and can do some rearranging of the staff."

"All right," Rhonda said. "We'll be a team."

"Great." Carly smiled. "I'm going to do everything I can to make the B and B a success."

"I hope it works," Rhonda said. "If it doesn't, we'll all know you tried your best and that's what matters."

Carly accepted the words in the spirit they were given— or at least in the spirit she wanted them to be given. She leaned forward and hugged her mother. The soft scent of Chanel No. 5 surrounded her.

"You'll see," she said. "It's going to be great."

And it would be. Just as soon as Carly stopped the money hemorrhage, got a few more guests and figured out what she was going to do with her daughter. Then it would be great.

Her small moment of celebration lasted for as long as it took to climb to her daughter's room. After a quick knock, she stepped inside. The bedroom was empty, but she heard a chair squeak in the small parlor.

Carly didn't want to have this conversation. She wanted things to be as they had been two or three years ago. Before her daughter had become so difficult and demanding. Sure, it was just a teenage thing, but why did she have to suffer, too?

Squaring her shoulders, she crossed the floor and entered the second room. Tiffany sat in a chair by the window. She didn't look up as Carly entered.

"It's not my fault," the teen said before Carly could speak. "You're messing everything up and I'm reacting to that. If we'd stayed back in Santa Monica, none of this would have happened."

Carly didn't know what to address first—the obvious lie that if they hadn't moved Tiffany would have behaved perfectly, or the complete lack of responsibility.

"So this is my fault?" she asked incredulously.

"Yes." Her daughter glared at her. "You're making me act this way."

The words were different, but the intent was the same. Painfully the same, and familiar. It took Carly a second to place it and when she did, she didn't know if she should laugh or cry.

"Oh, my God. You're exactly like my mother," Carly said in horror. "You don't take responsibility for anything and you're completely selfish."

"What?" Tiffany yelped. "That's not true."

Carly barely heard her. She pulled out the desk chair and sat down. Her brain seemed to be swelling by the second. Was it true? Was it possible?

"You're exactly like her," she repeated, more to herself than to Tiffany. "You blame me for your actions, you can't see any view but your own. How did this happen? Did I do it? Did I grow up a certain way based on my mother? Did my hyper sense of responsibility mean you didn't have to be responsible for anything?"

Had she screwed up her daughter as much as she'd been screwed up herself? Was this the legacy she had inadvertently passed on?

"Is it just your age?" Carly asked. "Or is it your character?"

Tiffany stood and waved her arms. "Hello. Still in the room. Stop talking about me as if I'm not here."

"What? Oh. Right." Carly looked at her daughter. "Because this is all about you."

Tiffany stomped her foot. "Stop saying that. I'm not selfish."

"And the last time you thought about anyone was when? You accused me of ruining things so your father left. Here's a news flash—it takes two to make or break a marriage. I'm willing to accept my responsibility in what went wrong, but your father has his, as well. We were equal partners in what happened. You can continue to blame me, but that doesn't change the truth. As for what you did—there's no excuse.

You hurt me because you don't care about me. I'm working my butt off to make your life better and all you can see is what's wrong with it."

She rose. This revelation about her daughter deserved some serious thought. If she was contributing to Tiffany's center-of-the-universe thinking, she was going to have to change how she interacted with her daughter. She headed for the door.

"Wait," Tiffany called. "What about me?"

Carly turned and stared at her. "What about you?"

"Aren't you going to punish me? For what I said." Tiffany looked both angry and afraid.

"Will that make you feel better?" Carly asked. "Will that take away some of the guilt?"

Her daughter nodded.

"Then not just yet."

Carly returned to her room and started to organize the papers on her desk. First up, she needed her own office. There were several available spaces downstairs. She would clear one out and move her stuff in.

Thank goodness her laptop was relatively new. She wouldn't have to buy a new computer anytime soon. She could—

She set down the folder she'd grabbed and leaned back in her chair. She was really going to do this. Her! She was going to turn this business around and make it a success. Whatever happened, wherever they ended up, it would be because of her hard work, her ideas, her vision. No one was making her do this and no one was offering advice. It was totally and completely up to her.

The idea of being that much in charge was both terrifying and freeing. Sure, if she failed it was public, big-time, and had a huge impact on many lives. But if she didn't… If it worked, then it was something she could point to with pride.

The need to share the slightly thrilling, slightly scary moment had her reaching for the phone. But who would she call? Maribel was busy with her family, and all her L.A. friends had turned out to be less than friendly.

"I wish you were here, Mary," she murmured aloud, but the ghost didn't appear. Not that she actually expected her to. Ghosts weren't real, right? Except Carly needed the ghost. Having a haunted B and B had opened doors for her. Without a "shimmering essence," she was unlikely to turn the business around.

A problem to deal with later. Right now she could celebrate her pending business venture with a trip downstairs to pick out her office. She could move in that afternoon, then come up with a schedule. In a perfect world, she would spend mornings working on growing the business and afternoons learning all the ins and outs of the B and B. Not that her life was going to be that tidy, but still, she could dream.

She stood to head out when someone knocked on her bedroom door. As the person on the other side was likely to be either her mother or daughter, she briefly thought about pretending to be somewhere else.

But in the end she sighed, then called, "It's open."

Tiffany stepped into her room. Her eyes were red and swollen and her lower lip trembled.

Carly had always considered herself a soft touch. Still, she didn't say anything. Maybe being a soft touch had contributed to her daughter's lack of responsibility.

"Yes?" Carly asked.

Tiffany flinched. "I'm sorry."

Carly waited. Right now those two words weren't good enough.

Tiffany swallowed. "I'm sorry I called you a bad word. I shouldn't have done it. I was mad."

"You hurt me. I love you more than anyone in the world. I would die for you. I know you're going through a lot and it's unreasonable to expect you to completely understand I'm going through some things, too, but you have to learn that you can't always blurt out what you're thinking. There are consequences for words and actions."

Tiffany began to cry. "Do you hate me?"

"I've never hated you. Sometimes I don't like you very much."

Her daughter seemed genuinely shocked. "But you're my mom."

"I know that. I love you. I always will. But liking you is different."

"B-but you have to like me." Tears spilled down her cheeks. "I'm sorry, Mom. I'm really, really sorry. I know I can be a brat and I'll try really hard to do better. I just get so mad and it gets big inside."

And Carly was a safe target. She opened her arms. Tiffany threw herself into them and held on tight.

"I'm sorry," she repeated.

Carly stroked her hair. "I accept your apology."

Tiffany sniffed. "Really? You're going to punish me now?"

"Absolutely."

"Oh, good."

Carly smiled at that. "Whoever thought you'd be happy with the idea of being punished?"

"Yeah. Don't tell anyone. So what's it going to be?"

"All the wood furniture in the public rooms need to be polished."

Tiffany stepped back. "There's a ton."

"Probably closer to two tons. You'll have a week to get it all done. After dinner I'll show you where the supplies are and how to do it."

"Okay."

Now that the ugly stuff was out of the way, Carly wanted to share the rest of her news. "Grandma agreed to my plan. We're going to stay here and make the B and B work."

"Really." Tiffany sounded more cautious than excited. "And that's good?"

"I think so. I know you're hating school right now, but you'd have to start over anywhere we went. At least it's pretty here, and we have a cool house. You'll make friends. Imagine the slumber parties you could have here."

Tiffany brightened at the thought. "That would be good. Maybe a real party. You know, with boys."

"Hmm, maybe not for another year or so."

"Oh, Mom."

"Yeah, yeah, I know. I'm a serious drag. But here's the good part. I'm going to be doing a lot of advertising for the B and B. I want your help on that. You can design the graphics and work on the ads. That sort of thing. It will be your chore. We'll work out a schedule, and if you're spending more time on it than we decide, I'll pay you."

"Really? That's so cool."

"I'm glad you think so."

Some might question her decision to seek input from a fifteen-year-old, but Tiffany had inherited all of Neil's marketing sense and was a whiz on the computer.

"There's a great computer lab at school," Tiffany said. "Maybe I can hang out there at lunch and do some work on this. It's not like I have anyone to talk to."

"I appreciate your cooperation," Carly said, ignoring the dig about school. She knew that would get better fairly quickly. "This is going to be fun. And when you're grown up, you'll love having this place as part of your history."

"I'll inherit it, right?" her ever-thoughtful, ever-sensitive daughter asked. "When you're dead, I mean? Then I can sell it and use the money to buy a really great car."

"I'm sure none of us can wait."

Carly typed on the keyboard and then pushed the enter button. The numbers on the computer screen wiggled and danced, then quickly rearranged into a simple profit-and-loss statement. She studied the bottom line and grimaced. Bad. They were still hemorrhaging money, but at least doing so was helping them achieve something.

"Is this a good time?"

She looked up and saw Maribel standing in the entrance to her office.

"Absolutely." Carly saved the file, then turned toward her friend. "The whole numbers thing makes me crazy. Some days I know I can do it and others I just want to run screaming into the mist, never to be heard from again."

Maribel sank onto the chair next to Carly's desk and handed her a file. Then she reached around and began to rub the small of her back.

"It's only been three weeks," her friend reminded her. "Give yourself a break. You've already made a ton of changes."

"Thanks. How are you feeling?"

"Seriously pregnant. I'm reaching the stage where everything hurts."

"You can stop working anytime," Carly reminded her. "Your daughter has graciously agreed to fill in for you while she's on summer break from college."

"That's because I didn't raise a fool," Maribel said with a smile. "Lisa has figured out she can make more working for you *and* be done with her workday by eleven in the morning. That leaves her plenty of time to hang out with her friends." Maribel leaned back in the chair and rested a hand on her belly. "I've given her all the recipes and I'll be just a phone call away."

"I'm not concerned," Carly told her. "We'll be fine."

"I know. It's just I feel bad missing out on all the fun. After years of the same old same old, new things are happening. Oh, speaking of which, here are the menus I worked up. Your idea for box lunches from town is a good one, but we can definitely make them cheaper ourselves. Even with a part-time person devoted to them, we come out ahead."

Carly flipped through the pages her friend had brought. Although she'd contacted a deli in town to provide box lunches, she'd wondered about having them made on-site. It gave her a little more flexibility, although it added to her stress level by giving her another thing to worry about.

"What do you think?" she asked.

Maribel grinned. "Wow. Someone wants my opinion on more than the location of the soccer ball or a backpack. I'm flattered."

Carly chuckled. "I know that one. But I mean it. I don't think I'd start this up until you were ready to come back to work. I'd need your help. Are you willing to take on supervising a helper?"

"Ooh, management. Sure. I could handle that. I wouldn't mind putting in a few extra hours a week."

"Good. I'll go over your numbers and figure out what I want to do," Carly said. "I'm leaning toward moving our sandwich operations here."

"If you do, I have a couple of cookie recipes I want to try. I've been playing around with them and if I can get them the way I want them, we could include them in the lunches." Maribel tucked her hair behind her ears and cleared her throat. "Okay, it's more than that. I've been thinking maybe we could go in on the cookie thing together. Sell them here under a special Chatsworth-by-the-Sea label. Split the profits."

"I like it," Carly said. "We could have them in the guests' rooms when they arrive, then sell them. We could get into some kind of limited mail order. Of course not right now. I'm not sure I can deal with one more thing."

"Right back at you," Maribel said. "But let's talk about it again after the baby."

Carly flipped forward a few months on her calendar and wrote "cookies." "Think I'll know what that means?"

"Hope so. I'll remember even if you don't." Her friend touched her arm. "Are you doing okay?"

"Yeah. I am. It's insane. When my mom agreed to all this, I told her I'd be working sixteen-hour days, and I wasn't kidding. There's a lot of work. But I'm pulling it together."

Carly pointed to a binder on her desk. "Those are menus from local restaurants willing to deliver. I have a two-day seminar next week and local civic groups lined up. The model–airplane club booked every room for the long weekend in ten days. And there is a group of horror writers coming here for a retreat at the end of June."

Maribel grinned. "Horror writers?"

"It's the ghost thing. I guess they think they'll be inspired. In fact all of our guests, except the model–plane guys, are here because of Mary. I just wish she'd make an appearance."

"Sort of a personal haunting?"

"Yeah. I haven't seen any sign of her since I've been back."

"I've *never* seen her," Maribel said with a laugh. "Remember? You saw her all the time when we were kids. I just felt a chilly brush and tried not to feel slighted that it wasn't more."

Carly tried not to ignore the fact that she was wishing for the moon. "Having a ghost in residence is a huge selling point. That appealing fact is responsible for most of our new bookings. But a ghost? For real?"

Maribel shrugged. "You used to believe."

"Then I grew up. But I would swear I saw something. I know I felt it."

"You and me both. Maybe you should go on the Internet and see if there's a way to lure a spirit here. You don't specifically need Mary. Pretty much any spirit would do." Maribel laughed. "I can't believe I just said that."

"It *is* crazy."

"But you'll go investigate?"

Carly nodded. "A ghost would be cool. But a friendly one."

"Right. Maybe you could take applications."

The two women laughed together.

"But do me a favor," Maribel said. "Wait until I'm out of here to try anything. I'm not really ghost-friendly."

"Fair enough."

Carly glanced around the large office she'd made for herself. After painting the walls a pale yellow, she'd moved in an old desk, a large table for additional workspace and a couple of bookcases. Next door was a conference room she'd decorated with comfortable chairs from the attic.

"I'm really doing this," she said, both pleased and stunned by the way things were working out.

"You're not just doing it, you're doing it well." Maribel glanced at the open door and leaned close. "A couple of days ago I overheard your mother talking to one of her friends. She mentioned you had already doubled the bookings. I think she's impressed."

"I'm glad. Not that she would ever say anything to me."

"Of course not. My mom is exactly the same. I promise myself I won't be like her when my kids are out on their own, but I'm afraid I will be. How does that happen? How do we turn into our mothers?"

"Not a clue." Carly didn't want to think she was anything like her mother, but she had a feeling they had more in common than she wanted to admit.

"Maybe I'll do better with this one," Maribel said, glancing down at her stomach.

"You did great with the others."

"I did okay. I learned from each of them. After all this time one would think I would be perfect, but I know that's not true."

"Yeah, I make plenty of mistakes." Carly glanced out at the gardens. "Do you think it's the least bit possible that our kids understand we're trying to do our best?"

"Not a prayer."

"You're right. I would never have believed that of my mom." Carly still didn't.

"It is a mother's lot in life to be misunderstood and under-appreciated. That's why we get our own day." Maribel pushed herself into standing position and groaned. "I'm going to go home where I can lie down and remember what it was like when I could see my feet."

"Okay. Have a good afternoon."

"You, too."

Carly turned back to her computer and opened the spreadsheet. She wanted to finish this projection, then start calling some of the local bridal fairs. If it wasn't too late, she would buy a booth and plan on selling the B and B as a great place to hold a wedding. But before she could finish entering the information into her program, the phone rang.

"Chatsworth-by-the-Sea," Carly said. "May I help you?"

"I would like to speak with Carly Spencer please."

"That's me."

"Mrs. Spencer, this is Mrs. Beecham, the vice principal. I have Tiffany in my office."

"What?" Carly's stomach flopped over and dove for her toes. No. This wasn't happening.

"I'm sorry to inform you that your daughter has been cutting class. Is it possible for you to come to the school anytime soon?"

Carly had already logged out of her program. "I'll be right there."

It had only been three weeks, Carly thought grimly as she parked on the street, then hurried in the main entrance.

Three weeks. Tiffany had never once gotten in this kind of trouble at her old school.

Worse, Carly had thought things had been improving with her daughter. Tiffany had made a couple of friends, including a girl who had stayed for dinner a couple of nights ago. There was even a boy she liked—Jack something. She mentioned meeting him in the computer lab and how she hoped he liked her. So why this?

Carly followed the familiar halls to the vice principal's office and went inside. Tiffany sat on a bench outside a closed door. She rose when she saw her mother.

"You didn't bring Grandma," she said, sounding both scared and relieved.

"No. I didn't tell her." Carly hadn't wanted to hear the lecture. "I'll explain things to her after I understand them myself."

Tiffany grabbed her arm. "It's not what you think. It's not bad. I didn't do anything wrong. Well, not bad-wrong. Mom, I can explain. It's not my fault."

"How many times have I heard that sentence before?"

"But it's true."

The door opened and Mrs. Beecham stepped out.

The woman was in her early thirties, attractive and well dressed. Not exactly the dried-up old prune Carly remembered from *her* days at the school. Apparently administrators had changed in the past twenty-two years. But the rules hadn't, and if Tiffany was cutting class, there was going to be hell to pay both here and at home.

"Mrs. Spencer?" the vice principal asked with a smile. "It's very nice to meet you, although I'm sorry it has to be under these circumstances."

"Me, too," Carly said as they shook hands.

Tiffany tightened her grip on her arm. "Mom, I'm really, really telling the truth. I didn't do anything wrong."

"Why don't you let us discuss it?" Mrs. Beecham said pleasantly. "Would you prefer your daughter in with us or would you like to have her wait out here?"

Tiffany's blue eyes pleaded for admission to the meeting. Carly hesitated. The situation was a new one. She still couldn't believe this was happening. Tiffany had acted up before, but she'd never done it at school. Skipping classes? Was it possible.

"She can join us," she said, not sure if she was making the right decision.

"Thanks." Tiffany moved close. "I can explain everything."

Mrs. Beecham frowned. "You'll have to be quiet if you're to sit with us," she said sternly. "Do I make myself clear?"

Tiffany shivered slightly and nodded.

Carly followed the vice principal into her bright and cheerful office and took one of the two chairs on the visitor side of the desk. Several plaques hung on the wall, honoring the school for academic achievement. There were mentions of the various universities Mrs. Beecham had attended and Carly was a little surprised to see her first name was Heather. Somehow women named Heather had never been so authoritarian before. At least not in her world.

"Tiffany has missed her class after lunch twice this week," Mrs. Beecham said. "I can see by her transcripts that she was never in this sort of trouble before, which is why I wanted to have you in, Mrs. Spencer. We don't want to start a negative pattern here in Tiffany's new school."

"I don't get it," Carly said, turning to her daughter. "You're cutting class after lunch? What's going on? Are you leaving campus?"

"That's not permitted until one is a senior," Mrs. Beecham said quietly.

Tiffany ignored her. "I'm not going anywhere. I've been working in the computer lab. On stuff for the B and B. That's what I've been trying to tell you. I was working on the computer doing graphic designs. I lost track of time and didn't realize I should be in class. I messed up and I was late. But here, if you're more than ten minutes late, it counts as an unexcused absence. Which means they're saying I cut class, but I was really there."

Carly turned to Mrs. Beecham. "Is that true? Is more than a ten-minute tardy an unexcused absence?"

The other woman nodded. "It may seem harsh, but we want to make sure the students are in class, learning. People strolling in ten or fifteen minutes after the bell disrupts the class for everyone."

Carly saw her point—sort of. But if a kid was late to class, it seemed wrong to tag her with cutting school.

"I'll make sure Tiffany understands it's important to be in class on time," Carly said. "What is her punishment?"

"Two days of detention."

Tiffany gasped. Before she could say anything, Carly shot her a warning look.

"All right. Thanks, Mrs. Beecham. I assume you have

some system in place so that Tiffany can get back to class without being marked down for truancy?"

"Of course. I'll write her a pass."

"Great. If I could have a minute to speak with her in the hall, I'd really appreciate it."

"Of course."

"But I—"

Tiffany started to speak. Carly grabbed her hand and pulled her to her feet.

"We'll be right outside," she said. "I'll send her in to get the note."

"Good. Thank you so much for coming right away. I feel it's very important to nip this sort of thing in the bud."

"Of course. Sure. Have a nice day."

Carly led Tiffany into the hallway and closed the door behind them.

"It's not fair," Tiffany wailed. "I can't believe this is happening because I was late."

Carly found herself wanting to agree, yet unwilling to side with her daughter against the vice principal.

"I don't necessarily agree with the rules, but it's good to know what they are so you can avoid getting into trouble the next time."

"But I was doing stuff for *you*."

Carly put an arm around her. "I know, and I really appreciate it. But I'm thinking maybe it's time to spend your lunch hour doing something else. Trust me—you don't want a career of detention."

"I can't believe she's making me do that. I'm not some loser."

"Agreed, but it could be worse. It could be three days."

Her daughter grimaced. "I wasn't doing it on purpose. You know that, right?"

"I do. I've seen how engrossed you get in your work. I believe that you didn't hear the bell."

Tiffany looked relieved. "Thanks, Mom. This was all so horrible. She called me out of class and everything. Talk about total humiliation. I thought I'd just die."

Just then a tall, skinny guy with short brown hair and shoulders broad enough to support the world rounded the corner. He jogged toward them.

"Tiff. Jeez, I'm really sorry." He noticed Carly and skidded to a stop. "Oh, hi. Are you Tiffany's mom?"

"Yes. Carly Spencer."

"Hey. I'm Jack. I've been hanging out with Tiffany in the computer lab. This is totally my fault. I have the computer lab right after lunch so I've learned to tune out the bells. I should have been paying attention and made sure she got back to class on time."

So this was Jack—the boy Tiffany had been talking about. He was charming, in a puppy-dog kind of way. Carly liked how he took responsibility—something her daughter could learn to do.

"I've been helping her with the graphic designs," he continued. "She's really talented."

Tiffany stared at the floor and blushed. "No, you are," she mumbled. "Jack's come up with some great ideas for colors."

He shrugged. "I'm really interested in the house, Mrs. Spencer. I've heard about it for years, but I've never been. The ghost thing. Totally cool. I've been doing some research on ghosts and paranormal phenomenon. I've even bought some equipment, you know, to help find it."

Tiffany looked at him. "My mom's seen the ghost."

"For real?"

"Not recently," Carly said. "That was years ago. You should come out and look around."

His face brightened. He glanced at Tiffany and seemed to almost glow. "Thank you for asking. I'd like that very much. Look, um, I have to get back to class. I just wanted to let you know that it wasn't Tiffany's fault."

He smiled at her, winked at her daughter, then loped away.

Carly watched him go. Okay, he was a good kid with decent manners. She liked that and she liked him. Of course saying that was a really bad idea.

"He's older, isn't he?" she asked instead.

"Just by a year. He's sixteen." Tiffany sighed. "He has his license. Do you think he likes me?"

"I don't know. Maybe. I'm not sure about him, though."

Tiffany rolled her eyes. "You don't like anyone I like. So why did you invite him over?"

"So I can keep an eye on him and you."

"I hate my life."

"I'm sure you do. Look, go get your note from Mrs. Beecham and head to class. I'll be by after your detention to pick you up."

Tiffany nodded, but before she turned away, she asked, "What's my punishment at home?"

Carly almost asked "For what?" when she remembered the tardiness. She weighed the options and decided to go with her gut.

"You've never done this before," she said. "I think there are extenuating circumstances. Your detention is enough."

Tiffany's whole face brightened. "Yeah?"

"Yeah."

Her daughter flung her arms around her and hugged her hard. "You're the best, Mom."

"I am pretty cool, aren't I?"

Carly had barely taken two steps when she saw Mr. Everwood, aka Steve, approaching.

"We meet again," he said, looking handsome in a math-teacher sort of way. "I heard about Tiffany. I think the tardy rule takes things a little too far, but I don't make the rules."

"Me, either. But it's handled."

"How are you settling in?"

"Getting there. I'm working hard at the B and B. It's fun, but challenging."

"I heard there were some changes."

"That's true."

"I'd love to hear the details. How about over dinner?"

The man was too smooth by far, Carly thought.

"I, uh, dinner." With Mr. Everwood? Could she really do that? "Um, sure. Great."

"I'll give you a call."

She nodded and started backing toward the main entrance. "I know you know the number. Thanks. I, uh, I have to get back to work. Good to see you."

"You, too, Carly."

She turned to bolt, but before she could get up any speed, he called her back.

"How are we doing on the whole 'calling me by my first name' thing?" he asked with a grin.

"It's much better."

"You're lying."

"Okay. I'm working on it."

"Keep practicing."

Carly watched her mother debate which side to come down on. Tiffany shouldn't be late to class, but this was her beloved granddaughter and she had been working to help the B and B.

"You've spoken with her?" Rhonda asked.

"Yes, and she has detention for two days. That should be unpleasant enough to remind her to get back in class on time."

"Are you punishing her?"

Carly debated how to handle the situation. Right now she couldn't face another run-in with her mother on how to raise Tiffany.

"I was going to," she said carefully. "But then I remembered what you always said—that the punishment should fit the crime. As Tiffany wasn't trying to skip class and get away with anything, I think the detention is enough."

Rhonda considered the answer, then nodded. "I agree. She's basically a sweet girl. With a little more direction and parenting, she'll grow up into a fine young woman."

Carly clenched her teeth, then did her best to relax. Remember the bigger picture, she told herself. Better to keep things pleasant in the family, at least during all the changes in the B and B.

Besides, she knew one sure way to make her mother forget all about Tiffany.

"I ran into Steve Everwood while I was at the high school," she said as she poured them each a glass of lemonade. "I think he's going to call and ask me out to dinner."

Rhonda's shock was priceless. Carly wasn't sure if her mother was surprised that a man would be interested or that Carly would talk about it.

"Well, good for you," Rhonda said as she took a glass. "He's supposed to be very nice. He has a steady job and everyone says he was good to his late wife. You knew he was a widower, didn't you? He's not divorced. I've heard he does what he can to get women in bed and then he dumps them, but I doubt you'll have a problem with that."

There was so much information in her mother's short speech, Carly didn't know what to respond to first. Was her mother implying she wouldn't have a problem with Steve's amorous nature because he wasn't likely to be interested in her that way, or because she was such a slut that she could easily handle it? And what was up with making a point of him being a widower rather than divorced?

Well, at least she had the distraction she'd wanted.

"I'm not sure if I want to go out with him," Carly said. "He was my teacher in high school. That makes the whole thing kind of weird."

"That was nearly twenty-five years ago. What does it matter now?"

Technically not yet twenty-two years, Carly thought.

"Besides, you'll be forty soon," her mother added. "You'd better accept any invitations that come your way."

"Before I'm too old," Carly said, not sure if she should laugh or scream.

"Exactly. You could do worse than him."

"Good to know." How thrilling that she had yet to hit bottom.

CHAPTER 7

"This is all your fault," Rhonda complained loudly.

At least that's what Carly *thought* she was saying. She'd never been very good at reading lips and it was impossible to hear actual words over the whine of twenty or thirty remote-control model airplanes swooping and soaring off the cliffs.

The sound was incredible—part chainsaw, part lawn-mower, but at a pitch designed to send onlookers into madness.

She motioned for her mother to follow her back into the B and B where they could speak in relatively normal tones.

"What was that?" she asked when she'd closed the door behind them.

Her mother glared at her. "I blame you for that. The noise is horrible. How long are they here for?"

"Three nights." Carly did her best not to look too happy, but in truth, she was giddy with delight. "Three whole nights with the B and B full and local restaurants catering the meals. We get a cut of that, you know. A smooth fifteen percent off the top."

"I don't like it. I already have a headache."

Carly did, too, but she figured it was a small price to pay for wild success.

Okay, maybe not *wild success,* but a really big step in the right direction.

"We're lucky to have them," she said. "Their usual hotel had a lot of damage after last winter's storms so they were looking for a place. We have everything they want, including the cliffs where they can fly their planes. They're just one chapter of a fairly large national organization. We could have clubs like this here all the time."

Her mother stared at her. "You say that like it's a good thing."

"It is. Just think of the money. Plus, I've been able to put together some special activities on a small scale. We have that lecturer coming in tonight to talk about the history of the house. That should be fun. If he's any good, I'll book him regularly."

Maribel had turned her on to a professor at the community college who had done a lot of research on Chatsworth-by-the-Sea and was considered the resident expert on the ghost.

Carly was looking forward to attending the lecture herself and maybe learning something. Like where Mary had been hiding out all these weeks.

She walked into the main office and pointed to the booking schedule posted on the far wall.

"We're booking up faster than I thought we would. Those ghost hunters are here next weekend. We still have the horror writers coming and there's a group that researches paranormal phenomenon coming at the end of the month. I've already received calls from three former guests who are interested in reserving rooms. They said the drive was longer than they liked for a weekend, but it was worth it for a chance to hang with a ghost."

Her mother studied the chart. "We're starting to fill up."

"I know. It's fabulous. If things keep going like this, we might break even for the month of August."

"So soon?"

"Don't get too excited. It's just one month, but we're moving in the right direction. I want to do some more brainstorming. I was thinking of a Regency-themed weekend. We could hold cooking classes and learn the dances from the time."

"You're certainly pushing our ghost."

"She's the best selling point we have. Without her, I couldn't make this work."

Her mother shook her head. "People are so silly about ghosts."

"As long as those people are interested in booking rooms, I don't care how silly they are."

It had only been five weeks, and already Carly could see her work coming to fruition. Talk about a great feeling. There hadn't been any more calls from the school about Tiffany, which was a good thing. Neil had actually called his daughter three times. Life was good. Now if she could grow the business steadily, she would be a happy camper.

"Has Steve called?" Rhonda asked.

Carly's good mood took a decided turn for the unsettled.

"Um, yeah. Last week. He asked me to dinner but we had that group in and I had to stay and supervise the evening."

"You turned down a date with him to stay home and work?"

The tone of her mother's voice implied she was not only

stupid, but she might have lost the only opportunity she would ever have to date again.

"The B and B has to get all my attention right now."

"You can take an evening off when a nice man asks you out to dinner. You're never going to get married again if you don't put yourself out there."

Had Carly been drinking, she would have choked. "What? Married? Why would I want to do that?"

"Do you want to spend the rest of your life alone?"

"Frankly, that doesn't sound so bad. Mom, I was married for over sixteen years. I'm kind of enjoying being on my own."

"What woman *wants* to be alone?"

"A lot of them." Married. Yuck. "I'm still recovering from my time with Neil."

"The best way to get over a bad fall is to get right back on the horse. I would have myself except no one could measure up to your father."

"I'm through riding." Although Maribel's comment about sex popped into her head. It had been a really long time. She might not want to commit to any one man, but some time in bed had a certain appeal.

Of course having sex with a man meant getting naked. The last time she'd done that with someone new, she'd been twenty and pretty damned hot. While she wasn't hideous now, she was a couple of days shy of forty and she'd had a child. No one would look at her body and use the word *perky* to describe anything. There were stretch marks and squishy bits and some odd bulges she couldn't get rid of.

Obviously the solution was to find a way to have sex with

her clothes on. Or in very, very subtle lighting. Or with someone so incredibly desperate that he would only feel amazing gratitude that she was willing to be with him at all.

Carly's reluctance to date Steve came back to bite her in the butt less than five hours later. And it started so innocently, too.

"Jack asked me out," Tiffany said that night over dinner.

The clear evening was blessedly silent, what with all the model plane folks busy eating their catered dinner in the main dining room.

"That's nice," Carly told her. "You know the rule."

"But it's not fair. I can't help it if I'm not sixteen yet. If you'd had me earlier, I could be sixteen now and go out with him."

"Yes. And although I did specifically plan my pregnancy so that fifteen years later I could ruin your life, the answer stays the same. No dating until you're sixteen."

"Just because you're not interested in men, Carly, is no reason to infringe on your daughter's happiness," Rhonda said as she passed the salad.

"Yeah," Tiffany said smugly.

Carly clutched her fork while the shower scene music from *Psycho* played in her head.

"Thanks for the thought, Mom," Carly said, wishing there was wine with dinner. "But Tiffany is too young to be out alone with a guy." She turned to her daughter. "You're more than welcome to have Jack over here where you two can hang out in a very supervised way."

"You mean so you can spy on us."

"Pretty much," Carly admitted cheerfully.

Tiffany rolled her eyes as she turned to her grandmother. "She thinks we're going to have sex. We're not. I know all about it and I'm not interested."

Carly completely believed her. At that age, she'd been far more interested in romance than sex. Right until some slightly older guy had kissed her senseless and then touched her breasts in a way that had made her want to explore the possibilities.

"Tiffany seems very trustworthy," Rhonda said.

"I agree. But my decision stays the same. No dating this year."

"But I *hate* having Jack over," Tiffany complained. "He's so interested in the stupid house and the stupid ghost. He wants to check out all the rooms with some dumb equipment he bought so he can figure out where she is. I swear, he's more interested in that ghost than in me."

Which made Carly really like the boy.

"Plus, he wants you to be with him, so you can tell him where you've seen the ghost," Tiffany added, sounding outraged.

"Your boyfriend isn't interested in your mother," Rhonda said, patting her granddaughter's arm.

"I know. It's just weird."

Carly changed the subject by asking about Tiffany's progress on the new letterhead. From there, they moved into a spirited discussion on the best kind of swimsuit for summer and if they should sell "beach packs" to guests wanting water—a towel and some suntan lotion. The meal ended without anymore mention of Jack, dating, or Carly's inability to attract men.

When her mother and her daughter had disappeared—

Rhonda to open the mail and Tiffany to check out the latest fashions on the Style network—Carly retreated to her office where she leaned back in her chair and breathed in the silence.

This was good, she thought, hoping her pleasure in the moment didn't jinx it. She was working hard and it was paying off, big-time. Sure, she still had five billion things to do, but in the meantime, she was happy and making progress.

Then her mother walked into the office and put a letter on her desk.

"We're going to have a new guest," Rhonda said.

"Okay. And this is important, why?"

"Because he's going to try and ruin us. This always happens. Why can't they just leave us alone?"

Carly sat up in her chair and reached for the letter. It was addressed to her from an Adam Covell. He wanted a large room with a view for three weeks, during which time he would be conducting experiments on the house.

"Experiments?"

"Keep reading."

Carly scanned the rest of the letter. "He's coming to debunk the myth? What? He's a ghostbuster?"

"Apparently. They show up from time to time."

This Carly didn't need. "What are we going to do?" she asked, more to herself than her mother. "Are we expected to produce a ghost? I don't have one right now."

There hadn't been any "shimmering essences" since she and Tiffany had returned. As much as Carly wanted to believe her childhood sightings, there wasn't any proof.

"We haven't had one ever," Rhonda told her. "Sometimes

I worry about you. You've been talking about the ghost like this for some time and I couldn't figure out why. It's not real. It never has been. This man is here to ruin us and I don't think we can do anything to stop him."

Carly clutched the arms of her chair. "No one is going to ruin us. I won't let him. Besides, there was something once. I remember seeing things, feeling a presence. Maribel felt it, too."

Rhonda sat down and took her hands. "I know you think you did. When you were little we talked about Mary all the time and I think that made her real to you. But anything you saw was just our usual tricks."

"What?" Carly pulled free and stood. "What tricks? I'll admit believing in ghosts is a stretch of the imagination, but I saw her. Or something shimmery. I saw her walk through walls. I heard her voice."

Rhonda sighed. "I'm so sorry. I never meant for this to hurt you. The stories about the house being haunted have existed for as long as the house has been here. I remember hearing them when I was growing up. People were always interested in the fact that the place was haunted and the family has kept that interest going. It's good for business."

Carly felt odd defending the fact the house was haunted when she wasn't a hundred percent convinced. But she wasn't willing to reject the possibility. "But over the years, dozens of people have tried to prove there's no ghost and they've all walked away believers."

"I know. There are things that can be done to make people believe. Our family has been fooling the public forever. But it's not real. It's never been real. What you're remembering is all the stories, Carly. What we talked about. Mary isn't real and the house has never been haunted."

She didn't want to hear any of this, so she excused herself and walked out of the office. As she moved down the hallway, she studied moldings and doorways and antique pictures. What had, just a few minutes before, seemed charmingly eccentric, now just looked old and dusty. She felt the walls beginning to close in on her.

Carly walked to the edge of the property and stood staring out at the sun sinking over the ocean. The waves were orange and red and gold, the sky nearly white. It was breathtakingly beautiful, but all she could think was that she couldn't take one more kick in the teeth.

She'd lived through an unhappy marriage, staying because she thought it was the right thing to do. She'd endured a divorce, the loss of most of her friends, selling her house and furniture, a move here, only to find out the B and B wasn't going to be a haven after all. By God, she would *not* give up her ghost.

As soon as the thought formed, she felt her lips twitch. Then she started to laugh. *Giving up the ghost.* She'd never understood what the expression meant, and still didn't, but it was appropriate. She wasn't giving up on Mary.

Maybe it hadn't been real to anyone else, but it had been

real to her. She wouldn't allow some would-be ghostbuster to take that away from her.

She returned to the house and found her mother in her room.

"What do you mean, you faked Mary," Carly asked. "How come I remember stuff?"

Her mother shook her head. "Your father and I used to fight about your belief in the ghost. I wanted to tell you the truth, but he thought it was charming. And he did a lot of things to convince you she was real."

Carly suddenly understood Tiffany's emotional outbursts at the unfairness of her world when the grown-ups around her did their best to destroy her happiness.

"No," she said, trying to stay calm, but feeling panic build. "Daddy would never have lied to me."

"It wasn't a lie, Carly. It was…something to make you feel special. Come with me."

Her mother led her to the tower Carly had always escaped to when she'd been a kid. They climbed the stairs to the dusty room where Carly had curled up to read. But instead of going inside, her mother showed her a small secret compartment in a wall. After pressing a hidden latch, the door swung open, revealing a kind of slide projector. As Carly watched, her mother turned it on.

"Go back into the tower room," Rhonda told her.

Carly hesitated, then did as she asked. Shock swept through her as she realized a shimmering presence stood gracefully in the corner of the room.

"Mary," she breathed as sharp disappointment cut through her. It wasn't real. None of it had been real.

"There are three or four slides," her mother said. "Your father would use different ones at different times. He worried you were too solitary, and having Mary around gave you a friend."

Carly couldn't believe it. She returned to the hallway. "What else did he do?"

Rhonda turned off the projector. "There are dozens of tricks. We have specially prepared rooms for nonbelievers where we can change the temperature at will. We can mist their room so they feel a chilly presence. There are tables that tilt, walls that rotate. I'll show you everything before this Adam Covell arrives. I'm sure we can convince him just like we've convinced the others."

"Okay. Yeah. We should probably talk about it," Carly said, still surprised by all the trickery. "Thanks for showing me this."

"Are you all right?" her mother asked.

"Fine." Not really, but what was she going to say? "I'm going back to my office. See you in the morning."

She left her mother in the tower and made her way downstairs.

Intellectually she understood the pain of learning that Mary wasn't real came from a whole lot more than just the loss of a memory. It was the final straw in what had been an emotionally difficult year.

But it didn't feel that way. Disappointment threatened to crush her.

She'd been walking around wondering when Mary was going to show up. She'd called out to her several times and had even started investigating ways to get a ghost to appear.

All of which made her feel stupid. She'd been so sure. She'd depended on the reality of having a ghost. She'd—

Carly walked from her office to the side door, then made her way back to the cliffs. Once there, she turned back. The massive old house rose four stories into the evening sky. Huge and beautiful and very, very expensive to keep going.

Disappointment flared into anger. Without the ghost, she didn't have a viable business. She'd been selling Chatsworth-by-the-Sea as a haunted B and B. No one was all that interested in a slightly rundown, very old, former English manor. Without Mary, they were sunk.

Carly might have come here because she didn't have any other choice, but now she was committed. She liked the house and she liked the idea of returning to her roots. After nearly six weeks of hard work, she'd seen plenty of progress. No way was she going to uproot Tiffany and start over in some other place all because of a hotshot guy who thought he was Bill Murray in *Ghostbusters*.

"There is no way in hell you're taking this away from me, Adam Covell."

Carly found her mother in her private sitting room. Tiffany sat next to her on the small chintz-covered sofa. Her daughter's forlorn expression told Carly that she'd been given the news.

"You said we've been fooling other ghostbusters for years," Carly said.

"Oh, there are dozens of ways. There's an old journal full of ideas. I can't remember more than what I told you. Give me a second."

She rose and walked into her bedroom. A few minutes later, she appeared with an old wooden box. "It's all in here."

Carly took the box. "I'm going to find out all I can about our guest and figure out what we can do to defeat him. The success of the B and B depends on us being haunted."

Tiffany's eyes widened. "You're going to lie about Mary?"

"If I have to. It's a matter of survival, and apparently there's a long tradition of it in this family." She clutched the box tightly to her chest. "Tomorrow, as soon as you get home from school, we'll have a family meeting and figure out a plan. Between now and then, I'll go over what's in here and check out this Adam guy on the Internet. Fair enough?"

Tiffany and her grandmother nodded. "We'll be there," Rhonda said. "We'll be ready to kick some ass."

Jack joined their meeting the following afternoon. Carly wasn't sure about discussing such a sensitive issue in front of him, but he insisted on being a part of things.

"I can help," he told her. "I know technology. Maybe I can come up with some ideas or figure out ways to make them work. Please?"

He looked so serious and sincere, she thought wistfully. But what really sold her was Tiffany's pleading expression. After all, fooling Adam would allow her to spend time with Jack, which wasn't exactly as good as dating, but pretty close.

Carly set her papers down on the coffee table in front of the sofa in the rear parlor they'd temporarily taken over.

"Technical help would be nice," she said. "As you all know, we get most of our business because we're haunted. We're featured on the national ghost registry as a haunting that has never been disproved. It's like getting a five-star safety rating. But if one of the top ghostbusters disproves the haunting, we're removed from the registry and marked as a hoax. Not good for our bottom line."

"No kidding," Jack said.

"What are we going to do?" Tiffany asked.

"Fight back. I spent a lot of time on the Internet, and Adam Covell is going to be difficult to defeat. Apparently he comes from a long line of people interested in debunking rumors about paranormal phenomenon. His grandfather made a living doing it and wrote a lot of books." She held up the one she'd checked out of the library that morning.

"I couldn't find out very much on Adam himself," she continued. "He doesn't do this with the same enthusiasm as his grandfather, but he's just as deadly. He wrote papers on two supposedly haunted houses in Virginia. One was a restaurant and the other an inn. Both closed within a year of his report."

Rhonda caught her breath. "A year? We can't let that happen. Carly, did you go over those papers I gave you?"

"Every one of them." She set the box on the table. "We're going to assign Adam to the special bedroom. It's been fitted with two secret entrances, a misting system and its own heating and cooling units."

"Why?" Tiffany asked. "What will that do?"

"The heating and cooling will allow for fast temperature changes," Jack said eagerly. "Misting him will give him a chill. And you can use the secret entrances to take stuff in and out of his room." He looked at Carly. "Is that right?"

"Yes. It's exactly right. We want to keep Mr. Covell on his toes."

"Can we poison him?" Rhonda asked.

Carly stared at her mother. "What are you talking about? We want him impressed, not dead."

"Oh, I didn't mean kill him. But if he had an upset stomach the whole time he was here, he couldn't do his best work."

Fooling a man was one thing, but compromising his health was another. "No poison," Carly said firmly. "Our goal is make sure our guest believes he's been thoroughly haunted. Then he'll go away and we can get on with our lives."

They talked for another half hour. Carly passed out assignments, including several for herself. She wanted to make sure the special equipment was in working order.

When she was alone in the parlor, she drew in a deep breath. As much as she knew she had to convince Adam there was a ghost, a part of her simply wanted to give up and cry. How could she have lost such an important part of her past so easily?

She supposed that in the scheme of things, believing in a ghost in the first place was a little stupid. No one else did. But Mary had been a part of her memories for a long time. She'd accepted her because, to Carly, she'd existed.

And now she'd not only lost someone she'd thought of as a friend, but she might be losing the B and B.

"Not gonna happen," she told herself. They had a plan. More important, they had desperation on their side. She was reminded of the old story about a rabbit being chased by a hound. When the rabbit got away, the hound was teased for being too slow. He'd pointed out that while he'd been running for his supper, the rabbit had been running for its life. She and her family were the rabbit and there was no way in hell that hound was going to catch them.

"Do you like it?" Tiffany asked anxiously.

Carly picked through the cheerful basket of office supplies her daughter had bought for her. "I love everything," she said with a laugh. "You know I can't resist things like folders and paper clips."

They sat at a table, outside, facing the ocean. The afternoon was warm, the sky a blue only found on the California coast. After a late lunch of all of Carly's favorites, they'd moved on to celebrating her fortieth birthday with presents and a large cake.

Carly fingered the gold bracelet her mother had bought her. The delicate links made her feel feminine—a nice change from her constant attempts to be businesslike and in charge. She'd been concerned that finding herself almost divorced, alone and forty would be too depressing for words, but so far she was doing fine.

A testament to the human spirit, she thought as a large black SUV pulled into the parking lot.

She glanced over as the door opened and a man stepped out. He was tall, with too-long dark hair and a lean, hard body designed to make women look twice.

Her gaze swept over his flat stomach and broad shoulders before settling on a face that was both chiseled and incredibly handsome. His large, dark eyes defined soulful, while his mouth made her think about kissing in ways she hadn't in maybe twenty years.

Gorgeous, she thought, breathlessly. Young…too young, but gorgeous.

He saw them and waved, then strolled over. Carly liked the way he walked—all purposeful stride and narrow hips.

"Afternoon," he said in a low voice that made her want to sigh. "I'm Adam Covell and I'm looking for Carly Spencer. I have a reservation."

"I'm Carly," she said. "Welcome to Chatsworth-by-the-Sea."

She rose and held out her hand. When he shook it she felt definite sparkage, as her daughter would say.

Adam looked her over and grinned. "Nice to meet you."

Oh, yeah, she thought cheerfully. Happy birthday to me.

"If you'd just sign the registration card," Carly said after she'd led Adam into the house and to the main desk.

He glanced over the preprinted lines, then signed his name with a bold, black slash of letters.

"Don't you want to yell at me?" he asked. "Most owners do. They take me to task and call me names."

"I had that planned for the second half of our evening," Carly told him, still caught up in his appearance. She couldn't remember the last time a guy had gotten her attention on such a physical level. Was it her? Had the divorce freed her to look in a way she never would have let herself before? Or was it more than that? Was Adam simply one of those guys who captured a woman's interest and didn't let go?

He topped her by about six or seven inches. Even casually dressed—in jeans and a tucked-in T-shirt—he exuded confidence and power.

Yum, yum, she thought, even as she knew she was flirting with a danger she would never embrace. He couldn't be much more than thirty. Should she ever get the courage to do the naked thing, it was going to be with a guy a whole lot more desperate than this one. She doubted Adam had ever spent even one evening unwillingly alone.

"I will admit that if you're trying to ruin us, it seems tacky to actually stay here," she admitted as she handed him a key, then led the way to the elevator.

"I do it for two reasons," he told her. "First, I need to be close by to figure out how you're faking out your guests. Those kinds of tricks require a lot of personal observation. The second reason is to contribute to the business cash flow. It's the least I can do."

"Gee, so you want to help before you try to put us out of business. How generous. *And* you're calling me a liar. What a popular guest you must be everywhere you go."

"'Liar' is harsh."

"But it's what you mean."

She pushed the up button and turned to face him. His dark eyes seemed to stare into her soul. She wanted to swoon right there on the hardwood floor and hope that he would catch her.

"I grew up here," she said, instead of collapsing. "I have memories of time spent with our ghost. She used to come in my bedroom and read with me. We walked in the garden. We were friends."

A slight exaggeration, she thought, as she smiled brightly.

"You really believe in your ghost," he said, sounding faintly surprised.

"As much as I believe in you."

The elevator doors opened and she stepped inside.

Adam followed her and set his small suitcase on the floor.

"Not much luggage for a three-week stay."

"The rest of it is in my rental. I have a lot of equipment I'll be setting up."

Oh, joy. A techno-ghostbuster. Just her luck.

"Have you ever found a ghost?" she asked.

"No. They don't exist. Not even your Mary."

"You know her name?"

"I know everything about her. Mary Cunningham. The second daughter to a baron. She married at eighteen, moved to this house, never had children and died at twenty-two. From all accounts, her death was caused by food poisoning."

They reached the third floor. Carly stepped into the hallway.

"I never knew how she died," she admitted.

She paused in front of his door and held out her hand for the key. When he handed it to her, their fingers brushed. She felt more sparkage. It was like being sixteen again. Maybe hanging around Adam would help her relate to her daughter better, she thought with a grin.

"This is one of our larger rooms," she said as she pushed open the door and entered. "You're on the corner, so you have a perfect view of the ocean and the cliffs to our north."

She walked around the big, open space, showing him the armoire, the television and remote, the entrance to the small bathroom.

"Breakfast is served from seven until nine-thirty during the week and until eleven on weekends. We'll provide a box lunch with a day's notice. There's a menu in your desk. As for dinner, we don't have a restaurant, but you can either drive into town or call one of the restaurants and have something delivered. That list is in your desk, as well."

"You have it all covered," he said with an easy grin. "Nice place."

Sure. Right before he destroyed it. "Why us?" she asked. "Why don't you go debunk some other place and leave us alone?"

"You have the most highly documented haunted house in the area. I've wanted to come here for a long time, but I knew I would need at least three weeks. I had to wait until my schedule permitted."

"Lucky us."

He crossed to the window and stared out. "Is she your daughter?"

Carly joined him and glanced down at the lawn. Tiffany sat with her grandmother. Jack had joined them.

"Yes."

"She's pretty. She must get that from you."

The compliment made her laugh. "Very smooth. Get to me through my daughter. I'll give you points for being good, but don't expect to win me over."

He turned to her. "You can't blame me for trying. But now that I've shown my hand, you'll probably want to keep a close eye on me."

She opened her mouth, then closed it. Was he *flirting* with her? On purpose?

"You'd better stay on the straight and narrow," she said. "Or I'll send my mother after you. Trust me, you don't want that."

"You're right." Adam leaned against the window frame and crossed his arms over his chest. "You have beautiful eyes."

She resisted the sudden need to flutter her eyelashes at him. This guy was good—and way too experienced for her.

"I'll bet you say that to all the girls."

"Only when it's true."

She felt definite heat low in her belly—the first flickering interests of sexual desire.

That can't be smart, she thought. Adam was too good-looking and way out of her league. It was probably best to make a speedy retreat.

"I hope you enjoy your stay here," she said, backing out of the room. "Call down to the desk if you have any questions."

"Will do."

She nodded and left. It was only after she was in the hall that she remembered he was trying to discredit her and that she shouldn't make friends with the enemy. If he was going to spend the next three weeks proving the ghost didn't exist, Carly was going to spend just as long trying to show him she did. There was no way she could be attracted to him.

Except she was, and damn if it didn't feel really good.

"So?" her mother asked as Carly approached the picnic table. "What did he say?"

"Hi, Jack," Carly said as she took her seat. "He was very polite, very nice and very insistent that we didn't have a ghost. Apparently he has a bunch of equipment in his SUV. I have a feeling he's a technical kind of guy."

"We can beat him," Jack said with the confidence of a sixteen-year-old who has yet to experience serious defeat. "He's toast."

"Hope so."

"He's very handsome," Rhonda said. "Those dark eyes. Was he charming? He seemed charming."

"He was okay," Carly said as she picked at a roll. No way was she going to discuss her suddenly squishy insides with her mother or her daughter.

"You're right, Grandma," Tiffany said dreamily as she stared at the house. "I mean he's really old and everything, but he was hot."

Jack narrowed his gaze. "You liked him?" he asked in outrage.

Tiffany seemed to surface. She glanced at Jack and smiled. "Not like that. He's practically old enough to be my dad." Then she glanced at Carly and her smile widened.

Carly shook her head. Great. Adam Covell had been in residence all of fifteen minutes and he already had the three generations of women lusting after him. What would happen over the next couple of weeks?

"Maybe you can go out with him," her daughter said.

Before Carly could answer, Rhonda chimed in. "Nonsense. She's already dating Steve Everwood."

Tiffany's mouth dropped open. "You're dating my math teacher? Mo-om. No. You can't. That's just too twisted for words."

Tell me about it, Carly thought. "I'm not dating anyone. In case neither of you has noticed, there aren't any guys around here. So no one has to panic."

"But you will be dating Steve," Rhonda said in a way that made it sound a lot more like a statement than a question.

"I'm not so sure." Carly still had trouble thinking of the man as "Steve." She had a feeling it would be better to hold off on any dating until she could work her mind around his first name. Plus, "I'm really busy with work. I don't have time."

"You need to make time," Rhonda told her.

Not likely. "Until that happens, let's focus on what's important. We have to make sure we stay one step ahead of our new guest. By the time he leaves here, I want him totally convinced we have a haunted house with a beautiful and active ghost in residence."

Early the next morning Carly headed out to the garden to pick herbs for Maribel. In her friend's present condition, asking her to bend over was just plain cruel. Besides, Carly enjoyed the quiet of the early hours, before guests were awake and the predawn mist had cleared away.

She collected a basket from the mudroom and stepped out into the cool morning. The sun had yet to clear the mountains behind the B and B, but the sky was bright blue and birds took flight overhead.

She rounded the corner toward the herb garden when the sight of a man by the toolshed stopped her in her tracks. Someone was up very early.

"Morning," Adam called when he saw her.

"Good morning. What on earth are you doing?"

He had just pushed a tall metal pole into the ground. On top was a small platform. He attached a blinking device to it, tightening screws to hold it in place.

"Setting up sensors," he said. "Don't worry. I'll sign whatever you want, saying you're not responsible for my equipment. If it gets hit or knocked over, I won't sue."

She eyed the odd, blinking gray box with the dozens of switches. "What if it gets stolen?"

He grinned. "It has a tracking device, so it's easy to find the thief."

Too bad. Of course if she casually tossed it into the ocean, he wouldn't know it was her. But she wouldn't—for two reasons. First, it was wrong. Second, she hated to pollute the water, and Lord knew what kind of toxic metals were in that thing.

He finished his work and wiped his hands on his jeans, which drew her attention to his butt. Nice, she thought with more than a little appreciation.

He looked good—a long-sleeved shirt rolled up to the elbows, the worn jeans that hugged all the interesting places. Funny how she'd never been one to pay attention to a man's appearance before. Neil was okay-looking. Sure, when they'd first met she'd thought he was cute, but that hadn't been on her list of requirements. Yet with Adam, she had trouble getting past the handsome face and great body to the man inside, so to speak. In fact, she wasn't sure she was interested in the man inside. Which meant there was something seriously wrong with her.

"So what do your sensors do?" she asked as she crouched down in the herb garden and snipped off some basil.

"I'm measuring changes in energy. Are there sudden electromagnetic bursts? Is there an energy field that can't be explained away by an engine or wave generator?"

"You can tell that sort of thing from that little box?"

"Sure. I've set up four more just like it all around the property."

"For someone who doesn't believe in ghosts, you have some fairly serious equipment."

"This is nothing. You should see what I have in my room."

Carly snipped off a few more basil leaves. Had that been an invitation? Did she want it to be?

"How did you come to be in this profession?"

He chuckled. "You mean why am I a ghostbuster?"

She sat back on her heels and looked at him. "Yeah. It's not something they discuss in those guidance sessions in high school."

"I learned from my grandfather. He was really into the whole paranormal thing. When I was a kid, he would take me out with him to various houses."

"Randolph Covell," she said, remembering her Internet research. "He was fairly famous in the field."

"You know about him?"

"I've heard a few things. So you've been dabbling in this all your life and you've never once found a ghost?"

"Not even a near-miss. They don't exist."

So she'd recently heard. Carly supposed it was easier to believe there weren't ghosts than there were, but she still hated the idea of giving up her memories of Mary.

She moved on to the rosemary and cut off a few stalks. "If this is just a hobby, what do you do in your regular life?"

"I develop solid fuels for boosters that send satellites into space."

She tilted her head. "Which means what?"

"I'm a rocket scientist."

Of course he was, she thought glumly. Couldn't they have

gotten a ghostbuster existing on the dull-normal side of the IQ chart? But no. They had to get a rocket scientist.

"Tell me there isn't any solid fuel sitting in your bedroom," she said. "We're interested in staying right where we are."

"Not to worry. Although I do have a great thermal imaging system."

"What's that?"

"It takes pictures of my room at regular intervals, but instead of using regular film, it measures changes in temperature. So if something cold or hot passes through, I'll have a record. The room is set at sixty-eight degrees. Your body temperature should be about ninety-eight. So if you went into my room and moved the furniture around, you'd show up on the thermal imaging, even in the dark."

Interesting. That meant they would have to modify their plan. "I would never do that," she said primly as she cut a little more rosemary, then stood and collected her basket. "Mary is going to do all the work of convincing you."

"I hope so. I would like to be wrong once."

"Somehow I doubt that. Have you ever been wrong?"

His dark gaze seemed to linger on her face. "Dozens of times."

She felt a definite pull, as if he was willing her to step into his embrace where he could grab her and kiss her senseless. But as she was reasonably confident the only thing senseless was her, she restrained herself.

"It's about time for breakfast," she said brightly. "Let me take you inside and show you the dining room."

She led the way into the house. "Just through there," she said as she paused in the doorway.

None of the other guests was down yet. Her mother and Tiffany were already seated at a table in the corner. When Rhonda saw Adam, she waved him over.

"Mr. Covell, do join us. You're up early this beautiful morning."

"Mrs. Washington. A pleasure."

Her mother beamed. "Oh, you can call me Rhonda. And you met Tiffany yesterday, didn't you?"

"Yes. Of course. Hi."

"You can sit here," Tiffany said, pulling out the chair next to her.

Her grandmother beat her to it by standing and ushering Adam to the seat beside her. "You'll have a better view from here, Adam."

Carly sighed and turned away. The man was nothing but trouble.

Back in the kitchen she found Maribel slipping a quiche into the oven. Fresh muffins and scones sat cooling on a rack.

"I heard there's a new guy," her friend said as she straightened.

"Oh, yeah. He's here to prove our ghost isn't real and create trouble all at the same time. Even as we speak, my mother and my daughter are fighting for his attention."

"That good-looking, huh?"

"You bet. And charming. And here to destroy us. So I'm going to do my best not to get friendly."

Maribel leaned against the counter. "But you're tempted?"

Carly grinned. "More than a little. There's something really appealing about him. But he's too young and I'm not in the market."

"How young?"

"Early thirties."

"You've just turned forty. That's doable. Guys do it all the time."

"Oh, and you're saying that makes it right?"

"Sure." Maribel waggled her eyebrows. "Think of it as standing up for women everywhere. Being strong. Giving men a taste of their own medicine."

"Thanks, but I don't think so. Besides, I don't even know what I'd do with the guy. Date him? I haven't been on a date in nearly twenty years. I wouldn't know what to do. And if we're talking about sex, forget it. He's far too pretty. I'm sure his last bed partner was twenty-two and perfect."

"Guys have a thing about older women. They believe we can teach them the secrets of being a good lover."

"In this case, he's sadly mistaken."

"You should think about it."

Carly shook her head. "I don't have time. Besides, I'm guessing all the attraction is one-sided. Adam would no more consider dating me than he would ask out my mother."

"I think you're wrong."

"I really appreciate the support. You're a sweetie for saying all this."

"Well, one of us has to be having a thrilling life," Maribel said as she straightened and headed to the counter. "I'm just getting bigger by the second."

"But soon you'll have a baby."

Her friend's expression softened. "I know. Isn't it a miracle?"

"Absolutely."

Carly could think of a lot of words to describe getting pregnant the year she turned forty, and *miracle* wasn't one of them. As she had thought the first time she realized her friend was "with child"—no way, no how. She was happy to have Tiffany, but she wasn't interested in starting over with a newborn.

Not that it was an issue. Even if there was an interested guy, who was to say her eggs were still functioning? No doubt they'd long since turned to raisins and were just living out their lives in semiretirement.

She crossed to the small linen closet by the pantry and pulled out several dish towels. After wetting them down, she put them in the freezer.

"Don't ask," she said when Maribel looked at her. "I have a plan."

"Okay. Are you going to tell me what it is?"

"Not until I'm sure it works."

Carly didn't know if her friend knew about the ghost scam, but she didn't want to talk about it. She figured the fewer people who knew what was going on, the better.

After putting the still steaming muffins into several baskets, she carried them into the dining room.

It was midweek, so the B and B wasn't all that full. There was one management off-site for a company that made some type of hoses. She hadn't been able to figure out if these were for the garden, cars or other things. She left a basket of muffins on their table, then crossed to the older couple in the corner.

"Morning, Mr. and Mrs. Abelson," she said brightly. "How are you enjoying your stay?"

"It's all wonderful," Mrs. Abelson told her as she patted her husband's hand. "Frank and I think this place is simply charming."

"Thank you."

The Abelsons were celebrating their forty-seventh wedding anniversary. Carly envied the obvious affection between them and the way they still held hands. Good to know that some marriages lasted.

She headed for the last table, where her mother leaned so close to Adam that she was practically in his lap. He seemed to be handling it all with an easy confidence that convinced her there was no point in feeling badly for him.

"Fresh muffins," she said as she set the basket on the table. "How is everything?"

Adam looked at her. "Great. Are you joining us?"

"No. I have some work I need to get to. But you seem well occupied."

Rhonda patted his arm. "We're keeping Adam entertained, aren't we, Tiffany?"

The teen giggled.

Rhonda glanced at Carly. "Adam was telling us he's not married. Isn't that interesting?"

As the older woman seemed to want him for herself, Carly wasn't sure whether the information was supposed to inspire or impress.

"It's great," she said, going for cheerful and not sure if she got there. "Huh, maybe I should look at a singles' event for the B and B. Something to think about."

She smiled and headed out of the dining room. After pouring herself a mug of coffee from the carafe by the registration desk, she walked toward her office, all the while trying to figure out plans to defeat Adam Covell. There had to be a way to convince him there was still a ghost in residence.

When she entered her office, she carefully closed and locked her door behind her. She didn't want Adam strolling in as she went over the papers and notes on how other eager ghostbusters had been fooled. Of course not many of them had come equipped with thermal imaging systems.

There were the misters, she reminded herself. After the towels she'd tossed in the freezer froze, she would take them into the crawl space and wrap them around the misters. The sudden burst of supercold air would give the imagers or whatever they were called, something to photograph.

Rearranging the furniture was a must, of course, but how to get around the system?

She glanced at her watch and then reached for the phone. With luck Jack wouldn't have left for school yet.

He picked up on the first ring. "Hello?"

"Jack? It's Carly Spencer, Tiffany's mom. Do you have a second?"

"Sure. What's up?"

She told him about Adam's background and all the equipment.

"Man, I hope he lets me see it," he said.

Carly smiled wryly. "I'm guessing all you'll have to do is ask. He's very approachable. But try to remember you're on our side."

"I know. Sorry."

"So how do we get around this stupid thermal imaging

system? I want to rearrange the furniture without being caught. But if he can measure body temperature, we're in trouble."

Jack chuckled. "Not necessarily. Did you ever see a movie called *The Thomas Crown Affair?*"

"The first one or the second one?"

"There were two?"

"Yeah. The first one was before my time, too. You're talking about the one with Pierce Brosnan."

"Yeah. In it he uses a heater to raise the temperature in a room until it reaches body temperature. That way anyone moving around would be invisible."

"I love it!" she told him. Talk about clever. "I'll get to work on that right away." With the separate heating and cooling system for that room, she wouldn't even have to have a maid put in a heater.

"Well, could you wait to heat up his room when I can help?"

"Sure. I appreciate it, Jack. You're brilliant."

"Thanks, Mrs. Spencer."

She hung up and smiled. They were going to win this one, she told herself. High-tech equipment or not, they would have Adam Covell on the run.

Carly pressed along the molding by the last door on the third-floor hallway. She heard a click, then felt something release. A concealed door swung open, showing her a narrow staircase leading up about six stairs.

"Okay, this is creepy," she muttered to herself.

"Go on," her mother said from her position behind her. "You'll be fine."

Easy for her to say, Carly thought. She wasn't the one climbing into total darkness. Still, it had to be done.

She clutched her flashlight in one hand and the plastic bag filled with frozen dish towels in the other and started up the stairs. At the top she turned and looked back at the open door. Some of her tension eased when she saw a release mechanism. At least she didn't have to worry about getting trapped in between floors. While she didn't think she had a problem with claustrophobia, this was not how she wanted to find out.

At the top of the stairs, the ceiling closed in. She crouched down and started crawling between joists. Up ahead light spilled in from a series of small windows. It was dusty and quiet up here, but she didn't smell anything icky, or hear rustling. Thank God. Seeing a mouse—or worse, a rat—would send her over the edge.

A narrow pipe snaked along beside her. Carly followed it until it stopped by a simple lever. When she bent closer to the pipe, she saw little nozzles at the end and a crack that allowed her to peer down into Adam's room.

"Found it," she called back to her mother, careful to keep her voice low even though Adam had left to go into town less than twenty minutes ago.

"Do you need any help?"

Carly glanced around at the cramped quarters. "I'm fine." She pulled the still-frozen towels out of the bag and wrapped them around the pipe. Once that was done, she sat there staring at her handiwork. Okay, so how long would it take the frozen towels to chill the pipe?

"What do you think?" she asked. "Ten minutes?"

"That should do it."

Carly made her way back to the hallway where she and her mother paced until the appropriate time had passed, then Carly returned to the secret passage and the hopefully chilled pipes. She pressed down once on the lever.

A definite *hiss* filled the silence. So some sort of mist had drifted into Adam's room. About five seconds later she heard a faint beeping coming from equipment below.

Not knowing if the sound was good or bad, she quickly unwrapped the pipes, then scurried back to the hallway.

"Something happened," she said. "He's got beeping machines."

"Good. They probably picked up the sudden drop in temperature."

Carly hoped that was the case. But with Adam being so into the whole science thing, she wasn't sure the mist trick would fool him.

"We're going to have to find a way to get him out of the house for longer," Carly said. "Heating the room up to body temperature has to be done slowly. Jack thinks we need at least two hours to heat it and two hours to cool it off. I wish I knew of some event he wanted to attend. But he hasn't mentioned anything."

"I invited him to join us for dinner tonight," her mother said. "We can talk about it then."

Carly shoved the still-frozen towels into the plastic bag. "Why did you invite him to dinner?"

"He seems like a nice man. He's alone. I was being polite."

"He's trying to ruin us. If he's successful, there's no way I can make the B and B pay. We'll have to sell."

Her mother shrugged. "I'm sure that won't happen. My point is during dinner we can find out if he has any interests and then suggest things in the area he might like."

Carly didn't actually object to Adam joining them for dinner; she just thought it was strange for her mother to ask. Still, he was pretty enough to look at that she would enjoy the distraction.

"If we can't get him to go bird watching or something, maybe we can convince him to go to San Francisco," Carly said. "His home address is in Virginia. Maybe he's never been to this coast before."

"We'll have to ask that, too," Rhonda said. "Now you go freshen up for dinner. You'll want to look your best."

Carly glanced at her watch. It was barely one in the afternoon. Even *she* didn't need that much time.

She closed the hidden door and made sure it latched in place, then excused herself to go to her office.

"I'm going to work for a while before I tackle the 'freshening up,'" she said.

"If you think that's wise." Her mother waved her fingers and headed toward the stairs.

It wasn't enough that Adam threatened their livelihood. Apparently he also threatened their sanity, something already in short supply around here.

Despite her best intentions to ignore the impending meal with Adam, Carly found herself in her bedroom a half hour before dinner. With her mother in charge of the cooking, there was little for Carly to do but show up. Or in this case, stare at herself in a mirror and wonder where the lines around her eyes had come from.

She needed a facial, she thought, as she leaned close and pressed her fingertip against the skin over her cheekbones and around her jaw. Or maybe just a new face. Her complexion looked dull and blotchy. Honestly, in the past few weeks, she'd reduced her morning and night beauty routine to face washing, some eye cream and a moisturizer with a built-in sunscreen.

"What's up with my eyelashes?" she asked as she studied the thin, pale hairs. Didn't she used to have more of them?

Her eyebrows were okay, she thought as she picked up tweezers and pulled out a few stray hairs.

She glanced down at the faded T-shirt she wore over jeans

and decided she didn't want to deal with her body right now. Better to just be depressed about her face and let it go.

After she'd showered and washed her hair, she returned to her room, where she passed over her jeans for a pair of black slacks and a nice blouse. After blow-drying her hair—using a round brush to give it a little volume—she opened her makeup bag and pulled out a bottle of base.

"Let's see if I remember how to do this," she murmured.

Ten minutes later, she'd applied base, blush and powder and done her eyes. Three coats of mascara seemed to plump up her skimpy lashes. She slipped on the two-tone hoops she'd always liked and grabbed her watch. A pair of casual sandals completed the look.

Telling herself she *hadn't* gone to all this trouble for Adam wasn't something she could actually make herself believe. Okay, maybe she had, but it was more for the practice than anything else. Looking at Adam was like looking at those huge, expensive Lladró pieces. The ones that took up an entire table. Sure they were stunningly beautiful and everyone had a fantasy about owning one, but they weren't something everyone could afford.

But she could window-shop.

She took the front stairs down and walked into the main foyer. Jack was already there, his arm around Tiffany. Adam stood by the bottle of wine her mother had left on a tray. He saw her and smiled in a way that made her bare toes curl ever so slightly. She moved toward him, but before she could actually get there, the front door opened and Steve Everwood walked in.

Several things occurred to Carly at once. First, she didn't

care if it was against the law and that she would go to prison—she was going to kill her mother for this. Second, that she was more disappointed than was reasonable, and third, talk about the makings for an uncomfortable evening.

"Carly," Steve said warmly as he moved toward her. "Thanks for asking me over to dinner."

As she hadn't issued the invitation, she could only smile at him, even when he took her hand in his, leaned close and kissed her cheek.

Tiffany made a choking sound, which pretty much summed up what Carly felt.

"Mr. Everwood just kissed my mother," Tiffany said in a not-so-low voice. "I'm going to die."

Steve grinned at her daughter. "That's as far as it's going, kid. You can relax."

Tiffany wrinkled her nose. "It's still gross. So if I don't tell anyone what I saw, can I skip the next exam?"

"Sure. If you want to get an F." He winked at Tiffany. "Kissing moms isn't against the law."

"It should be."

Steve chuckled, then turned to Adam. "Hi. We haven't met. I'm Steve Everwood."

Adam glanced from him to her. Carly didn't know what to say or why she felt compelled to explain anything.

"Mr. Everwood, ah, Steve, is a math teacher at the high school," she told Adam. "In fact he was my math teacher when I went there."

As the words spilled out of her mouth, she desperately tried to call them back. Tiffany shrieked.

"He was your *teacher?* We have the same teacher? And

you're going out with him? Mo-om, you can't. It's all too weird."

Jack touched his finger to the tip of her nose. "Tiff, it's fine. They're both adults. They can have a mature relationship if they want."

"Says who?"

"Just go with it."

While Carly appreciated the *intent* behind the rescue, she wasn't sure she appreciated the actual rescue itself. She and Steve weren't dating. Sure he'd asked, but she'd always said no. Currently the only one issuing invitations seemed to be her mother.

Rhonda walked in from the kitchen. She, too, had spent some time primping. She wore a silk blouse over black slacks and had curled her hair. Talk about twisted, Carly thought, when you figured they were both interested in the same guy.

"Oh, good," Rhonda said. "You're all here. Carly, don't make our guests stand. Everyone should go into the parlor. Or, since dinner's almost ready, let's move into the dining room."

She bypassed the large dining room used by their guests and led the way into the private, more formal room just next to the kitchen.

Carly took in the good china, the fine linens and the salads waiting on each plate and had the sudden suspicion that the reason she hadn't been asked to help with the cooking was that the meal had come from one of the restaurants in town.

Rhonda directed them to specific chairs. She claimed the

one at the head of the table, with Adam on her right and Steve on her left. Jack sat opposite her, Tiffany sat next to Adam and Carly sat next to Steve.

Rhonda passed Adam a bottle of chilled chardonnay. "If you wouldn't mind opening this for me. I'm not very good at these kinds of things. My late husband used to take care of things like that." She sighed softly, as if the pain of the moment nearly overshadowed any possible pleasure.

"I think I can manage it," he said as he took the cork-screw and went to work.

Steve turned to Carly. "Your mother sets a beautiful table."

"Yes, she does."

He glanced at the salad. "And she's a great cook."

"You bet. Wish I'd inherited that ability from her, but I'm into simple cooking."

"You do okay, Mom," Tiffany said. "Except that one time you tried to feed us duck. It was horrible."

"The duck or the thought of eating it?" Adam asked with a smile as he pulled the cork free and poured the wine.

"I never tasted it. How could I eat something I'd have as a pet?"

Carly agreed, but Neil had insisted she work on perfecting a recipe. He'd wanted fancy dishes served whenever he brought people from work home for dinner.

"You married?" Steve asked Adam.

"Divorced," he said easily.

Carly was surprised. She hadn't known that. Plus, he was hardly old enough to have had that many life experiences.

"Really," she said. "Me, too."

"Steve's a widower," Rhonda said pointedly.

Carly got the momspeak message instantly. Death wasn't anyone's fault. Unlike divorce, which was a clear mark of failure.

"Guess we'll have to wear a scarlet *D* on our chest," Adam said with a wink.

"I'll have sweatshirts made up," she told him.

"What's with the *D*?" Tiffany asked.

"Like an *A*, in *The Scarlet Letter*," Rhonda said.

"It's a book," Adam added, leaning toward the teen. "We had to read it back in high school. It's old and…well, boring."

Carly grinned. She hadn't enjoyed the story, either. "But serious literature. You had to give them that."

"English wasn't my thing," he admitted. "Now give me a couple of hours on the football field and I was happy."

She could imagine him playing. "I thought you were the science guy."

"That, too. But I kept it a secret. I didn't want anyone to think I was a nerd."

Unlikely, she thought. Not with that face and body.

"Jack plays football," Tiffany said proudly. "He's the quarterback."

"Backup," Jack said. "But I'll be a senior next year and I'm going to be first string."

"Good for you," Rhonda said. "It's important to do well in sports."

Carly looked at her mother. Since when? But she didn't want to get into it now, not when Adam kept looking at Steve and Steve kept glaring back.

"How long have you lived here?" Adam asked Steve.

"About twenty-five years. I came right out of college. Got

my first job at the high school and liked it enough to stay. Where are you from?"

"Back east. I'm in Virginia right now, but I've moved a lot with my job."

"No roots, huh?" Steve asked, his tone implying a lack of roots was close to a felony. "Most people want to settle somewhere."

"I've never been all that interested in settling," Adam told him.

Carly glanced at her mother. Okay, this was getting out of hand. Rhonda looked worried and mouthed, "Do something."

Carly grabbed her wineglass. "I'd like to propose a toast. To friends, old and new."

The men stopped eyeing each other and joined in the toast. When the glasses had been set down on the table, Carly turned to Steve and asked with as much interest as she could summon, "You mentioned the new computer labs on campus. Tell me about them."

Dinner was long. Too long for a meal of salad, pasta and sorbet. Every time either Steve or Adam started to tell a story, the other interrupted with a completely unrelated topic. Tiffany laughed too much at one of Adam's jokes, which had made Jack sulk. Carly had found herself trying to occupy Steve to keep the peace, when she really wanted to listen to Adam. Not only did she not get what she wanted, she had a feeling she'd given Steve more encouragement than was safe. Her suspicion was confirmed when he stood and said he had to be going, then asked if she would walk him out.

"Sure," Carly said, her entire dinner forming a tight, hard knot in her stomach.

Once they walked out of the B and B, Steve moved close and took her hand. Just like that. She did her best to relax and tried not to think about how long it had been since a man other than Neil had touched her that way. But it was difficult to stay calm when she was busy trying not to hyperventilate.

"Thanks for asking me over," he said, as if unaware of her panic. "You turned me down so many times, I figured you weren't interested."

She glanced at him and forced a smile. The man was being nothing but nice. It was hardly his fault she'd forgotten how to interact with the opposite sex. "It's not that. Not exactly. Between settling Tiffany and making some changes around here, I've been running around like a crazy person."

"Are you going to have some time for yourself soon?"

Eek! How did she answer that? Steve seemed really nice. Was it his fault he didn't make her toes curl? Wouldn't she be an idiot not to find out if she liked him? Not that she was interested in anything serious. At least she didn't think she was. Around Adam, Steve wasn't all that thrilling, but by himself he wasn't so bad.

"I can probably sneak away for a couple of hours," she said, then instantly wondered if she should have.

"Then I'll definitely call this week."

"Great."

They paused by his car—a black sedan. He released her fingers and put his hands on her shoulders.

Oh. My. God.

He was going to kiss her. She could tell by his intent gaze and the way the corners of his mouth turned up in anticipation. A kiss. Yikes! Did she want this? Did she want her first post-Neil kiss to be from her former math teacher?

Before she could decide or he could make his move, the front door of the B and B opened. Adam stepped out with Tiffany and Jack. Light spilled onto the gravel parking lot.

Carly instantly stepped back and folded her arms over her chest. "Okay. Well, this was great. Thanks for coming."

Steve looked at the trio, then back at her. "Next time," he promised.

She smiled but didn't speak. What was there to say? She didn't know what she felt or what she wanted, except possibly more wine.

She walked toward the front of the B and B, then turned to wave as Steve drove away. Tiffany and Jack wandered off toward his car—where Carly was sure there would be a whole lot more going on. As she walked by Adam, he grabbed her arm.

"Did I interrupt anything?" he asked. "Should I apologize?"

"No, on both counts."

His fingers burned her through her blouse and made her want to throw herself at him. Oh, yeah, definite tingles, she thought. Now why couldn't that happen with Steve?

She pulled free and walked into the house. Apparently getting older didn't mean getting smarter—at least not where men were concerned.

"Dad wants to see me," Tiffany announced as she danced into Carly's office late on Thursday. "He's coming to San

Francisco and I need you to drive me there. It's so cool, because I only have a half day at school tomorrow. He's getting in around two and we can meet him there just after. We're staying at a hotel and I have my own room."

Carly looked up from the ads she'd been approving. "Sounds exciting," she said, pleased that Neil had finally come through. Although he'd gotten better at the phone calls, it had been nearly three months since he'd seen his daughter.

"It is. Oh, Dad said he'd drive me back so you don't have to worry about that. He said we're going to the wharf and there's like a whole Ghirardelli chocolate-factory place. Isn't that the best?"

"I think you'll have a great weekend. I'm glad."

Tiffany spun in the center of the room, then came to a stop. "I don't have anything to wear. None of my clothes are right for San Francisco. We have to go shopping."

"I don't think so. You have lots of pretty things. Plus I bought you several new things when we moved here."

"But I've worn them all."

"And you can wear them again. No one in San Francisco has seen them."

Tiffany puffed out her lower lip. "You're not a lot of fun anymore," she said.

"Tell me about it. But I have an idea. We'll trade. I'll go to school, hang out with your friends and spend the weekend away. You can stay here and run the B and B and deal with Grandma. Then we'll see who is the most fun."

Tiffany ignored that. "Where's the luggage?"

"In the storeroom. But before you lose yourself in packing, I want you to finish your homework. Somehow I doubt you'll get to it this weekend."

"Oh, Mo-om. You worry too much."

"You don't worry enough. Homework," she said, pointing to the door. "I'll get your suitcase out and give it to you after you're finished."

Tiffany rolled her eyes, then turned and left. Her step was decidedly less bouncy on the way out.

Carly waited until she was gone, then stood and went in search of her mother. Was this trip to San Francisco the break they'd been looking for with Adam? They needed to get him out of the house for a few hours so they could work on re-arranging the furniture in his room.

So far, he hadn't said anything about the misting incident, but based on his opinion of the whole paranormal phe-nomenon, she doubted it had convinced him.

She found her mother in the kitchen, checking their wine inventory.

"We need more chardonnay," Rhonda said as she counted bottles in open cases. "It's our most popular wine."

"I'll put a call in to the rep," Carly said. She'd recently acquired a wine rep who took their orders, then had the wine delivered. Not only did they get a better selection than that offered at the local discount store, but she was able to take advantage of winery incentives.

"Neil called Tiffany," she said. "He's spending the weekend with her in San Francisco."

"Oh, that's nice. She needs to be with her father more. A man's influence is so important."

Carly had several thoughts on the subject, the first being she didn't think Neil was all that great an influence, be he male or not. However, that wasn't the point.

"I'm driving her to the hotel tomorrow afternoon. She only has a half day at school. It's a couple of hours there and a couple of hours back. I thought I'd ask Adam to come with me."

Rhonda blinked at her. "Adam? Why would you do that?"

"So you can raise the temperature in his room. I'll call Jack and see if he can come in to rearrange the furniture."

"I don't see why you're the one spending the afternoon with Adam," Rhonda said with a sniff.

Insanity ran in the family. Carly had always wondered and now she knew for sure.

"Okay. Fine. You take Tiffany into town and drop her off with Neil. Then you can take Adam with you and hang out together."

Her mother's gaze narrowed. "Now you're being ridiculous. Why would I want to do that?"

Because you're acting like a jealous lover! Carly wanted to shriek the words aloud, but she held back. Adam made them all crazy. There was something about the guy that twisted female minds in a very unflattering way.

"I'm open to either scenario," she said honestly. "Maybe you'd enjoy the trip to the big city."

"I don't want to see your ex-husband. No, I'll stay here. You go."

The last two words were uttered on a very long sigh. Payment to follow, Carly thought, knowing there was no way around it.

"Just call before you come back," Rhonda told her. "If we're not done, you can stall him."

Carly wasn't sure how she was supposed to stall Adam, but she would deal with that issue at the time.

"Okay. I'll go ask him if he wants to go."

"He's out by the cliffs," her mother offered helpfully.

"Thanks."

Carly walked out of the house, toward the ocean. As she saw Adam sitting on a bench, facing the water, she slowed her step. Talking about asking him to join her in the city was one thing. Actually doing it was another.

What excuse could she give? How did she phrase it? Would he take the invitation wrong? Okay, unless he suspected her of trying to get him out of the house so they could do their best to trick him into thinking there was a ghost, then probably not.

"Hi," she called as she approached.

He looked at her, then smiled a slow, seductive smile designed to make her knees go weak. It worked, too.

"Hi, yourself. What's going on?" he asked.

"Not much."

She paused by the bench and looked out at the vast Pacific. The water was flat—a sheet of blue and green and gray that stretched out as far as the eye could see. Whatever else might go wrong in her life, at least this was always right.

She wasn't sure how to open the conversation. Should she talk about the invitation? Hint? Only he couldn't possibly get a hint, so it was probably best to just jump right in.

"I'm taking Tiffany to San Francisco tomorrow," she said, staring at the view rather than at him. "She's spending the weekend with her father. I thought maybe you'd like to come along. After I drop her off, we could look around the city some."

He stunned her by grabbing her hand, which forced her to look at him.

"I'd like that," he said. "We could have dinner down by the wharf. It's one of my favorite places."

"Oh, you've been before?"

"Lots of times."

She was pretty impressed that she was able to form an entire sentence, what with his thumb brushing against her fingers. Back and forth, back and forth. She felt both tingles and heat. And they were climbing up her arm and heading for other, more interesting, body parts.

Oh, no, she thought as she pulled her hand free of his. No way was she going to get all attracted to him. Talk about a disaster. He wasn't her type—not that she'd figured out her type yet, or even if she wanted one. Either way, it wasn't Adam. He was too…too…

"How old are you?" she asked before she could stop herself.

"Thirty-three."

She'd known he was younger, but she'd hoped he was one of those guys who just aged really well.

"I'm forty. That's seven years," she said, watching him closely so she could see him flinch. She figured a good flinch or recoil would take care of her tingly issues.

"Okay."

She waited, but that was all he said.

"That would make me older than you. Seven years older. I have a teenage daughter."

He grinned again, and damn if her knees didn't get all weak and bendy.

"I can do simple math," he said in a mock whisper. "Kind of goes with the rocket scientist thing. And I still want to have dinner with you."

"Fine. Then we'll have dinner. We're leaving about two-thirty."

"I'll be ready."

She nodded tightly and walked back to the house. Her body felt hot and parts were more damp than they should have been. She waited until she was safely inside before stomping her foot. She would not, *not,* be attracted to this man. Her only interest in him lay in convincing him there was a ghost in residence. Aside from that, he didn't exist. She would hate every minute of their time together. It would be slow and painful and probably boring, because, seriously, what was there to talk about with someone that young?

More important, she thought, as she crossed to the elevator and pushed the up button so she could go to her room, what was she going to wear?

Neil had chosen a relatively inexpensive hotel a couple of miles north of the wharf. While Adam graciously agreed to drive around the block to save them from the hassle of finding parking, Carly walked her daughter into the foyer and used the house phone to call for Neil.

Her ex-husband came down immediately. Tiffany launched herself at her father and started to cry. Carly chose to take a more impersonal approach.

As father and daughter embraced, she studied the man she'd married. In some ways, he was intimately familiar. She knew every inch of his body, from his thinning reddish-brown hair to the birthmark on his right instep. She'd loved him, hated him, fought with him, cooked for him, made love with him and thought she was building a future with him.

"Hi," he said as he released Tiffany, who clung instead of letting go.

"Neil." She probed her heart, searching for some feelings, but there didn't seem to be any left. Could she really already not care?

"Want to see her room?" he asked. "I did what you

said—got her the one next to me. It's got two double beds and everything."

"I'm sure she'll be fine."

If she wasn't, Tiffany had the number to the house and wouldn't hesitate to call.

"Have a good time," she told them, gave her daughter a quick kiss on the cheek, then walked out of the hotel. Even as she wondered if she should stay and talk, she reminded herself that she and Neil had run out of things to say a long time ago. Better that he and Tiffany reconnect.

She found Adam waiting, his rented SUV double-parked. She climbed into the front seat.

"Go okay?" he asked as he pulled into the street and headed up the hill.

"Fine. I hope Tiffany has a good time."

"I'm sure she will. What about you? Are you looking for a good time, too?"

Despite the teasing tone to his words, Carly felt her stomach tighten. She wanted to scream that, yes, yes, she was very interested! Extremely interested. Good time, bad time, just so long as they were both naked and touching everywhere.

As stunned by the thought as by the graphic images that accompanied it, she cleared her throat before speaking. "I, uh, have always enjoyed the wharf and Pier 39. Want to start there?"

"Sure."

Forty minutes later they'd parked in one of the large structures across the street and were strolling along the pier. The scent of salt air mingled with grilling meat and fresh popcorn. It was a beautiful late May afternoon, and tourists crowded the area.

Two little girls ran toward them, their parents in hot pursuit. Adam grabbed her hand to pull her out of the way and when the family had passed, he didn't let go.

"Was it strange seeing your ex again?" he asked as he laced his fingers through hers.

Not as strange as this good-looking younger guy holding her hand, she thought, determined to act as if this was completely normal and happened to her all the time.

"Not so much strange as sad. We were together for a long time and now all that is gone. Except for Tiffany, it feels like a waste."

"Do you miss him?"

She glanced at Adam, who was staring out at the water.

"No. I don't love him. I haven't in a really long time. Plus, even if I did have some things to get over, the B and B has given me plenty of work to keep me busy and time to think. There's nothing like an afternoon of folding laundry to clear the mind."

"I'll have to try that sometime," he said with a chuckle.

"Oh, sure. Like that's ever going to happen."

"The house has been in your family a long time," he said.

"Nearly a hundred and fifty years. I can't imagine a world without it. I grew up there and it was a great childhood. So much space, interesting people coming and going. I didn't have to go into the world, it came to me."

"So why did you leave?"

She glanced at him. "You're asking a lot of questions."

"I'm interested."

Gee, when was the last time a man had said that to her?

"Okay. But only because you asked. I left when I grew up. I wanted to see the world for myself. I moved to L.A. with my friend Maribel."

"The cook who makes the fabulous scones and muffins?"

"That's her. We were going to make our mark on the world. She lasted three weeks, then went back and married her high school sweetheart and started having babies. I went to college for a couple of years, then got a job planning events. Mostly big Hollywood parties and movie premieres. A lot of fun, but tons of pressure."

"When did you give it up?"

"When I had Tiffany. There were a lot of late hours and I didn't want to be gone from her. I tried wedding planning, but that meant being gone every weekend, so I ended up managing a doctor's office. After the divorce, I came back here."

"Are you glad you did?"

"Some days." She hesitated.

He pulled her over to the railing and stared into her eyes. "What?" he asked. "What aren't you telling me?"

"That the business isn't doing that well. It was in trouble when I arrived and I'm doing everything I can to make it successful. We're rebuilding our regulars and trying new things, like management seminars and off-sites and having special groups in. I have some horror writers coming in a few weeks and several culinary weekends and weeks. I'm trying to book a few weddings, some big parties, that sort of thing."

"How's it going?"

"Pretty well." He was so close, she could feel the heat of his body. "The thing is, our ghost is a big draw. Without that, we're just some old house on the coast in an out-of-the-way place."

"You need Mary to be successful."

"Exactly."

His dark gaze never wavered. "Then I hope she's real."

And she had been hoping for more. Like an agreement to stop trying to prove Mary wasn't. Of course that didn't make any sense. Adam didn't owe her anything.

He shifted a little closer. They weren't exactly touching, but it was a near-miss. She could feel his chest just millimeters from her breasts, and any second now his thighs were going to brush against hers.

"Who ended the marriage?" he asked.

"What?"

"You and Neil. Who ended things?"

"Oh. Um, he did. He left to go find himself."

"Was he lost?"

Carly laughed. "Apparently. Neither of us had been happy for a while, but I didn't think that was a reason to leave. I thought 'forever' really meant that. He didn't. I tried to tell myself that him leaving me to search for himself was better than him leaving for a younger woman, but I'm not so sure."

"He'd be crazy to leave you for someone else."

"As we discussed earlier, I'm forty."

"So? You make forty look good."

Man, oh, man did he have a way with words. "Thanks."

"I'm not kidding. You're amazing."

She felt the trembling start and knew it was a really bad idea to let things go any further so she slid a little to the left and turned to stare at the water.

"You mentioned you were divorced," she said, hoping she sounded more calm than she felt. "What happened in your relationship?"

"We didn't get along as well as we thought." He moved next to her and rested his forearms on the railing. "We were both twenty-seven and all our friends were getting married, so we figured we should, too. Within a couple of months of the wedding, we knew we'd made a mistake. Rather than stay and make each other miserable, we split up."

As simple as that, she thought. "I guess not having kids helped keep things less complicated."

"Sure. Kids would have changed everything. We'd both wanted to wait on that. Maybe because deep down we weren't sure it was going to last."

"You have plenty of time to start a family," she said. Yet another reason it wouldn't work between them. He would want children and her reproductive system had already gone into semiretirement.

"I'm sure you'll meet someone," she told him, going for perky and positive.

"Me, too," he said with a meaningful tone that left her breathless…and terrified.

"So, um, where do you want to eat dinner?" she asked. "There are a lot of great restaurants around here. I guess we should think about dining early because it's a long drive back to the B and B."

He turned to face her and placed his hand on her forearm. "Do I make you nervous?"

What kind of a question was that? Was it reasonable? Was it fair?

"'Nervous' is strong," she said. "How about *uneasy?*"

"That's better?"

"I'm not sure if it's better, but it's different."

"Why?"

"Because they're not the same feeling. 'Nervous' is—"

He squeezed her arm. "No. Why do I make you uneasy?"

"It's a really long list and I'm not sure we have the time."

He gave her that slow, sexy smile. "I have all the time you need."

"See, that's one of the reasons. You say things like you just said. It's confusing."

"Because you don't know if I'm coming on to you or not."

He wasn't asking a question, which was good, because she wasn't about to answer even if he was. Jeez—was there anything he *wouldn't* talk about? She didn't remember the men in her life being this self-assured. Was it a generational thing? Or was it the difference between a guy at twenty-two and one over ten years older?

He leaned close enough to brush his lips against her cheek, which he did.

She'd barely had a chance to realize what he'd done when he shifted so that he could speak directly into her ear.

"I am hitting on you."

The time between leaving the pier and heading over to the wharf to pick a restaurant for dinner passed in a blur. Carly was sure they'd walked and even talked, but she had little or no recollection.

No doubt the combination of his light kiss and the claim that he was coming on to her had scrambled her perimenopausal synapses until they became disconnected or over-loaded or whatever it was synapses did when they failed. When she resurfaced, she and Adam were being shown to a waterfront table by a cute twenty-year-old in a short skirt. The girl/woman gave Adam the once-over followed by a smile that offered more than good service at the restaurant.

"Nice place," Carly said as she picked up the menu, then set it down. Eating seemed impossible. As she wasn't driving, maybe liquor was the answer.

"It's one of my favorites. Everything is good here."

A waiter set a basket of bread on the table, along with a small cup of butter. Carly inhaled the faint scent of sour-dough and thought about how her jeans could be tight by morning. She did her best to ignore the bread, while giving the waiter her drink order.

"Vodka tonic with a lime," she said. Usually she ordered it "tall" which meant more tonic and less vodka, but tonight she was going for false courage. Or at least enough of a buzz so she didn't actually care.

"You okay?" Adam asked after he'd ordered Scotch. "You've been quiet."

"I'm fine. I was just thinking we've been doing all this talking about me. What about you? Tell me about your work."

"Solid fuel science is mesmerizing," he teased. "I wouldn't want to tell you everything at once. It's like a great story—you have to draw it out."

"Now you're making fun of me."

"No. I'm pointing out that what I do is really interesting to me, but the rest of the world could easily sleep through the explanation."

Fair enough. She'd never been all that interested in the hows and whys of things. She just wanted them to work.

"It's a very specific specialty. How did you pick it?"

"It picked me. I was doing my postgraduate work in fuel cells, when a buddy asked me to help him with some experiments. I got hooked and had to change direction. Not something my parents wanted to hear, since I'd already been in college six years."

"You have a Ph.D.?"

"Two."

Of course he did. And she had those two scintillating years at a community college. They were practically twins, separated at birth. Not that she wanted to be related to Adam. That would mean her thoughts were not only inappropriate, they were also icky.

"Where do your parents live?" she asked.

"Arizona. Scottsdale."

"Oh, they're retired."

He shook his head. "My dad's only fifty-five. He's an engineer and works for an aerospace company out there. Mom has her own business, outsourcing payroll."

She supposed the good news was she was closer in age to him than his father, but still. Only fifty-five? She had friends that age.

"Your parents are really young," she said.

"You worry too much," he said. "So what if there's an age difference?"

"It's a big deal. We have nothing in common."

The waiter appeared with their drinks. Adam asked for a little more time before they ordered.

When they were alone, he picked up his glass. "We have more in common than you think. We want the same thing."

I... He... You...

Her brain shut down. She felt it and heard the audible click. One second there were thoughts, and the next—nothing. Not even a flicker of a concept.

"Carly?" Adam waved his hand in front of her face. "Are you okay?"

"Fine," she managed, then swallowed about a quarter of her drink.

"Did I say too much?"

"Oh, yeah. Don't do that again."

"So we should stick to nice, neutral topics and pretend this isn't happening."

She raised her glass and clinked it against his. "I'll drink to that."

As they walked back to the parking garage Carly was pretty pleased with herself. She'd survived dinner with Adam and it had actually been fun. He'd kept his word, so they'd talked about things like movies and places they'd traveled and family holiday traditions. She'd managed to keep her liquor to the single cocktail and a glass of wine, so while she felt a teeny, tiny buzz, she wasn't actually drunk.

Because drunk could be dangerous. Drunk could make her do things or want things or say things that could get her in a lot of trouble.

She wasn't sure if she was more worried that Adam would take her up on her offer or that he would be gentle and sweet as he turned her down. Both would be fairly hideous and she wasn't in a place where she could handle that kind of pain.

They entered the parking garage and headed for his SUV. Although he hit the remote to unlock the doors, he still walked around to her side of the vehicle.

But instead of opening the door, he stopped right next to her, cupped her face in both hands and kissed her. Just like that. No warning. Not even a hint.

Carly didn't know what to do. A strange man's lips were on hers. Everything was different—his height, his touch, his scent, even the way he gently brushed back and forth, slowly, ever so slowly.

She felt awkward. Her arms hung at her side. Was she supposed to touch him back? It had been too long since she'd kissed anyone but Neil. Apparently she'd forgotten what to do. How humiliating was that?

He raised his head and smiled at her. "How you doing?"

"Fine. Great. Peachy."

The smile grew into a grin. "Peachy?"

"Uh-huh. Probably not a word you've heard before. It's because I'm old. Older. Different vocabulary."

"I've heard peachy. Just not in this context."

He dropped his hands from her face to her wrists, grabbed her hands and put them on his waist.

"It would be nice if you liked this," he said quietly.

Pronouns exploded in her head again, but she ignored them. She ignored everything except the feel of soft cotton over his hard body. She pressed her fingers into his sides and met some seriously muscled resistance. This was a guy who worked out. Oh, yeah.

This time when he lowered his head to kiss her, she was prepared. Sort of. She closed her eyes and concentrated on the feel of his mouth against her mouth and allowed herself to get lost in the possibilities.

He wrapped both arms around her and drew her close, even as he angled his head and swept his tongue against her lower lip.

The unspoken request provoked an involuntary response. She parted for him. Even as she tried to accept the fact that they were touching *everywhere* from their shoulders and their thighs, she felt his tongue sweep inside.

Then they were kissing—seriously kissing. Something she hadn't done in the past until at least the second or third date. But they weren't dating, she reminded herself. And she wasn't seventeen anymore. So the hell with it.

She ignored the questions, the rules, the what-ifs and let herself drown in the sensations.

And boy, howdy, there were plenty. How his firm chest squished her breasts and made them ache, but in a really good way. How possessively he held her, as if he wanted to feel her, and keep her against him. The firm, yet gentle kiss that teased and aroused and made her wet and hungry.

Had kissing improved in the past twenty years or was Adam just really good at it?

Before she could figure out an answer, he drew back and looked at her. She liked the passion she saw flaring in his eyes, although she would have liked a little more proof that he was, well, interested. Despite the body pressing, she hadn't been able to feel, um, it.

"That was nice," he said as he brushed his fingers against her face.

"I thought so, too."

He kissed her cheek, then stepped back and opened the car door.

She climbed inside. The drive back was silent. Adam put in a CD and told her to close her eyes. She tried that, but every time she let her lids flutter closed she relived the kiss and she wasn't sure that was such a good idea. To her it had been fairly close to a life-changing event, but what had it been to him? No doubt he pretty much kissed every woman he met. He was young and gorgeous and she would do well to remember that he was just passing through.

"You're back late," her mother said when they stepped out of the SUV and walked up the front steps. Rhonda hovered by the front door, looking both annoyed and intrigued.

Adam smiled at her. "We had dinner on the wharf. Did I keep Carly out too late?"

"No. Of course not," Rhonda said, and playfully patted his arm. "She's a grown woman. She practically has a grown daughter."

That made Carly wince. Tiffany was only fifteen, a long way from being grown.

He looked at her. "Thanks for inviting me. I had a great time."

"Me, too."

She wanted to say more, but what? Besides, her mother was right there, listening. He nodded at them both, then took the stairs two at a time.

Was he going to do that all the way to the third floor? she wondered, getting tired just thinking about it.

"What were you doing?" her mother asked in a low angry voice. "You were supposed to keep him occupied, not go gallivanting."

Carly took a step back. "We drove to San Francisco and dropped off Tiffany. Then we had dinner."

"I know how long it takes to eat a meal."

"What exactly are you accusing me of?"

Rhonda tugged at her shirt. "Nothing. I just don't want you to make fool out of yourself."

Great. "How did the furniture moving go? Did Jack come over?"

Rhonda hesitated, as if she wasn't going to accept the change in subject. Then she spoke. "Yes, he was by. We moved the furniture around. Not a whole lot, but just enough for Adam to notice. It was incredibly hot in there."

"Good. We needed it to be body temperature. Has the room cooled off?"

"It should have. We'll see what Adam has to say about all this. I hope it convinces him."

"Me, too." Although she had her doubts. The man had two Ph.D. degrees. Was that fair?

Carly stretched. "I'm going up to bed, Mom. See you in the morning."

Instead of answering, her mother stared at her.

"What?" Carly asked.

"It's Adam, isn't it? You're getting involved with him."

"I'm not, but even if I was, what's the big deal?"

"He's too young for you."

Carly almost said "You, too," but held back. "There's nothing you have to worry about."

"But there is something?"

"No. There's nothing." Just a kiss and she wasn't going to share that with anyone else. "Night, Mom."

Unlike Adam, she took the elevator to the third floor, then walked to her room. Once inside, she pulled back the drapes to expose the night sky and the light of the moon. Then she flopped back on her bed and stared up at the dark ceiling.

She wanted Adam. Sexual need filled her until she ached from the hunger. How long had it been since she'd felt that? The last two years of her marriage had been completely sexless. Oh, she and Neil had done it plenty of times, but she'd just been going through the motions. She hadn't experienced passion or desire. She hadn't felt anything.

She'd thought that it was her body changing, that as she got older, the hormones or whatever it was that created that sensation of desperate desire had simply dried up.

Apparently not. She was both restless and edgy.

She stood and walked back to the window where she pressed her hands against the glass in an effort to cool her body. How ironic that she'd had years of accessible sex and she hadn't been interested, but now that she didn't have a man around, she was hungry with longing. Wasn't that just always the way?

Was Adam interested? She wanted to think he was, but she wasn't going to test the concept with anything like an invitation. Besides, even if he wanted her in theory, reality was very different and possibly unpleasant.

There were stretch marks from her pregnancy, a few very

unattractive spider veins and old breasts. Seeing her naked could emotionally scar Adam for life, and she didn't think she could live with the guilt. Plus, once he'd seen her, he wouldn't be able to get it up and then where would she be? Depressed *and* unsatisfied.

Maybe a man closer to her age would be better. Someone like…Steve. He could—

Carly stared out at the darkness. She blinked twice as she turned the thought over in her head. Was she saying Steve was okay but Adam wasn't? But Steve was at least ten years older than she was and she was only seven years older than Adam. By her own definition, Adam was the better choice.

Except Steve was older and Adam was younger. Which meant she was giving in to sociological pressures that condoned an older man and younger woman but not the reverse. Which made her a hypocrite and just the sort of person she disdained and far too much like her mother.

Carly gave a soft laugh. She was also on the verge of going crazy. Apparently her mental heath was that tenuous. Sad, but true.

Well, the good news was that wanting sex as much as she did meant she was very much alive and hormonally healthy, if there was such a thing. She'd been kissed senseless by a very cool guy, and even if nothing else happened, she would also have that.

Now if she just had a ghost.

Despite Carly's brave thoughts about the sociological unfairness of a society that trained women to believe that older men were more desirable by virtue of their age, if for no other reason, she did her best to avoid Adam for the weekend. As the B and B was full, staying busy and out of his way was amazingly easy. She made sure she worked hard enough on Saturday that she physically couldn't stay awake when she fell into bed that night and woke up bright and early Sunday to help Maribel with the brunch.

By four on Sunday, she was exhausted and wondering if she needed another plan. It didn't seem to matter how much she organized, cleaned, polished or planned, she couldn't stop thinking about Adam and their kiss. Worse, she'd wondered constantly if she was too old, too fat and too saggy to ever interest a man.

"Something I have to get over," she told herself as she finished proofing the ads she was sending off to two travel magazines. Not only didn't she have the time or energy to worry about that kind of stuff, it made her tired. She was forty—shouldn't she be able to accept herself for who and what she was?

She stuck the ads in the envelope, made a mental note to overnight them in the morning, then left her office to go hang out in the front parlor. Tiffany was due back any time now and Carly wanted to check in with Neil and make sure everything had gone well.

Fifteen minutes later, Neil drove up in his rental car and Tiffany bounced out of the passenger side.

"Hey, Mom!" she called as she ran up the front steps. "I'm back. Did you miss me?"

Carly hugged her daughter, then held her at arm's length to study her face. She had on a little more makeup than usual and her hair had been teased into a halo of semicurls, but otherwise she looked pretty much the same.

"It was very quiet without you," Carly said as she grinned at her daughter.

"I knew it would be. Oh, I bought you some bread."

Tiffany raced back to the car and danced impatiently while her father opened the trunk. While he pulled out her small suitcase, Tiffany grabbed a bag and ran to the steps.

"It's this really big deal in San Francisco. They sell it everywhere. I had some at dinner last night and it's really good."

"Thanks." Carly took the bag and sniffed the delicious, fresh-baked, sourdough scent. Instantly her stomach rumbled.

Neil carried the suitcase to the steps and put it down. "Hey," he said. "We had a good time."

He sounded so surprised, Carly wanted to cuff him. If he'd spent more time with his daughter, he would know that when she wasn't being a typical teen, she was a great kid.

"I'm glad to hear that," Carly said. "What did you two do?"

Tiffany grinned. "We went to the wharf, and that pier place."

"Pier 39?"

"Yeah. And we took the trip out to Alcatraz. That was pretty cool, but kind of icky. Prison doesn't look as fun as it does in the movies. Oh, and Dad got me this. Isn't it so cool?"

As Tiffany spoke, she pulled up the hem of her T-shirt and exposed the small gold hoop in her belly button.

Carly felt her temperature climb about a hundred and fifty degrees. Anger flared until she knew she could incinerate anyone in her path with just a glare.

"Tell me that's not real," she said in a low, harsh voice.

Tiffany gave a little shrug. "Dad said it was fine."

Of course he did, Carly thought, as she turned on her ex-husband.

"What were you thinking?" she demanded. "Neil, *we* agreed no body piercing until she was eighteen."

"I didn't agree to that," he said. "What's the big deal?"

She wanted to choke him. Right there, right that minute, she wanted to wrap her hands around his throat and squeeze the life out of him. But she didn't. Not only would it set a really bad example and possibly send her to prison, she didn't think she was physically strong enough to actually hurt him.

"It's a huge deal. We discussed the whole issue several times and we were concerned about what a pierced belly button said about Tiffany. You were totally on board with me. Neil, there are rules for a reason."

He simply looked uncomfortable and Tiffany looked so

smug, Carly wondered if maybe not spanking her as a child had been a mistake.

Carly turned on her daughter. "This isn't over, Tiffany."

"I have it now and there's nothing you can do about it."

Want to bet? But Carly didn't say that. Instead she figured she might as well get all the bad news at once.

"Did you do the homework you were supposed to finish before and didn't?" she asked.

Tiffany smiled again. "Dad said I didn't have to."

"What?"

Neil winced. "I said it could wait, Tiff. Not that you could blow it off."

"You've got that right." Carly narrowed her gaze into the laser stare that always made her daughter uncomfortable. "Get upstairs right now and do your homework."

"But I don't want to."

"Do you think anyone here cares about that?"

Tiffany looked at her father. "Dad, tell her not to make me."

"No way." Neil took a couple of steps back. "You, ah, probably should have done it before."

Tiffany glowered at them both before sighing heavily, then grabbing her suitcase and heading inside.

When the front door closed behind her, Carly turned on Neil. "What the hell were you thinking? Dammit, Neil, this wasn't some teen movie you were playing in. You're Tiffany's father. You need to set an example and establish some rules. I know it seems really great to just be the buddy, but the only person that helps is *you*. In the end, Tiffany is left with an unrealistic picture of what the world will be and no skills with which to handle her life."

"You're such a drag," he muttered. "I took her. Isn't that good enough?"

He stood on the gravel, kicking at rocks, his hands shoved into his pockets. He looked closer to thirteen than forty-three, but without the little-boy charm.

"No," she said firmly. "It's not good enough. We have to present a united front. You had to know this was a bad idea."

"I don't get the kid thing."

"She is your *daughter*. Of your flesh. How can you not love her with every fiber of your being?"

"I love her."

The silent "sort of" echoed in her ears.

She didn't know how to get through to him. What combination of words would make him understand how important this was?

"You need to be her parent, not her friend. If you aren't willing to sometimes be the bad guy, you're hurting your daughter in more ways than you can imagine."

"Fine. Whatever. Are we done here?"

She'd never hated Neil before. Not when he'd disappointed her in their marriage, not when he'd told her he was leaving, not when she'd had to move out of her home and uproot Tiffany.

But she hated him now. She could excuse his actions within the context of their marriage, but she would never forgive him for refusing to give a hundred percent where Tiffany was concerned.

The front door opened and Adam stepped out.

After avoiding him for nearly two days, Carly had almost convinced herself that the attraction she felt wasn't real. But even in the middle of her rage, she was able to appreciate his lean good looks and how his smile made her heart beat faster.

"Am I interrupting?" he asked.

Neil jumped forward. "No. Not at all. I was just heading out." He frowned. "Adam, right? Tiffany mentioned you."

"Right."

The two men shook hands. Neil glanced between Adam and Carly.

"He's staying here?" he asked, as if not sure how to put the puzzle pieces together.

"He's here because of Mary," Carly said, knowing that Neil was now off the hook and would make his escape while there was a third party around to offer protection.

"Mary?"

"The ghost," Adam told him.

Neil rolled his eyes. "You're not still peddling that dumb story, are you?" He turned to Adam. "She loves that ghost. Thinks she's real. She has all these stories from when she was a kid and Mary was there. What a bunch of crap. Who believes in ghosts these days?"

"I do," Carly said icily, suddenly anxious to have him gone. She pointedly glanced at her watch. "Unless you want to talk about Tiffany some more, you should probably be going."

"What? Okay. Sure. Oh, I told Tiffany I'd see her in two weeks. I won't get the boat until the middle of next month, so I have time."

Great. Wow—everyone should be so thrilled about Neil's commitment to his daughter.

"You're buying a boat?" Adam asked with obvious interest.

"Yeah. A sailboat. She's real sweet, completely updated. I'll have to get in a better nav system, but that's about it."

"Neil's planning to sail to Hawaii," Carly said cheerfully.

Adam looked at the other man. "You have an understanding employer."

"Oh, he doesn't work," Carly said. "He's trying to find himself and a job gets in the way."

Neil narrowed his gaze. "It's not like that."

"Really? What's it like?"

Before he could answer, two cars pulled into the parking lot. Carly recognized them both. Jack showing up presented a minor problem, what with Tiffany about to be grounded, but Steve was a whole other issue.

Why was he here? She didn't think her mother had invited him over, which meant he'd decided to show up all on his own. Great—her ex-husband, the guy who had kissed her socks off and her former math teacher who might or might not be interested in her, all on the same porch. It was a very special moment.

Neil turned toward the cars. "Is that Jack? Tiffany talked about him all weekend. He seems like a nice enough kid, but I want to talk to him. If he and Tiffany are going to date, then he has to respect her."

Carly resisted the need to stick her finger in her ear and wiggle it around. "They don't date."

Neil looked at her. "Sure they do."

"Uh, *no*. They don't. She's too young and she knows that. No car dating. My God, she's only fifteen."

Jack walked up the stairs. "Hi," he said, nodding at Carly and Adam.

She drew in a deep breath. "Neil, this is Jack, Tiffany's friend. Jack, this is Tiffany's father."

Jack stiffened, then held out his hand. "Hi, Mr. Spencer. Nice to meet you."

Steve walked up the stairs and grinned. "Are we having a party?"

"Seems that way," Adam said, eyeing the other man. "What brings you out here?"

Steve put his arm around Carly's shoulders and pulled her in close. "Just being neighborly."

Carly felt everyone's attention on her. Neil looked both shocked and hurt, which once again gave her ideas about strangling him. Not that there was anything going on between her and Steve, but so what if there was? Neil had been the one to walk out on the marriage.

"Okay," Carly said, moving away from Steve, "time out. This is getting too complicated." She turned to Neil. "I'm glad you want to see Tiffany again in two weeks. I think it's great. But between now and then, you and I have to talk about ground rules."

"You're so uptight, Carly," her ex said. "You gotta loosen up."

"Where my daughter is concerned, that will happen when hell freezes over. Speaking of which—"

She glanced at Jack who immediately moved down a step. "I didn't do anything."

"I know. But Tiffany is grounded, so you can't see her now and she's going to lose her phone privileges for a week." Carly wasn't sure what to say about him seeing Tiffany— Jack had been a big help on the ghost front. And he wasn't the one who had misbehaved. "I may let you come over some evening this week. I don't know."

Jack shifted uncomfortably. "Sure thing, Mrs. Spencer."

The teen glanced longingly at the house, then nodded at the adults and went back to his car.

"You're tough," Steve said with a smile. "Good for you."

Neil glared at him. "I'm outta here. I have a long drive back to L.A. in the morning."

"Goodbye," Carly said, knowing the only way she and Neil were going to have a meaningful conversation about Tiffany was if she, Carly, physically tied him down and tortured him until he listened. While the visual was pleasing, she hated that he was so unwilling to take a little responsibility.

Now there were only two guys and herself. Carly looked between them and wondered what she was supposed to say. Steve touched her arm.

"I guess I should have phoned first," he told her. "Life is complicated here."

"It is. Especially now."

"No problem. I'll give you a call in a couple of days and we can pick a time to go to dinner."

With Adam standing so close, she felt awkward. What was the correct response? What did *she* want to say? Nothing occurred to her, so in the end, she nodded lamely and watched him walk away.

Adam crossed his arms over his chest and leaned against the railing. "This is getting interesting," he said.

"Maybe for you, but I find everything about this situation a nightmare." She started to walk past him.

He grabbed her arm. "Carly, wait. I haven't seen you in two days."

"I know. I've been sorting some things out."

"What did you decide?"

"I haven't a clue."

"Maybe we should go to dinner sometime."

"Maybe."

"You could try to sound a little more enthused."

Probably, but the concept was beyond her right now. "I have to go deal with Tiffany."

"Okay. We'll talk later."

She wasn't sure if that was a promise or a threat. She nodded and walked into the house. It wasn't that she didn't want to be with Adam—of course she did. Except for his refusal to believe in Mary—which made sense, considering she liked everything about him. But there were difficulties. And right now her daughter was a priority.

She took the elevator to the third floor, then climbed the stairs to Tiffany's tower rooms. She knocked once and waited for a reply. When there wasn't one, she pushed the door open.

Tiffany sat in a chair by the window. She stared out at the view, although Carly doubted the beauty of the ocean was really on her mind. Her expression was closed and Carly had a feeling this wasn't going to go well. Which was fine with her—she was in the mood for a fight.

"You know better," she said, keeping her voice low. She might be ready to take her daughter on, but she always tried not to scream. "You were extremely clear on the rules and you disregarded them. Just as bad, you played your father against me. You took advantage of the situation for your own personal gain. I'm not only angry, but I'm deeply disappointed in you. I thought you were more mature, but I can see I was wrong."

Tiffany glared at her. Carly wanted to think the part about her being disappointed had made an impact, but she couldn't tell.

"I don't know what you're so mad about," Tiffany said.

"Really? From your perspective, you did everything right?"

"Dad said I could get my belly button pierced. Doesn't he get to make rules, too?"

"Not that one." Carly narrowed her gaze. "You went behind my back, then you acted as if I would be happy about it."

"I'm not going to feel bad," Tiffany said, coming to her feet. "Your rules are stupid."

"In your opinion."

"In everyone's opinion!"

"Not mine, and I'm the most important someone in your life." Carly moved closer to her daughter. "You're fifteen years old. While I'm interested in your opinion on some matters, this isn't one of them. You will follow my rules and you will pay the consequences for not doing so when you know better. You deliberately defied me, Tiffany. I won't stand for that."

"Yeah? What are you going to do about it?"

"I'm so glad you asked. First, I want you to take out the belly button ring right now."

"What?" The teen's eyes filled with tears. "No! You can't make me."

Carly shrugged. "You're right. I *could* call your father back and have him and Adam hold you down so I can take it out myself. If that's what you'd prefer, let me know. Your dad is heading back to San Francisco and I'd like to catch him before he gets too far."

"You're mean."

"About this. Oh, yeah. Take it out, Tiffany."

"No."

Carly walked to the phone sitting on the nightstand. She picked it up and dialed Neil's cell number.

"Hi, it's me," she said when he'd answered. "I'm sorry to bother you, but I need your help with something."

"Here!" Tiffany thrust the belly button ring at her.

Carly took it and held in a sigh. She hadn't wanted to ever have this conversation with her daughter.

"What's up?" Neil asked. "Carly? Are you there?"

"I am. Never mind. Sorry to bother you. See you in two weeks."

"Okay. Bye."

She hung up the phone and turned back to her daughter. Tiffany stood with a tissue pressed against her belly button.

"I'll probably get an infection and die," she said dramatically. "Then you'll be sorry."

Carly ignored that. "Put some antiseptic on the holes," she said as she bent down and unplugged the phone.

Tiffany shrieked. "What are you doing?"

"Taking away your phone for a week. This one and the cell." She held out her other hand. "Give it to me or I'll get it myself."

Tiffany grabbed her backpack and held it to her chest.

"No. You can't…" Her voice trailed off. She reached inside and pulled out the phone.

"I hate you," Tiffany said, her voice low and angry. Rage burned in her eyes. "I hate you."

Weariness settled over Carly. She took the cell phone and tucked it in her pocket. "Right now you're not my favorite person, either."

Carly put the confiscated phones in her office, then walked into the kitchen. It was time to set out the appetizers and wine. As her mother was off for the afternoon, it was up to Carly to take care of it.

She opened several bottles of red and white wine first, then poured herself a big glass of cabernet sauvignon. After drinking about a third of what she'd poured, she turned on the oven and got out the puff pastries Maribel had left for her.

Adam walked into the kitchen. Without saying anything, he walked to the sink, washed his hands, then took the covered plate from her and put the rest of the pastries on the cookie sheet.

"What are you doing?" she asked.

"Helping."

"Why?"

"You look like you could use some."

Did that mean *pathetic?* She wasn't sure she could stand that.

"You're dealing with a lot right now," he said.

"You noticed."

"Hard not to. I don't want to add to that."

"I appreciate that, but why do I know you're still going to?"

He shrugged and carried the cookie sheet over to the oven. "What's next?"

She set him to work cutting up cheese, while she diced fruit.

"I'm surprised Neil isn't a believer—in Mary," he said.

"For a man who worked in advertising for twenty years, he has a surprising lack of imagination."

"Is that required for someone to believe in ghosts?"

"No. Seeing one can make even a cynic a believer."

He looked up from the cheese. "I've never seen one, Carly. And while I appreciate the effort you're making, it's not working."

She froze, knife poised to slice through a papaya. "What does that mean?"

He gave her a smile that could only be interpreted as tender, which, under any other circumstances, she would have appreciated.

"Raising the temperature in my room so the thermo-imaging wouldn't read the people rearranging the furniture was original. I give you full points for that. I keep a temperature monitor in my room. I know how fast it went up and back down again. I also have a motion-activated video-tape set up. It caught the whole thing."

Carly felt her cheeks flush. A camera. So he'd seen everything.

"The misting was interesting. How did you get it so cold?"

"I don't know what you're talking about."

He put down the knife and circled around until he stood next to her. "I like you a lot. I think I made that clear when we were in San Francisco. You're sexy as hell and I won't deny that

I'd like to do something about it. But this isn't personal. It's about science and how the universe works. There are no ghosts."

"You're wrong," she said, feeling weak at the knees, and not because he stood so close. This was about watching her life disintegrate right before her eyes.

"I wish I was," he said as he touched her cheek. "I don't want to do this to you."

But he would. Because that was his job, or at least his hobby.

"You should go," she said as she stepped away from him.

"Are you asking me to leave the kitchen or the house?"

"Just the kitchen." There was no point in him leaving the B and B until she was able to convince him to keep quiet about the place or make him believe in Mary.

"Okay."

He bent down and kissed her cheek. She did her best not to react to the physical sensation, but apparently her body had already hardwired itself, where Adam was concerned. Every nerve went on alert and parts of her were very interested in something more physical.

She ignored the sensations of need and hunger and turned her back on him. After a couple of minutes, she heard him walk out of the kitchen. Only then did she move to a chair and collapse.

There had to be a way out of this. There *had* to be. Unfortunately she couldn't see what it was.

The group seemed less cohesive than it had before, less confident. Carly knew part of the problem was that Tiffany was still angry with her. They were only three days into the weeklong grounding, which would have been okay if Carly hadn't taken away phone privileges. She accepted that, for a teenager, not having a phone was close to death. But Tiffany had to learn there were consequences to her actions.

Rhonda was also there, but her interest in the fake-ghost project seemed to be wavering. Only Jack was excited and happy, no doubt because he got to spend some time with Tiffany.

"Adam wasn't convinced by anything we've done," Carly said when everyone had found a seat in the small, back parlor. She'd already closed and locked the door, just in case Adam returned from his walk early.

"Not even the furniture moving?" Jack asked.

"Nope. Apparently he had a video camera set up and saw the whole thing."

"Well, that's just ridiculous," Rhonda said angrily. "Isn't there a law against taking pictures of people without their permission?"

Carly shrugged, not sure how to answer the question. She figured there was no point in mentioning that going into Adam's room for the sole purpose of tricking him wasn't exactly aboveboard, either.

"We're going to have to come up with some other ideas," Carly told everyone. "Any suggestions?"

"We should just give up," Rhonda told her. "We tried and we weren't successful. We can make this place work without the ghost."

Carly shook her head. "We can't, Mom. I wish it were different. About seventy percent of the new bookings are because of the ghost. One of the culinary weeks is devoted to food from Mary's era. We can't make it on thirty percent of full. Without Mary, we're not worth visiting. If we give up, then we might as well simply close our doors and sell."

Jack looked stricken. "You'd do that?"

"We wouldn't have a choice."

He looked at Tiffany who seemed to be equally unhappy at the thought.

"There has to be something," her daughter said.

"I'm open to suggestions."

"Magnets," Jack said as he sat up straight in his chair. "Isn't Adam checking on electromagnet energy?"

"I think so."

"Then we can rent a big magnet—an industrial-size one. We can bring it up in the elevator, plug it in and turn it on. That will zap his equipment in a huge way." He paused. "It's going to be noisy, though. I think a magnet that big would require a generator. It couldn't run off house currents."

Carly saw the possibilities at once. "Why don't you take that one?" she said. "I think it's a great idea. Find out where we can rent one and all the stuff we need to make it work. But it can't be bigger than the elevator."

"Good point." He made a couple of notes.

Carly considered other options. "I wonder if there's a way to create cold spots in his room," she mused. "I'll look for that on the Internet. Maybe in some joke shops."

"Locks," Tiffany blurted. "Remote locks. We could activate them somehow and lock him in a room. Or out of it."

"That's great!" Carly said.

She grinned at her daughter, who smiled back until she remembered they weren't speaking. Then her smiled faded.

"Whatever," she said, sounding bored. "I don't really care what you do."

Jack leaned close to Tiffany. "It's a great idea."

She smiled at *him*.

Carly made some notes. "Okay, we have a new plan. Jack, you'll research the magnet and get back to me. Tiffany, how about looking for remoteactivated locks? I'll find out about cold spots. Mom—"

"I'll keep Adam occupied," Rhonda said. "I don't think you should spend any more time alone with him."

Carly felt both Jack and Tiffany turn in her direction.

"Fine by me," she said, and meant it. Right now her life felt plenty full. She wasn't sure she could handle one more thing, and Adam certainly qualified as that.

As promised, Steve called and invited Carly to dinner. She wasn't sure if she wanted to go on an actual date with him, but she wasn't sure she didn't, either, so she'd accepted.

Now that she'd gotten used to the idea of him as a contemporary instead of a teacher, she could admit he was nice and funny and okay, while he didn't make her heart race or her body shake the way Adam could, he was still a fun guy. Sex wasn't everything, right?

Oh, who was she kidding? After the past few years of lackluster lovemaking with Neil, she felt she was due for something spectacular. So far, Adam seemed to be in the running for that—although she wasn't sure if she had the courage to give in if asked.

Steve…well, she wasn't so sure about him. Yes, he was attractive, but so far there hadn't been any tingles. Of course there hadn't been much chance for close encounters. She would have to see how the night went.

She ran a brush through her hair one more time, then gave herself a quick once-over. A pale summer dress skimmed her body to just above the knee. Her sandals were relatively new and purchased for their cuteness rather than their practicality. She debated bringing a sweater, then chose fashion over comfort and left it behind.

At exactly six twenty-nine she went downstairs and found Steve in the foyer, talking to Rhonda. He looked up as she entered and smiled at her.

"Hi," he said as he walked toward her. He paused at her side and kissed her cheek. "You look gorgeous," he murmured in her ear.

"Thanks."

He looked pretty good, too. Not as overtly handsome as Adam, but still appealing in a charming, older-man sort of way. She was happy to see him and looking forward to the evening. Both good signs.

Carly waved to her mother and walked out with Steve. When he held open the passenger door of his black sedan, she had the feeling of being watched from the house. She glanced back over her shoulder, half expecting, half hoping to see Mary at one of the windows. But there wasn't anyone. No person and no ghost. Maybe she should simply accept that Mary hadn't existed. As much as she wanted things to be different, they weren't and she should probably get used to that.

The restaurant Steve chose had once been a winery. There were still old barrels stored up in the rafters and the scent of grapes lingered in the paneling. They were shown to a quiet table in the corner where they had a view of the lush courtyard.

Steve ignored the menu and leaned toward her. "I've been looking forward to this for a while."

"Really?"

"Sure. I was intrigued that first day when you brought Tiffany to school."

"Oh, good. So I don't have to worry that you thought about me before that."

He grinned. "I'm not that twisted. A teacher thinking about a student? Not my style."

"Twisted? Interesting word choice."

"Hey, I learn plenty of hip talk in class."

She leaned close. "You know we don't say hip anymore, right?"

"I'd heard that. But I'd always liked the word."

She smiled. "Good to know." She fingered her menu but didn't pick it up. "I was surprised you were still here. I know what you said about liking the town and putting down roots, but still. It's not the big city."

"I grew up in Chicago. When I graduated from Northwestern I had two goals—to never shovel snow again and to live near the ocean. I have both here. Then I got married and had kids. We didn't want to uproot them, and to be honest, I didn't want to uproot myself. I guess I could have had more ambition, but I don't."

Wanting a simpler life looked okay on Steve, she thought. "You make a difference," she said. "That matters more than ambition. You touch those kids every day."

"Not every day. Maybe once a week. When things are going well."

She laughed. "Fair enough. How old are *your* kids?"

"Brad, the youngest, is in his first year of college. The twins, Katie and Mark, graduate next year. She's going to be a kindergarten teacher and he's applying to law school."

She winced. "That's a lot to pay for."

"It's not a problem. Bonnie had a large life insurance policy. It's going to put the kids through college and then some."

"I'd heard your wife died. I'm sorry."

"Me, too. We had a great marriage. She was diagnosed with liver cancer in September and gone before Christmas. In some ways it was easier that it was so fast. She suffered a lot less. Selfishly, I wanted her around a whole lot longer."

"I'm sure you did."

None of her friends had lost a spouse. That was supposed to happen to parents and friends of parents.

"How long has it been?" she asked.

"The kids were still pretty young. It was hard. Bonnie's mom moved in for a few years. People thought I was crazy asking my mother-in-law to come live with us, but she was terrific. She picked up the slack, gave Katie a woman to talk to and got us through the worst of it."

"Where is she now?"

"Enjoying her well-deserved retirement in Sun City. That's down south. She has a lot of friends there and it's close enough that we can all visit."

He shook his head. "This wasn't how the conversation was supposed to go. I was going to dazzle you with my wit and charm."

"What makes you think you haven't?"

He raised his eyebrows. "Then you have really low standards."

She laughed. "I don't get out much."

"Any dating since the divorce?"

"No." When would she have found the time? Plus there

weren't exactly dozens of men lining up to spend the evening with her.

"So I'm the first?"

She nodded, knowing she couldn't really count her dinner with Adam. She'd invited him for the express purpose of getting him out of the house for the failed furniture rear-ranging. As for the kiss afterward, she wasn't thinking about it anymore, let alone talking about it.

"Speaking of living with relatives, how are you doing with your mom?" he asked.

Carly wrinkled her nose. "It's okay. Some days are easier than others. I'm sure Tiffany would say I make her as crazy as my mom makes me, but I can't imagine it."

"You're in a unique situation," Steve told her. "Your mother is a lovely person, but she's also a professional victim. No matter what happens, it's never her fault."

The waiter appeared just then and asked for their drink orders. Carly thought she'd asked for white wine, but she wasn't sure. She was too stunned to think.

Steve had nailed it. In two words, he'd summarized her mother in a way she'd never been able to do. Of course—a professional victim. That explained so much. Everything really.

"Are you all right?" Steve asked when the waiter had left.

"What? Oh, yes. I was thinking about what you said. You're so right—she *is* a professional victim. Why does being able to name the condition suddenly make it easier to deal with?"

"Not a clue," he said.

"Maybe it makes me feel I'm less crazy."

"Are you crazy?"

"Sometimes."

"Then I'm glad I could help."

Whatever concerns or tensions she'd had about the evening faded away. Suddenly she wanted to know everything about him.

"Okay, enough about me and my mother," she said. "What do you do for fun around here?"

Nearly two hours later Carly set down her fork and groaned. "I ate way too much. I'm going to have to make up for this by never eating again."

"I'm glad you liked everything," Steve said, looking amused.

"What?" she asked.

"I never thought you'd get through that whole slice of prime rib, let alone the banana cream pie."

She glanced down at her empty plate. "Yes, well, I was hungry."

"Apparently."

Oh, no. Had she broken a dating rule? "Do women still not eat when they go out with men?" she asked. "I remember that from high school, but I figured because we were older, it didn't matter."

"I'm glad you enjoyed your meal, and of course you're allowed to eat. Not enough women do."

Oh, great. "So your other women are superskinny?"

Steve paused in the act of pouring them each another glass of wine. "Okay, I sense several potentially dangerous pitfalls in that sentence. Number one, I don't have 'other women.'"

"That's not what I've heard," Carly said breezily. She could certainly feel the two glasses of wine she'd already had and was about to indulge in a third. *So* not like her, but then it felt fun to be someone else for the night.

"I've heard you're quite the ladies' man. I was even warned about you."

"Really? What was the warning?"

"That you'd probably try to seduce me, but not to expect a real relationship."

As soon as the words were out, she covered her mouth with her fingers.

"I did *not* say that," she mumbled.

Steve grinned. "I'm afraid you did. Interesting. I didn't realize I had such a reputation. I don't know if I should be flattered or insulted."

"Flattered," she said, dropping her hand back to her waist. "That's how it was meant."

"Why don't I believe you?"

"Not a clue." She did her best to look completely innocent. "So, why don't you tell me more about your summer trips to that village in Mexico? I think it's so great you take those teenage boys with you and then you all build housing for the poor."

"There's nothing more to tell. Let's stay on the subject of my seducing you."

"Not a good idea."

He looked at her as if trying to decide if he should pursue it or not. Carly crossed her fingers that he wouldn't. Right now she was a little drunk and very confused. She'd come into the dinner with clear-cut ideas about not being attracted to Steve, and now she found she was. The feelings were different from her wild, visceral reaction to Adam, but still in-triguing. Jeez, who would have believed that less than three months after her divorce she would have thoughts about getting involved with two different guys? Not that either had actually asked, but there were possibilities, and she liked that about them.

"I didn't realize you were such a lightweight," Steve said. "You're swaying in your seat after only two glasses of wine."

"Three," she said, pointing at the full glass in front of her.

"You haven't drunk that one yet, and I'm thinking you probably shouldn't. Who knows what would happen?"

She grinned.

He shook his head. "That does it. Less liquor for you."

"I would have thought you would like me drunk."

"I like to think I'm the kind of guy who can get his girl without help from alcohol." He flagged down the waiter and asked for the check.

"What about our walk on the beach?" she asked. "You said we were going to do that."

"I think we should save that for another time. I don't want you falling in."

"I'm not that drunk."

"You could have fooled me."

Carly didn't remember much about the drive home. She enjoyed her buzz and her newfound interest in Steve. When he parked in front of the B and B, she turned toward him in eager anticipation of his kiss. But instead of pulling her close and laying one on her, he lightly touched her cheek.

"Thanks for dinner," he said.

"That's my line. I had a nice time."

"Me, too. We'll have to do it again."

He smiled at her and got out of the car.

Carly blinked in confusion. That was it? He wasn't going to kiss her? Why? Hadn't he had a good time?

He opened the passenger door and she stepped out into the cool night.

"You didn't kiss me," she said before she could stop herself.

"I know," he said with a chuckle. "This is your first dating experience since the divorce. I thought I'd take it slow."

That was so nice, she thought happily. He was really nice. She liked nice. And him.

"Okay," she said. "It's not like I'm going anywhere."

"Good to know."

He walked her to the front door, lightly kissed her cheek, then opened the door and gave her a little push inside.

"I'll give you a call in a couple of days," he promised.

She waved her fingers at him and wondered if men calling when they said they would really happened these days, or if the male of the species was as undependable as she remembered.

She stepped into the empty parlor. The wine buzz had faded enough to make her rethink her question about him kissing her, and she was grateful that he'd held back. She didn't know what, if anything, could happen with Steve, but whatever it was wouldn't be helped by rushing. Far better to—

"How was your evening?"

She turned toward the voice and saw Adam sitting on the bottom stair.

The buzz returned, but it had nothing to do with wine and everything to do with the man.

Funny how it didn't matter that he was casually dressed or slightly rumpled or even too young. Just looking at him made her all soft and wet and wanting. As if she were melting from the inside out.

"Dinner was good," she said, trying not to stare, yet not able to look away.

"Steve, huh? So there *is* competition."

"Oh, there's not," she said before she could stop herself, then figured she might as well dig the hole deeper. "I mean I like Steve. He's a really great guy. But it's not the same."

Adam rose. "How is it different?"

"He's the kind of man women want to marry, and you're the kind of man women want…"

"Want? Want to what?"

She could get lost in his dark eyes. She heard the phrase a hundred times, read it a thousand, and it finally made sense. She wanted to lose herself in *him,* in what he could do and how he could make her feel.

"There's no 'to,'" she whispered. "That was the end of the sentence."

"Oh."

He moved closer, until she had to tilt her head back to meet his gaze.

"So you want me," he whispered, even as he bent down and pressed his lips to the side of her neck.

She'd planned to say no. She'd planned to tell him that she meant women in general, not her in particular. But instead she closed her eyes as she felt the warmth of his firm, yet soft mouth brush against her sensitized skin.

Shivers and tingles and goose bumps raced all over her

body. A moan started low in her chest and gradually rose until she had no choice but to let it out. She swayed, reached out for something stable and encountered…him.

The second she put her hands on his shoulders, he surged forward and wrapped his arms around her. He pressed his mouth to hers in a demanding kiss that had her clinging to him even as she parted her lips and circled his tongue with hers.

Passion didn't begin to describe the need that exploded between them. One second there was rational thought, with her worries about her saggy breasts and dimpled thighs, the next nothing mattered but Adam and his touch. She didn't care about her appearance, or the fact that his last lover had probably been a twenty-two-year-old supermodel. She didn't think about appropriate or inappropriate or right or wrong.

"Come to my room," he murmured as he kissed his way along her jaw.

Carly felt too aroused to play hard to get. She had a brief thought that she couldn't remember the last time she'd shaved her legs, then she figured she couldn't worry about that now.

"Okay," she breathed.

He led her to the elevator. The short trip allowed them to hold on to each other, even as they kissed over and over. When the doors opened, she was conscious enough to make sure there weren't any other guests in the hallway before following him to his room.

Adam unlocked the door and motioned for her to precede him. When they were both inside, he turned on a lamp and turned off several complicated-looking pieces of equipment.

The video camera! He'd taped Jack and her mother moving furniture around.

"Are you—"

"All off," he said as he flipped the last switch.

She watched monitors, lights and displays go dark.

"But just so you don't worry." He walked to a long power strip and pulled the plug out of the wall.

His genuine concern made her smile, while the lingering effect of his kisses made her want him. She walked over and wrapped her arms around him.

"You're one of the good guys," she said.

"I try to be."

He cupped her face in his hands and began to kiss her again. Even as he slipped his tongue inside her mouth and made her squirm, he urged her backward. She went with the movement until she felt the bed behind her.

Before she could actually think about what was happening and get nervous, he dropped his hands to her waist and his mouth to her neck.

There was something to be said for a patient man, she thought, as he licked and nibbled his way down the V of her dress. Neil always acted as if the preliminaries were simply something he had to get through so that he could get off, but Adam took each step with enthusiasm. He moved slowly down her chest until he reached the curve of her breast, then he lightly kissed the sensitive flesh.

He shifted to her other breast, then moved higher and higher until she had to let her head fall back so he could nibble along the other side of her neck.

While his mouth kept her gasping and lost in sensation,

his hands began a dance of their own. He stroked up and down her back before slipping down to her fanny. He cupped the curves and squeezed. She instinctively arched her hips forward, which brought her in contact with his body.

He was hard. She felt the thick ridge against her belly. Delight filled her.

"You want this," she said as she opened her eyes and looked at him.

He frowned. "Why wouldn't I?"

"Oh, give me a minute and I'll give you a hundred reasons."

"Carly, you're beautiful. You move with a sensual grace that leaves me weak. I love your face, your body, the feel of your skin."

Her heart stopped. No one had ever said anything like that to her before. Not even as a joke.

"Okay," she said breathlessly. "We can do it now."

He chuckled. "Not yet."

He kissed her. She let herself get lost in the pleasure of what he did to her. When he reached for the zipper on her dress, she silently urged him to go faster. When the garment fell to the ground and he cupped her breasts in his large hands, she gave a sigh of thanks.

He moved with the confidence of a man used to pleasing women. He circled her breasts, exploring them through her bra, nearing the nipples, but never touching them. Closer and closer until she finally grabbed his wrists and moved him into place.

His thumbs swept over the tight peaks. They both moaned. Heat made her ache and swell until she thought she couldn't wait another second.

"Adam," she breathed.

"Me, too."

He stepped back and reached for the hem of his T-shirt. While he peeled it off, she stepped out of her sandals, then sat on the edge of the bed to take in the show.

He was as beautiful without clothes as she'd imagined. Hard muscles made him look more like a perfect sculpture than a man, right up until he pulled off his boxers and his large erection jutted out toward her. That looked real enough.

In that moment, as she stared at his nakedness, she realized she'd only been with one other man. She'd gotten close with a few guys at college, but she'd been a virgin when she'd met Neil. There had only ever been that one penis in her life.

She reached out to touch Adam. He stood perfectly still as she brushed her fingers against the hard tip, then stroked the length of him. So smooth, she thought. Soft, soft skin surrounding hard desire.

He looked different than Neil had. About the same length, but thicker. The hair at the base was dark instead of red. She leaned in and licked the head of his arousal.

Different taste, she thought even as Adam sucked in a breath.

"You probably shouldn't do that again," he said in a strained voice. "I'd rather not lose it."

She laughed. "As if that's a danger."

He crouched down in front of her. "Don't say that. Don't even think it. I want to be with you. Believe that."

Before she could figure out what to say in response, let alone speak it, he stood and moved onto the bed, pulling her with him.

Then they were a tangle of arms and legs and his hands were everywhere. He unfastened her bra without looking. Even as he slipped it off, he bent down and sucked on her nipples.

Fire raced through her in flames of need. She forgot to be unsure or embarrassed or even wonder if she'd been doing it wrong all these years. She held on and tried to catch her breath when he slipped off her panties and eased his fingers inside her.

Too much, she thought hazily. Too much felt too good. He explored all of her, pausing at the parts that made her gasp and cling and squirm. He rubbed faster and faster until the ground gave way and she flew into her orgasm.

It went on and on until she wondered if it would ever stop. Then he was kissing her and shifting. He grabbed a condom from the nightstand and slipped it on, even as he kept kissing her. Then he was inside and she felt herself tightening, pushing, reaching.

She came again. He pumped in and out of her, each thrust filling her with more pleasure. She wrapped her legs around his hips, urging him deeper. It was too good. It was incredible. She couldn't breathe, couldn't speak, couldn't do anything but feel him on top of her, in her.

At last he gave one hard pulse and stilled. Every muscle in his body tensed.

"Carly," he gasped as she felt his release. He stared at her and she would swear she could see into his soul.

It had been the best sex of her life. Okay, sure that was probably due to a long stretch of doing without and the thrill of a new partner. Or maybe it was turning forty and that sexual peak thing she was always reading about in magazines. Whatever the cause, she felt content and boneless.

"I have to get back to my own bed," she said after Adam had rolled off her and pulled her close. "Either my mother or my daughter finding me here would raise too many questions."

He kissed her shoulder. "I promise you that neither of them make regular appearances in my room."

"Good to know, but I still should be going."

The thing was, she didn't want to move. She wanted to make love again, this time more slowly. She wanted to feel those sensations again. She wanted him inside of her, claiming her with a mastery that made her feel both feminine and empowered.

He placed his hand on her breast and rubbed his fingers against her nipple.

"What about round two?" he asked.

There was a round two? She hadn't experienced that since the early days with Neil.

"I was thinking about it," she admitted, "but I wasn't sure you'd be able to, um, well…"

He leaned over and kissed her. "And if I can?"

He shifted slightly. Something very hard and promising poked her thigh.

"I can go back to my room later."

"That's my girl."

Carly spent the next morning walking around trying not to grin like a fool. She was relaxed, refreshed and delightfully sore. Could life get any better?

Adam cornered her in the laundry room, where she was doing an inventory count on sheets. He came up behind her and grabbed her by the waist, turned her in his arms and kissed her senseless.

"Last night was incredible," he murmured. "When can we do it again?"

"What are you doing at midnight?" she asked.

He grinned. "Your room or mine?"

"We could try my bed this time. I think it's been a long time since it's seen any action."

"I'll be there." He kissed her again. "I told you I have to run into San Francisco, right? I'm meeting a guy from work for lunch. He thinks he's made a couple of important breakthroughs."

"You mentioned it, yes."

"Good. I don't want you thinking I'm bailing on you."

He was so earnest, she thought happily. As if her feelings

mattered. Okay, this could never last, but she had a feeling it was going to be really good in the short term.

"You're sweet to worry about me. I'll be fine."

"I might be late. If we get to talking about solid fuels, who knows what could happen? But I'll be back by midnight."

She shivered in anticipation. "I'll be waiting."

"Good."

They kissed again before he left. As soon as he walked out of the laundry room, Carly counted to twenty before going up the stairs and calling for her mother.

"Let them know I'm on my way," she said. "I'm going to pick up Jack, then drive directly to the equipment rental."

She and Adam might have just done the wild thing an amazing three times in a single night, but that didn't mean she wasn't still going to try to convince him that the ghost was real. With Adam gone for several hours, she and Jack would put his electromagnet plan into action. With luck, that would do the trick.

No one had actually considered the dimension and weight of the magnet, Carly thought, as she and Jack wheeled the heavy cart onto the elevator.

She stepped back and stared at the device. "It looks like something out of a science fiction movie," she said. "Is this going to work?"

"It'll be great," Jack promised.

Tiffany hovered in the hall. "Should you guys ride up in the elevator with it? Won't that be too much weight?"

Carly looked at the metal device, the cart and the small elevator. "Good point. We'll take the stairs."

She leaned in, pushed the button for Adam's floor, then jumped back. Jack, Tiffany and she raced up the two flights, then hurried down the hall to meet the elevator when the doors slowly opened.

It was early afternoon and all their guests seemed to be out enjoying the sunny Saturday weather. Good thing, she thought as Jack slipped in behind the magnet and pushed. Carly and Tiffany grabbed the front of the cart and pulled. The large wheels began to slowly turn. If anyone saw them right now, they would run screaming for the hills.

"What is this supposed to do?" Tiffany asked.

"In theory, it will disrupt Adam's equipment and convince him there's been some kind of ghost dropping by," Carly said as she pulled with all her might.

The heavy cart finally rolled free of the elevator. She went around back to help Jack push as they urged it toward Adam's room.

"It's been two weeks, Mom. If he doesn't believe now, he's not going to."

"I'm not giving up," Carly said, between gasps as she pushed harder.

At last the cart was in place. Jack strung the thick power cord out a window and down to the portable generator that had been provided to run the magnet. He went downstairs and a few minutes later the entire house shook as he started the generator.

Tiffany raced to the window. "Ready?" she yelled. She turned to Carly. "He's giving me a thumbs-up. Go for it, Mom."

Carly flipped the switch on the jumbo magnet. For a second there was only a faint hum, then the afternoon exploded into a cacophony of thumps and crashes and screeches as throughout the house metal objects did their best to fly toward the magnet.

Carly swore under her breath. Obviously she hadn't thought this through. A particularly loud crash made her wince, but she left the magnet on for a full minute before turning it off.

Tiffany stared at her wide-eyed. "What just happened?"

"To be honest, I don't want to know."

The damage was mostly minor. Several metal cooking utensils and pans had flown out of open shelves and up to the ceiling, only to crash to the ground a minute later when the magnet was turned off. Serving trays had taken the same journey, as had all the paper clips in Carly's office. Her file cabinets had walked halfway across the floor. Drawers stood open. Her lamp was a casualty of attempted flight.

"It's so weird," Tiffany said when she ran into the office. "My bed is nearly out the door."

"Probably the metal frame. What about other stuff?"

"A few of my belts are on the floor. Jack says you need to check your computer disks. The floppies could be messed up."

Carly sank into her chair. "I don't want to know what the guest rooms look like. I sure hope this worked."

"We still have the locks to try," her daughter reminded her. "The automatic ones. They'll be fun."

Carly nodded, but she wasn't convinced. What if Adam didn't believe? What if she couldn't convince him?

"You're quiet," Adam said around one in the morning, when they'd finished making love and were simply trying to catch their breath.

"I was wondering how your day went. Did you have fun?"

Had he noticed that a giant magnet had gone off outside his room?

"It was good. I won't bore you with the technical details about what we discussed, but I think Will is on to something."

"Good."

He bent over her and kissed her. "Giant magnet, huh?"

She did her best not to show any emotion as she looked at him. "I have no idea what you're talking about."

"My equipment is all messed up and my floppies are trashed. Only one thing could have done that."

"A ghost?"

He chuckled. "No. A magnet. A really big one. How did you get it in the house?"

Her heart sank. Sure, the sex was good, but what did it matter in the face of her family's financial ruin?

"Why can't you just believe?" she asked as she sat up. "Ghosts are real."

"No, they're not. We both know that, Carly."

"I don't." She moved to the side of the bed and reached for her clothes. "I don't know that for a second. You can tell me what your monitors say all you want. I don't care. I remember her. Mary is a part of my childhood. She was here, in this house. I've seen her and I don't care what anyone says. I believe, and if you don't, it changes everything."

He raised himself up on his elbow. "Is that the price of this relationship?"

"What relationship? You're here for another week, then you're leaving." She pulled on her panties, then grabbed her T-shirt. "How can you do this to me?"

"Do what?"

"Ruin me. If you go out and write your paper, or whatever it is you do, this B and B will lose over half our business. We'll never make it. My mom will sell. This house had been in our family nearly a hundred and fifty years. You don't have the right to take that away from us."

"I'm not. I'm simply telling the truth. I'm sorry about the house, but I don't believe you're going to lose it. You're stronger than you think."

She wasn't. She could feel herself getting weaker by the second.

"I've worked so hard and there's so much left to do." She pulled on her T-shirt, then grabbed his hands. "Adam, please. Don't do this."

"I care about you, Carly, but I won't lie."

"I'm not asking you to lie. I'm asking you to keep quiet."

"They're not that different."

"They are to me." She released him and turned away. "There's nothing I can say to change your mind?"

"No. I'm sorry. This isn't about you."

"Then who is it about?"

He didn't say anything for a long time. Finally she heard him get out of bed and pull on clothes. "You want me to go?"

"Yes."

She wasn't sure if he meant to leave her room or the B and B. Did it matter? Sure, she would miss him when he left, but she would miss the house more. To have come so far, only to lose everything now.

"I'm sorry," he said as he walked to the door. "I never meant to hurt you."

"Too bad. If that had been your plan, think of how successful you could feel right now."

She waited until he was gone, then she collapsed back on the bed and buried her face in a pillow. How could everything have gone so wrong so quickly? And how on earth did she make things right?

"Mom?"

Tiffany hovered outside Carly's office. Carly looked up from her computer, where she'd been searching for small towns with good schools. If they had to move again, she wanted to make sure her daughter had a chance at a great education.

"What's up?" she asked, trying for cheerful and not sure she'd succeeded. The past two days had been one giant hurt that she'd tried to keep to herself.

"I don't know. You seem different. Are you okay?"

Carly smiled at her daughter. "I'm fine, but you know what I need?"

"What?"

"Some time away from here. Let's go into town and have ice cream for dinner."

"Really? Just the two of us?"

"Absolutely. Only don't tell Grandma."

"I won't. She'd totally freak."

Thirty minutes later they sat across from each other with two large chocolate sundaes between them.

"Bon appétit," Carly said.

Tiffany giggled and took a big bite. "This is great."

"I'm sure we'll both have stomachaches later, but it will be so worth it."

"You bet."

They ate in silence for a few minutes. Carly felt the first stirrings of a sugar rush. Maybe it would be enough to get her mind off Adam.

He'd chosen not to leave the B and B, so she'd spent the past two days avoiding him. She'd canceled the order for the remote locks—they wouldn't fool him—and resigned herself to the demise of their status as a haunted house. After running the numbers without Mary as an enticement, she'd discovered what she already knew—no ghost meant no profits. It was well and truly over.

"Jack feels bad the magnet didn't work," Tiffany said. "But he had a good time helping."

"I'm glad. He's been great." She glanced at her daughter. "You guys have been together for a while now."

"Nearly two months." Tiffany ducked her head and blushed. "It's my longest relationship ever."

"You're growing up."

"Enough to car date?"

"Nope."

"Mo-om!"

Carly set down her spoon. "I know you think I make up these rules to make you unhappy, but it's not true. I love you and you're the most important person in my life. I want to do everything I can to keep you safe."

"But Jack would never hurt me."

"I think he cares about you a lot, but that doesn't mean he can't hurt you without trying. Boys are different."

Tiffany rolled her eyes. She leaned forward and lowered her voice. "We're in a *restaurant,* Mom. Don't you dare bring up sex now!"

"I'll whisper," Carly said softly. "But it is about sex. Because Jack cares about you, he wants things. Sexual things." The fact that he was sixteen meant he would want those things even if he didn't care, but she wasn't about to get into that.

"He hasn't tried anything."

"He hasn't had a chance. But if the two of you were alone, in a car or at someone's house, it would be so easy. You start out kissing and one thing leads to another. Eventually you're going to have to make those choices on your own. I know that. But not at fifteen. You're not ready, and neither am I."

"But this shouldn't be about you. What about my life?"

"I want you to have fun, but that doesn't mean you can do what you want. I love you too much not to have rules."

"Rules aren't good."

"They can be. They can save you. Tiffany, I would give my life for you. I'm also willing to have you hate me from now until you go off to college if that's what it takes. That's how much I want you to have a good life."

She thought she might have gotten through, but she wasn't sure. Especially when her daughter sighed and said, "I'm still mad about the belly button ring."

"Me, too."

"But everyone has one."

"Name me twenty girls at school who have one."

"Okay, not everyone."

Carly smiled. "Name me ten."

Tiffany sighed again, then grinned. "How about one?"

"You are *so* not getting a belly button ring on my watch."

"Fine. I'll put it on my to-do list for when I turn eighteen. I'm gonna be really busy that day."

"I'll bet you are."

Tiffany grinned. "Want to come with me and get one yourself?"

"We'll talk."

Carly walked into her bedroom that evening to find Adam sitting on her bed. She came to a stop, not sure if she should be happy, angry or simply order him out.

"I don't want it to be like this," he said before she could speak. "I hate that you're mad at me."

"Do you expect me to be happy with what you're going to do?"

"I expect you to understand." He stood and moved toward her. "Dammit, Carly, we have something special here. Are you going to let that go because of some fake ghost?"

He was furious. She could see the temper in his eyes.

"What are you talking about?" she asked.

"Us. What we could have together."

Was he insane? "There's no us. You've been really sweet to me, and I appreciate that, but Adam, you live in Virginia. I'm here. At least until I have to move. You're seven years younger than me."

He grabbed her arms. "Do you really think that matters?"

"Of course."

He swore again and released her. She couldn't believe he was so upset.

"I thought this was just about sex," she said. "I thought—"

"What?" His gaze narrowed. "That I didn't care? That this was all just an easy game for me? That you were one more notch in the bedpost?"

Honestly? "Yes."

"No!" He cupped her face in his hands and kissed her with a desperation that made her knees go weak. "I care about you, Carly. More than I have cared about anyone in a long time. You're amazing. I want us to make this work."

What *us?* What *this?* She couldn't get her mind around the fact that he thought they had a future.

"For how long?" she asked. "At what point will you want someone younger and newer?"

"Why does it always have to be about age?"

"Because age matters. I'm forty. I have a fifteen-year-old daughter. You're going to want kids someday and I'm not interested in doing that again. I don't even know if I *could* get pregnant, but I can tell you I don't want to."

"I've never been that interested in kids."

Ha. Like she believed that. "You say that now, but you'll change your mind."

"So you won't have a relationship with me because of something that might happen in the future?"

There were other things, too, although she couldn't think of them now. Truthfully, she'd never allowed herself to consider a future with Adam. Sure he was great and pretty much everything she'd ever wanted in a man, but *so* not for her.

"I can't deal with any relationship right now," she told him. "I just got a divorce. I'm not looking to get involved."

"So this is just bad timing?"

"Some of it. Plus I know you think you're in the right on the ghost thing, but I don't want to be with someone so willing to ruin me."

His eyes darkened. "That's too bad because I can't be with someone who wants me to lie for her."

"I don't want you to lie," she began, then stopped. Wasn't not telling the truth as he saw it a lie of omission? "I guess I do."

"I won't."

"I know." Perhaps in time she could appreciate his honesty, but right now it was just too hard.

"I'm leaving in a few days. I don't want it to end like this."

"How do you want it to end?"

"With a promise for the future."

"I can't give you that. There's too much in my life right now. I don't know what's going on. If the B and B closes, I don't even know where Tiffany and I will live."

"Then come back to Virginia with me. I have a house. There's room."

She stepped back. "I've known you less than three weeks. I can't move in with you. Even if I wanted to, what kind of example does that set for my daughter? I'm having a hard enough time trying to keep her following the rules now."

"But I…" He reached for her. "I care about you."

She stepped back a second time. "Sometimes caring isn't enough."

"It has to be."

For the first time, she actually felt every one of the seven years that stretched between them and then some. He was so earnest and determined. As if he could will things to be the way he wanted.

She'd learned a long time ago that wanting had very little to do with anything.

"I'm sorry, Adam. It's not." She walked to her door and held it open.

He stared at her for a long time, then he shook his head and walked out into the hallway.

"You'll regret this," he said.

He might be right. There *was* something between them. There had been from the first second she'd seen him. But for now, her gut told her it was time to let him go.

The only good thing about feeling so crappy was that she didn't want to eat, Carly thought three days later as she sat at her desk and reached for her fifth cup of coffee. Maybe she could drop a couple of pounds and have to buy all new clothes because her old ones were hanging on her. It could happen.

Adam was leaving that afternoon and she had yet to speak with him. She hadn't—not since their last, very painful, encounter. She didn't know what to say.

She doubted he would want to know he was the best lover she'd ever had. Not only was that not much of a compliment, she had a feeling he wanted their time together to be about more than sex. And it was. She had feelings for him, but she didn't know what they were. Everything had happened too fast. She was too close to her divorce. He wanted the impossible, all the while planning to destroy her.

And she'd thought her life was complicated before.

She returned her attention to the spreadsheet in front of her. Once again she tried to make the numbers work without the ghost. If they could get enough business *before* word got out, maybe people would keep coming because they enjoyed the experience. Or if they could—

"I really like what you have done with the house. All those bookings. Isn't that lovely? I haven't seen the board so full in ages."

Carly froze in her seat. The voice was unfamiliar. Soft, female, British. Not sure she believed she'd heard it, terrified to turn around and see nothing, she could barely breathe.

"Have you seen Maribel? She's so round. In my day a woman was never allowed to show herself while she was in such a delicate condition. How things have changed. Carly? Are you all right?"

Carly swallowed, grabbed the arms of her chair and slowly turned to her left.

There, shimmering in the middle of the office, stood a slender young woman of twenty or so in a pale floor-length dress. Everything was the same, Carly thought in amazement. The way the fabric moved slightly, as if disturbed by a light breeze, the intricate braids in her hair, the glow, as if she were lit from within.

"M-Mary? Is that really you?"

"Of course." Mary turned from the bookings board and smiled. "I'm glad you're back. It wasn't the same around here after your father passed away. Oh, how rude. I never said I was sorry. I know how much you loved him. You must have been very sad."

Carly pushed to her feet. Her heart raced and her legs shook. Was this really happening? "I, ah, was. My mom's had a difficult time, as well. We… Where have you been?"

"Traveling." Mary pressed her lips together. "I don't mean to speak out of turn, but your mother can be difficult. Always dithering."

"Okay. You're real, right? You're really here?"

"Of course I'm here. You've known me all your life. Why would you question my presence?"

"I just… You were gone for so long and my mother told me you never existed. That what I remembered were just stories I'd heard or made up."

Mary sniffed. "No imagination. That's why I never appeared to her."

Carly laughed. "Are you staying? I have had so many people asking about you."

Mary folded her hands together at her waist. "That depends. How are things here these days?"

"What? Oh, I'm taking over. My mother is going to retire to Las Vegas in a few years. That's in Nevada."

"I know. I've visited a few times. Interesting place. Well, if you'll be here, I would very much like to stay. Travel is so tiring at my age."

"I would imagine."

Her mind whirled. This was real. Mary had returned. The

house had a ghost. Carly wanted to dance with delight, she wanted to scream and cry and she didn't know what. But she also didn't want to upset Mary by "dithering."

"There's been an interesting development while you've been gone," she said, trying to stay calm. "A gentleman is staying here. Adam Covell. He doesn't believe in ghosts. In fact his purpose is to discredit the B and B. He's going to write a paper. I've been trying to convince him you're real, but it hasn't worked."

"How intriguing. Tell me about this man. Is he young?"

"Younger than me. Very handsome."

"You smile when you say that. Is he of some import to you?"

"I don't know. I like him a lot, but… It's confusing."

"Men generally are." Mary smiled. "Have you been intimate with him?" She held up a slender, glowing hand. "I know, I presume with that question. You have every right to refuse to answer, but I hope you will not."

Carly grinned. "Oh, yeah. We've been intimate."

"How lovely." Mary's smiled widened. "I was married for a time, before my demise. At first the intimacies of the marriage bed were quite distasteful, but after a time…" She paused and delicately cleared her throat. "I will only say that I did not turn my husband away."

You go, girl, Carly thought. "He's leaving in the afternoon. Can you help me convince him you're real?"

"It will be my pleasure."

Carly took the elevator to Adam's floor. Mary would, of course, make her own way there.

She was real, Carly thought with equal parts delight and amazement. She hadn't made it all up. Mary was still very much a part of her past.

She'd already thought about several things they could do together and she very much wanted her friend to meet Tiffany. Talk about an interesting relationship if the two of them hit it off.

Still smiling at the thought of the nearly two hundred-year-old ghost and her fifteen-year-old chatting about boys and fashion, she stopped in front of Adam's door and knocked.

He opened it at once and when she saw him, she was stunned by the dark circles under his eyes.

"What's wrong?" she asked.

"What the hell do you think?"

She wanted to believe he was upset at the thought of leaving her, but that didn't make sense, did it?

Without saying anything, he grabbed her arm, pulled her inside, shut the door behind her and kissed her.

She felt herself responding to his touching, wanting him with more passion than was humanly possible to contain. She tried to get closer, to make his need and her need meld.

"How can you say there's nothing between us?" he asked bitterly as he stepped back.

"I guess I can't."

"What?" He stared at her.

"I have feelings for you," she said slowly. "I just don't know what they are."

He growled and pulled her close again. "You're damned annoying. Do you know that?"

"I'm aware it might be a possibility. But before we get into this, I have someone I want you to meet."

She moved away and turned to see Mary standing in the room. The ghost looked amused.

"Am I interrupting?" she asked politely.

"Not really. Adam, this is Mary."

Carly waited for his shriek or gasp or something. Instead he picked up a shirt he'd already folded and tucked it into the open suitcase on the bed.

"Nice to meet you."

Carly stared at him. "Adam, she's a ghost."

He didn't bother looking up. "Nice trick with the lights. How are you doing it?"

"I'm not doing anything. She's really a ghost. This is Mary. I told you about her. She's been traveling and now she's back."

He glanced at the shimmering presence again and shrugged. "I like the detail with the costume."

Mary frowned. "I am not wearing a costume, Mr. Covell."

"Uh-huh."

Carly wanted to stamp her foot like a two-year-old. How could Adam not believe?

"It's all right," Mary said soothingly. "Mr. Covell, if I may have your attention for a moment?"

Adam glanced up as Mary glided through the wall, then returned.

"Hologram," he said, sounding particularly unimpressed.

Mary nodded, then levitated a chair and turned it slowly in the air.

"I saw that when I was eight and my parents took me to Disney World."

"I've been there," Mary said as she lowered the chair. "Lovely, lovely place. All those happy children." She turned her attention to Adam. "You, sir, are most difficult."

"Thanks."

"He thinks he's really smart," Carly said.

Adam smiled. "I *am* really smart."

Carly ignored that and pointed at his equipment. Various lights were blinking and several gauges seemed to be vibrating.

"Doesn't that mean anything?" she asked.

"Nope. I have to get everything recalibrated when I get home. Your magnet really screwed it all up."

Oh, wasn't that just perfect!

"Mary, you have to think of something. If Adam doesn't believe in you, my mother is going to have to sell this place."

Mary sighed. "Not more new owners. It took me nearly fifty years to adjust to your family." She eyed Adam. "Very well. Although I do protest having to go to this length. It is very disconcerting and far too great an intimacy when we have such a short acquaintance."

She seemed to draw herself up to her full height, then she glided purposefully to Adam. He watched with interest, but didn't seem the least bit afraid. Not even when she slipped right inside him.

Carly gasped. What on earth?

At first nothing happened. Then Adam stiffened, went completely white and swore. Mary left him as smoothly as she'd entered. She paused in the center of the room and stared at him.

"I trust you are now more inclined to believe I exist."

Adam staggered a few steps, then sank onto the edge of the bed.

"Holy Mother of God," he breathed. "What the hell just happened?"

Carly rushed over and sat next to him. "Mary sort of merged with you. Are you all right?"

"He is perfectly fine," Mary told her. "Just a little muddled by the experience." She raised her eyebrows. "He's very fond of you. Were you aware?"

Adam shook his head, then turned to Carly and grabbed her by the shoulders. "She's a ghost."

Carly grinned. "I believe I mentioned that earlier."

"No. A ghost. A real ghost. We connected. I know her history, her thoughts. I know about her family." He stared at Mary. "You're real."

"For someone with as much education as you have, sir, you're not very bright, are you?" She shook her head. "My work here is complete. Good day."

She glided through the wall and disappeared.

★ ★ ★

"I don't want to leave," Adam said as he loaded his equipment into his SUV.

"Mary isn't going anywhere," Carly reminded him. "She's promised to make an appearance from time to time, just to keep the guests on their toes. I think she's looking forward to it."

"I still can't believe she's real."

"Having your body momentarily inhabited by a spectral phenomenon is enough to convince even the staunchest cynic?"

"Absolutely." He pulled her close and kissed her. "But I was talking about not wanting to leave you."

Carly didn't know what to do with that information. "Adam," she began, before he cut her off with a quick kiss.

"Stop. I know exactly what you're going to say and I don't want to hear it. I'll be back to convince you in a couple of months."

"You don't have to do that."

"I want to."

She had to admit his intensity was appealing. While she wasn't sure what she wanted from the future, having Adam around wouldn't be so bad.

"Just so we're clear, I'm not interested in getting married again," she told him.

He grinned. "You say that now, but I'll change your mind."

"I don't think so." She was more interested in sex than something permanent.

"Don't go falling for any math teachers while I'm gone."

"You don't have to worry about that."

"But you'll be dating him."

"Occasionally." Steve had called and asked her out for Friday.

Adam shook his head. "That guy's too old for you."

He kissed her again, then climbed into the SUV. After opening the window, he leaned out.

"I'm coming back," he promised.

"You know where to find me."

Carly hung up with the reporter and grinned. Ever since Adam's article on the house and Mary had been posted on the national registry Web site and had been picked up by several newspapers, she'd been flooded with calls. Everyone wanted to hear the story and then come stay for the night. They were booked solid every night through the summer and every weekend through the first of the year.

"Not bad," Carly said aloud as she added the reporter's name to the growing wait list. He'd wanted to bring his wife up for their seventh anniversary.

The phone rang again. If this kept up, she was going to have to get a full-time assistant.

"Chatsworth-by-the-Sea, may I help you?"

"I need to speak with Carly Spencer," a woman said.

"This is Carly."

"Oh, hi. I'm Annie Carter. My daughter is in school with your daughter. I was calling to find out what you knew about the party last Friday night."

"Party? I don't know about a party. Tiffany spent the night at a friend's house."

"Jessica something?"

Carly got a bad feeling in her stomach. "That's right. But I called and spoke with Jessica's mother."

Annie sighed. "So did I. Unfortunately the person we spoke with was Jessica's older sister who thought this was all pretty funny. There was a huge party at the house. It lasted until all hours and there were boys there. Some from college."

The bad feeling doubled in size and Carly got very, very angry.

"I appreciate you telling me, Annie."

The other woman chuckled. "Okay. I tell by the tone of your voice that you're pissed, too."

"More than pissed."

"I can't believe my daughter lied to me."

"Right back at you," Carly said. "Tiffany is in for some serious grounding."

"I hear you. I just wanted to let you know about the party. I have a couple of other parents to call. Oh, doesn't your daughter know a boy named Jack?"

"Yes. They're friends—semi-boyfriend and girlfriend."

"He was there, too."

Carly's anger grew until it threatened to explode. It nearly doubled in size. She said goodbye, hung up and threw a pen at the wall for good measure.

She couldn't believe it. How could Tiffany have done this to her? She'd thought things were better between them. Obviously she'd been seriously wrong.

She stood and stalked out of the office, only to run into her mother. "Have you seen Tiffany?" Carly asked her.

"She's upstairs in her room. She said she had a lot of homework and wanted to get it finished before dinner." Rhonda smiled. "I think our little girl is finally growing up and learning to be responsible."

"Oh, I think our little girl is terrified I'm going to find out about her Friday-night activities and wants to make sure she doesn't get in too much trouble by being a sweetie now."

"What happened?"

"Tiffany lied about spending the night at a friend's, and instead went to a boy-girl party that lasted until who knows when. Plus, her girlfriend's older sister played mom when I called to confirm there would be adult supervision."

"Then she's going to be in big trouble," Rhonda told her.

"Oh, yeah. I'm going to talk to Tiffany."

Rhonda nodded. "I'll take care of the appetizers and wine."

Carly glanced at the clock. It was nearly four. "Thanks, mom. I appreciate the help. You're the best."

Rhonda looked faintly surprised, then smiled and left for the kitchen. Carly took the elevator to the third floor, then climbed the tower stairs. She knocked once on Tiffany's door, then entered.

Her daughter sat at her desk, hard at work on her homework.

"Hi, Mom," she said cheerfully. "I'm nearly done here. Want me to help with the appetizers when I'm finished?"

If only this pleasant, happy child was really her daughter. But alas…

"I just received a call from a parent of one of the girls at your school. Apparently there was no sleepover Friday night. There was a boy-girl party. You went with Jack." Carly felt her temper flare again. "You lied, Tiffany. You flat-out lied. Then Jessica's older sister pretended to be her mother to fake me out."

Tiffany stared at her. Utter shock widened her eyes. "What? No. That's not…"

Carly held up a hand. "Don't make the mistake of lying to me a second time. That will only make things worse."

Her daughter pressed her lips together, then pushed to her feet.

"But it's not fair. How did anyone find out? We all swore we weren't going to say anything. Who blabbed?"

"I haven't a clue. But here's the thing. You can kiss your sleepover privileges goodbye. You're grounded for the next month. You will lose phone privileges and you won't be seeing Jack."

"What?"

"He was there, too. I expected better of the two of you." Oddly enough, she was almost more disappointed in Jack than Tiffany. She expected her daughter to try to get away with things, but she'd thought he was different. Which was silly. He was sixteen. Just because he didn't screw up in front of her didn't mean he wasn't a regular kid.

"But I have to see Jack."

"No, you don't."

"This is so unfair."

"There's more to your grounding, but I haven't figured out what it's going to be," Carly said, keeping her voice calm. "You chose to lie, you chose to mislead me and you chose to break the rules. You made every bit of this happen and now you're going to face the consequences."

"I hate you!" Tiffany screamed.

"I'm sure you do." She unplugged the phone that had only been recently restored from the last grounding. After collecting Tiffany's cell phone from the nightstand, she turned to leave.

"Just so we're clear, I'm calling Jack's mother to tell her about the party."

"What? You can't. This is too embarrassing."

"Should have thought about that before. Consider yourself stuck on the property here until the second week of July. I suppose you can leave to see your dad, but that's it."

"You can't do that. It's nearly summer vacation."

"Huh. You're right. You should have thought about that before."

Carly stepped out into the hallway. Something hard slammed into the door, but it didn't phase her in the least. For once she didn't mind that her daughter was upset with her. Tiffany had screwed up and now she would face the consequences. It was time to make sure there was only one professional victim in the house.

"I don't like these people one bit," Rhonda said as she peered out the kitchen window. "The way they dress, and their music. They'll probably murder us in our beds."

"I think they'll be more creative than that," Carly said. She poured herself a second cup of coffee. "They're horror writers, Mom. They're fine."

Her mother sniffed loudly. "They're odd."

"I know, and I'm okay with that."

Funny how she was. Tiffany hadn't spoken to her in nearly three days and she had a feeling Jack was pissed at her, as well, but that was all right, too.

"Neil's here," Rhonda said. "What do you suppose he's going to do with Tiffany this time?"

"I haven't a clue." Carly carried her coffee out to the front porch and waited for her ex-husband.

When he strolled up the steps, she smiled. "Hi. Tiffany's in a bad mood because she's grounded for a month." She told him about the party. "I'm sure you think I'm being too tough, but I would appreciate your support by not telling her that. Also, please don't take her shopping this weekend. She's still grounded."

Neil nodded. "I know, I know. No belly button rings, no late nights, no inappropriate movies. Jeez, Carly, don't you ever get tired of being an adult?"

"Sometimes, but it's too late to go back."

"Not necessarily. My boat's nearly ready to go. You could leave all this and sail with me to Hawaii."

"What?" He couldn't be serious.

He shuffled his feet. "It could be fun. Like it was before."

"Before when?"

"You know. Back when things were good between us."

Before she had grown up, she would bet. "Thanks for asking, but I'd rather stay right here."

He frowned. "Why?"

She leaned against the front of the porch. The railing would need painting again soon. There was a broken washer, a full house and the produce delivery was late. Maribel had gone on maternity leave and her daughter freaked out every single morning before she started baking. Carly knew it would be a long two months until her friend returned to work. And it was summer—their busiest time.

She seemed to go from crisis to crisis. But wasn't that life? A day-to-day world where very little was in her control? And isn't that what made it wonderful?

She might have come here because she'd had nowhere else to go, but she was staying for far better reasons.

"I like my life, Neil. I don't want to run away."

And if she did, it wouldn't be with him.

"What is there to like?" he asked, obviously genuinely baffled by her statement.

She thought for a second, then grinned. "Everything."

SANDWICHED
by
Jennifer Archer

Jennifer Archer has survived manoeuvring through life in seven different states, raising two teenage boys and, this year, her very first hot flush – all without serious medication. She is the author of four novels and currently resides in Texas with her school sweetheart, whom she married more than twenty-five years ago. Jenny is at work on her next novel, while awaiting the words every mother longs for, 'Mum, I finally graduated and found a job! I'm off your payroll!' She loves to hear from her readers through her website, www.jenniferarcher.net

Like the women in *Sandwiched*,
I have lived under one roof with some fabulous females
for many years. This book is dedicated to them with love
and gratitude:

My mom, Joan Browder,
who is patient and supportive, loving and wise.
You mean the world to me.

And

Linda Heasley, Charla Walton and
Angie Prince – sisters by fate, friends by choice.
My life would not be nearly so fun
or interesting without you.

Thanks to my editor, Gail Chasan, who is a
dream to work with; and to Tara Gavin and all the
wonderful people I've met at Harlequin.

Thanks to my agent, Jenny Bent, who
challenged me to make the proposal stronger, and stuck
out the tough times with me.

Thanks to the Thursday night Divas,
who offered wine and whine sessions,
encouragement and their invaluable expertise
and suggestions: Dee Virden Burks,
Jodi Koumalats, Marcy McKay, DeWanna Pace,
April Redmon and honorary Diva (whether he likes it
or not) Robert Brammer. And to the
long-distance Divas, Britta Coleman and
Candice Havens, who encouraged from afar.

Thanks to my friend Ronda Thompson,
who met me at Schlotsky's and saved my sanity
by helping me figure out how to structure the dreaded
synopsis.

And as always, thanks to my husband, Jeff,
who didn't complain when the alarm went off
every morning at 5:00 am; and to my son Jason who
sometimes remembered to call and let me know he was
going to miss his curfew (again);
and to my son Ryan, whose funny phone calls from
college gave me nice breaks away
from the writing.

CHAPTER 1

Cecilia Dupree
Day Planner
Saturday, 11/1

1. Unpack Mother.
2. Grocery store.
3. Shop for Erin's concert dress.

Instead of filing for divorce, I should've buried Bert in the backyard, in the spot beneath the willow where our bulldog likes to pee.

I realize my mistake on a Saturday morning while driving home from the Donut Hut. The sun shines bright in a lapis-blue sky; the autumn air is as sweet and crisp as my mother's famous gingersnap cookies. It seems a shame to go back to the house so soon on such a gorgeous day, back to Mother and a bedroom full of boxes containing her things. So I decide, instead, to take a little drive.

After rolling down the windows, I choose a chocolate long john from the doughnut sack then proceed to lick off the icing. Which might give you a fairly clear idea of what's lurking at the back of my mind, though I have a difficult time admitting, even to myself, why nibbling the pastry gives me such an inordinate amount of pleasure. I pretend I'm only attempting to satisfy my sweet tooth but, after more than six months of sleeping alone, deep down I know better.

Since the separation, I've spent my days and nights trying to keep up with my teenaged daughter, checking on my widowed mother, putting in long hours at a demanding child-and-family counseling practice. No time exists for sex; at least that's what I tell myself. So I avoid anything and everything that might remind me of what I'm missing.

It isn't easy.

In case you haven't noticed, sex is everywhere these days. Television. Movies. Books. Doughnut sacks. Even my late Friday and Saturday nights of safe, celibate solitaire have turned traitor on me. After a couple of months alone with the card deck, the King of Hearts has started to look appealing; I'd swear he has a frisky gleam in his eye.

But back to Bert and why I should've buried him.

Somehow or another, I wind up on his street this Saturday morning. And just in time to see him step onto the front porch of his condo with a young, buxom redhead attached to his side. The girl doesn't look much older than our daughter Erin, the only worthwhile thing Bert ever gave me during our nineteen years of marriage.

It's the kiss that does me in. I can't tear my attention away from their passionate lip-lock, from Bert's hands kneading and caressing that tight, round, voluptuous butt. Because of that kiss, I don't see the curve in the road. I hit the curb, run up onto the sidewalk, jerk to a screeching halt only inches from a mailbox in front of the condo across the street from Bert's.

That forces my attention away from the kiss. Bert's too, apparently, because before I can catch my breath, he's beside my window, looking down at me with the smug, disdainful sneer I know so well.

Swallowing a creamy bite of pastry that, luckily, I didn't choke on, I meet his gaze and attempt to act as if nothing is at all unusual about my minivan, aka "the grocery getter," being parked on his neighbor's walk. "Hello, Bert."

"Cecilia." His eyes shift to my lap where the prior object of my desire now sits in a smear of chocolate, soiling my gray, baggy sweats.

Bert, I notice, wears boxers. No shirt. His feet are bare. He's lost weight and bulked up since the last time I saw him barelegged and bare-chested. Muscles bulge I never knew existed. My once soft and pudgy soon-to-be ex looks buff and disgustingly great, which only makes me wish all the more that I'd chopped him up into little pieces and planted him beneath the willow tree. Maxwell, our bulldog, would've loved me for it. The dog never cared much for Bert. I imagine he'd take great pleasure in a daily tinkle over the remains of the guy who called him "girly-dog" and once kicked him for eating out of the trashcan.

When I realize Bert sees me sizing up his pecs, I shift my attention to beyond his shoulder where a little red convertible backs out of his drive. "How upstanding of you to volunteer to teach the Girl Scouts mouth-to-mouth resuscitation."

Bert doesn't even flinch. I guess nothing embarrasses him

anymore after being caught by me in the arms of Tanya Butterfield, our neighbor's twenty-one-year old daughter.

"You're looking good," he says, eyeing my sleep-mussed hair and the pimple on my chin, compliments of my frequent flirtation with chocolate. I always thought blemish-free skin would be one of the few perks of perimenopause. I thought wrong. This morning, I left for the Donut Hut straight out of bed and didn't bother to use a comb or wash my face, much less put on makeup to cover the zit.

Bert sweeps a finger across the side of my mouth and comes away with a glob of icing. "I see you gave up on your diet."

Before I can think of a barbed comeback, an old man steps out of the house in front of the mailbox I barely missed demolishing. He stands in the yard wearing his pajamas, arms crossed, glaring at me over the tops of his reading glasses.

"Hello, Mr. Perkins," Bert calls out. "Everything's okay. She missed your box. I'll have her off the sidewalk and on her way in no time."

Bert steps away from the van, and I put it in Reverse then back out into the street. I consider shifting into drive, slamming on the accelerator and leaving him choking on exhaust. But Bert's arrogant declaration to pucker-faced Mr. Perkins changes my mind. He'll have me on my way in no time? We'll see about that. No one controls Cecilia Dupree. Not anymore. I press on the brake and wait for him to walk back over.

"So…" Bert bends down to look into the window again, leveling one forearm on the edge and his gaze on mine. "What brings you to my neighborhood at 8:00 a.m. on a Saturday morning, CiCi?"

Birds twitter and cheep, serenading my humiliation. "Yesterday Erin and I moved Mother out of Parkview Manor
Retirement Village and into the spare bedroom. Today we're
unpacking. I went to get breakfast."

"I'm not exactly on your route home."

There is no way in Heaven or Hell I'll admit that I've
ended up on his street because I've been thinking about him
day and night for the past week. Our wedding anniversary
passed uneventfully three days ago and, the truth is, I'm
having a tough time learning to live single.

Seeing Bert doesn't help matters. While he has obviously
been working out at a gym, dating, *having a life,* I've been
paralyzed. Unable to move forward. Wallowing in the pre-
divorce doldrums while feeding my face with whatever I can
find in the fridge to fill the hollow spot inside of me, the
gaping hole Bert left behind.

Don't get me wrong; I stay busy. During the day, my life
is chaos. And most every evening, I'm at the kitchen table
studying patient files. When I've had enough of that, the
King of Hearts and I fool around a little until Erin comes
home from wherever she spends her spare time these days.
When it's time for bed, old movies on late-night TV keep
me company until I drop off to sleep.

It's not so much that I miss Bert; I miss what felt familiar.
Being one half of a couple. Having a warm body in the bed
beside me at night. Lately, I've even been tempted to give
in to Maxwell's sad eyes and let him sleep on the bed at my
feet.

Determined to salvage my pride, I lift my pimpled chin
and meet Bert's stare straight-on. "It's been so long since

Erin's heard from you, I was afraid you might've skipped town. I thought I better swing by and make sure your car was still in the driveway." I hope it doesn't occur to him that I could've just picked up the phone.

"Erin's cell's always busy. I'll try her again today."

Shifting the van into drive, I motion toward the old man who still stands in the yard, arms crossed, watching us. "Tell your neighbor I apologize."

Bert smiles. "Say hello to Belle for me. I'll miss her cooking this Thanksgiving and Christmas. She's okay, isn't she?"

"Mom's fine. For the most part, anyway."

He frowns. "For the most part?"

"Her eyesight's getting worse. I think she's depressed about it. She doesn't socialize at all. She's stopped cooking for the other apartment residents, and you know how Mom loves to cook. Anyway, Erin and I talked it over and decided she'd probably be happier and more active living with us. We've hired a woman to come over and be with her during the day."

"That's a big step. I admire you for it."

"Yeah…well." I shrug. "I do my part for the elderly of the world, you do your part for the youth."

"Youth?"

I nod toward his condo. "The mouth-to-mouth?"

Bert surprises me with a blush, which gives me a small measure of satisfaction as I drive away, this time leaving *him* alone and embarrassed.

Sweet justice.

Around 11:00 a.m., Erin declares her work duties done, blows her Nana a kiss and takes off for her best friend

Suzanna's house. They plan to eat lunch at the mall, then spend the afternoon shopping for a dress for Erin's yearly holiday orchestra concert. I'd planned to go along, but too much is left here to do, and Erin didn't seem to mind if I begged off.

Mother shakes her head as she watches Erin go. She mutters something about families eating together, about homemade meals and how life was better back in the old days when my brother, Jack, and I were kids.

The mention of Jack makes me want to crush the box at my feet. Nothing's changed. Even as a kid, my brother could always find clever ways to weasel out of his responsibilities. I have to give it to him this time; moving eight hundred miles away just before Dad's heart attack is his best scheme yet. I want to be here for Mother. Still, some backup would be nice. Even long distance, you'd think Jack could help with the decision-making, with trying to boost Mother's frame of mind. But, no. His idea of involvement is a fifteen-minute phone call once per week.

As I drag the box to Mother's bedroom and start unpacking clothing, knickknacks and books, my early morning drive-by comes to mind. So. Bert has a life. Not only a life, a *sex* life. Women actually find him appealing. Maybe he really wasn't just a mercy lay or a boredom diversion for our neighbor's not-so-innocent young daughter.

And that pisses me off.

All these months while I've been raising our child alone, coping with all the stress that goes with having a teenager, juggling family and career, struggling with ending our failed marriage and putting it behind me, Bert and his penis have been out on the town. Literally.

Mother's humming drifts to me from the kitchen where she's putting away her gourmet cooking utensils, pots, pans and bakeware. The sound makes me pause. I can't recall hearing her hum like that since Dad died almost a year ago. The anniversary of his passing is a week away. Next Saturday.

The humming pleases me…and makes me feel guilty. The truth is, I haven't come to terms with her moving into my house. I love her and want the best for her. But is her moving in best for Erin and me? I haven't lived full-time with a parent since I left home at the age of eighteen for college. I'm accustomed to doing things my own way, not Mother's. And Erin is finally starting to have friends come around. She likes her independence and privacy, and so do I. But did all that walk out the door when Mother walked in?

"You okay in there?" I yell.

"I'm making headway, Sugar, but it's going to take a while," she calls back. "Your cabinets are a mess! You could die of starvation before you found a pot to boil water in or a pan to scramble an egg."

"Which is why I don't boil water or scramble eggs."

"For heaven's sake! What do y'all eat?"

"Takeout." I pry open a box filled with colognes and bubble bath and other bathroom stuff. "Frozen dinners."

"What about breakfast?"

"Breakfast? What's that?"

Even the two walls separating us can't block her sigh. "No wonder Erin's so skinny, poor thing. Now that I'm here, I'll take care of that."

I drag the box toward the adjoining bathroom, reminding myself that this is what matters. Family pulling together during tough times. My mother's happiness in the winter years of her life. Not my pride or privacy or independence. And most certainly not Bert's extracurricular activities.

I groan. *Bert.* I can get over the fact that he has a social life and a sex life and I don't; I *will* get over it. Nothing good ever came of sex anyway. Well, nothing but babies and orgasms, but I'm long past the baby stage of my life.

As for orgasms, let's just say Bert never put much stock in the motto "it's better to give than to receive." So, while I could argue that some is better than nothing at all, I haven't really given much up in that department. Anyway, if not for raging hormones, Bert would've lost interest in me when the first date ended. It wasn't my brilliant mind he probed in his bachelor apartment when we were seniors at the University of Texas.

Hefting the box onto the bathroom vanity, I start pulling out floral-scented bottles and small brown medicine vials.

"CiCi?" Mom calls from inside the bedroom.

"In here."

My petite, plump, pink-cheeked mother appears in the bathroom doorway, a bright smile on her face, her eyes unnaturally huge behind the magnified lenses of her glasses. She holds my thick, white plastic cutting board, which she lifts up in front of her. "Not that it's any of my business, Sugar, but don't you think it's time you threw this ol' thing away?"

I blink. Rarely, if ever, do I use the board, but still it's mine, and after her previous criticism of my kitchen organizational skills, I'm starting to feel a bit defensive. "What's wrong with it?"

"I'm blind as a bat, but even I can see there's mold growing on it." Mother wrinkles her nose. "It isn't sanitary."

"It's sanitary. I bleach it after every use. The green just won't come off."

"Surely you can afford a new cutting board."

"Why should I spend the money when that one's still perfectly functional?"

Mother gives me The Look. You know, The Look? Head tilted to the side, one brow raised, lips pursed?

I realize how ridiculous I sound, a forty-one-year-old woman arguing with her mother over a moldy cutting board I haven't seen in months, maybe years. So what if her scrutiny of my life and home makes me feel fifteen again? I don't have to act fifteen. "Okay, okay. Get rid of it," I tell her.

Mother's sweet countenance returns. She steps toward the trashcan by the desk in the corner and drops the plastic board inside. "Thank you so much for making space for all my things. I can't wait to start cooking for you and Erin, and it isn't the same if I don't have my own pots and pans."

I reach into the box, run my hand across smooth, cool glass, over peeling labels and bumpy plastic. "It'll be great having your home-cooked meals again. Cooking's just another of your many domestic talents I didn't inherit."

With my gaze still on Mother, I pull out another item.

Mother's gasp is quick and sharp. The color drains from her face, then rises again, bright red now rather than pink. Her eyes blink. Rapidly.

I glance down at my hand and immediately drop the object I'm holding. I'm no expert on vibrators, but I'm pretty sure I know a neck massager from…well…the *other kind*. The one on the floor at my feet is not for sore muscles, I can promise you that. Flesh-colored, it has a switch on the side that must've engaged when it hit the bathroom tile because the dismembered member pulses and vibrates and buzzes.

"Um…" I can't tear my gaze from the quivering body part, which fake or not, is quite impressive in size and energy. "Uh—"

"Well, for heaven's sake!" Mother's voice is high and panicky. "How did my bread beater get packed with my bathroom things?"

"Your *bread beater?*"

The next thing I see is her hand wrapping around the *thing,* which is an action I would've been happy never to witness in this or any other lifetime. She lifts it from the floor and turns off the switch while I reluctantly peer up at her.

My mother no longer blushes or blinks. In the space of a few seconds she has pulled herself together. She couldn't look any more prim or proper if she stood in front of her church choir to lead a hymn. Squaring her shoulders, holding the "bread beater" in front of her chest like a baton, she meets my eyes.

"That's right. My bread beater. Haven't you seen them advertised? It's a clever new device that kneads dough, easy as you please."

"Well…" I clear my throat. "Isn't that…something."

Mom turns and starts off through the bedroom. "I'll just go find a place for it in the kitchen."

I watch her go, then shift my attention to the mirror and stare at the dumbfounded expression on my face. I picture

Erin going after a fork and finding Mom's newest kitchen gadget in the silverware drawer.

First Bert, now Mother. Wouldn't you know it? At the age of seventy-five, even she has more of a sex life than I do.

LATER IN THE EVENING, after a trip with Mother to the grocery store, she cooks a dinner that brings back memories of all those childhood meals she mumbled about earlier. She, Erin and I actually sit at the kitchen table rather than at the coffee table in the den, my usual place to dine. We carry on a conversation instead of watching the news.

Afterward, stuffed with savory fried chicken, garlic mashed potatoes and fresh green beans, Erin and I clear the table while Mother takes off to watch *Wheel of Fortune*. An apple cobbler bubbles and browns in my oven; Mother left the oven light on, and I glance at her culinary masterpiece with longing each time I pass by. I'm not sure why, maybe it's the foreign aromas of cinnamon and spice drifting through my kitchen, but I'm unusually relaxed and content as my daughter and I load the dishwasher together.

"I'm going to rent a movie, then watch it at Suzanna's," Erin declares when we finish.

"Before you leave, I want to see your concert dress."

"I didn't find one. I'll try again tomorrow or next week."

"Make it some time I can go with you."

Erin crosses her arms; her eyes shift away from mine. "It's no big deal. Suzanna will help me."

Okay, I admit it; for the second time in one day I feel like an overemotional teenager. Only now, instead of butting heads with my mother, my best friend is replacing me with someone else. I can't help it; silly or not, I'm jealous.

"What about that book report you said was due on Monday?"

"I'm not doing homework on a Saturday night. I'll work on it tomorrow."

"Be home by eleven." I eye her tight hip-hugging jeans, the inch of bare flesh between them and her T-shirt. Revealing so much skin is a new look for Erin. A fashion side effect of her friendship with Suzanna, I imagine. Though I don't like the change, I've decided not to make a big deal of it. I counsel families with kids younger than Erin who are promiscuous, have alcohol problems and worse. If an exposed navel is the most I have to deal with, I count myself lucky. I'll just keep an eye on her and make sure that's as far as it goes. "Got your mace?" I ask.

She gives me the eye-roll she spent middle school perfecting. "You know it's on my key ring."

"Just make sure you keep it in your hand if you're returning the movie and walking through the store parking lot after dark."

"I know, Mom." She hugs me and laughs. "You've only told me a million and one times. Anyway, there's a movie drop. I won't even have to get out of the car."

"Let Maxwell in and feed him before you go."

After Erin leaves and *Wheel of Fortune* ends, Mother and I watch *CNN* together while eating ice-cream-smothered pie. Maxwell peers at us with pleading eyes. He sits in front of the sofa, whining quietly each time I lift my spoon. Mother gives me The Look again when I place my bowl on the floor to let him lick it. I laugh at her and proceed to fold a couple of loads of laundry.

I'm placing a stack of clean underwear on Erin's dresser when I see the novel on her bedside table. I figure it must be the assigned book for her report since I've never known my daughter to read a novel unless it's required. I hope she's not getting sidetracked by her newfound social life and putting off the report until the last minute. But I remind myself that, though she's spending more time with friends these days, it's still not in Erin's nature to procrastinate. She's a typical only child. Fairly responsible as teenagers go.

I walk over, pick up the paperback, read the title. *Penelope's Passion*. A hazy cover creates the effect of looking through steam at a woman's naked back. A man's hand lifts the damp, curling tendrils of hair at the nape of her neck. I have my doubts Erin's English teacher chose this particular read.

Settling at the edge of my daughter's bed, I open the book to a random page.

Penelope sensed rather than heard the captain's approach. Pulling the sheet to her breast, she watched the door…and waited. Her heart fluttered like hummingbird wings, her stomach felt as unsteady as the ship, tossed and swayed by the turbulent sea.

Flickering candlelight painted shadows on the walls. For only a moment, Penelope glanced away to watch them dance, and when she looked back, he stood there…filling the doorway…his dark eyes devouring her, looking more a pirate than captain of a ship. His unbuttoned shirt revealed a powerful expanse of muscled chest. The sight of it made

Penelope aware of her own chest, bare beneath the bed sheet. Her only garment had mysteriously disappeared while she bathed, so she'd had no choice but to retire naked.

Penelope lifted her chin. "Do you intend to rape me, Sir?"

The captain pulled off his shirt as he stepped into the room and closed the door behind him. "Since you now share my name, I intend to consummate our marriage."

She kept her gaze on his face, too nervous to glance lower at his body, afraid if she did he might see the excitement in her eyes when she looked up again. "And if I refuse you, Captain?"

He chuckled, his smile quick and heart-stopping. Then he reached for the buckle on his belt and moved closer to the bed.

Penelope could no longer refrain. She glanced at his broad chest, then lower still, down his flat, muscle-corded belly to the thin line of dark hair that trailed to the top of his breeches. Her breath caught, her stomach tightened involuntarily and a warm, sweet ache spread like heated honey through her limbs. To her shame, she yearned to touch him, yearned for him to touch her in all the places no man ever had, or should.

"Dear Lady," he said, his voice a deep, arousing caress, "you won't refuse me."

"Well, hell," I mutter, closing the book. Penelope isn't the only one with a warm, sweet ache.

First Bert, then Mother, now Erin.

Maybe the person who came up with the old saying, "if you can't beat 'em, join 'em," knew what he or she was talking about.

Tucking *Penelope's Passion* beneath my arm, I leave Erin's room. At the end of the hallway, I poke my head around the corner into the den where Mother sits knitting and watching TV, with Maxwell snoring on the rug at her feet. The knitting needles click out a rhythmic beat.

"I think I'll turn in early and catch up on some reading."

Mother's needles pause. The clicking stops. She looks up at me. "I hope for once you're reading for pleasure instead of for work."

The corner of my mouth spasms as I think of Penelope's captain. "Purely for pleasure tonight, Mother. You have my word."

CHAPTER 2

To: Erin@friendmail.com
From: Suz@friendmail.com
Date: 11/1 Saturday
Subject: Tonight
Hey. Meet me at the mall at 11:30. We'll eat, then shop for something to wear out tonight to The Beat. You're going. No excuses.

I look at the outfit spread across Suzanna's bed and wish I'd never checked my e-mail this morning. The skintight, one-sleeved red-and-black striped top will leave one shoulder completely bare, while the pleated black pinstriped miniskirt is barely long enough to cover my scrawny butt. But the worst of it all sits in an open box; a pair of ankle-high, pointy-toed red boots with buckles on the sides and short spiked heels.

This afternoon at the mall, I gave into Suzanna's arm-twisting and bought it all. It seemed like a good idea at the time. The outfit was great for laughs in the dressing room.

But the thought of actually wearing it in public makes me want to puke up Nana's fried chicken.

My stuff has been in the trunk of my car since I left the mall. It's bad enough having Mom to deal with, but now I have Nana, too. It's not like I don't want her to live with us; I do. But I'm afraid if the two of them saw these clothes, Mom would go ballistic and Nana might have a heart attack. And two against one makes it that much harder to defend yourself. I'm sure Mom didn't have this sort of outfit in mind for my concert. Which, now that I think of it, I totally forgot to shop for. The concert, that is.

"This all goes back," I say, shaking my head and turning to face my friend. "It's not me at all. It's more like something you'd wear."

Suz grabs the top and holds it up in front of me. "Oh, get over it. You're just nervous. You're gonna look *amazing.*"

"I'll feel like a skank."

"Are you saying I dress like a skank?"

"No. I'm saying that you can pull off wearing slutty things *without* looking skanky. I can't."

Suzanna tosses the satiny top in my face. "That's just stupid."

I catch the shirt and start to refold it. "It doesn't matter what I wear tonight. If I'm with you no guy's going to notice me anyway." Not that they pay me much attention when Suz *isn't* around. It's just worse when she is.

"That's only because you're so quiet. They probably think you don't *want* to hook up."

"Okay." I sit at the edge of her bed, wishing she'd turn off the rap music, which I hate. "Then explain why it is that guys who've never met me, guys who don't know I'm quiet or that you're outgoing, completely look past me whenever you and I are together? Even before we ever open our mouths?"

Suz rolls her eyes. "As if."

"It's true."

"If it is true, which it isn't, then maybe it's because…" She pauses to nibble her lower lip. "Well, I hate to say this, but maybe it's because you dress like an orchestra member."

"I *am* an orchestra member."

"Exactly." Suzanna flips back her long blond hair.

"Playing the cello doesn't have anything to do with the way I dress. Lot's of girls who aren't in orchestra dress like me."

"They probably can't hook up, either."

"What's wrong with my clothes?" I glance down at my jeans and T-shirt, bought last week, though they aren't my style. "I'm showing skin." I point at my belly button. "See?"

Suz eyes my jeans. "At least they aren't your usual. Baggy, khaki or black."

"Samantha Carter dresses like a *nun* and she has boy-friends. My clothes aren't the problem."

"Then what?"

I lay the folded skank-top on the bed beside me, cross my arms and stare straight at her chest. "Remember yesterday after school when you ran up to me in the parking lot while I was talking to Todd Blackburn about our science project?"

She nods. "What about it?"

"When he saw you coming, he forgot I existed. At first I thought it was your bouncing ponytail that threw him into a trance. Then I realized your hair wasn't the only thing bouncing."

Her eyes widen. "*Shut up!* I wasn't bouncing!"

"Yes you were! And Todd wasn't the only guy in the parking lot who noticed. Instead of 'follow the bouncing ball,' it was 'follow the bouncing boobs.'"

"That's disgusting." Suzanna's face flushes, which is a total surprise since nothing much embarrasses her.

"Well, if that's the problem," she says, "I can solve it."

"If you tell me to stand up straight and stick out my personality, I'm out of here." Back before Nana quit sewing, she'd say that to me. She'd be fitting a dress or whatever, pinning it at my shoulders or under my pits and getting all bent out of shape because I was slumping.

Suz makes a face and starts for the door. "Wait here."

While she's gone I turn off the music and swipe a piece of mint gum from her dresser. I think how weird it is that two people so different wound up friends. I moved to Dallas as a sophomore two years ago when Dad expanded his business. Since then, I've been pretty much alone when it comes to a social life. I hate my school with all its little groupies. Until Suz transferred in at the beginning of the year, I didn't have a best friend. The truth is, I didn't have any close friends at all. Just kids I hung out with sometimes. Other girls from my orchestra class, usually. Most of them quiet, goody-two-shoes nobodies. Which is probably how people think of me, too. I didn't share secrets with anyone or talk on the phone 'til late at night. I never laughed so hard I peed my pants. Mainly, I studied a lot, practiced my cello, made the honor roll and spent time with Mom.

Then Suzanna showed up and everything changed. She

lives nearby in a Dallas suburb. Suz isn't exactly honor roll material, but she knows how to have fun. She should've graduated last year, but she didn't pass a couple of classes. Instead of retaking the first semester of her senior year at her old school and being totally humiliated, her parents let her transfer. I still can't figure out why she chose to hang out with me. At her old school, she was a cheerleader with more friends than she could keep track of. She says they've all taken off to different colleges. I'm pretty sure some of them made her feel stupid for not graduating, though she's never come out and said it.

Some friends.

I think she realized that. Or maybe she's just had enough of the whole "high school popularity" thing. Whatever the reason, she latched on to me the second she heard me playing cello in an empty classroom one day after school, and she's never let go. Okay, so sometimes I feel like her ugly stepsister. But at least I have fun now that I'm not hanging with Mom 24/7.

I'm dabbing some of Suz's spicy perfume on my neck when she walks back into the room and hands me two pale pink oval blobs. "What are these? Dead jellyfish?"

"Silicone inserts," she says. "They're Katie's. She takes after Dad. I take after Mom."

Katie, Suzanna's fifteen-year-old sister, is so flat she's almost concave. "She actually wears these?" I press the blobs against my 32-A's. The inserts even have nipples. Hard ones.

"Sometimes she does."

"Well, I can't," I say. "I won't."

"Why not?"

"It's false advertising for one thing. For another," I pinch the nipples, "I'd look like I'm chronically cold."

Suz snickers.

"Besides, if a guy's only interested in me because he thinks I have big boobs then maybe he's not worth knowing."

She sits beside me. "Let me explain guys to you. They can't help it. They're drawn to ta-tas like flies are drawn to picnic tables. It's the way they're wired."

I lay the blobs on the bed beside the red boots. "In that case, I have no hope."

"Not true. You just have to trick them into noticing you so that they'll stick around long enough to get to know you better. Once they do, and they realize how funny and smart you are, your booblessness won't matter so much."

I stare at her. "Yeah, right."

Suz sighs. "Okay, maybe not. I've never met a guy our age that mature."

I think of Dad. Mom doesn't know I figured out about him and the sleazoid who lives next door. But I'm not stupid. I saw how his eyelids got all heavy-looking whenever he saw her out in the driveway wearing only a little bikini top with her short shorts. I heard how his voice changed whenever they spoke, how his deep drawl got deeper and more drawn out, like the words were coated with molasses. "I'm not sure they're ever that mature," I say to Suzanna. "Even the old ones."

Suz sighs. "We'll have to concentrate on something besides funny and smart then." She studies me. "You have great eyes. I wish mine were big and brown. And your hair…" She twists it up on top of my head then lets it fall. "I like the color."

"You have a thing for muddy brown?"

She makes a face. "It's chestnut."

"Whatever you say."

Suz picks up an insert. "Quit being so negative and just have some fun with these, why don't you?" She tosses it at me. "At least try them on with the clothes."

Five minutes later, I strut back and forth in front of Suzanna's full-length mirror laughing like a crazy person. "Hey, dressing like a slut is sort of fun."

"Ohmigod! You're *so* not slutty-looking. I swear! You look like a model. You *have* to buy some of those thingies to wear all the time. They look *real!*"

Jumping up and down, I watch them jiggle. I laugh so hard tears run down my cheeks. I admit to Suzanna that I think I might like pretending to be the girl in the mirror for just one night.

"Then let me change clothes and we'll get out of here," she says, clapping her hands together.

My stomach twists. I wipe my eyes. "I want to, but I can't."

"What now?"

"My mom. She'll freak if she finds out I went to The Beat."

"We won't be drinking. If you're under twenty-one, they put a band on your wrist so the waiters won't serve you."

"I'm not eighteen yet. I can't get in."

"My cousin Trevor works there. He'll be taking cover at the door tonight. He'll let you through."

"I don't know. I could be eighteen and swear not to drink, and Mom still wouldn't let me go."

"Come on, Erin. Please? All the college guys go there. When I went with Trevor last weekend on his night off we had a blast."

"I want to…."

"Then do it! I like your mother, but she's so strict. You're not a little girl anymore, and if you don't stand up to her and make her see that, you'll never get to have any fun. What does she expect you to do? Sit around with her and your grand-mother on weekends? You might as well just skip the next twenty years of your life and go straight to the old folks' home."

"I can't stand up to her. I know my mother. I'll lose."

"I think you should try. It's either that or go behind her back."

I imagine telling Mom I'm going to The Beat. After she gets over the shock of it she'll forbid me to leave the house. I imagine saying that she can't stop me. Then I think of my car, which she bought, the gasoline, which she pays for, the allowance she puts in my pocket. She has plenty of ways to make my life miserable.

"I choose going behind her back."

Suz raises her brows. "Ooh-kay."

"It's my only chance of going." I glance at my watch. "We're not going to have much time. I have to be home by eleven on weekends, and it's nine now. By the time you get ready and we drive out there, we'll have to leave again."

"Eleven? Your Mom *is* strict." Suzanna frowns. "Things don't really even get going until after eleven. But don't worry." She thinks for a few seconds then smiles. "I have a plan."

It's easier than I thought to sneak the sack of new clothes into my bedroom.

"Erin? Is that you, Sugar?" my grandmother calls from the den when the front door slams.

"Hi, Nana. Be right there." I stuff the sack under my bed.

Even before I get to the den, I hear music playing. The kind with a lot of brass and piano, with some guy's silky voice weaving through it. I'm sort of weirded out when I find Nana on the floor with Maxwell tucked up beside her. Leaning against the sofa, she scratches his belly, her eyes closed, her glasses on the coffee table beside her. Socks cover her feet, and her toes tap the air to the beat of the song. I don't know why seeing someone her age sprawled out on the floor with her shoes off seems strange, but it does.

For a minute, I just stand and stare at her, afraid to break the mood. It's like her mind is someplace besides this room, in a different time, a happy one if the smile on her face is any clue. It may sound stupid, but I almost feel like I'm spying on something private, something I shouldn't disturb. Deciding I should just tiptoe away, I start to turn.

Nana's eyes flutter open. She squints. "Oh, Erin." Lifting her hand from Maxwell's belly, she places it on the sofa. "Come sit and talk with me."

Maxwell raises his head and whimpers until she touches him again. I understand. I remember the comfort of being cozied up to her. When I was little, we'd sit together in the rocker and she'd read to me. She smelled soapy clean.

Suzanna waits outside for me, three houses down the block. The excitement she offers tugs me one way at the same time Nana's warmth pulls me the other. I hesitate then cross the room, settling on the sofa beside where she sits on the floor. "I thought you might be asleep."

"No, just resting my eyes." She sits up straight, reaches for her glasses then slides them up the bridge of her nose. "How was your evening? Did you have a nice time with your friend?"

"We just talked and tried on clothes."

"Your mother said you rented a movie."

"I did, but we didn't watch it yet. Maybe tomorrow." I glance toward the door to the kitchen. The lights are off. "Where's Mom?"

"She turned in early to read." Nana covers her mouth and yawns. "I think I'll take a quick soak in the tub then do the same. I'm having some trouble settling down after all the day's excitement." She reaches up to me. "Would you give me a lift?"

I stand and face her. Nana's hands are dry and powder soft. As I pull her to her feet, I try to figure out what excitement she's talking about. "Did something happen while I was gone?"

"Happen?" Nana's brows pull together. "Your mother and I just ate pie and watched television. I couldn't have stood much more after all the unpacking and putting away. And then there was the trip to the grocery store. And the

cooking." She pats my arm. "Mind you, I'm not complaining. It's a joy to be busy with my family."

I hug her, realizing the excitement she talked about was
just the move. Shame tightens my throat. This day meant a
lot to Nana. I guess I should've known that, but until now,
I didn't. I probably should've stuck around instead of going
to the mall with Suzanna.

Ending the hug, I stand back and look at her. "I think I'll
go to bed, too. I'm sort of tired." I almost choke on the lie.
What started out smooth and clear is all twisted and cloudy
now. I didn't expect my escape route would have ruts, guilty
feelings to dodge along the way.

"I love you. Sleep tight," Nana says. "Stay warm."

"Love you, too." Heat creeps up the back of my neck. My
heart beats too fast. "I'll put Maxwell out."

Max trots toward the front door, his bottom twisting in
the prissy way that always used to earn him a rude comment
from Dad. "Oh, no you don't." I hook a thumb in the direction of the backyard and lead him that way. Once outside,
he squats to pee, then lifts his head and sniffs the air, as if he
smells freedom beyond the fence and wants to explore. I
watch him a minute, thinking of Suzanna waiting out front,
of the night ahead. Then I go back inside.

I decide I better cover all my bases. A light shines under
Mom's bedroom door so I knock and tell her I'm home.
Usually, she tells me to come in and we talk for a while. By
some miracle, this time she doesn't. She sounds sort of funny,
like she's startled or something. We speak through her closed
door for a few seconds then say good-night.

Twenty minutes later, after changing clothes and fixing my

hair and makeup, I'm halfway out my bedroom window when the buckle of one spiked-heel boot catches on the inside latch. I have my free foot on the ground, the snared one raised high above the sill. I'm leaning forward, mooning the street. The temperature outside has dropped from comfortable to chilly. A breeze lifts the pleated hem of my miniskirt and scatters goose bumps across my butt. This is more than a rut, this is a major pothole.

Leave it to Suz and her great ideas.

I hear an engine and look over my shoulder. Her Honda Civic passes slowly by with the headlights turned off. She's supposed to wait down the street, but since I'm ten minutes late, I guess she got worried.

Before going through the window, I tossed my purse out. It's on the ground beside my foot. My cell phone's inside of it, ringing nonstop. It's a quiet muffled trill, but I panic anyway, sure Mom or Nana will hear it. My breath comes fast; I'm so scared I'm dizzy.

The second the phone goes quiet, I hear Nana humming on the other side of my door. I quit struggling with the boot buckle and stand still in spite of my cramped thigh. Her bedroom is next to mine; she probably finished her bath and she's headed there.

I'm shivering from coldness and fear when I finally hear Nana's bedroom door close. The humming stops. I twist my foot from side to side to work on the buckle again.

The bushes alongside the window rustle. I gasp, but see it's just Suzanna.

"Jeez!" I hiss. "You scared the crap out of me."

"Sorry," she whispers. "What are you doing?"

"Practicing to be a Dallas Cowboy cheerleader. What does it look like I'm doing? I'm stuck."

"Here." Suzanna squeezes in beside me. "Let me see." She leans in through the open window, reaches up, wiggles the latch with one hand while wiggling my boot buckle with the other. In no time, I'm free.

"I knew these boots would cause trouble," I mumble, pulling my leg from the sill, stumbling as I put my foot on the ground. "I feel like I'm playing dress-up."

"You are."

I reach for my purse as Suzanna slides the window closed. She grabs my hand. "Let's get out of here."

Her car idles at the curb. Giggling, our ankles wobbling on our spiky heels, my silicone boobs bouncing like her real ones, we run across the dark lawn toward it.

CHAPTER 3

From The Desk of
Belle Lamont

Dear Harry,
Last night was my first at home with Cecilia and Erin. With remnants of our life together packed away in boxes around me, I dreamed of your roses. The dream was so vivid that, as I woke, their cloying scent filled the room and I felt the velvet petals brush my cheek.

I miss you so. Now, more than ever, I need your strong arms around me, your whisper of reassurance, your rational advice.

Just moments ago, I looked out my bedroom window and saw Erin sneaking out her window. She and another girl were dressed to kill—an appropriate cliché in this case since I know it would kill her mother to see her in a skirt so short and heels so high. Her father, too, if Bert even cares anymore. Sometimes I wonder.

The two girls made a beeline across the yard, climbed into a car and sped off, leaving me here wondering about my role in all this. My duty. Do I go to Cecilia and tell her? Or do I bite my tongue? Wait up for Erin, listen to what she has to say, then try to talk some sense into her? I'm leaning toward the latter. I have Erin's cell phone number, and I can always call her if she's not in by midnight. Besides, Cecilia's too strict with the girl. In this day and age, an eleven o'clock curfew on a Saturday night for a young woman of almost eighteen is going overboard if you ask me. Of course, Cecilia didn't.

I think our daughter lives in deadly fear that if Erin's allowed to be a normal teenager, the girl will put her through the same grief Cecilia put us through at that age. Which would serve CiCi right; I'm sure you'll agree. I say that with a smile on my face!

I don't think poor Erin has ever had a date. How could she when she's stuck beneath the weight of CiCi's expectations that she act like a middle-aged adult when it comes to everything except boys? With the opposite sex, she's supposed to stay ten years old and uninterested.

Being a man who raised a daughter, you'd probably be tempted to agree with Cecilia on that. But I'd have to remind you that at eighteen, I'd already received a marriage proposal. From you. You smooth-talked me into tying the knot, and I had already dated enough young men to know that you were the one for me.

So, there you have it. Only one day living under our daughter's roof and already I worry about overstepping my bounds. Though, to do whatever's best for Erin, I'll gladly suffer the wrath of both her and her mother. I only wish you were here to help me decide what is the best thing to do. Was this a mistake? My moving in with the two of them? Maybe I'm being selfish, but I need them. And they need me, though they don't know it. They need me, Harry. CiCi lives life in a blur. Because of it, she's missing out on so much, and so is Erin. Which is why it's a good thing I'm here.

But do they want me here? They act as if they do, but I'm not certain that isn't pretense to spare my feelings. Is their love for me sturdy enough to weather so much togetherness?

*I realize something now that I didn't last week, or even yester-
day. This won't be simple. For them or me. Maybe it goes against
nature for parents and their adult children to live in the same house.
Maybe Cecilia and I, maybe all mothers and daughters, are only
meant to know one another as parent and child, not as grown women
with more shared fears and desires than we care to admit. Which
brings to mind a certain bread beater incident.*

*That blasted nasty Jane Binkley and her silly birthday gag gift!
I swear, I thought I'd thrown the thing away, but CiCi found it in
my things. I'll spare you the embarrassing details. Suffice it to say,
I had to think fast to come up with a story. And even then, I didn't
fool Cecilia.*

*Back to the subject at hand. After you left, I thought Parkview
Manor was a good solution for me, the answer to CiCi's worries
about me living alone and so far from her. I didn't mind moving
there, really. Like I've said before, Parkview isn't a nursing home;
good heavens, I'm not ready for that. It's simply a community of
retirees, but they do have a nursing staff on the premises in case
they're needed. Still, it wasn't what I'd hoped.*

*One day I may have to accept moving back to Parkview Manor
or someplace like it. But for now, while I'm still able to care for
myself and able to help CiCi with Erin, I couldn't bear to spend
another day in the place. Gather that many old men and women
together in one building and what do you get? A big ol' bunch of
busybodies with too much time on their hands, that's what. Why,
just last week, Ellen Miles tried to pry gossip out of me about Jane
Binkley. I didn't waste a minute before setting her straight. I told
her I don't make a habit of talking about other people's business.
"Just because my apartment is next door to Jane's and I'm privy
to most of the woman's coming and goings," I said, "doesn't mean*

I'll tell you or anybody else about the late hours men spend over there, or about all the giggling I often hear on the other side of my wall."

I swear, Harry, you should have seen Ellen's face! Her eyes bulged and she slapped a hand over her mouth like I had offended her, instead of the other way around.

Busybodies aside, Parkview just isn't for me. It doesn't seem natural to see only old, wrinkled faces day by day, to go out into the courtyard and never hear children laughing, to never see or speak to young families playing together or taking bike rides or walks around the neighborhood. A happy, healthy life requires a certain mix of ingredients. Babies and children. Teenagers. Middle-aged people and old folks. Most of those ingredients are missing at Parkview, and what remains is a very stale cake.

The only things I liked about the Village are a few dear friends I met and the reading group, which I formed and CiCi led. She's promised we can go on with it, that we'll keep meeting each week and she'll still read aloud for those of us with eyes too weak.

Speaking of my eyes, Cecilia would probably tell you a different story about my ability to take care of myself. Because my sight's getting worse, she's hired a baby-sitter to stay with me during the day. She won't listen when I tell her that, other than driving and reading and the like, I'm as self-sufficient today as I was five years ago and the five before that. My new glasses help with my vision. My only complaint is that the magnification is so strong my eyeballs look as if they might pop out of their sockets. I'm trying not to be vain, but sometimes I'm glad you can't see me like this.

I'll be thinking of you every moment next Saturday, the anniversary of our last day together. The truth is, I still think of you almost all the time on every day. I try to concentrate only on the *good times, but often my mind drifts to the difficult times, too. Oh, how I wish we had had more patience with one another. Why did we spend even one precious moment on pettiness, jealousy or pointless blame? Because of your stubbornness and the resentments I collected like rare coins, we wasted minutes that could've been spent making joyful memories. If only we had it to do over.*

That said, I must admit that sometimes I even miss our arguments. I miss your hard head, our standoffs. Without them, there'd have been no making up. And making up was the sweetest thing, wasn't it?

I'm asking Cecilia to drive me to Cleburne and by our old house next Saturday to check on your prize roses. If the weather held, they always lasted at least through mid-November. I hope that's true this year. I missed having you give me the first bloom this season. It was always my favorite gift from you, especially during our tough times. It seemed a promise that everything was all right between us. That you were sorry, or I was forgiven, or you'd given in and life would go on.

Saturday, when we turn the corner onto Bentwood Drive I will see your tender smile in the blooms. And I'll remember.

As always, your yellow rose,

Belle

CHAPTER 4

Cecilia Dupree
Day Planner
Wednesday, 11/5

1. 9:00—Hoyt Couple—New patient appt.
2. 1:00—Mom's Parkview reading group.
3. Call Bert. Remind him he has a daughter.

By nine-thirty-five, I'm wondering if Mr. Roger Hoyt will ever open his twitching mouth and start talking. He sits stiff and straight as a ruler beside his wife of twenty years, hands clutching the chair's arms like he's on a roller coaster that's about to take off. His expression tells me his tie is too tight. Only, he isn't wearing a tie.

"Mr. Hoyt…Roger. May I call you Roger?"

"Sure. Why not?"

Cut to the chase, I decide. Ask him point-blank. I lean forward. "Cindy has said that she feels you don't love her anymore. That you're bored with her." I catch his gaze, hold it. "How do you feel? Are you bored with your wife? Have you fallen out of love with her?"

Roger Hoyt reeks of fear, or it might be his aftershave; I'm not sure. He glances at the woman in question and clears his throat. "I still love my wife. It's just, well, I'm not *in* love with her. Not anymore."

Cindy's lower lip quivers.

I flash back to the moment Bert made the same admission to me, and I sympathize with Cindy Hoyt. "Okay, Roger. When did you realize this?"

He clears his throat again. "I can't put my finger on an exact moment. It just sort of happened over time. We stopped having fun together, stopped talking about anything except the kids and the bills. That sort of thing."

"So, you're saying you're more like brother and sister now?"

"Yeah, but we still…you know. We're more than brother and sister, but it's not enough." He shifts in the chair. "I want more."

"You've got commitment, the security of family, but no passion?"

He nods.

I turn to Cindy. "What's it like for you to hear all this?"

"It hurts." She blinks tear-bright eyes. "But he's right. We don't have fun anymore. We don't really talk. And our sex life has suffered. But I think we can work things out if we try."

I watch for Roger's reaction. Interesting. Cindy sees it, too, and looks down at her lap.

"Roger, when Cindy just said that, you cringed. Why?"

"I don't know. I, um, I guess I'm not sure if I want this anymore. I—"

Cindy sits straighter; her expression hardens. "That's just what I thought, Roger. Do you think I haven't noticed how much time you've been spending at work?" She turns to me. "I think he's starting something with his secretary."

"I am not!" Roger's face flames.

"Not an affair," Cindy adds quickly, anger replacing the hurt in her voice. "Not yet. But I saw the e-mails, Roger. I saw them. The woman couldn't be more than twenty-five." She crosses her arms and leans back.

A switch flips inside me. I stare at Roger and cross my arms, too. "Would you care to tell me about these e-mails between you and...?"

"Bitsy," Cindy hisses. Our eyes meet then narrow in unison. In unity.

"So, Roger, you and Bootsy have been flirting with infidelity through e-mails, is that—"

"Betsy. Her name is Betsy. I—we're—" Roger scoots to the edge of the chair. Glares at Cindy. At me. "We're not...I..." He stands. "Fuck this! Fuck it! I won't sit here while a complete stranger and my wife gang up me."

Oh, no! No! Damn it! What's wrong with me? What am I doing? I reach my hand toward him. "Calm down, Mr. Hoyt. No one's ganging up on you."

"Oh, really?" He paces and tugs at his collar, at the tie that isn't there. "What would you call it then?"

"I didn't mean to upset you, I was simply asking a question. Perhaps I should rephrase."

"Perhaps you should." He flops down in the chair.

"It seems that the two of you are at a point of decision, would you agree?"

Roger's Adam's apple bobs. He and Cindy look at one another. The two of them nod.

I tap my index finger against my thigh and study the immature jerk, trying to see deeper. Will he choose some temporary, ego-boosting fun with little Miss Bootsy who, judging from the looks of Roger, is probably only after his money? Or will he decide to make an effort to revive what he once had with the mother of his children, this intelligent, attractive woman he chose to marry? This woman who has washed his dirty socks and underwear, stuck with him through the early, sparse-money years after he started his business, believed in him when he didn't believe in himself.

Realizing my thoughts pertain to my own marriage, not necessarily the Hoyts', I take a deep breath. This is about them, not me. "Both of you need to spend some time thinking about what you really want, what's really important to you." I zero in on Roger. "Do you want to preserve your commitment or move on to something else? Think hard about that. This affects not only your life, but also Cindy's. And your children's lives, too. It's not a decision to be made lightly."

I turn. "And you, Cindy." Her efforts to control her emotions trigger my own. My throat knots up; I tell myself to breathe. "If Roger stays, are you willing to work on the marriage? Can you put your suspicions and bitterness away and trust him again? And if he chooses to leave, what will you do? Your life will change dramatically. How will you deal with that? It's something to ask yourself."

We end the session. And while Roger doesn't promise to come back next week, he does say he'll consider it.

In the meantime, I have a lot to think about, too. It's clear I still have Bert issues. I thought I'd worked through the worst of them, buried the pain, cynicism and anger in a deep, dark grave. But judging from what just happened, they're all still alive. And thriving.

The paperback novel lies open in my lap. *A Room For Eleanor*. The current literary rage. Four hundred pages of angst and introspection.

Perching my funky new reading glasses on the bridge of my nose, I glance down at the page. The final chapter, thank God. If I have to spend one more week reading about the depressed and depressing Eleanor, I'll need a room, too. At the psychiatric pavilion.

I look up for a moment, scan the group of four women, all wearing glasses of some kind or another, and one man whose vision must be better than mine, since he's lens-free. Ten folding chairs sit empty behind them. We started the club a year ago with fifteen members. Fourteen women and Oliver something-or-other, the sharp-eyed old charmer who sits at the end of the first row beside my mother. The club has dwindled to these five people; I don't know why.

Lifting the novel, I begin to read aloud from chapter twenty-three.

"Eleanor locked the bathroom door, turned to the mirror then lifted the tweezers to her right eye. 'No more,' she whispered, plucking one lash then another and another, numb to the pain. 'No more…'"

As I read, my mind drifts to my session with the Hoyts this morning. I almost crossed the line, let my personal feelings affect my professional objectivity. I transferred my anger at Bert to Roger Hoyt. That scares me. I have no business counseling couples if I can't keep my own emotions out of the equation. I should've made every effort to connect with the man, prove myself to him, gain his trust, not put him on the defensive.

> *"She turned on the faucet and water spilled out, over her hand, into the tub, warm, soothing water to wash away the pain. And Eleanor whispered, 'No more…'"*

It's just that, when I saw the Hoyts sitting across from me, middle-aged, miserable, together yet miles apart, I felt I was looking at a photo of Bert and myself from a year ago. Then Roger Hoyt finally started to talk, and I saw my own feelings reflected in his wife's eyes. Humiliation. Self-doubt. Fear. For a second…okay, maybe more like five minutes, I envisioned the two of us tackling the balding Don Juan, strapping him to the sofa, face-up, castrating him with a dull pair of fingernail scissors.

Not good. Not good at all.

> *"The water surrounded Eleanor; her legs, her body, her face, filling her with peace, with truth. All her life, she had tried to avoid what she knew in her heart. 'No more,' she thought now. 'No more.'"*

I yawn. Okay, so maybe I do have an idea why the reading group has dwindled.

Halfway through the second scene, a loud snuffle brings my head up.

Mary Fran Hawkins and Frances Green, otherwise known as "The Frans" since they share not only similar names, but also an apartment, snore in rhythm, their chins on their chests. Mary Fran's book is on the floor. Frances still holds hers open, though it's migrating toward her knees.

I guessed the first second I met them that The Frans are lesbians, but Mother refuses to discuss it. According to her, it's an inappropriate assumption on my part and none of our business one way or another. But whether she'll admit it or not, I'm sure she knows it's true. Like she's always telling me, her eyesight's bad, but she's not blind.

Between The Frans and my mother, Doris Quinn files her nails and hums quietly to herself. Not a single silver hair on her head is out of place. She's a tiny, twittery, totally feminine woman. Always upbeat. Always ready to bat an eye at any man who happens to glance at her. Eager to sympathize with their hard luck stories. I can imagine Doris being the "other" woman in her younger days. The equivalent of Roger Hoyt's Bitsy or one of Bert's baby-faced…

There I go, doing it again. Transferring my anger at Bert to someone else. Comparing a sweet, romantic woman of eighty who loves people and life to one of Bert's bimbos.

At the end of the row of book lovers in front of me, jolly Oliver something-or-other, his book face-down in his lap, grins as he whispers something to Mother. She blushes, but pretends to ignore him, her gaze fixed on her copy of A Room For Eleanor, which she holds in both hands upside down.

"Eleanor opened her eyes, gazed up through the rippling water. Life shimmered above her, painful, chaotic, unpredictable life. She—"

"The End," I say five paragraphs before the final line. I slap the book closed. The noise snaps The Frans to attention.

"So, what did you think?"

Doris stops filing her nails and sighs. "Remarkable. A masterpiece." She presses a palm to her chest. "The ending…" She sighs. "It makes a person think, doesn't it? There was so much wisdom in it, so much hope, so much—"

"Bullshit," Mary Fran mutters, rubbing sleep from her eyes and eliciting a snicker from Frances.

Doris flinches. "I beg your pardon?"

"I thought it was an interesting selection, Cecilia," Mother cuts in before Mary Fran can elaborate. "Another fine choice on your part. Very thought-provoking, as Doris said."

Oliver smirks at her. "Come on now, Belle. It was a real stinker, and you know it."

Doris points her fingernail file straight up. "Perhaps one person's odor is another's perfume."

The Frans snort.

"Thanks for the show of support, Mother. You, too, Doris. But I have to agree with the others." I tap a finger against the book's cover. "I don't get it. The book's been at the top of the bestseller lists for over a month."

Oliver winks at me. "There's no accountin' for taste, CiCi." He scans the room. "No offense, but we're gonna have to liven things up around here or pretty soon you'll be reading to a bunch of empty chairs."

I'm surprised by the look of distress that passes across Mother's face at his comment. Wondering about it, I reach down for my briefcase then place it in my lap. I pop the latches, open the lid, pull another *Oprah*-esque book from inside. "I'd planned this for our next selection." I hold the book up so the group can see the bland cover.

Everyone groans. Even Doris and my mother.

"Okay. I'm open for suggestions."

As they debate whether the next title should be a mystery, a family saga or an action adventure, I return both books to my briefcase. That's when *Penelope's Passion* catches my eye. The story has become my new addiction; I can't get enough of it. Or, to be honest, I can't get enough of the captain. I've been trying to squeeze in a paragraph or two between patients whenever possible. I tell myself it's a healthy diversion from reality. What's the harm in a little fun?

Well, I'll tell you.

Yesterday I met with two of my regulars, a sixty-year-old shoe salesman and his wife of thirty-five years. They blame his mother's penchant for going barefoot and wearing red toenail polish when he was a boy for his obsession with women's footwear and feet. Toes specifically. He's partial to sucking them and struggles to restrain the urge at work. While they talked, I caught myself thinking about a scene in *Penelope's Passion* where the captain and Penelope make love for the first time. In my daydream, though, I was Penelope.

Pathetic, I know. My mind should be on my patient's abnormal preoccupation with Jimmy Choo shoes, not on being seduced by some make-believe macho man. Still, the toe-sucker left my office happy, so I suppose it didn't hurt that my mind wandered a bit while he talked.

Studying the wrinkled faces before me, I remember Mother's bread beater, which I've nicknamed "BOB," as in battery-operated-boyfriend. Maybe she isn't the only one here, me included, who misses intimacy. These senior citizens would probably appreciate a healthy diversion, too. The next best thing to sex I've found. Some relatively harmless fun. I'm betting even The Frans' relationship could use a shot in the arm.

"Ladies," I say in a raised voice to be heard over the chatter. I stand, put my open briefcase on the stool and clap my hands. "Ladies! You, too, Oliver."

The talking stops. They all look up at me.

"What do you think about this?" I pick up Erin's book, turn it over, read the blurb on back....

"When Lady Penelope Waterford stowed away on The Voyager
She wanted only to escape an arranged marriage
To be carried away in the arms of a powerful ship
Toward a fresh start in a new, untamed land.

When Captain Damian Stonewall set sail
He wanted only to deliver his cargo on time,
To see his crew safely to the opposite shore
And collect the money owed him.

The captain never suspected he harbored a passenger
Or that one glimpse of her creamy skin, flaming hair
And flashing blue eyes would force him to question

His priorities and tempt him to break his own rules.

The lady never expected she might be forced to marry
The hot-tempered captain who found her hiding, soaked
And exhausted, below deck. Or that his touch would
Make her tremble with lust as well as with anger.

But as land disappears from sight
And the wind rages around them
Penelope and the captain discover their biggest
Surprise of all:

A passion more vast and powerful than the sea...."

I lower the book to my lap and look up.

Doris whispers, "Oh, my."

The Frans snort, then smile at each other.

Oliver chuckles. "Now you're talkin'."

Mother looks from my briefcase, to the book, to me. She lifts an eyebrow.

Shrugging, I smirk at her. "Ladies and gentleman, I believe we just found our next selection." I turn the book around to show the group the sexy cover. "I give you, *Penelope's Passion*."

A hush falls over the room, but is broken seconds later by the sound of an ear-piercing alarm.

I hope it isn't someone's pacemaker going off.

My kitchen smells like chicken and dumplings tonight. I think Mother's trying to fatten up Erin, but I'm sure it'll be me who ends up waddling, not my teenaged daughter. She can exist on a diet of French fries without gaining a pound.

We've fallen into a routine. One instigated by Mother. She cooks. We eat as a family at the table. Erin and I clean up. I'm amazed it's lasted an entire five nights; I don't know how she managed to recruit Erin in the first place, much less keep her coming back. But, though I enjoy the family time, I'm also a tiny bit jealous that my mother pulled off what I couldn't. Since this school year began, my offers of a home-cooked meal have been turned down. Erin's either had other plans for dinner or says she'd rather get takeout. I realize I'm not Julia Child or even my mother when it comes to the kitchen. But I whip up a decent omelet, and my spaghetti's not bad. I add spices to the Ragu.

"Did you talk to your dad today?" I scrape chicken into the disposal, then hand the plate to Erin.

"Yeah. He called right after school."

Right after I called and gave him an earful. If that's what

it takes for Erin to receive some attention from her father, so be it. I'll bug that man from now until he drops dead.

Erin places the plate into the dishwasher. "Did someone straighten up my room?"

I laugh. "If so, they didn't do a very good job."

"I'm missing a book."

"Penelope's Passion?"

A blush stains Erin's cheeks as she reaches for another plate. "Yeah."

"I borrowed it and forgot to put it back. Sorry. When we finish up here I'll get it for you. I'm planning to read it at Nana's group so I'll be buying my own copy and copies for all the members."

Pausing with the plate in her hand, Erin's eyes widen. *"Mo-ther!"*

"What?"

"You're joking, right?"

"No. Why?"

"You *can't* read that to people their age."

I wet a dishcloth, turn off the faucet and wipe down the counter. "Why not?"

"There's *stuff* in it."

"You think your generation invented *stuff*?"

Erin lowers the plate she's holding. "But, they're *old*."

Mother enters the kitchen, headed for the breakfast nook and the hutch where she keeps her knitting basket. "Listen here, smarty-pants," she says to Erin in a teasing voice. "We old people could teach you youngsters a thing or two about romance. There's a lot to be said for wooing."

"Wooing?" Erin scowls.

"That's right, wooing." Mother tucks the basket under her arm and smiles. "Candy and flowers. A walk in the moonlight. Stolen kisses on a front porch swing."

I want to sigh. It sounds so old-fashioned. And wonderful. In my dating days, an evening was considered romantic if the guy paid for the movie without trying to cop a feel afterward. How did my generation miss the boat? The one with champagne, candlelight and a string quartet?

"When I was young," Mother continues, "the boys pursued the girls, not vice versa. At least not in such an obvious way like I see today. We didn't call them on the phone or chase after them. A young man came to a girl's house and met her family before any dating went on." She pauses to give us The Look. "And I might add that he came to the front door."

Erin tucks her lower lip between her teeth, and for a second, I sense a silent message passing between my mother and my daughter. But then a memory hits me full force, and I realize the message is for me, not Erin.

"Oh, I get it." I lean against the counter and cross my arms. "You're taking up where Dad left off, is that it? You're not ever going to let me forget about that time when I was seventeen and he caught Dave Baldwin outside my bedroom window."

"According to your father, the boy reeked of beer." Mother chuckles. "Harry was fit to be tied."

"You can say that again." Shaking my head, I look sideways at Erin. My laugh sounds nervous even to me; I hope she doesn't notice. "And after your grandpop put the fear of God into poor Dave, he tore into me like I was the one who'd been drinking beer. Which, by the way, Dave hadn't been drinking, either." *It was strawberry wine.* "I never convinced your granddad of that, though."

Mother joins us at the sink. "He thought—"

"I know, I know, he thought I was going out the window." I glance at my daughter again. She's reading the instructions on the dishwashing detergent, which strikes me as odd, but lately everything she does strikes me as odd, so I blow it off. "Just so you know, Erin, I wasn't about to sneak out." *Not that night, anyway.* "Dave and I were just talking. But your granddad never believed that, either. And for the rest of his life, he never tired of teasing me about it."

"Suzanna and I are going back to the mall to look for a concert dress tonight," Erin says, as if she hasn't heard a word of our story.

"What about *See Dick Run?*" Erin and I always watch the popular reality-TV program together on Wednesday nights. Without fail. The show is completely ridiculous. Twenty steroid-enhanced jocks compete in physical challenges to win a week in paradise with a life-sized, walking, talking, breathing blow-up doll. At least, *I'm* convinced her head is full of air. But Erin loves the show, so I pretend I do, too. It's one of the few routines we still share. And, okay, I'll come clean; I'm caught up in it, too. It's silly fun.

"Would you tape it for me?" Erin talks over her shoulder as she hurries out of the kitchen. "I don't have time to watch tonight."

"Sure." I try to sound unaffected. "Don't forget it's a school night. Be home by nine."

"Nine-thirty," she calls from the entry hall. "The mall doesn't even close until nine."

"You know the rules."

"Jeez!" The front door squeaks open; I hear the rustle of her jacket as she slips it on. *"Whatever."*

The door slams, and I feel the distance growing between us in more than just a physical way.

At the sink, I rinse the dishcloth, avoiding my mother's gaze.

"About that incident with Dave at the window," she says.

"Good grief, are we back to that?" I wring out the cloth, then gather a stack of mail from the counter and shuffle through it. "It happened twenty-some-odd years ago. Could we just forget it?"

"Maybe you *shouldn't* forget such things. What's that you always say? What goes around comes around?"

"If you're implying what I think you are, Mother, don't worry about it. Erin's a hundred times smarter and more levelheaded than I was at seventeen. She isn't the least bit boy crazy."

Hoping to escape a lecture, I take the mail and head for the backyard.

The patio light provides enough of a glow that I'm able to read.

Max looks up from his bowl and blinks at me, then returns his attention to his food.

I settle into a wicker chair, flip through the mail again, then place all but one piece on the patio table. The evening is cool, but not uncomfortable. It's already dark out, but I don't care; I'm numb and blind to everything except the texture of the expensive envelope beneath my fingertips and the return address in the upper left corner. *Gosset, Dusseldorf and Klein.*

Shooing away a fly, I turn the envelope over to open it, but can't bring myself to lift the flap. "This is it, Max," I say, eliciting a tiny moan from him. He stops munching and trots over. "The end of life as I knew it. No more Bert. Hurray!" My throat tightens. Erin might as well be gone, too. From now on, it'll just be Mother and me.

It won't be so bad, I tell myself. Who needs men anyway? Who can trust 'em? I'll learn to knit. That's something Mother and I can do together. Night after night. In front of the television. *Wheel of Fortune*. Mother will cook delicious meals for me. What better way to fill the emptiness than with smothered steak and buttermilk biscuits? Blackberry cobbler? She might even make my favorite chocolate éclairs. I'll gain so much weight that I have to buy my clothing at the tent and awning store. Which won't be an issue anymore since I won't be trying to impress a man. Think how comfy I'll be. How content. Fat and happy.

And alone. With Mother.

Max yelps. I look down at him. He tilts his head to one side. His brown eyes appear sympathetic.

"I'm sorry Max." I sniff. "It won't be just Mother and me. I'll have you, too. Since Dad's gone, you're the only male in my life worth bothering with, anyway. At least you don't leave dirty underwear on the bedroom floor."

His butt wiggles, like he's trying to wag his nubby tail.

"Your ass is cute, too. And you never expect me to kiss it."

He nuzzles his cold nose against my hand. "In fact, you're the best-looking guy I've seen in a long time." As I size him up, I have to admit, he is. His coat is smooth and shiny, his body looks strong, his eyes are sad, but clear. He comes from a long line of prize-winning English bulldogs, and it shows.

"I think you've got potential, Max," I say, perking up a bit. "A good-looking stud like you? I bet if your services were for sale, every bulldog hussy this side of the Mississippi would be panting at your doghouse door. Someone in this family besides Bert might as well get some action." At least I'd get paid for Maxwell's philandering.

Max prisses over to the grass.

"Another point in your favor. You don't leave the toilet seat up when you pee."

He hunkers down.

"Really though, Max." I swat at a fly. "You might want to start lifting your leg. I don't know what the hussies would think of a squatting stud."

When Max finishes his business and comes back over, I scratch between his ears. "I might even enter you in one of those stuffy shows. I bet you'd take home the blue ribbon."

With one final scratch to Max's head, I return my focus to the envelope. I open it, pull the paperwork out, unfold it, then set it aside, facedown. Why not see what else came in the mail and put off the inevitable? I make my way through bills, flyers, an invitation to a party to celebrate an associate's twenty-fifth wedding anniversary. Good for her. Thanks for rubbing it in. I reach for an envelope from Erin's school. The letter inside is for parents of seniors. A meeting's planned next week to discuss graduation plans; announcements, caps and gowns, the class party. Already.

A wave of sadness sweeps over me.

Erin. She's not a little girl anymore. But she's not as grown up as she thinks she is, either. She's pulling away from me, but still requires my guidance. More than ever. But I need a different approach now that she's older.

With a sigh, I return to the legal papers. Can't put them off forever. Maybe I've been looking at this divorce all wrong. Maybe it's a new beginning rather than an ending. A chance to discover new interests. To rediscover old ones. To do something for *me,* for a change. I should redefine my relationship with Erin, focus more on my career, spend more time with Mother. Can't all that be enough?

When I flip to the last page, Bert's signature jumps out at me. Then mine. I suck in a breath of cool air.

My tears taste salty and bittersweet as I stare at the document that ends my old life and launches a new one.

New and improved.

CHAPTER 6

To: Suz@friendmail.com
From: Erin@friendmail.com
Date: 11/6 Thursday
Subject:Judd
Hang up your phone! I've been trying to call you! I'm hyperventilating! He's coming over again! Right now! If you get this message, call me on my cell at midnight in case I need an escape. ~ Erin

Stuffing my phone into my jean pocket, I hurry to the closet and look inside. What was I after? I scan the shoes on the floor, the clothes on hangers. My mind whirls, my heartbeat's skipping. I am seriously having a panic attack.

I tug off my girly pajamas, the ones Nana gave me for Christmas last year, and wiggle into my newest pair of hip-hugger jeans, the skintight T-shirt I bought yesterday, and a pair of pink rubber flip-flop thongs.

After hurrying into my bathroom, I get started on my face. Blush on my cheeks. A little red lipstick, then a whole lot more. I blot my lips on a square of toilet tissue then apply mascara. Several coats. My hand shakes so much that the wand bumps my cheek, smearing black across it. "Not now!" I snarl, as I reach for the toilet paper roll again and knock over a perfume bottle. It clatters as it falls, making my heart thump all the harder. The last thing I need is to wake up Mom or Nana.

When my cheek is finally clean, I bend over at the waist and ruffle my hair, then straighten again and spray it. I step back and take another long look at myself in the mirror. Something's not right…something… I glance down at my chest. The jellyfish!

I return to the closet and put on a bra, then find the silicone inserts I borrowed from Suz's sister. When they're in place, I check my reflection again.

A girl I don't recognize stares back at me. A girl with wild hair, too much makeup and a big set of *ta-tas,* as Suz always calls them. A phony. A fake. A Britney Spears clone with brown hair instead of blond. Exactly the kind of girl I can't stand. So why am I doing this?

I cross my arms, turn away from my reflection. Because I'm sick of being boring, straight-laced Erin. Because I'm tired of sitting home with Mom while everyone else is out having fun. Because Judd wouldn't give the real me a second look.

Judd. Judd Henderson.

I met him Saturday night at The Beat. He's twenty, about to be twenty-one, a junior at North Texas. He thinks I'm also twenty, and that I'm a junior at S.M.U. At the club, he didn't look twice at Suz, though she stood right beside me. He walked straight over and asked me to dance.

We danced all night. Then, when his ride was leaving and he had to go, he kissed me. Nothing major, just brushed his mouth against mine and said he'd call.

He did. Night before last at ten. I almost died. He wanted to come over so I had to come up with an excuse really fast. I said I was sick. Strep throat.

He said he was sorry and promised not to kiss me. Not on the lips, anyway.

Just the thought of him kissing me again anywhere, especially with Mom and Nana close by, almost gave me explosive diarrhea, so I said that, according to the doctor, the strep throat was highly contagious and he shouldn't even come in the house.

So what did he do? He came to my window.

Like, how romantic is that? *Totally* romantic, if you ask me, no matter what Nana says. I'm pretty sure she hinted about Judd yesterday in front of Mom. She must've seen him at my window. At least she didn't come right out and say it. Which I can hardly believe.

Anyway, for maybe the best forty-five minutes of my life, Judd smoked cigarettes and talked to me in a low voice through the window screen. He told me he likes how I act all quiet and shy, but my look says something different. I didn't tell him that my "look" is the act, and that quiet and shy is the real me.

Before he left, Judd laughed and said hanging outside my bedroom window made him feel like he was back in high school. I said it did me, too. Then I remembered that I *am* in high school, and I felt even phonier than I do now.

Judd promised to call again to check on me and, a half

hour ago, he did. Since I can't pretend to be sick forever, and he'd probably think it weird that a twenty-year-old woman would have to sneak out of the house to meet a guy, I told him Mom caught my strep throat and that the house is still pretty much off-limits. So, I'm meeting him out front at eleven-thirty.

Except for the strip of light beneath Mom's bedroom door, the hallway outside my room is quiet and dark. I decide it might be safer to go out my window again instead of risking her hearing the front door open and close. That way, I won't have to worry about the security alarm, either. I duck back into my room and lock myself in. What I'm really doing, though, is locking Mom and Nana out.

Ten minutes later I'm beside Judd inside his pickup truck, which is parked at the curb in front of my house with the engine and headlights off.

Judd turns down the music. "You sure you don't want to go somewhere?"

I shake my head. "I still have homework to do. I can't stay out long."

He pulls a pack of cigarettes off the dash and offers me one.

"No, thanks." I point at my neck. "The strep. I mean, I'm well and everything, but I don't want to push it yet."

"Oh, yeah. I forgot. I won't smoke, either, I guess." He tosses the pack back where he found it. "Sorry I didn't call yesterday. School and work have been kicking my ass."

"Where'd you say you work?"

"At the convenience store on campus." Judd reaches across the seat, tucks my hair behind my ear. "Just part-time. Until I graduate."

"Oh." I nibble my lower lip. *Oh? Oh?* Why can't I think of anything else to say? It's like my mind erased the second he touched me. "I don't work."

"Maybe you should." He smiles. "Then you could rent a place with some friends and we wouldn't have to sit out in front of your mom's like a couple of teenagers." He looks out the window at the house then shifts back to me, tracing the curve of my ear with a fingertip. "Let's go for a ride. I passed by a park on the way here."

My heart does a backflip. "I can't. Really."

I have the strangest feeling. Like there's this hum of energy between us, a current of electricity stretching from Judd to me, connecting us. Being this close to him makes me excited and freaked at the same time, though I don't know what I'm freaked about. It's not like we weren't even closer on the dance floor Saturday night. But this feels different. Tonight, we're alone.

Judd takes my hand and jerks his head, nodding me over. "Come here."

I scoot across the seat, closer to him. He puts his arm around me, and I tilt my head back and gaze up at him. No guy has ever looked at me the way he is, like he's seeing me inside out and naked and memorizing every detail. I could fall right into his dark, narrowed eyes, but something tells me I'd never find my way out again. I don't want to turn away, but I'm afraid not to, afraid I'll lose myself, as weird as that sounds. So I move my focus to his lips. They're not too thin, not too full, nicely shaped, parted a little. Beneath the lower one, there's a soft shadow of beard stubble.

When I got into the car, I was sort of cold, but I'm not

cold now; that's not why I shiver. His fingers stroke my arm, right beneath my shoulder, scattering goose bumps across my skin and making the muscles in my stomach pull tight.

"Erin," he says, and then his mouth is on mine, soft and firm at the same time, warm, drawing me in, tasting of cinnamon gum and menthol as our breaths mix. It's not like I've never been kissed before; I have. But never like this, like I've stepped onto a roller coaster and there's no stopping it, no turning back. My control is whisked away on a rush of air while another part of me comes alive. The world outside blurs until the only things vivid are Judd and me; the texture of his hair between my fingers, the pull of his cinnamon lips and musky male scent, a soft scrape of beard against my cheek.

Quiet, insistent sounds come from deep in his throat. He shifts our positions so that I slide down some, my head pressed into the seat back, and he is centered between the dash and me. I feel surrounded, enclosed, cocooned by his hard body, his arms. His warm, dry hand cups my chin then skims my face, across my collarbone, my shoulder, down the side of my breast. Before I realize what he has in mind, his fingers inch beneath my T-shirt and he's touching my stomach, making my body hum and vibrate...*vibrate*....

I jerk back, away from Judd, into reality. I reach for my buzzing jean pocket. Talk about good timing.

Judd frowns and leans back. "What's that?"

"My phone. I...um...turned off the ringer." My hands shake as I pull it from my pocket and push the talk button. "Hello?"

"Erin?" *Suz. Thank you, thank you, thank you.* I cringe when I think what might've happened if she hadn't called.

I understand now what it means to be swept away, like they always say in the romance novels I've started reading. When Judd kissed me, I felt I could only hold on tight and hope to land safely, like he pushed all the buttons, controlled the speed, decided if my heart beat faster or slower. While I was caught up in his taste and scent, in the magic his hands made, losing my self-control felt like a rush. But now that I'm able to think again, it scares me, too.

I slide closer to the door. "Oh, hi Mom. What's wrong?"

"Are you okay? You sound— Ohmigod! He's with you right now, isn't he? Were you—"

"No, that's okay." I glance at Judd. He stares at me and rakes a hand through his hair. "I'll be right in."

"Call me back," Suz whispers.

"I will. It'll just be a minute." I break the connection.

Judd lifts his hand to the back of my neck. "What's up?" Grinning, he glances at his lap. "Besides the obvious, I mean."

I can't help myself; I look down, too, then up again. Quick. I'm glad it's dark in the car so Judd can't see my face, which I'm sure is bright red. Or maybe he can. He laughs quietly, and I wonder if I'll ever breathe right again, if my heartbeat will ever slow down. "It's my mom. She…um…she's running a fever. She needs me to bring her some medicine."

Each new lie is easier than the one before. It's as if I've had this hidden talent for deception all my life, but didn't figure out how to use it until this year. I'm not sure how I feel about that, proud that I have something in common with Dad, or ashamed.

"Man, your mom must really be sick if she can't even get her own medicine."

"She is."

He moves closer, leans over me, presses me into the back of the seat again, his chest against mine, crushing the jellyfish his fingers crept toward only moments ago. I'm dizzy with dread at the thought of Judd's reaction if he finds out the truth. I'll die from humiliation.

"Come back out," Judd whispers. His mouth brushes across my lips, soft as butterfly wings, making me even dizzier, confused. How can you crave something and dread it, too?

"I need to study."

"Please." His tongue feels warm and wet against my lips, soft and irresistible.

I force myself to reach for the door handle. "Not tonight."

He grasps my arm. "Tomorrow night, then. I'll pick you up."

"No!" I catch my breath as his brows pull together. "I mean, I'll meet you. At The Beat. I'll go with Suzanna."

Judd's fingers press into my flesh, not enough to hurt, but enough to get my attention. "I want you to go with me."

I turn to the window, look out at the house. Maybe it's time I stood up to Mom for once. Show her I'm not her baby, anymore. What can she say? It's not like I've never been on a date; I have. Before we moved here. School dances. Once with two other couples to a movie. She and Judd will meet, then we'll leave before either one of them can say too much. Before she figures out how old he is, or he figures out how young I am.

I turn to Judd. "Okay. Be here at seven. I warn you, though, my mother still thinks I'm seventeen."

He grins and gives me another kiss before I open the door. "See you tomorrow night."

"I'll be ready."

My knees shake as I step from the car and, when I stand, I feel a weight drop from my chest. Seriously. I press my forearm across my waist just in time to catch the silicone insert before it slips free of my shirt and falls to the ground.

"Suz?"

"Tell me everything!"

I kick off my pink flip-flops. "We made out in his car in front of the house."

"Shut up!"

"I'm serious." Pulling the phone from my ear for a second, I tug my T-shirt over my head. "I don't know what I was thinking. Everything got completely crazy. I mean, he had his hand under my shirt and I was wearing Katie's stupid fake boobs and—"

"Ohmigod! What did he say?"

I toss the silicone blobs onto the bed. "Thanks to your phone call, he didn't make it far enough north to discover that what he thinks are the Grand Tetons are really the Great Plains."

Suz giggles. "What do you mean, thanks to my call? Fake boobs or not, you would've stopped him." When I stay quiet for a few seconds, she says, "You would've stopped him. Right, Erin? You hardly know the guy."

I puff out my cheeks, let the air seep slowly from between my lips. "I don't know, Suz. I mean, everything was happening so fast, and I wasn't thinking about anything but…"

Dropping to the edge of the bed, I close my eyes and clutch the phone tighter. "Oh, God. What am I going to do? I said I'd go out with him tomorrow night. He thinks I'm something I'm not. *Someone* I'm not. And when I'm with him, I am. I don't even know myself. I wish I'd never let you talk me into dressing up like some hoochie and going to The Beat."

"He's not picking you up at the house, is he?"

"That's the plan. I'm taking your advice and standing up to Mom." I imagine Mom's expression when she sees Judd, and my stomach clenches. He looks his age. I'll have to get him in and out of here fast.

"She might surprise you. Your mom seems pretty cool and laid-back about most things."

"She is. Except when it comes to me. Since she and Dad split, her friends have been meeting over here about once a month for dinner. You should hear what they laugh about when they think I'm not listening. Sex…men. You wouldn't believe some of the jokes they tell after a couple of pitchers of margaritas."

Suz laughs. "Maybe you should get her drunk before Judd shows up."

"That's not a bad idea."

"It'll be okay, Erin. Just stay firm with your mom and keep your head on straight with Judd."

"Easy for you to say. You haven't kissed him."

"Wow." Suz sighs. "That good, huh?"

"Better." I sigh, too. "Maybe I should just tell him I want to slow down. That I just want to have some fun and not get so serious."

"Erin…I forget how little you know about guys. They don't see things like we do. I promise you that in Judd's mind y'all *were* just having some fun."

I hear a *click click click* at her end of the line, like her fingernail taps against the phone. "If you're really worried about what might happen," she continues, "then maybe you should just end it now. Call Judd and tell him you can't go. From what I saw of him the other night, I *figured* he might be a player. I just didn't want to say anything until I was sure since I could tell you liked him so much."

"But I don't want to end it." I fall back onto the pillows. "That's what's so crazy. I mean, I'm afraid of what's happening, but I like it, too."

For a few seconds, all I hear is Suzanna's breathing, then, "Tell me when and where you're going tomorrow night. I'll show up and watch out for you. You know," her voice changes to a teasing tone, "in case I have to step in and slap some sense into you."

I sit up. "Would you really show up? I'd feel so much better if you were there."

"Are you kidding? You know me. I live to snoop in other people's business."

At seven the next night, I'm watching out my window when Judd pulls up. I throw on my jean jacket to hide my inflated chest then wobble on my spiked heels toward the entry hall.

In the den, Nana sits on the sofa with Mom, teaching her how to knit. "Is he here?" My grandmother sounds more excited than me. Which is no big surprise, since I'm mostly terrified.

"Yeah." I don't stop to look at them. "Stay there. I'll get the door."

From the corner of my eye, I see Mom stand and start toward me.

Nana squeals like a twelve-year-old girl at a slumber party. "I can't wait to meet him."

"I can't, either," Mom says from behind me.

The bell rings. I reach for the doorknob.

"I can't... *Wait!*"

The change in Mom's voice stops me.

"Erin Dupree, don't you dare open that door. Turn around. What are you wearing?"

I look at her over my shoulder. "*Mom,* don't do this to me. Not in front of Judd."

Her expression looks the same as the day Dad moved out. My heart twists. I don't want to be anything like him, but maybe it's in my genes to hurt the people who love me, to lie and deceive. Did Dad feel trapped by her expectations like I do? Is that why he left?

"Where did you get those boots?"

I glance down at the red leather.

"Your hair…your face…you look—"

"My age, for once, instead of like a little girl."

She makes a strangled sound. "Not unless you're a teenaged hooker."

I turn my back to her and throw open the door. "Oh, hi, Judd!" His grin falls and his eyes widen when I grab his arm and pull him inside. "Meet my mom."

"Hello." He nods at her then gives me a sideward glance when she doesn't answer.

"And there's my grandma." I point. "See? Peeking around the corner?"

Nana steps out. "Hello, Judd. I'm Belle Lamont, Erin's grandmother." She smiles. "It's so nice to meet you."

Judd clears his throat. "You, too, Mrs. Lamont."

Nana adjusts her glasses. "So you're a classmate of Erin's?"

"No, I go to—"

"We met through Suzanna." I nudge Judd toward the open door. "Don't wait up for me!"

Mom snaps out of her zombielike state. "Just a minute."

I sigh. I guess her developing a sudden case of laryngitis was too much to hope for. "What?"

"We need to talk." Her eyes narrow to slits. "Now."

My insides quiver like Jell-O, but there's no way I'm backing down. I narrow my eyes, too, and stare right back at her. "Wait for me in the car, Judd, I'll be right out."

"Sure." He glances from Mom to Nana and says, "Nice to meet you."

I close the door behind him.

"You're not going out looking like that." Mom's voice rumbles, like she's about to erupt. "You're not going out period. Not with him. He smells like an ashtray. He must be twenty years old."

I cross my arms. "Almost twenty-one. And I *am* going out."

Mom stares at me like I'm a stranger. One she doesn't trust. But behind her disapproval, I see more. Fear and confusion. For once, my smart mom the therapist, the woman with all the answers, doesn't know what to do.

For a second, I feel myself waver. We've always been close, *too* close, maybe. She's always been so proud of me, but there's no way I can ever live up to her dreams. I've made myself crazy trying, and what did it get me? Nothing but a bunch of perfect grades that don't mean much to anyone but her.

Well, no more. I'm finally doing something just for me. I open the door again. "See ya."

She grabs my arm. "Erin…you are not leaving this house."

I jerk away. "Watch me."

"Now, Cecilia…Erin…" Nana steps between us. "Arguing won't accomplish anything. You two talk this over rationally like the grown women you are."

"Erin is not a grown woman, Mother. She's—"

"Almost eighteen," Nana interrupts. "The age I was when your father and I became engaged."

Mom jabs a finger at Nana. "Don't you dare take her side!"

"I'm not taking anyone's side, Sugar." Nana blinks worried eyes at Mom, then smiles at me, but looks all nervous and twitchy, like it's up to her to smooth things over and she's not sure she can. "Erin, why don't you run and wash your face and change into something more appropriate. I'll go tell Judd you'll be a while."

I shake my head. "Sorry, Nana." Then I close the door and walk toward Judd's idling car as fast as my spiked-heel boots will carry me.

The second I slip in beside him, my cell phone rings. I pull it from my purse, look at the display, see that the call's from our home number. Mom or Nana. I turn off the sound.

Judd pulls away from the curb. "What was that all about?" He offers me a cigarette.

Music blares from the stereo speakers. I shake my head "no" and stare out the window. "My mom." I huff a laugh. "She's certifiable."

"She really does act like you're still in high school."

"More like middle school."

The scent of burning tobacco drifts to me, followed by a swirl of smoke. Trying not to cough, I look across at Judd. Now's the first time I've seen him when it's not pitch dark. The cigarette's propped in one corner of his mouth. A tiny white scar slices his tan forehead, right above his right brow. His eyes look a little sleepy. Steering the car with one broad hand, he taps the wheel with the other. He looks sort of dangerous, like everything forbidden but tempting wrapped up in one hot package. For me.

Judd takes the cigarette from his mouth and grins. I melt inside.

Tonight will be worth any torment Mom puts me through as punishment. I refuse to worry about her or anything else.

Judd reaches across and unbuckles my seat belt. "Come here."

I smile and slide closer to him.

No worries. None at all.

Twenty minutes later, we're inside The Beat, standing in line to pay our cover, and I don't see Suzanna anywhere. What if she doesn't show up? What if Mom followed us? What if I see someone I know and Judd finds out I'm a fake?

What if…what if…what if? So much for no worries.

The club throbs with sound. "Judd…that's not Suz's cousin checking—"

"Don't worry about it. I've got you covered." He pulls an ID from his pocket and hands it to me.

The name and address on the laminated driver's license aren't mine. The photo, either, but the girl and I look enough alike that anyone glancing at the picture would think I've just changed my hair. The year of her birthday makes her twenty-one.

Judd leans down to my ear. "Memorize it." He nods toward the guy at the front of the line who's checking IDs and collecting money. "In case he drills you."

I don't want to do this, but what can I say? He thinks I'm

as wild as my outfit. Admitting to him that I'm afraid of getting caught, that I don't drink anyway, would pretty much clue Judd in that I'm not the girl I've pretended to be. He'd dump me right here.

Taking a deep breath, I repeat my alias name, address and birth date over and over again in my mind, telling myself I'm only queasy because of the loud music and the thick smoke blanketing the room. I was nervous last week when I came here with Suz, but tonight's worse. Tonight I'm Judd's date. I'm breaking a law so that I can drink. And Suzanna's not beside me, giving me courage and keeping an eye on me.

When we reach the front of the line, the guy doesn't ask any questions. He glances at the ID, at me, then does the same with Judd and takes our money. I drop the license into my purse.

A wire cage decorated with colored twinkle lights hangs suspended above the center of the dance floor. Identical cages dangle from every corner of the room. Girls dance inside of them, dressed in retro clothes; shiny white patent leather boots, skintight neon pink hip-hugging short shorts, fishnet stockings, bikini tops. Glow-in-the-dark paint covers every inch of exposed flesh; peace signs, flowers and other symbols, reminding me of the *Austin Powers* movies.

Judd holds my hand and leads me through the crowd toward an empty table. I scan every face we pass, looking for Suz, my pulse pumping along with the music. I recognize a couple of guys from school. A football player whose name I don't know. A blond guy from my English class last year. They wouldn't know me. We never talked, but I remember the blonde being sort of a cutup. Funny and cute, but out of my league. What guy isn't? At least when I'm the real me, the other half of my newly split personality.

Judd pulls out a chair. "How's this?" When I nod and sit, he settles in across from me, waves a waitress over and orders a beer, then asks what I want.

I blurt the first thing that pops into my mind. "A lemon-drop martini." Once, I saw a movie where the main character drank them. They sounded good. Besides, maybe the lemon will disguise the taste of the alcohol. And the glasses seemed small compared to a beer can. Surely I can down a couple without getting wasted.

When the waitress leaves, Judd leans across the table and smiles at me. "You look hot tonight."

"Thanks." It's hard to breathe for reasons other than the smoke. I am hot, but not the way he means. His eyes make my skin burn. And the room *is* stuffy.

"Why don't you take off your jacket?"

I feel like I'm losing my last link to safety as I slip out of the denim and drape it over the back of my chair.

When I look up, Judd's eyeing my chest. The corner of his mouth spasms. He pulls a cigarette from his pocket and lights up.

For some reason, I don't know what to do with my hands. I cross my arms, uncross them. Lace my fingers together on the tabletop then lower them to my lap. I nod at the pack that Judd tossed center table. "I think I will have one of those."

"Help yourself."

My hand shakes as I pull out a cigarette and stick it between my lips. I don't think Judd notices. He lifts his lighter and strikes a flame. I've watched other people smoke, so I know what to do. Suck on the filter until the tip glows orange, draw smoke into my mouth. I stop short of inhaling. Still, I cough on the exhale. "The strep," I rasp, squinting through the haze at Judd. "My throat's still raw."

He laughs then looks past me, raising a hand. "Hey!" He pushes back his chair and stands. "I see some friends. Be right back."

My coughing fit starts the second he's out of earshot. I hold the cigarette to my side and gulp in gasps of air not much clearer than what I sucked through the filter. After another practice hit, then another and another, I'm finally able to pretend-smoke without the cough.

As the waitress delivers our drinks, Judd heads back to the table with two guys trailing behind him. He introduces us and they start to sit, but we're one chair short. "No problem, dude," Judd says to the guy left standing. "Erin can sit with me." He scoots my drink in front of him.

The two guys stare as I push out of my chair, walk around the table and lower myself onto Judd's lap. It's like I'm the main character in a play, or something. *Suz, where are you?* Finally I know how she must feel all the time. It's not like I thought, all this male attention. I feel divided; the new, wild, carefree me loves it, while the old, sensible, careful me wants to escape to someplace safe and hide. It's just like when Judd kisses me; I'm excited and uneasy at the same time. I feel powerful in a weird sort of way, but uncomfortable, too. I mean, a little attention is nice. But this is too much. How do I act? I feel exposed.

I feel something else, too. Pressing against the underside of my thigh. I look back at Judd. His mouth quirks up. I want to die.

While the guys talk around me, I take a drag off the cigarette and focus on the martini glass. They don't include me in the conversation. In fact, the only part of Judd that seems aware I'm around is the part I'm sitting on.

White granules ring the martini glass rim. I touch them, bring my finger to my lips. Sugar. Lifting the glass, I drink half of the contents in two big gulps. It's good, both tart and sweet. Just like a lemon drop. Just like Judd.

I take a sip. One more. Two.

After a while, Judd pulls me closer against him. His arm's around me, just above my waist. He nuzzles the side of my neck. "You're thirsty tonight. How about another?"

"Sure. Thanks."

When the waitress comes over, he orders then continues talking with his friends while I scan the club for any sight of Suzanna. The colored lights around the dance cages seem brighter than before; the music sounds better.

My martini arrives; it's yummier than the first. I don't just hear the music now, it pulses inside me. I move my shoulders to the beat, feel the press of Judd's forearm against my rib cage, cradling what's above. His thumb strokes lightly back and forth across the space between my armpit and my breast.

One of the guys at our table nudges the other. They sneak glances at my chest and grin at Judd like he won the lottery. That might have bothered me fifteen minutes ago, but now it seems funny. Hilarious. They think they're so smart, and I'm a total dumb ass. Too bad, they've got it backward. I want to find Suz so we can have a good laugh.

"Excuse me." I stand and smile down at Judd. "I'm going to the restroom. I'll be right back."

"I'll have another drink waiting for you." He's trying not to laugh at me, I can tell. I don't know why, since the joke's on him, not me.

On my way through the club, I get caught in the tangle of people by the bar. The blond guy from English class stands among them. Just like all the other guys, he checks me out. But his expression shifts to surprise when he reaches my eyes. His brows pull together, like he thinks he might recognize me, but he's not sure. I turn away and push through the crowd.

Inside the restroom, it's quieter. I go into a stall, put the toilet lid down and sit. I dig through my purse, looking for my phone. I'll just call Suz and ask where she is. The phone's vibrating when I finally find it. The display tells me it's her. I push the talk button. "Where are you?"

"Erin! Finally! I've been trying to call you all night. Mom and I had a fight. She took my car keys. I'm sorry. Are you okay?"

My head feels disconnected from my body. My stomach's woozy. Leaning forward, I hug my knees and giggle. "He has a *stiffy*," I whisper into the phone.

"*What?*"

"Judd." I snort. "*You know.* He has—"

"Ohmi—Erin! You are messed up! What have you been drinking?"

"Martinis. Only two so far. Judd's ordering me another one."

"*Two martinis?* Those are strong. And expensive!"

"Judd's paying." I lower my voice. "He got me a fake ID."

"I am not believing this guy. He's just trying to get you drunk! Ohmigod, you are so naive. I knew you shouldn't go there with him. You hardly know him, Erin. Call a cab and get out of there."

"That's stupid. Nothing's going to happen. I'm okay. We haven't even danced yet."

"Last night when you *hadn't* been drinking you weren't sure you could say 'no' to him."

She's right. "Okay…a couple of dances. Then I'll tell him to take me home. I'll say I'm sick or something." I do feel sort of sick. The toilet's spinning like a merry-go-round.

"No more drinks," Suz adds. "And don't let him kiss you. Promise?"

"I promise." And I mean it, too. About the drink part, anyway.

"I'm calling you in thirty minutes. If you're not out of there, I'm stealing the car keys and coming after you. Mom will just have to get over it."

When I leave the restroom, Judd's waiting outside the door. "Did you fall in?"

"I shouldn't have downed those drinks so fast."

He laughs. "You wanna dance? Cade and Sean will watch your purse."

"Sure." He takes my hand, gives me that sleepy-eyed smile I can't resist. Suz couldn't be more wrong about him. Away from his friends, Judd's different. As sweet as he was when we talked through the window earlier this week. As nice to me as he was last night.

The first dance is fast. I move with the music, feeling more free than I ever have, less self-conscious, like the girl in the cage above my head. Maybe it's still the martinis, or maybe it's because of the way Judd looks at me, I don't know. What I do know is, I like the feeling.

A slow dance plays next. I love the feel of Judd's arms around my waist. I close my eyes, my head against his shoulder. He kisses the side of my neck. His hands slide down, press against my butt, skim up my sides. North to the Tetons.

I open my eyes. Woozy again. Unsure. I'm starting to think his hands are metal and these boobs I'm wearing are magnets.

I lift my head, see the guy from English class, staring at us.

"Don't." I look up at Judd, pull away some. "Don't touch me like that. People are watching."

"So, what?" He pulls me to him again, lowers his mouth to kiss me. "Nobody cares."

I turn away. "I care. Take me home. I feel sick."

Irritation flickers in Judd's eyes. "It's just because you drank too fast. It'll wear off."

"I'm serious. I want to leave."

His arms drop away from me. He steps back. "Fine then. Go. I'm staying." He walks off, leaving me alone on the dance floor.

I feel like I'm lost in a foreign country, surrounded by people I don't know. The table where I left my purse seems miles away. Since I don't want to face the guy from English class, I weave through dancers to exit the dance floor at the side. Judd's not at the table. Nobody is. My purse sits on the floor by a chair, available for anyone to steal. How stupid could I be? As if a couple of guys are really going to baby-sit my stuff.

Grabbing it, I bolt for the door. I don't know how I'll get home. Right now, I don't care. I just want out of here.

The second I'm outside, I burst into tears. I take deep breaths of cool, clean air, hoping it will clear out my head, my lungs, this dirty feeling inside me. In the parking lot, I find a car beneath a streetlight and lean against it. I'll call Suz. She'll tell me what to do. Not that her bright ideas didn't help get me into this mess in the first place. I open my purse and dig through all the clutter for my phone.

"Erin."

I glance up. Judd walks toward me. He doesn't look mad anymore, just bummed, like I've been nothing but a pain, not the good time he expected. Poor him.

Returning my attention to my purse, I keep on digging.

"Come back inside. I'm sorry I yelled at you." He stops in front of me. "You drank too much, too fast. I figured you could handle it or I wouldn't have kept buying them for you."

As if. He really does think I'm stupid. My fingers push aside a pack of gum, my sunglasses. Where is that phone?

Judd touches my chin. My eyes stay on the purse. "I said I'm sorry."

Is he? He sounds sincere. I meet his gaze. And I'm confused all over again. One second I think he's the biggest, scheming jerk on the planet, the next second I want him to kiss me.

Which he does.

His lips whisper across the sides of my closed mouth, whisking away my doubts. My purse slides to the pavement as I wrap my arms around his neck and start kissing him back.

That's when everything changes.

Judd backs me against the car, and his mouth presses harder against mine, bruising my lips. I try to turn my head, but he moves with me. "Stop," I mumble against his lips. The word sounds muffled, but I know he hears.

Just like last night, his hand slips beneath my shirt.

I manage to wedge my palms between us, to push against his chest. "No." He doesn't budge. "Don't!"

Keeping me trapped against the car, Judd leans back. "Now what?" His face is hard and impatient.

Panic shoots through me. Then my temper kicks in. I push him again, and he steps away. "Now *nothing,* that's what. I asked you not to touch me like that."

"As if you're some sweet little virgin." He barks a laugh. "You wanted it. You've given me every signal."

"That's not true!"

Or is it? Nothing's clear to me anymore. I just wish he'd leave so I can puke. Or maybe I should just puke on him. "Is that the only reason you asked me out? So you could get your hands on these?" I point at my chest. "Well here, I'll make it easy for you." Reaching into my shirt, I grab a jellyfish and sling it at him. It smacks his forehead.

Judd flinches, stares at me a second, then stoops and picks up the silicone blob. "You've gotta be shittin' me!"

"Have a great time!" I yell at him, then pull out the other one and throw it at him, too. He ducks and it lands on his foot. "Enjoy yourself. That's what you wanted. They're all yours."

I'll buy Katie another pair.

Judd picks up the other one. "What did you expect, wearing these?" He tosses them back at me. "And look at the way you dress. You're nothing but a tease."

I will not cry. I won't. Not in front of him. What *did* I expect? Maybe I am a tease. Maybe that's what I've turned into.

Judd laughs under his breath then jerks his head to the side. "Come on. I'll take you home."

"Don't worry about it."

He stares at me a minute before turning and starting toward the building. "Whatever." His laughter trails behind him as he walks away.

I pick up the inserts and my purse then sit on the car's hood. Let the owner come gripe me out and call me names. Who cares? I'm used to it. I mean, supposedly I'm a naive, teenaged hooker tease. What could be any worse?

When I finally find my phone, I'm crying so hard I can't see to punch in Suz's number.

"Hey."

I look up. The guy from my last year's English class stands in front of the car, holding my jacket. "You forgot this."

Wiping my face with the back of my hand, I take it from him. "Thanks."

"You okay?"

"No." I'm sobbing again, sobbing and totally humiliating myself. As if I haven't already. "How long have you been out here?"

"A while. I know that guy. I thought you might need some backup."

I squeeze one of the jellyfish in my lap and wish for a quick death. Right here, right now. "I guess you saw the whole thing, then. You probably think I'm a tease, too."

He shakes his head. "What you did...you were amazing. So was the look on his face." He grins. "You didn't need me or anyone." Offering his hand, he helps me down off the car. "I'm Noah Sherwood."

My nose runs. I sniff. "I'm—"

"Erin. I know. We had senior English together last year."

I blink at him, surprised he even noticed me, much less knew my name.

"You were just a junior, though, right?" he asks.

"Yeah." He knew that, too? I put the blobs in my jacket pocket then slip it on. "I took the class a year early."

"Must be nice to be so smart."

"I'm not so smart, really. Just motivated. By my mom, mostly."

He has a great laugh, the kind that makes me want to laugh with him.

Noah nods at the building. "I'm surprised to see you here."

"Not half as surprised as I am to be here."

The tears start again. Noah must think I'm a total geek. "I don't know why I came here with him," I sob. Which isn't completely true. I just wanted to have some fun. To have a guy notice me for once and want to be with me. "I'm not even sure who I am anymore…or what I want."

"I know what you mean." He pulls a wadded up napkin from his pocket and gives it to me. "Sometimes I feel that way, too."

"You do?"

"Yeah."

I'm not sure about the napkin. It's stuck together in the center.

"It's clean," Noah says. "Other than the dried up chewing gum, I mean."

I laugh. He does, too. I blow my nose then cry some more.

"Hey, if you don't stop that, they'll have to put flood warnings out on the area lakes."

He's funny. And cute. He doesn't look the least bit dangerous. Which is okay with me. I've had enough danger to last me a while.

"You need a lift?"

Before I can answer, my phone buzzes inside my pocket. When I answer it, Suz says, "Are you on your way home?"

"Not yet."

"I'll come get you."

"That's okay." I smile through watery eyes at Noah. "I have a ride."

CHAPTER 8

From The Desk of
Belle Lamont

Dear Harry,
So much has happened since my last letter.

I fired my baby-sitter. Cecilia was fit to be tied, and we had words,
I'm sorry to say. I held my ground, Harry. That woman (the sitter,
not CiCi) refused to stay out of my kitchen. I swear, you'd think
I'm ten years old the way she hovered over me whenever I cooked.
Yes, my vision's bad, but I can whip up a meal with my eyes closed,
and I told her so. I've convinced CiCi to give me a two-week trial
run at home by myself. If I don't burn down the house, maybe her
mind will be eased.

In happier news, twelve new people called to order a book for
Wednesday's meeting. Twelve! Can you imagine? And four of them
men. You know how I abhor rumors, Harry, but one is circulating that
Doris Quinn delivered homemade cookies to the Parkview pool hall,
made a few suggestive comments about the book, batted an eyelash
or two, and that was that. Mind you, Doris isn't a floozy like Jane
Binkley. Just a hopeless romantic and a brazen flirt. Or that's what

I've always thought. When I told The Frans about the pool hall, though, they said they've heard stories about Doris's past that would make a sailor blush. You never can tell about a person, can you?

Enough about Doris. It's Cecilia who concerns me. I hope this less highbrow book is a sign she's going to stop being so serious about everything. Since Bert left, the only time I've seen her let down her hair, so to speak, is when her girlfriends, whom I've come to think of as the Margarita Martyrs, came to dinner Friday night. But that was little more than a man-bashing session that started with my shrimp nacho appetizers, iced tea and commiseration, and ended with sopapillas, margaritas and dirty jokes.

At least the get-together took Cecilia's mind off Erin for a while. That is, until the girl came home as tipsy as her mother. And on a motorcycle driven by a different young man than the one with whom she left the house. That's right, our Erin had a date. And of course, Cecilia didn't approve, primarily because the boy's an old geezer of twenty. I'm not making light of Cecilia's concerns. I simply wish our daughter didn't jump to conclusions so fast. Shouldn't Erin have a chance to explain herself before CiCi passes judgment? Of course she should.

After a tense yelling session—threats and punishment issued by CiCi, tears and door-slamming from Erin—the two have hardly spoken to one another. Erin hasn't ventured from her room this weekend except to have lunch and a tense, quiet drive with us to Cleburne yesterday.

Cecilia is on a painting frenzy. Her beige bedroom's fast becoming Grape Nehi purple. Tacky beyond words, but I'm taking a cue from Maxwell and keeping my mouth shut.

Oh, Harry. I'm twisted up inside. All this conflict takes me back to CiCi's senior year in high school. I lost my way for a while back then. You didn't know that, did you? I lost my way, my self, and didn't come back until months after she'd left for college.

Jack was already a senior at the university and hundreds of miles from home. CiCi was so busy with school and friends that we rarely saw her, remember? When we did, it seemed we were always at odds over something. Cecilia felt she didn't need us anymore. You handled it better than me. I knew it was normal for her to pull away, but I couldn't stand that she didn't want to spend time with me. Oh, I was proud of our kids, proud of us for raising them to be self-sufficient and independent and ready to take on the world. But I often felt like a penny in a parking lot. Forgotten and worthless.

I wanted to tell you what I was going through, but I couldn't bring myself to. My emotions seemed so self-indulgent, too silly for me to mention. So I kept them to myself until the day we left Cecilia at school.

Do you remember how I cried for weeks after? How the tears would start at the oddest moments? The first time, you cried, too, though you tried to hide it. Well, you didn't fool me, Harry. Not for a second. I can still see us driving away from her dormitory, pulling over when we were out of sight of it, holding each other while the traffic sped past.

When we dried our eyes and took off again, you moved on in other ways, too. But I couldn't. Not for months. I'd see your smile and hear it in your voice when I'd burst into tears. You thought I only missed Cecilia and Jack. I did, but more than that churned inside me.

Sometimes I'd jerk awake in the middle of the night with a feeling of such urgency, such helplessness and worry, with an ache as heavy and full as my breasts once felt when the children were babies and would cry in the night to be fed and held. But there was no release for this ache. No sense of being needed. Only need. Mine.

For more than twenty years I'd poured every ounce of myself into a task so important, so all-consuming, and it was over. I had given all I had and was drained dry of everything except a love so full it seeped from my pores. I wondered sometimes if it would just evaporate, go to waste somewhere up there in the atmosphere, or could Jack and Cecilia feel it across the miles? Did it drift from me to them, wrap around them in an invisible embrace when they needed reassurance?

During those moments in the middle of the night, I'd reach out across the darkness and there you were, next to me. In your arms, I found safety, comfort and more. I found my way back. I know you didn't fully understand my grief, but you were there, as steady and reliable as the change of seasons. And that meant everything.

But what about Cecilia? Her divorce from Bert has been final-ized. The papers are signed. Sometimes I hear her crying in the night. Who can she reach out to for comfort as Erin pulls away?

A year has passed since you left. Can you believe it? Sometimes it seems so much longer, other times, as if you left only last week. Months ago, I stopped being angry with you for leaving me all alone. Now I'm only sad and lonely. Missing you.

Yesterday, we drove to Cleburne and by our house. Your roses are gone. The neighbors, those nice young newlyweds the Langleys who moved in three years ago, said that the new owners plan to build a room onto the house soon and most of the bushes had to go. They only left one at the side of the house, and it was barren, almost dead from neglect.

CiCi, Erin and I stood at the curb and cried, holding each other. We didn't care if the Langleys saw. The truth is, they cried, too.

You're not coming back. I know that now. Somehow over the past twelve months, I tricked myself into believing you'd show up some evening, suitcase in hand, and tell me you were home for good. Or that I'd wake up one morning and discover this has all been a terrible dream. But none of that's true.

Your roses are gone, and so are you.

Regardless, letting go is hard, so I'll continue to reach out to you through these letters. They keep you near to me somehow, and I don't know what else to do.

As usual, I've gone on too long. I love you, Harry.

As always, your yellow rose,

Belle

CHAPTER 9

Cecilia Dupree
Day Planner
Wednesday, 11/19

1. Check paper for Max's ad.
2. 1:00—Mom's Parkview reading group.
3. Decline blind date with Mrs. Stein's second cousin's great-nephew.
4. Buy new bedspread to match purple walls.
5. Unground Erin.

The second week the Parkview group meets to read Penelope's Passion, there's an expectant energy in the room, a charged silence similar to the moment the curtain parts on opening night at a sold-out play. I glance up. Not an empty chair. Books are open and right side up. I turn the page....

"How dare you lock me in here!" Penelope refused to let him
see her tremble, though her wet dress clung to her, molding

every curve and raising goose bumps on her skin. She met his dark gaze, saw amused sympathy glittering within it.

"Dear Lady." The captain chuckled, a deep sound she felt more than heard. "I'm not locking you in, I'm locking the men out. For your protection. Besides, you should thank me that you have quarters at all. And the finest quarters on this ship, at that. Mine. You'll find the bed to be quite comfortable." He strode past her, slow and sure as a tiger. Then he sat on the bed and patted the mattress. "It's large enough for two."

Penelope raised a hand to slap him.

The captain caught her wrist midswing and laughed....

A tiny gasp brings my head up. Doris Quinn, who listens rather than reads, sits at the edge of her chair with her eyes closed. Perfectly manicured fingers press against her lips. Beside her, Jane Binkley, the Parkview Manor Mae West according to Mother, fans her cleavage with a bookmark. Two new male recruits, one a silver-haired Paul Newman type, the other a wiry, sunken-cheeked Don Knotts look-alike, nudge one another and grin.

I return my attention to the page....

"Such poor manners, Lady Waterford. Have you so little appreciation for your host?" The captain drew her to him.

Penelope held her breath. His eyes no longer contained sympathy, amused or otherwise. Anger simmered within their depths. Anger...and something else. Something that had her softening against him until she was nothing more than clay in his hands, pliant, helplessly available for him to mold to his will.

Captain Stonewall pulled her closer still, and she felt the hard length of his manhood press against her midsection....

A snort is answered with a snicker. I don't look up. I know The Frans when I hear them....

"Since you've taken it upon yourself to stow away on my ship," the captain murmured, "I intend to make your voyage as enjoyable as possible." He traced the shell of her ear with a fingertip, skimmed the line of her jaw, paused at the pulsing hollow beneath her throat. "Nothing but pure pleasure until the day we dock."

A sigh sifts through the room, a giggle follows, a whisper then a chuckle or two.

I close *Penelope's Passion* and look up. "Okay, that's it for today. Next week we'll continue with chapters ten through twelve. The floor's open for discussion."

As the back-and-forth banter begins, I look at Mother. She looks back at me, shaking her head. A smile twitches her lips as she slips off her glasses to polish the lenses with the hem of her blouse. Her cream-colored silk. When I picked her up at lunchtime, I didn't notice she'd worn it. Strange. The blouse is a bit dressy for reading group. Oh, well. I have to give her credit. She's doing okay on her own at home during the day. Really, why should we pay someone to stay with Mother when we have Mrs. Stein next door, who checks on her daily, whether I ask her to or not?

"Captain Stonewall is such a strong, dashing hero." Doris's

voice flutters with dreamy admiration. "He's a man who knows what he wants."

"And knows how to get it," Jane adds with a sultry laugh.

Doris nods her agreement. "If he lived in our world today, I wonder what he'd do?"

"Time." Mary Fran's voice is as bemused as it is cynical. "For rape, most likely."

A heated discussion ensues as to whether or not the captain's behavior is forceful or merely seductive.

I shift my focus to jolly Oliver who sits in his usual place beside Mother. Today his arm stretches across the back of her chair as if it belongs there. I stare a minute, but he doesn't budge. He doesn't even squirm. Instead, he looks directly at me, winks, then smiles.

So. What's that all about? Now I'm the one squirming.

"Excuse me, Miz Dupree?"

"Hi, Mr. O'Dell. What's up?" I ask the paunchy, red-faced man who is suddenly standing beside me.

He cuts a glance over his shoulder at the group, then blinks puppy dog eyes at me. They're always as sad as Maxwell's, even when he smiles. "While they debate, I wondered if I might ask you a personal question?"

"Of course you can."

"If you'd rather I make an appointment, I understand."

"No, that's all right. If we need more time later, we can schedule it."

He coughs. "I've been wondering how soon is too soon for a person to start dating after losing a spouse?"

"That depends on the person. How long has it been since Mrs. O'Dell passed away?"

"Six years."

I want to hug him. "Is there someone you're interested in seeing socially?"

His face flushes scarlet. "Iris Shelby." Turning, he gives a discreet nod in the direction of a heavyset woman I've come to know well.

Iris has steel-gray scouring pad hair, a double chin, lumpy knees and elbows. And she's the epitome of all that's missing in Herbert's life. Happiness bubbles out of her like fizz from a shaken soda can. Her eyes are as lively as a young girl's, and when she laughs, which is often, she throws back her head and gives it her all.

"I can't find my nerve to ask her out," Herbert whispers. "I'm eighty-two years old. It's been sixty years since I dated a gal. I don't remember how. And even if I did there's the problem of me not driving anymore. Doesn't seem proper to ask a woman on a date, then make her do the driving."

Screw professional propriety. This man needs a hug, and I'm going to give it.

Before I can, a knock sounds at the door, and Bill Burdette, the Parkview Manor Retirement Village manager, pokes his head into the room. "Sorry to interrupt, everybody. CiCi, could I have a word with you in my office if you have a minute?"

"Sure, Bill." I tell Herbert I'll call him tonight, then stand and look out at the small crowd. "Keep on keeping on. If I don't make it back before time's up, I'll see you all next week." I meet Bill at the door and we start down the hallway. "What's up?"

He fingers his jacket lapel. "We have a bit of a problem,

I'm afraid. Mrs. Quinn's son and Mr. Rayburn's daughter are here with a complaint about your current book selection."

"What?" I make a face. "I'm reading to adults, not a class of ten-year-olds."

Pausing at his closed office door, Bill says, "Grown children of elderly parents often treat them like they're in elementary school." He shakes his head. "Just listen to their concerns, CiCi. I'm sure when they meet you and hear what you have to say, they'll calm down."

"They aren't calm?"

Bill's eyebrows lift.

My stomach falls. "Refresh my memory. Which one is Mr. Rayburn?"

"Good-looking guy. Silver fox. Sharp blue eyes."

I nod. "Paul Newman."

"Right." He puts on his happy face and opens the door. "Mr. Quinn, Mrs. Kiley...I'd like you to meet Cecilia Dupree."

I smile. They don't. We shake hands.

"Cecilia's been kind enough to take time away from her busy counseling practice this past year to volunteer as hostess for Parkview's weekly reading group."

"It was my mother's idea." I sit in a chair next to Doris Quinn's scowling son, then explain how the group started and why we've continued it even after Mother moved out. I try another smile, without effect. "I read aloud because several of the members have problems with their eyesight. It's seemed to work well for everyone so far."

Mr. Rayburn's daughter crosses one crisp khaki-covered leg over the other. "Who chooses the books?"

"When we started, the members planned to choose, but no one could agree, so they decided to let me. Of course, I'm always open to their suggestions."

Mr. Quinn lifts a copy of *Penelope's Passion* from his lap and waves it in the air. "And *this* is the sort of trash you deem fit for a group of seniors?"

Oh, shit. I sit up straighter. "Actually *Penelope's Passion* is the first romance novel we've read, Mr. Quinn. Normally, I select a title from the *Literary Pen*'s bestseller list, but the members were bored with such angsty reads. A lot of them dropped out. I thought they could use a change of pace, and they agreed."

Mrs. Kiley taps her foot against the floor and turns to Bill Burdette. "And do you approve of pornography being read to your residents on facility property?"

Bill clears his throat. "I only approved their use of one of our meeting rooms. I'm not involved in any other capacity with the group or their selection of reading material."

That a'boy, Bill. Dump this all on me. I scoot forward to the edge of my chair. "I assure you, the book we're reading is not pornography. It's a *romance* novel. There's nothing remotely degrading about it."

"Label it what you will, Ms. Dupree. Romance, soft porn, erotica. A spade is still a spade." With a jerk of his wrist, Mr. Quinn opens the novel to a book-marked page and reads in a dramatic voice, *"Penelope laced her fingers through his hair and pulled his head toward hers. Her lips parted, welcomed the warm velvet touch of his clever tongue, the feverish heat his kisses spread across her flesh. 'So soft,' he murmured."*

He pauses, looks across at me, narrows his eyes, then continues, *"The captain touched Penelope's throat, causing a shiver to ripple through her. His fingers fanned over one pale breast, circled her nipple in maddening strokes that made her breath catch, trailed down her bare stomach. And then he dipped—"*

Mrs. Kiley coughs. Loudly.

"Enough said." Quinn closes the book. "I believe that passage vividly portrays my point. It only becomes more explicit farther into the scene." He looks at Bill, whose face flames.

"Yes. Well." Bill glances at me, a plea for help in his eyes.

"Mr. Quinn…" I huff a laugh. "Tongue, breast, nipple and stomach are not dirty words. Besides, you read the scene out of context without knowing a thing about the story that led up to it."

His jaw muscle jumps. He crosses his arms.

"Haven't you ever watched any of the old swashbuckling movies of the forties and fifties? Errol Flynn?" I open my hands, palms up. "That's exactly what this is. A larger than life story. Melodrama. Adventure. Romance."

"Sex," he spits.

Okay. I've had enough of this prudish, pompous jerk and his uptight sidekick. Nobody here is paying me to act like a professional, so why should I? These people need to hear what I *really* think. Such as, maybe they should follow their parents' lead, since I've never met a couple in more obvious need of some spice in their lives.

I open my mouth to tell them, then come to my senses, square my shoulders, take a breath to calm my temper. "So the book has a sex scene or two. Studies support the importance of sexuality in people's later years. This novel might act as a substitute for the lack of intimacy in their lives or improve what they already have. Or it might just be good, fun entertainment." Leaning back, I smile.

Mr. Quinn continues to twitch and glare.

Mrs. Kiley appears horrified at the mention of elderly people and intimacy in the same sentence.

Bill's chair squeaks. "Maybe if the two of you explained the situation that brought the book to your attention. Mrs. Kiley?"

"It's Sue." She uncrosses her legs, crosses them again, blinks in rapid succession. "Yesterday afternoon I came by to visit Dad at the usual time. I always come on Tuesdays. But he wasn't in his apartment. I couldn't find him anywhere and he didn't answer his cell phone." She glances at the man next to her. "That's when I ran into Mr. Quinn in the hallway."

He gives her a halfhearted smile of support. "It's Donald."

She nods and smiles back at him. "Donald had just left his mother's apartment. She—" Sue studies her lap and starts blinking again.

"Mother didn't answer the doorbell," Donald continues, coming to her rescue. "I had a package for her, so I let myself in with my key. Music was playing in her bedroom and…" He squirms in the chair. "I heard laughter. Mother's and a man's. As you can imagine, I was stunned. I just stood there. I didn't know what to do. And then…"

"And then Mrs. Quinn and my father walked out of her bedroom and into the living room where Donald was," Sue finishes for him.

"*Danced* out. They were dancing. And wearing *robes*," he adds, his voice low and appalled. "In the middle of the day. Their *feet* were bare."

I chew the inside of my cheek. Bare feet and dancing! Oh, the scandal of it.

Sue glares at me as if she hears my thoughts. "Dad said they met at your reading group last week. The day you started that book. His friend Oliver had invited him to attend and he didn't have anything on his agenda so…"

Donald stares down at his knees. "They met *last week* and already they're…" He scrubs a palm over his face. *"Jesus."*

I cover my mouth to hide a smile. *Way to go, Doris. Paul Newman. What a catch.* When I regain some composure, I say, "I'm sorry. I don't see what any of this has to do with the reading group."

"It's this book," Donald snaps, tossing *Penelope's Passion* onto Bill's desk.

"They're lonely and vulnerable." Sue appears on the verge of tears. "And the book…well…it's titillating, to say the least. It might've put ideas in their heads."

"Good grief." I stand. For the third time today, I throw professionalism out the window. "They're human beings. Intelligent adults! Just because they're in their seventies doesn't mean they're brain-dead. They don't need a book in order to get *ideas.*"

Sue folds her hands in her lap. "They're in their *eighties,* not their seventies."

"Good for them. I hope they're having the time of their lives. And if I had anything to do with them getting together, good for me, too."

Donald Quinn bolts from his chair, turning his anger on Bill. "I don't care if this woman's a licensed therapist or not. You either ban this reading group from Parkview Manor, or form a committee to approve the books she chooses before they're read. If you don't, Mrs. Kiley and I are going over your head to file a formal complaint against this facility. I'm sure some of your other residents' family members would be happy to join us."

Donald Quinn and Sue Kiley leave the room together.

Sighing, I fold back into the chair and meet Bill's stare. His slackened face is pale. "Well…I guess he told you."

"CiCi…" He puffs out his cheeks.

"I know. I'll choose another book."

"And—"

"I'll bring it by so you and whatever committee you form can give it your blessing before we read it."

Bill drums his fingertips on the desktop. "I'll have to check into that. Forming that type of committee might raise liability issues for the Village."

"Are you saying you want us to disband?"

He nods. "For the time being, anyway."

"Fine." I stand up again. "I'll go tell the kids they're being censored by their children."

At six-fifteen, I step back to admire the new bedspread I bought after work. Plum and pale yellow. Bert would hate it, just like he'd hate the color I painted the walls. Nothing but neutrals for that man. Except when it comes to women, I guess. The flashier the floozy the better. Next week I might paint his beloved den sea-foam green or fire-engine red.

Erin pokes her head into the room and eyes the spread without comment. "I'm home." She turns to leave. The routine's been the same every day since I grounded her. She lets me know she's home from orchestra practice, goes to her room, comes out for dinner, then returns to her room for the rest of the night.

"Erin?"

She faces me again, crossing her arms.

"How was practice?"

"Okay."

"I've decided to let you off the hook a few days early. Just promise me no more drinking, okay? And no more dates with twenty-one-year-olds."

"He was twenty." When I scowl, she says, "Fine."

I toss a throw pillow onto the bed, then start from the room, pausing at the door to give her a hug. I'm surprised and pleased when she hugs me back.

Erin follows me into the backyard. It's cool out. The sky's a pearly gray. Twilight gray, I tell myself, though it's probably smog. I grab a dog brush off the patio table, whistle Max over, then sit in a chair and start to work on his coat. He sniffs the air, growls low in his throat when the poodle next door barks.

Leaning against the side of the house, Erin watches the movement of my hand across Max's back. "What are we doing for Thanksgiving?"

"The usual. Nana has a feast planned."

"Do you care if I have a friend over? Nana always makes too much anyway."

"Suzanna?"

"No, someone I just met. They don't celebrate Thanksgiving at their house. The parents are from Scotland."

I'm all for getting to know Erin's friends. "Okay. As long as Nana's fine with it. She's the cook."

After one final stroke of the brush, I lean back and inspect Max head to toe. His glossy coat gleams. His muscles ripple. He looks proud and strong, as dashing as Penelope's captain. I pat his rump. The hussies will swoon.

This morning, I called to tell my veterinarian Max is available if he knows of anyone looking to breed a female. I also called an ad in to the newspaper and sent one off to *English Bulldog* magazine.

I ask Erin to run get the newspaper so I can check to make sure the ad ran. When she comes back out with it, I scan the classifieds, locate my ad and then look up to find her watching me. Her nervous expression fills me with dread. "Something on your mind, sweetie?"

"Sort of." She nibbles the cuticle on her index finger. "Suz and I have been thinking."

Uh-oh. Suzanna and thinking are a dangerous combination.

"You know we both want to go to UT in the fall and, well, Suz is going to live in a dorm on campus, and the applications for housing are due soon, and I *really really* want to live on campus, too. With Suz."

I shake my head. "We already decided you'd live at home."

"*You* decided. You didn't ask me."

"You're not living in a dorm, Erin. It doesn't make sense. We live close enough to the university that it isn't necessary for you to move away."

"*Please,* Mom! We're not *that* close."

I fold the paper, lay it aside, push away from the patio table and stand. "I'm not going to discuss this right now."

Maxwell's water bowl's empty. I walk to the faucet, twist the lever and pick up the hose.

"But early applications are due *next week*. We'll miss out on the best dorms if we don't get ours in. Suz—"

"I said I'm not going to discuss this." Water streams into Max's bowl.

"Why not?"

"Because…" My throat closes. Because I don't think she's ready. Because she's not prepared to face the world on her own. Because dorms are havens for sex, alcohol and every other sin on the planet. I should know; I sampled them all when I lived on campus.

I draw a breath to finish my sentence, but I can't speak.

Because I'm not ready to let you go.

The truth hits me square in the nose. Is this about what I need or what Erin needs?

I swallow. "It's a waste of my money when you can just live here."

"Fine." She stomps to the back door, opens it just in time for my mother to stick her head out.

"Dinner's ready," Mother says in a singsong voice.

Ignoring her, Erin and I scowl at each other.

"I'll just ask Dad for the money then," Erin yells.

Mother blinks at her, at me, and then backs out of sight. Erin follows, slamming the door.

"Damn! Damn! Damn!" I shout kicking Max's bowl with each curse and slopping water over the edges.

Mrs. Stein, my neighbor, peeks over the fence, holding her poodle, Pom Pom. "CiCi? I thought I heard you out here."

"Hello, Mrs. Stein."

"Your shoes are getting wet."

I glance down. The running hose points at my feet, drenching them. "So they are."

Her eyes frown; her face doesn't, thanks to a recent round of Botox, I guess. "You never returned Jerry's call. My second cousin's great-nephew? The Bar Mitzvah?"

"I'm sorry. I can't make it."

"But he's a very successful man. And handsome. He still has most of his hair."

"Thanks, but I have other plans." I shrug. "Sorry."

She glares at me, then down at Max. Pom Pom yaps, sending Max behind a bush to tremble. Mrs. Stein and her dog disappear.

I kick the water bowl again. If Bert goes against me on this dorm thing with Erin, I *will* bury his body underneath the willow tree. Piece by piece. Except for *that* piece. His manhood, as Penelope would say.

Maxwell comes out from the bushes and nudges my leg with his nose. I lean down and scratch his head. "Max, old pal, by next fall you may have one very special chew toy."

After dinner the next night, I'm at the table reading a dog-show training manual and eating a piece of Mother's cinnamon devil's food cake when the phone rings. The man at the other end saw the newspaper ad. He wants more information. We have a lengthy conversation, then agree to get together over the weekend so he and his dog Gertie can size up Max.

Mother walks into the kitchen to get her knitting bag from the hutch as I'm hanging up. Before we can speak, the phone rings again. It's Bert, returning my call from last night. I tell him what's up with Erin.

"I don't mind giving her the money, CiCi."

"*I* mind." I lick icing off my fork. "I don't want Erin living in the dorm."

"It might be good for her."

"Who are you to say what's good for our daughter, Bert? I can count on one hand the number of times you've seen her in the past six months." I start to shake, inside and out. Mother pretends to be preoccupied with searching inside her bag for who-knows-what, but I'm sure she listens.

"I'm just trying to give Erin some space," Bert says in his oh-so-calm and practical tone. "You know, to sort things out."

"She doesn't need space, she needs to know that her father cares about her, that when you walked out on me you didn't walk out on her, too."

"You *asked* me to leave, CiCi. Remember?"

I stab the cake with my fork. He's right. Because I was angry. Because I thought he'd fight for our marriage, that he'd insist we at least try to work things out. Instead he acted defensive and all-too-eager to pack his bags. "You're embarrassed, aren't you, Bert? That's why you avoid her. You're embarrassed because you know Erin's on to you and what you did."

"And why is that, CiCi?" An undercurrent of rage buzzes in my ex's voice. "Did you tell her things to turn her against me?"

Good. Let him lose his temper for once. Let him be the one who goes off on a rant, not me. "I didn't tell her anything. Erin has eyes. She's not stupid. And if you're thinking of making up to her by giving her whatever she wants, that's a mistake. Erin needs you to be her father, not her best friend. She needs you to do what's best for her, not what's easiest for you." I ignore the nagging feeling that I should take my own advice.

Several tense, silent seconds later Bert says, "Okay, I'll tell her she has to wait a year before she can move out. That's fair, isn't it?"

The shaking subsides. I scrape a finger across the cake's icing. "I can live with that."

"And I'll spend more time with her. Call her more. I want to. I miss her. It's just…I can't stand the thought of her hating me."

"She doesn't hate you."

"Maybe. You're right, though. I haven't been there for her. Not enough. Even before we split. You've done a great job with her, CiCi. She's a good girl."

I hate it when he's nice, when he admits fault, when he compliments me. I don't want to remember Bert's few good qualities, only his many bad ones. "Thanks," I say and then we hang up.

"Where is that needle?" Mom continues to dig in her knitting bag. "Why, here it is." She holds it up for me to see.

I lick my finger. "How did you do it, Mother?"

"Do what, Sugar?"

"Hold everything together so well? Do everything right?"

She places the bag and needle on the table and crosses over to give me a hug. "I didn't do everything right. Far from it."

"You had a perfect marriage. I never once heard you and Dad have a real roof-raising fight. And I know as well as anyone that he could be hardheaded and stubborn as a jackass. Didn't you ever just want to strangle him?"

"Well, I wouldn't go that far, but we did have our squabbles now and then."

"But you always ended up letting him have his way. You always gave into him. You wanted to go to Hawaii on vacation but y'all never did. You went to Colorado. Every year."

She shrugs. "Your father loved to fish. He hated sand."

"Remember that bed you fell in love with? The brass one? How come you never bought it?"

"Harry thought all those curlicues on the headboard were silly." Mother laughs. "He said it was too feminine."

"So you just gave up. And you never complained about it. Weren't you the least bit resentful?"

"The bed wasn't important enough to cause a stir over, Cecilia. Neither was Hawaii."

I bite my lip. What's wrong with me? I shouldn't be jealous, even a little bit, of my mother's easygoing nature, the fact that she could keep a marriage running smoothly when I couldn't. "See, that's where you and I are different. I wasn't as big of a pushover as you, but I let Bert have his way most of the time, too. Then I stewed about it."

Mother lifts her chin. "I wasn't always a pushover. There were times when Harry didn't get what he wanted."

"Name one."

Her mouth quirks up at the corner. "You'd probably rather not hear this from your mother, but I feigned a headache or two in my day."

"Oh, that." I laugh. "Only one or two? See, I'm right. You were the perfect wife."

We sit across from one another at the kitchen table.

"No wife is perfect, CiCi. No husband is, either."

"You're just being modest. You were a model wife and a model parent, too. You cooked nutritious meals, made sure we spent time together as a family."

"People weren't in as big of a hurry back then."

"You hardly ever lost your temper with Jack or me, either. And still, when I went off on my own, I messed up."

"Nonsense."

I blink back tears. "So, what's going to happen to Erin? Bert and I have screwed up her life."

"Cecilia…" Mother reaches across and touches my hand. "I wasn't the saint you make me out to be. And as for losing my temper, if your father were here he could set you straight about that." She laughs, pats my hand, then sobers. "You haven't screwed up anything. Bert's the one who strayed."

I sniff. "I know, and I can't forgive him for hurting Erin. But I made mistakes, too. I didn't love Bert when I married him, not in the right way. You knew, didn't you?"

She nods once. "I suspected."

"It must've been awful for him, sensing I wasn't happy and not knowing why. Then, when he found those letters I wrote to Craig and never mailed…" I close my eyes. "I said terrible things in them. I told Craig I wasn't over him."

The memory of Bert's hurt eyes stabs me, the questions he asked, my lame reassurances. "I married Bert on the rebound. To help me get over Craig. To get over the miscarriage."

"Bert adored you. You cared for him, I know you did."

"But I didn't love him. Not then. That wasn't fair to him. I don't know, maybe I even got pregnant with Erin on the rebound, to help me forget about losing Craig's baby."

"CiCi," Mother says when I try to look away. Pressing my lips together, I meet her gaze. "You loved Bert. It was clear as could be on your face whenever you watched him with Erin."

"Eventually, yes. But it came too late for him."

I return to my dog-training manual, though my heart isn't in it.

"This talk of letting husbands have their way," Mother says, bringing my head up. "Is that what your purple bedroom walls are all about?"

I grin. "What do you think about candy apple-red for the den? Bert would hate it." And, I know I sound shallow, but that makes me love it all the more.

Thirty minutes later, I'm still at the table reading the training manual when the doorbell rings. Mother sits across from me, knitting.

"I'll get it!" Erin yells from the hallway. Seconds later she walks into the kitchen with her backpack over one shoulder. A blond-haired guy, also toting a backpack, is at her side. "Mom, Nana, this is Noah."

Dread rises up in me. It's the kid with the motorcycle. I only saw him from a distance the other night, but I recognize the blond hair. I stand as he approaches the table.

"Thanks for inviting me to Thanksgiving dinner, Mrs. Dupree." He shakes my hand. "I'm looking forward to it."

My eyes dart to Erin. So, her Scottish "friend" is male. She avoids my gaze.

"You're in for a treat," I say. "My mother's turkey and dressing will make your mouth water."

"Oh, such flattery, CiCi." Mother shakes Noah's hand and laughs. "Do go on."

Erin moves up beside biker-boy Scotty, hooks her arm through his, then gives me a look that dares me to comment. "Noah and I are going to do our homework together. You care if we use the kitchen table?"

Mother doesn't waste a second gathering her knitting so

I follow the model parent's lead, grab my manual and step aside. "It's all yours. So…you go to school with Erin, Noah?"

"I graduated." He and Erin dump their backpacks onto the table and sit side by side. "I'm at Tarrant County Junior College. We had English together last year, though."

We talk a minute longer, then Mother and I start from the room. "We'll leave you two to study."

In the den, Mother and I settle in on opposite ends of the couch. I toss the manual on the coffee table. "I don't like the looks of him."

She hands me two needles and a spool of yarn. "Why don't we pick up where we left off yesterday?"

"He has an earring."

"I didn't see one." Mother looks at my fingers. "Your hands are too stiff. Loosen up."

"You didn't see that stud in his left ear? How could you miss it?"

"Pay attention, Cecilia. Like this. Over, under—"

"What's he trying to pull by saying he's Scottish? His accent's as Texan as calf fries."

Mother's hands go still. "For heaven's sake, Cecilia, give the boy a chance. Erin, too."

The doorbell rings again. "What is this? Grand Central Station?" I start for the entry hall. "If this is that Judd kid, I'll—" I swing open the door, look up into a pair of cheery blue eyes peering from beneath a felt forties-style newsboy cap.

"Howdy do, CiCi."

"Oliver?" In the flesh. All six feet and three or four inches of him.

He removes the cap. "Belle around?"

"Uh…yes." I frown. Smile. Frown again.

He leans to one side, looks past my shoulder. "Could I—?"

I step back. "Um. Sure. Come on in."

I lead him into the den. "Look who's here, Mother."

Mother glances up from her knitting. "Oh." She lays her needles and yarn aside, stands, adjusts her glasses like she doesn't quite believe her eyes. "Oliver. How nice to see you."

He grins. "Why, Belle, you're looking fit as a fiddle tonight."

Mother blinks and flutters. "Don't be silly."

"No, I mean it. You're pretty as a peach."

I fold my arms. Good thing Mother's a gourmet cook. She hates baloney. She'll set the old fart straight in her tactful way.

"Oh, well that's so sweet of you to say." Tilting her head to one side, Mother smiles up at him. She looks flattered. Coy. Pretty. As a peach.

I frown at her as a memory plays through my mind. Daddy whistling *"The Yellow Rose of Texas,"* coming up behind Mother at the kitchen sink, her surprised laughter as he twirls her around. *You're my prettiest yellow rose, Belle.*

I step between Mother and Oliver. "Daddy always called you his yellow rose of Texas. Remember, Mother?"

"Of course I do, Sugar." Her voice is soft and as startled as her eyes.

Oliver looks around me, nods at the spot on the opposite end of the couch from Mother. My spot. The spot where Daddy always sat when he visited. "May I?"

I shake off an odd sense of panic, of defensiveness. "Sure. Have a seat."

He does. So does Mother. I stay put.

Oliver clears his throat. "I have an idea about the reading group. I want to offer my apartment as a meeting place. It may be on Parkview Manor's property, but I pay for it. Don't see as how anybody would have grounds to stop us from gathering there. And we could read whatever we choose."

Mother brightens. "That's a wonderful idea, Oliver."

From the direction of the kitchen, I hear Erin's and biker-boy Scotty's laughter, hers high-pitched, his deep. Studying? My foot.

"CiCi?" Mom's voice snags my attention again. "Isn't Oliver's idea wonderful?"

Nodding, I say, "I've been thinking, though. You don't really need me. You could get books on tape. I should've thought of that in the first place. It makes more sense."

"No!" they blurt in unison.

"I don't know about you, Belle," Oliver says. "But I get darned tired of conversing with machines these days. You make a phone call, you get a recorded message and are expected to leave one in return. You drive through at the bank, you get an electronic teller."

Mother nods her agreement. "People stay in touch by e-mail instead of by phone."

"And the list goes on and on," he says. "I like having you read to us, CiCi. Feels like the old days when we'd gather 'round the campfire and listen to someone tell a story."

I picture him in a flannel shirt, the sleeves rolled up, effortlessly splitting logs with a hatchet then tossing them into the flames. Mother admiring his flexing muscles.

"I agree," she says, a shy smile curving her lips. "It's more personal."

He winks at her. "More intimate."

She blushes and averts her eyes.

The sick feeling returns, the panic, the defensiveness. Don't fall for his good ol' boy charm, I want to tell her. Stick with "BOB." Your battery-operated-boyfriend will never break your heart. He'll always be there when you need him, and when you don't, you won't have to feign a headache since "BOB" is perfectly content in his bathroom drawer. "BOB" doesn't fish; he won't mind going to Hawaii. And he won't feel emasculated by a curlicue brass bed. No slinky lingerie needed for "BOB." You can turn him on, or off, with the flick of a switch.

"All right." I tap my foot, wishing I had a switch right now to turn off that gleam in jolly Oliver's eyes. "Your place it is, then. Same day, same time?"

He chuckles, pleased with himself. "That works for me. I'll let the others know."

I wait for him to stand and go. He doesn't. He twiddles his thumbs, looking like an overgrown kid on prom night.

"Belle, I thought I'd see if you might like to take a little drive. Maybe go for some ice cream."

Mother folds and unfolds her hands in her lap. "Oh my, no. I couldn't."

He grins. "Of course you could."

"Not at this hour."

"It's only seven-thirty."

She avoids looking at me. At Oliver, too. "I just ate an enormous dinner."

He claps his big, rough hands together. "Well, then. I'm right in time to buy you dessert."

Mother's eyes flash panic signals.

"We have devil's food cake," I say, helping her out with the pushy old coot. A burly, charming, lumberjack of an old coot, but a coot nonetheless.

"Yes!" Mother smiles her thanks and stands. "We have ice cream, too. I'll get it."

Oliver follows her. "I'll help you."

"No ice cream for me," I say, on his heels. "Just cake." If he thinks I don't know what he's up to, he's in for a big surprise. I'm keeping an eye on Oliver Winston. I'm not about to let him put ideas in Mother's head and take advantage of her loneliness, her vulnerability.

My pace slows when it occurs to me I heard those same words come out of Sue Kiley's mouth about her dad and Donald Quinn's mother. Lonely. Vulnerable. *Penelope's Passion* putting ideas in their heads. I made light of her concerns. In fact, I thought she was being ridiculous.

Erin and Noah don't even look up when we enter the kitchen. They sit, shoulder to shoulder, heads together, whispering and snickering over their open books. Funny, I don't remember the subject of math ever being so humorous.

Frustrated, though I'm not sure why, I go to the back door and let Maxwell in.

"Oh, Oliver..." Mother hands him the ice-cream carton, covers her mouth and laughs at something he says as I pass back through the kitchen with Max beside me.

Three slices of cake sit on the counter. "Which one's mine?"

They're too wrapped up in each other to hear me. All of

them. Mother and Oliver. Erin and biker-boy Scotty. "Hey, did you hear we're supposed to get a cold front this weekend?" No response. "A possible ice storm." Nothing. "I'm moving in with Mrs. Stein's second cousin's nephew and we're opening a toupee shop." Nobody cares.

Good grief and pass the chocolate; I give up. As the saying goes, three's a crowd. Or in this case, five.

I take a plate and head for the bedroom. I'll just keep the door open and my hearing turned up. Hormones have gone haywire in my house tonight. I don't trust anyone.

When I reach my bedroom, I set the cake on the night-stand and grab the new romance novel I started last night. I read ahead of the group and finished *Penelope's Passion*.

Gazing into Maxwell's sad eyes I hook a thumb at the bed. He whines as if to ask, *you sure you're not gonna swat my butt?*

"You're in the clear," I say. "Come on."

He takes the leap, then snuggles up next to my leg as I settle against the pillows, the novel in my lap. "They can keep the lumberjack and biker boy. You're all I need to keep me warm, Max." I fork a bite of cake, then open the book's cover. "Just you and Daniel Cade Colton, Texas Ranger."

And maybe someday soon, a "BOB" of my very own.

CHAPTER 11

To: Erin@friendmail.com
From: Noah@friendmail.com
Date: 11/21, Friday
Subject: Stuff
did i tell you how awesome you looked today at lunch? i hope it works out for you to hear my band tonight at the beat. oh, and don't worry about that a-hole being there. he and his buds got kicked out last week for fighting and they're banned from the place. you sure about thanksgiving? i don't think your mom's too crazy about me. who is scotty? forgot to tell ya she called me that once last night.
later, noah

To: Noah@friendmail.com
From: Erin@friendmail.com
Date: 11/21 Friday
Subject: re: Stuff
Did I tell you I think guys who play guitar are seriously sexy? I'll be there to hear you tonight. Can't wait! Suz

and I are going to a movie, I'll be home by my totally ridiculous curfew, then I'll go out the window, like always. Scotty? Who knows? My mom's having a midlife crisis or something. Ignore her. I do. And no way am I letting you get out of Thanksgiving! Thanks for picking me up at lunch. I know it's out of your way.
~Erin

I click Send then watch the message disappear into cyber-space. Seriously sexy? Guitar players are seriously sexy?

Leaning back in the chair, I close my eyes and groan. I am such a moron. Noah will think I'm making a move. I *am* making a move. But what if he doesn't feel that way about me? What if he just wants to be friends? I mean, we met two weeks ago, but we've never had a real date. And he hasn't kissed me yet, not really. Just a peck on the cheek sometimes, like today when he dropped me at school after lunch. Which, by the way, Mom doesn't know about. The times Noah's taken me to lunch, I mean.

Since day one, Noah and I have either seen each other or talked every night. He comes over a lot and we study or watch TV. A couple of times I've climbed out the window after curfew and we've sat in the yard and talked since he doesn't have a car, only a cycle. He held my hand last time. We didn't stay out long, though. The weather's getting colder. Which is probably the only reason he held my hand. Because his fingers were freezing.

So why does Noah tease me and flirt if he just wants to be friends? Like in his e-mail, saying I looked amazing?

That's flirting, isn't it? Maybe not. Maybe he's just being nice. Giving me a compliment because he feels sorry for me.

My cell phone rings as I'm logging off my e-mail. I see that it's Dad and don't answer. He took Mom's side when I asked him if he'd pay for me to live on campus next year. He said he'd rather I wait until I'm a sophomore.

I totally lost it. He's allowed to act my age, but I'm not? How fair is that?

Now Dad calls me all the time, like he's trying to make up for not helping me move out, not to mention everything else he's done. Sometimes he asks me to dinner or a movie. Sometimes he just wants to talk. Which is crazy since we don't have anything at all to talk about. Last week I caved and went with him to Pappadeaux's. Afterward, we stopped at this coffee shop for dessert and, surprise! His current girlfriend works there. Natalie. Or Nattie, as Dad calls her.

Puke.

Supposedly she's only working in the coffee shop part-time while she goes to college. Which tells me just how young she is. He's never introduced me to one of his girlfriends before. Maybe he thinks it's okay now since the divorce is final. Or maybe he's serious about this one.

Puke again.

All I need is a stepmom I run into every day on campus next year. Or to hook up with some guy and find out he used to go out with my stepmom.

Double puke.

I find Mom and Nana in the backyard. I sit beside Nana at the patio table. She's watching Mom trot Max around on a leash. Mom looks ridiculous running along beside him, her posture all stiff and straight, her steps perfectly spaced. She's been acting weird lately. Training and grooming Max all the time, painting the house wild colors. After her purple bedroom, she started on the den. It's so red it looks like someone got murdered with a chain saw in there. She makes me crazy, but still I feel bad for her, too. Dad really hurt her, and I know she's not over it. But what can I do?

"Oh, hi Erin," Mom calls out. "Watch this." She gives a short, shrill whistle, and Max stops trotting. Mom grins like he just did a cartwheel or something.

"That's impressive, Cecilia," Nana says. "You'd make your father proud."

Mom unleashes Max then walks toward us. "Erin, did I ever tell you that we always had a bulldog when Jack and I were kids, and that Grandpop used to enter them in competitions?"

"I don't think so."

Nana's laugh sounds light as air. "Up until your mother started high school and got too busy, she loved helping him train."

Mom's out of breath. She sits in a patio chair across from us. "Do you have plans for tonight? I thought we all might go out for Chinese."

"I'm going to a movie."

"With Noah?"

"Suz."

"Good. You're spending too much time with that kid."

I cross my arms. "Whatever, Mom. We've never even gone out. He just comes over."

"It's not a good idea to let one guy monopolize all your free time. Is he still coming for Thanksgiving?"

"Yes, is that a problem?"

"Of course not," Nana says. "The more the merrier. Less leftovers, too."

Mom gets all slit-eyed as she stares across the table at Nana. Her cheeks cave in, like she's biting the insides of them to keep from saying something. She turns to me. "When's the movie?"

"Seven-thirty."

"I guess it's just Nana and me for Chinese food then."

Nana coughs. "Sorry, Sugar, I forgot to tell you, Oliver is coming by tonight. He's singing a solo at Parkview's Christmas party this year, and he asked if I'd accompany him on piano. We're going to practice." She fans her face with one hand. "My goodness, it's hot out here."

"Hot?" Laughing and shivering, I turn to Mom. "You're not hot, are you? It's November."

I don't think she hears me. Her expression reminds me of Max's when we leave him in the backyard alone too long. For a minute, I forget I'm mad at her. "Hey, Mom," I say, trying to sound upbeat. "You should ask the Margarita Martyrs over."

She frowns. "The who?"

The surprised look on my grandmother's face makes me laugh. "Ever since y'all got together last time, Nana's called your friends that."

"I swear, Erin Dupree. Even as a little girl, you never could keep a secret," Nana says.

Our nosy neighbor pokes her head over the fence. Her dyed red hair is pulled back into a tight bun. Her lips are red, too, and her overtanned skin is stretched too tight across sharp cheekbones. I know she has to look in the mirror to draw on her eyebrows. What is she thinking? Is she blind?

"Hello you three."

Mom waves and wiggles her fingers. "Hello Mrs. Stein."

"I was in the yard and I couldn't help but overhear that you're footloose and fancy-free tonight, CiCi."

"Not necessarily," Mom says. "I haven't asked Max yet if he wants Chinese."

"You'll never guess who I ran into at the grocery store today," Mrs. Stein continues as if she didn't hear Mom's sarcastic comment. "The Calloways? Raymond and Lila? Used to live in the tan brick house at the end of the block? Well, I invited them to dinner and they asked if they could bring their son, Anthony. Remember him? He lived with his parents. Still does."

Mrs. Stein makes a tsking sound as she stoops to pick up her barking poodle. "Such a shame. Forty-three years old and never married. Such a gorgeous man, too. Almost pretty he's so perfect. And what a wardrobe."

When I giggle, both Mom and Nana nudge me under the table with their feet.

Mrs. Stein's nostrils flare when she looks at me. "Well, I take it you've heard all the talk about him. Raymond and Lila assure me it's not true. So anyway, CiCi, I was thinking how nice it would be if you'd join us tonight."

"I'd have to bring Maxwell."

Mom's joking, but I can tell by Mrs. Stein's shocked eyes, that she doesn't know that. She wrinkles her nose and holds her poodle tighter. "Pom Pom would be too nervous with him there. She's delicate, you know. Surely he'd be okay alone for a couple of hours while you and Anthony get to know one another better. What do you say?"

At ten o'clock, Suz parks in our driveway. She nods at an old-timey car at the curb. "Whose is that?"

"I don't know. Nana's friend's, I guess."

"It looks like something out of a black-and-white movie."

"So does Nana's friend."

Suz laughs. "Erin!"

"I didn't mean it that way. He's just, well…what's the word? A gentleman, I guess. He treats Nana like a queen. And he…" I try to find the right word, one you'd read in a romance novel to describe a man like Nana's friend. "He swaggers. You know, like John Wayne."

Suz laughs again. "I'll wait down the street for you. How long will it be?"

"Give me thirty minutes."

"Okay. I'll have time to get a cherry-lime then."

Reaching for the door handle, I turn to her. "Maybe Noah's just nervous. Maybe that's why he hasn't kissed me yet."

"You are so naive. Guys don't get nervous about stuff like that."

"How do you know? Why wouldn't they? We do."

Suzanna taps her fingers against the steering wheel to the beat of Avril Lavigne. "He's just messing with you. Trying to keep you guessing. That way, when he *does* kiss you, you'll be so relieved who knows what you might give in and do." She wiggles her eyebrows.

"You are such a dork." I open the door and step out. "See you in thirty minutes."

Piano music plays in the living room. *White Christmas.* I close the front door and head for the den.

Mom's watching the movie *When Harry Met Sally,* which she's seen a million and one times. "How was dinner at the Steins' with pretty Anthony?"

She lifts some sort of pastry from a plate on the coffee table. "I got a severe stomachache and had to call and beg off." Mom takes a bite and talks with her mouth full. "You're home early. You have another hour until curfew. Not that I'm complaining."

"We couldn't think of anything to do after the movie. Besides, I'm sort of tired."

"You've had a busy week. The Scot hasn't helped matters by coming over every night."

"Noah, Mom. His name is Noah. And he hasn't come over every night."

"Right. Sorry." She takes another bite. "Mmmm. Try one of these chocolate éclairs Nana made. They're so good they should be illegal."

"No, thanks." Mom finishes off hers then starts on another. If she doesn't watch it, she'll have to buy a whole new wardrobe. She's starting to look pudgy. "I think I'll go to bed."

The piano music stops.

"Wait," Mom says, her mouth stuffed with chocolate goo. She swallows. "Tell me about the movie first. Was it good?"

"It was okay."

"So, just you and Suzanna went?"

I should've known I wouldn't escape a pop quiz. "I already told you."

"Is that a 'yes' or a 'no'?"

"Yes." I glance up at the ceiling. "Jeez."

Nana and her friend come into the room. She walks, he swaggers. "Oh, Erin, you're back. You remember Mr. Winston, don't you?"

"Oliver," the old man says. "How are you, young lady?"

I like him already. I like anybody who interrupts my mother, the interrogator. "Good. How are you?"

"Fine as silk thread."

Yawning, I look at my watch. "Well, see you later. I'm going to read in bed."

"Maybe we can help Nana with the Thanksgiving baking tomorrow," Mom says before I take two steps.

"I'm going shopping. Besides, you can't cook."

Mom looks all offended. "Says who?"

Nana and I burst out laughing.

"Uh-oh," Oliver says. "You ladies are treading on shaky ground."

"Okay, you two." Mom smiles. She has a dot of choco-late icing above her top lip. "Then I'll go shopping with you. You and Suzanna haven't had any luck finding a concert dress without me."

"I found one. They did alterations. I'm picking it up."

Her smile falls. "Oh."

Why does she always have to make me feel so guilty?

As I head down the hallway I hear Nana say, "I changed my mind, Oliver. I think I would like to go for some hot tea."

"This late?" Mom blurts. "We have tea."

"In bags," Nana says. "For some reason, I'm craving the real thing, leaves brewed in a pot, with real cream."

I close and lock my bedroom door. No way am I living here when I start college. Mom's so needy all the sudden that even my seventy-five-year-old grandmother can't leave the house without her butting in. If I stay here, *Mom* will be seventy-five by the time she gets a date and *I'll* be the one on the couch stuffing my face with chocolate.

Memories of that last night with Judd twist my stomach when Suz and I walk into The Beat. I remind myself that everything's different this time. I'm dressed somewhere in between the old, boring me and the new, wild me, I'm not wearing so much makeup, and my hair doesn't look like I stuck my finger in a light socket, as Grandpop used to say. Oh, and no jellyfish tonight, either. They're back where they belong, on Katie's concave chest.

Suz's cousin isn't working the door tonight so I use the fake ID Judd gave me. Not that I plan to drink; I don't. Just the thought of a lemon-drop martini makes me woozy.

Music blares and pulses, but it's the piped-in kind, not Noah's band, Cateye. The three of them are on stage setting up. Noah wears jeans and a black T-shirt. The other two guys have on seventies-looking aviator-style sunglasses, even though it's dark in here.

As Suz and I weave our way through the crowd toward the band, I notice how thin and tall Noah is. Thin in a good way, all angles and wide shoulders, nothing soft about him.

When Noah spots me, he props his guitar against a speaker, says something to the bass player, hops down off the stage and comes over. He says hello to Suz as he takes my hand and eyes my hair and clothes. "Hey, I like the look." When he grins, I think I was wrong that nothing about him is soft; his eyes are. He gives me a quick kiss on the cheek. "You smell good, too. No cigarettes."

I laugh. "I decided to save my money and just breathe the secondhand smoke." It's like every ounce of energy in my body zooms in on the feel of his hand around mine. Warm. Dry. Strong. The tips of his long fingers are calloused from playing guitar.

"Who's your drummer?" Suz asks him. She's had her eye on the guy since the second we walked in.

"Tonto." Noah grins at Suz when he sees her checking out his friend. "Come on up, I'll introduce you."

We follow Noah onto the stage and meet the other two guys in the band, Tonto and Reese and then Suz and I leave to find a table since it's time for them to start their set.

They play old rock and roll, but put their own sound to it. Some of the songs I recognize from Mom's collection of old vinyl albums and eight-track tapes I used to listen to when I was little.

"They're good," Suz shouts over the noise.

I think so, too. Noah not only plays lead guitar, he sings. He doesn't seem the least bit embarrassed up there on stage. Not that he should be. He has talent. He looks hot, too. Now I understand why all those girls at rock concerts way back in Mom's day, or maybe even before, used to scream and cry and faint.

I'm not the only one who notices, either. The way the

hoochies at the next table look at Noah, I'm surprised there's not a big pool of drool on the floor at their feet.

Back off. He's with me, I want to say, but don't have the nerve. Besides, *is* he with me? I mean, yeah we're talking, but maybe that's all.

When the band takes a break, Reese heads for the bar and Noah and Tonto come over and sit with us. "You were incredible," I tell them.

Focused on Suz, Tonto drums the tabletop with his palms. "I hope the manager thinks so."

Noah balances on the two back legs of his chair and scans the room. "He says if this works out tonight, we might get a standing Friday night gig."

"I could use the cash," Tonto adds, taking Suz's glass of Coke when she offers it to him. "The pay's good here."

"You'll get the job." Suz gives Tonto her flirty smile while he gulps down her Coke. "The crowd was into you."

"Yeah. Some really old dude in the back was even busting a move." Tonto gives Suz back her drink, resumes drumming the table, and shifts his attention to Noah. "We need to get Miner back. Something's missing without him."

"Our keyboard player," Noah explains to us. "He quit last month." He turns back to Tonto. "Miner's through. He doesn't have time to play anymore since he's working a full-time job."

"Erin could play keyboard, couldn't you, Erin?" Suz tosses her hair like an actress in a shampoo commercial. "She plays piano."

Noah leans forward. The front legs of his chair hit the floor. "I thought you played cello?"

"I do. But I've had piano lessons since I was six." I don't

add that, unlike most kids, my mom never had to bug me to practice.

"You should hear her," Suz says. "She could play professionally."

I look away. "Whatever."

"She could." Suz offers Tonto another drink of her Coke and totally ignores me. "Trust me, she's a music genius. It's her thing."

The thing that's added to my loser status ever since I hit middle school. Face it, if you're in a rock band, you're cool. But join school band or orchestra and you can pretty much kiss any chance at prom queen goodbye. As if I'd want to be prom queen anyway.

Nodding his head and tapping his fingertips on the table, Tonto stares at me. "What do you think, Noah? We still have Miner's keyboard. She could practice with us on Sunday."

"I think that's a good idea." Noah smiles at me. "If you want to, I mean."

"Sure." I shrug. "Sounds like fun."

"Bring your cello, too." Noah stands. "We might come up with something."

At 2:00 a.m. when The Beat closes, Noah takes me home on his cycle, and Tonto follows Suz to her house in his truck, since it's late and she's alone.

I wear Noah's helmet and hold tight around his waist as the cool air rushes past us.

He parks at the curb at the end of my block and cuts the engine. Together, we walk six houses down to my yard and stand under the pear tree to the left of my bedroom window.

Noah sees me shiver. "Cold?"

"Sort of."

He opens his jacket. "I'll share."

I step closer and he wraps the jacket and his arms around me. He's five or six inches taller than me. I tilt my head back to look up at him.

"Thanks for coming tonight," he says, his breath warm against my face. It smells like peppermint. No cinnamon. No tobacco. No bad memories.

"I had fun." He looks into my eyes for what seems like forever, and I think *just do it,* but he doesn't. A story Nana told me about her and Grandpop's first kiss slips into my thoughts. Quick, before I can change my mind, I lift onto my tiptoes and kiss Noah, just touch my mouth to his and leave it there. Not long, but longer than the pecks he's given me.

When I pull away, my heart pounds so hard I hear it. Noah stares into my eyes again, and then his arms tighten around me. This time, *he* kisses *me,* so slow and gentle I feel like I'm floating. I lift my arms and encircle his neck, hold on to him. With Noah, I don't feel any fear or dread or pressure for more. I only feel his arms around me, his lips against mine, the beat of his heart keeping time with my own.

CHAPTER 12

From The Desk of
Belle Lamont

Dear Harry,
Happy Thanksgiving! What a wonderful day we had. I do so enjoy
cooking for our family. We missed Jack and his family. And we missed
you.

CiCi mentioned how much you loved my chestnut dressing. Erin
said nobody would ever match your deviled eggs, then realized she'd
insulted mine and got embarrassed about it.

Erin's friend, Noah, carved the turkey. While he did, I sensed
that, like me, CiCi and Erin thought about Bert, since after he and
Cecilia married, you turned the carving over to him. I know Erin
wished her father was with us; I think during that moment, Cecilia
did, too.

Erin's Noah is a friendly, outgoing young man. He seems to have
his head on straight, and he holds his own with CiCi, which is the
best thing of all and a hoot to behold. When she saw that I'd placed
Bert's carving knife on the table, she took off for the kitchen
mumbling something about Christmas rolling around before a kid

Noah's age could slice a turkey without an electric knife. When she came back, he'd already served her the first slice, me the second and was filling Erin's plate. In Noah, our daughter has met her match, I'm afraid. One thing is obvious; he's crazy about Erin, and the feeling is mutual. When they look at one another, I'm reminded of us when we were their age and falling in love.

What a beautiful gift, our love, our years together. I never realized how quickly the time would pass. When I was young, my mother always told me that life waits for no one. I didn't understand then, but now I do. I can either live it, or watch it streak by and leave me behind.

A while back, Erin asked if I thought young men get nervous about first kisses like girls do. I told her about ours and the weeks leading up to it. Sometimes it seems like just yesterday, that summer we met. In my memories, the days are fringed in gold, the long walks and cold swims, the sunshine and the laughter. Nothing else mattered except the way you looked at me. Oh, how I loved that look.

I told Erin how, after my family moved to town and into your neighborhood, you drove by my house for days in your brother's '41 Ford sedan before "just dropping by" to meet me. How three more days passed before you found the nerve to call and ask me out on a date.

I still laugh when I think of how you stuttered and stammered and beat around the bush. We talked for at least an hour about everything from our families to Dizzy Gillespie to Jackie Robinson playing with the Dodgers. Finally, Mr. Dryden broke in on the party line and said, "Son, I need to make a call. Ask her out and get it over with." And so you did.

We went to The Ghost and Mrs. Muir, remember? The theatre was so crowded we had to sit in the balcony. Gene Tierney and Rex Harrison were incredibly romantic. So were you. You held my hand *in the dark, and I just knew you'd kiss me before the night ended. But you didn't. Not then or on the next date or the one after that. I swear, Harry, you certainly knew how to make a girl suffer and doubt herself. You had me questioning everything from the scent of my perfume to the fit of my girdle.*

Then at the end of date number four, when you walked me to my parents' front porch, I took matters into my own hands.

Well, apparently either Erin followed my lead, or Noah found his nerve, because I saw them necking out front before he left tonight. So sweet. But it worries me, too. Can you imagine what CiCi would do if she found out about Erin sneaking out her window after curfew to meet that boy? Go into a tizzy, that's what.

Erin doesn't know I followed her to a nightclub where Noah's band played. I stood in the back and kept an eye on things. Not because I'm a busybody, but because I'm concerned for her safety. Blending in with a crowd of teens and twenty-somethings was no easy task, let me tell you. Don't worry. I didn't go alone. A friend took me. I know my limitations. I don't trust myself to drive anymore with these eyes.

Speaking of my friend, I've never lied to you, Harry, and I won't start now. His name is Oliver Winston. I hope you know I'd never betray your memory by allowing my relationship with him or any other man to become more than friendship. Still, I have to start living again. Watching Erin push her fears aside to dive headfirst into life, makes me realize I've been a coward, afraid of drowning. I refuse to piddle away any more of the time I have left. And I do so enjoy Oliver's company. I'm sure if the two of you met you'd hit it off in an instant.

Anyway, guess who Cecilia caught sneaking in after 2:00 a.m. on that night Erin went to the nightclub? No, not our granddaugh-

ter. Me. Unfortunately, my body isn't up to climbing in and out of windows these days, so I came through the front door. Not that I feel I need to sneak around. For heaven's sake, I'm a grown woman three-quarters of a century old! Still, Cecilia was beside herself. You always wondered if she heard anything you said all those times you got onto her as a teenager. She heard you, Harry. Loud and clear. Your words came out of her mouth. What a scolding she gave me! I half expected her to ground me and send me to my room.

As far as Cecilia knew, Erin was asleep through all this, and I didn't say otherwise. I'm still in a quandary about what to do about Erin's secret. Though I don't approve of her method of breaking away, I understand. Erin's ready to fly, but CiCi's determined to clip her wings.

Should I confront Erin and encourage her to stop breaking her mother's rules? To work things out with CiCi? I just wish she'd go to her and explain that she needs a bit more freedom. I'd like to believe that Cecilia would be reasonable, but I guess I'm being an idealistic fool. CiCi's anything but reasonable these days. Since separating from Bert, she's become so cynical it scares me. If she doesn't come to terms with what's bothering her soon, I shudder to think what color she'll paint the bathroom. Or my room, for that matter. The place is starting to look like a carnival fun house.

On a happier note, remember I told you the reading group was forced to disband? Well, we're meeting again in a different location. The Frans told Billie Jean Bilderback who told Ellen Miles who told me, that the problem had something to do with Doris Quinn and Frank Rayburn. When I mentioned that possibility to Jane Binkley, she said she'd heard rumors that the two of them are fooling around. Who knows if that's true? As I've said before, Jane has a bit of a dirty mind.

Then again, Doris is such an eyelash batter, I wouldn't put it past her. I'm not sure what her love life has to do with our reading group, but if I find out, I'll let you know. Until then, my love…

As always, your yellow rose,

Belle

CHAPTER 13

Cecilia Dupree
Day Planner
Wednesday, 12/5

1. 10:00—new patient consultation.
2. 1:00—P.V. reading group/finish Penelope.
3. Demand refund at dry cleaners for shrinking slacks.
4. 5:00—drop Max at Gertie's.

Mother and I huddle in our coats on our way to Oliver's apartment and the final three chapters of Penelope's Passion. Tiny lights twist around the lampposts that line the walkway through Parkview Manor's courtyard. The multicolored glow adds a warm festive touch to this nose-numbing, gloomy afternoon. A short distance away, at the entrance to the park, the duck pond gazebo also twinkles and blinks.

I wonder how many of Parkview Manor's residents will spend the holidays alone? It's too sad to think about. I guess I understand why people do crazy, desperate things in search of another chance at love.

I understand, but it doesn't mean I'll follow that path to frustration. I'd rather shave my bikini line with a dull, rusty razor than go on a date. Will I feel the same way, though, years from now when Mother's gone? When Erin's grown and on her own? Or will I grasp at any opportunity, no matter how foolish, that might land me a little companionship?

Which brings me to my ten o'clock appointment and the biggest opportunity-grasper of all time. Henry "you-can-call-me-Hank" Bocock. Fifty-six and going through his third divorce. Ex-rodeo cowboy turned rancher. Lover of snakeskin boots, starched open-collared shirts and gold neck chains to accent his furry throat.

As it turns out, my neighbor, the ever-so-helpful Mrs. Stein, my very own Cupid in a caftan, referred Hank to me, certain I might help him "get over Gloria." Funny, I got the distinct impression that Gloria was the last thing on Hank's mind. He seemed more interested in my legs than my advice. A fact I found amusing since, beneath my opaque black stockings, my calves are almost as hairy as his chest; I haven't shaved in four days. No, make that five.

But back to my point. In order to meet a prospective companion, (me), Hank shelled out a good amount of change for a therapy session he didn't need. Pretty creative of Hank, I must admit. Or Mrs. Stein; I'm not sure who came up with the idea. What the incident tells me, though, is that competition in the middle-aged dating world is fierce. I don't want any part of it. I'll stick with the safety of the tried, true and loyal to keep me company; Max, movies, the King (of Hearts, not Elvis).

I glance across at Mother. She hums "Winter Wonderland," a smile on her face.

"So what sort of novel do you think we should start next week?" I ask.

The humming fades into a *hmmm*. "Jane, Mr. Gaines and The Frans all called this morning. They want another romantic adventure." White puffs drift from Mother's mouth with each word she speaks. She secures the top button of her coat. "Oh, look. There's Jane now."

We both call out a greeting to Jane Binkley, whose wild, bushy hair is a different shade of blond today, and the Don Knotts look-alike ahead of us. Jane's hips swing as, arm-in-arm, they round the corner of the walkway connecting Parkview's bungalows to the apartment building. They yell "hello" and go inside. Don's step is so springy I wouldn't be surprised if his head hits the ceiling when he walks down the hall.

Mom tucks her gloved hands into her coat pockets. "According to Jane, others in the group want another romance, too."

"And you?"

"I wouldn't mind. Look how much our membership has grown since we started *Penelope's Passion*. It's wonderful, isn't it?"

Her eyes are as sparkly as the twinkle lights, as happy as I've seen them in a very long time. I tell myself her perkiness is due to the spirit of the season, or possibly a result of coming to live with Erin and me. But then I glance up at the building and see Oliver Winston standing at his third-story window looking down at us, and the truth slides like an avalanche right down to the pit of my stomach.

They've spent a lot of time together lately. The past two Friday nights, Mother's tiptoed in after 2:00 a.m., reeking of cigarette smoke. *Dancing,* she tells me when I ask where they've been. *Just friends. No big deal. No need to get upset.*

Right. Sure thing. If you think I believe that, stand on your ear. First my daughter, now my mother. And here I am, sandwiched in the middle like a pickle in a bun, trying to keep them from ruining their lives.

And feeling like a hypocrite.

Intellectually, I understand Mother's need for companionship. Like I told Donald Quinn and Sue Kiley about their parents, Mother's a grown-up, and I have no business butting into her love life. But I'm finding it's not so simple to be reasonable when it's my own parent flirting with love. It's not so amusing. Or sweet. Or easy to accept.

Up at the window, the old fart smiles and waves. Mother smiles and waves back. "Oliver says the reading group is the buzz of the village. Everyone looks forward to it. I swear, I think if we met every day instead of just once a week we'd still have a full house."

As I reach for the door to the building, it swings open and Bill Burdette, the manager, steps out. Squinting, he glances over his shoulder before aiming his gaze at me. "We need to talk."

"Okay." His serious expression tells me he's not preparing to ask me to tap dance at the Parkview Christmas program. "Go on up, Mother. I'll be there in a minute."

Bill waits for Mother to leave then steps outside and closes the door.

"Are you having a hot flash, Bill?" I shiver and laugh. "How about we have this discussion inside where it's warm?"

"I don't want anyone to hear this." He glances around again, sees that we're alone then says, "Iris Shelby and Herbert O'Dell eloped last night."

"No kidding?"

He shakes his head. "They're eighty-something years old. Both of them."

I lower my voice to a whisper and lean toward him. "Iris isn't pregnant, is she?"

"That's not funny, CiCi. I thought we had an understanding that the reading group was on hold."

"We're meeting in a private residence."

"Within this facility."

"In Oliver Winston's home, which he pays for. I don't understand why you're so upset. As long as it's legal, he can hold any kind of meeting he wants, and Parkview Manor's in the clear. Besides, what does this have to do with Iris and Herbert getting married?"

"They attend your reading group, don't they?"

"Front row and center every Wednesday." The cold numbs my toes. I stomp my feet to jump-start my circulation. "So?"

"Iris Shelby's son has power of attorney over her money. He writes the checks for her to live here, and he's not the only one. Many of our residents receive financial assistance from their children or have turned over legal control of their funds. If we piss off the kids, the parents could be forced to move someplace else. Then the Village loses money and my job's at risk."

"Calm down, Bill. Iris is only one resident." I step around him, open the door and go inside. My panty hose feel like they're about to cut me in two. I must have accidentally bought a size smaller than my usual medium.

Bill follows me down the hallway to the elevator, walking fast until he's at my side. "There's more." The elevator dings. The doors slide open and three women step off. Bill straightens, flashes his too-white teeth. "Seasons greetings, ladies. Bundle up if you're going outside. Jack Frost is paying us a visit today." His chuckle is loud and hollow, like a shopping mall Santa's at the end of a very long day.

I step onto the elevator. Bill joins me. I push *Three*. Bill's smile falls as the elevator rises.

"Saturday when the maintenance guy went out to the duck pond, he heard voices in the gazebo. "When he checked it out, he found Jane Binkley and Stanley McDougal inside getting it on." He shudders.

An image flashes through my mind. The shriveled-up old prune of a guy I saw with Mrs. Binkley only moments ago. Naked. In the gazebo. On Jane. I shudder, too. The elevator dings. I burst out laughing.

"Shhhh!" Bill blinks terror at me as the doors slide open. He blows out a long breath when we find the hallway empty.

"I'm surprised at you, CiCi. What if your mother was in that gazebo instead of Jane?"

I sober. "I'd be horrified."

"Then how can you laugh?"

"I know. But, the thing is, it *wasn't* my mother." As I start off toward Oliver's apartment with Bill on my heels, I struggle to control my humor, but do a miserable job of it.

"Pardon me for saying so, but I expected a more mature reaction from you."

"I'm sorry. It's just…it was something like forty-eight degrees on Saturday. They didn't get frostbite, did they?"

I notice a twitch at one corner of Bill's mouth. "According to the maintenance guy they spread Jane's chinchilla coat on the bench underneath them and covered up with her full-length mink."

"I hope the animal rights people don't get wind of this."

Bill glares.

I laugh again. Nothing but the best for Jane. I've seen her apartment. Very classy, from the artwork on the walls right down to the fancy brass toilet paper holder in the bathroom. So I'm guessing there must be more to skinny little Stanley McDougal than meets the eye. What that "more" might be, I'd rather not contemplate.

When I reach Oliver's apartment, I stop and turn to face Bill. Behind him, Roy West, wearing a cowboy hat and swinging a cane, escorts Ellen Miles toward us. Her rubber-soled shoes squeak against the tiled floor.

"CiCi," Ellen calls out. "You were right on target about me needing to get up off the couch and become more involved. Roy and I have been bowling on Mondays, coming to reading group on Wednesdays, doing water aerobics on Thursday mornings and going to the Village dances on Saturday nights. I have so much energy now I can't believe it."

Roy winks. "I'm having to double up on my vitamins just to keep up with the woman."

When they stop alongside us, Ellen takes my hand. "Thank you. I owe you so much."

I'm overcome by the gratitude I see in her eyes, as well as by the change in her. Ellen was lethargic and depressed only a few weeks ago when we first met. "You're welcome, Ellen. But you made the changes, not me."

Roy knocks on Oliver's apartment door. Someone inside calls, "Come in!" He releases Ellen's arm. "We'll leave the door open for you, CiCi," he says, his dentures whistling.

I glance inside.

Bill looks over my shoulder. "Notice anything unusual?"

In the past when I've attended Parkview functions, the women tend to gather on one side of the room, the men on the other. That isn't the case today. The scene inside Oliver's apartment looks more like a crowded cocktail party than a reading group. Couples talk and laugh together. Some hold hands.

"They're paired off," Bill says. "Almost all of them."

"Is that such a bad thing?" I try to sound self-assured, but inside I'm as conflicted as I've ever been.

"For the most part, yes," Bill says defensively. "But there is one bright spot in all of this. Sales of flowers, candy and condoms are up more than forty percent in the gift shop and store."

"Condoms?" I glance back at him. "You're joking."

"Nope."

"See? What are you worried about? They're practicing safe sex."

His brows lift. "The maintenance man said that before he interrupted Mrs. Binkley and Mr. McDougal in the gazebo, he heard her call him 'Captain.'"

I chew the inside of my cheek and try to look clueless. "So maybe Mr. McDougal was in the service."

"I've read the book, CiCi. I know all about Penelope and the captain. It's pretty steamy stuff."

Yeah, and I bet Bill enjoyed every sweaty word, but before

I can say so, commotion erupts inside the apartment, and someone yells, "Call 911!"

Bill and I push our way through the murmuring throng of people in the living room. They stare down at the center of the floor at something I can't see. I feel a hand on my arm and glance over to find Mother at my side.

"It's Frank Rayburn," she whispers, her face as white as the snowflakes dancing in the air outside Oliver's window.

"Everyone step aside, please," Bill yells.

The crowd parts, and I follow him to where Frank lies on the floor faceup. Mary Fran, a retired R.N., pumps Frank's chest and counts while Francis gives mouth-to-mouth.

Doris kneels at Frank's feet, her body trembling. "Not again. This can't happen to me twice." She looks up into my eyes. I take her hand and help her stand. "It isn't fair."

I ache for Doris. She should've guarded her heart after her husband died. But it's too late to tell her that now. Too late for Doris, but not for my mother.

Mother's eyes are closed, her palm pressed to her chest. I hope she learns a hard lesson from this terrifying moment. Nothing's worth the panic Doris feels right now.

In the distance, a siren's wail pierces the hushed winter day and suddenly, in my mind, I'm not holding Doris's hand, but Mother's, and instead of Frank on the floor, it's Dad. The past unfolds. Mother's desperate eyes, her cry, her body crumpling like a paper doll. And me completely helpless as something vital, something I'd convinced myself would last forever, slips through my fingers, and the world spirals out of control.

★ ★ ★

In the hospital Emergency waiting room, Mother and I sit on either side of Doris. Frank Rayburn's daughter, Sue Kiley, paces in front of us. Oozing dread from every pore, Bill Burdette sits in a corner and watches her.

It seems like hours before a young, female, frazzled-looking doctor walks in and takes Sue Kiley aside. They talk in quiet voices for a few minutes, then the doctor exits through the same door she came in while Sue gathers her purse and coat.

When Sue starts down the hallway after the doctor, Bill hurries behind her, calling her name. He catches up, stops her. I can't hear their conversation, only the sharp, angry tone of Sue Kiley's voice.

Doris excuses herself to join them and, after a bit of back and forth between her and Frank's daughter, she takes off with the woman.

I turn to Mother. "How are you doing?"

"One second you're laughing, the next your life changes. Just like that." She blinks at me. "I can't help thinking about your father. This brings it all back."

"I know."

"Poor Doris."

"She set herself up to get hurt again."

"By caring for Frank?" Mother frowns concern at me.

Tears burn the backs of my eyes; I don't know why I'm so emotional. Memories of Dad, I guess. "Frank Rayburn is close to eighty if he isn't already. Doris lost one man she loved. Why would she want to put herself through that again?"

"Oh, Sugar." She covers our joined hands with her free one. "That would be a miserable way to live. Not allowing yourself to care for anyone because you're afraid of getting hurt."

Bill saves me from a discussion I'd rather not begin by stopping in front of us and clearing his throat. I glance up at him, anxiety heavy in my chest. "Is Frank—?"

"Mr. Rayburn will be fine. He's awake and answering questions. It wasn't a heart attack. He just passed out."

"Thank God," Mother murmurs. For Doris's sake, she's stayed strong and calm, but now she starts to shake.

I wrap an arm around her shoulders. "You okay?"

She leans into me. "I am now."

I look up at Bill. "Why did he faint?"

"Apparently Frank's been taking one of those new drugs for…" He clears his throat again. "For sexual dysfunction and—"

"Oh…" Mother lifts a hand to her cheek.

"He didn't suffer one of those four-hour erection side effects the commercials talk about, did he?"

Mother blushes. "CiCi! For heaven's sake."

Bill looks at the floor.

I shrug. "I'm just asking. I'm guessing that could make a man pass out. You know, from lack of blood supply to the brain?"

"It wasn't that. Apparently he's on blood pressure meds, so he's not allowed to take anything for his…" Bill darts a glance at Mother. "His doctors won't prescribe anything for the dysfunction, so he borrowed some pills from a friend. The medication caused his blood pressure to drop. That's why he fainted."

I puff out my cheeks. "Wow. Not good."

"Sue Kiley is in full agreement with you on that point. She advised me to call Parkview's lawyer."

"As if you had anything to do with this." I shake my head. "Unbelievable."

Mother sighs. "Why is it people so often feel the need to cast blame?"

Bill scratches his head. "She advised that you call your attorney, too, CiCi."

"What?" I stand. "Why? What did I do?"

"She mentioned something about inciting irresponsible behavior among the members of the book group by exposing them to obscene reading material."

Mother gasps. "My word! *Penelope's Passion?*"

My head throbs. Lack of oxygen? From my waist-pinching control-top panty hose, perhaps? Maybe I'll pass out, too. Then I'll sue the panty hose manufacturer for inciting irresponsible flab constriction or something. Apparently a person can press charges for anything these days. "But I only have a divorce attorney. Robert Spinks. Ending marriages is all he does."

Mother pats my arm. "Don't worry, Sugar. This will blow over. You'll see."

"I wouldn't count on it," Bill says. "Sue Kiley's royally pissed." He sends Mother a sheepish glance. "Excuse my language, Mrs. Lamont."

"We'll ask your neighbor, Mrs. Stein." Mother talks fast, taking control of the situation since I can't seem to move or speak. "She'll know someone. She knows everybody."

I imagine my attorney-to-be, compliments of Mrs. Stein,

in gold neck chains, snakeskin boots and skintight black leather pants, with an extreme comb-over that flaps open to the side like a hinged door as he pounds the table and bellows, "I object!" Just what I need. A lawyer who's a combination of you-can-call-me-Hank, mama's boy Anthony and the balding Bar Mitzvah guy all wrapped up into one scary package.

I draw a long breath, blow it out slowly. "No thanks, Mother. I'll ask Robert. He'll refer me to someone."

At a quarter past five o'clock, I pull into Rod and Sally Coker's graveled driveway. The small ranch-style house sits on ten acres of land just outside of the city. I'm proud of myself for being only fifteen minutes late and just making one wrong turn. Finding the place was no easy feat for a directionally challenged person like me. I need landmarks, lefts and rights. As in, you'll pass a tan brick house before crossing a railroad track. Take a left at the first street after the dump yard. Instead, Rod Coker gave me, exit north on farm-to-market something or other. Go about three miles, then take the southwest fork in the road for another five or so.

In the back seat of my minivan, Max snuffles as he shifts around in his kennel. Most likely he fears he's headed for the vet and some poking and prodding, possibly even a stick in the rump with a sharp needle.

"Calm down, Max," I say over my shoulder as I turn off the ignition. "What are you griping about?" He doesn't have to worry about a lawsuit, Mother's romance or Erin's biker-boy.

Max rattles the metal door with his nose.

"You should thank me. You've got two weeks ahead of

nothing but sex and frolic in the country with the sinfully sumptuous Gertie, no strings attached."

He gives a plaintive cry.

"When it's over, you can just walk away. Never see her again. No child support. What a deal."

A blast of cold hits me as I step out of the car, open the back door, let Maxwell out of his kennel and leash him. Rod and Sally meet me in the yard. Both sixty-ish, he's as hard and calloused and stone-faced as she is soft and round and animated.

"You're here!" Sally stoops to welcome Max with a scratch to the snout. "Gertie's been waiting for you, big guy," she says in a baby-talk voice. "You two are going to make me some grand-puppies. Yes you are!"

Max makes a pitiful sound and looks up at me with irritated eyes.

Rod Coker shakes his head, lights a cigarette and grumbles something unintelligible.

His wife stands. "Oh, hush." She gently slaps a mittened hand against her husband's arm, her eyes on me. "Rod thinks bulldogs are worthless because they don't hunt or point or retrieve. I say there's value in being cute and lovable."

I nod and laugh.

Mr. Coker huffs and takes a deep drag of tobacco.

He strikes me as a man who appreciates a dollar as well as a diesel truck and a well-oiled gun, so I say, "The puppies should make you some money. Gertie's from a good line. So is Maxwell."

He blows out a stream of smoke. "That's the only reason I agreed to this."

Sally climbs the steps to the porch again and opens the screen door. "Gertie! Gertie girl! Maxwell's here."

The little black and white dog wiggles out onto the porch, then she and Sally come down into the yard.

Sally claps her hands together. "Why don't you take Max off the leash, Mrs. Dupree? Let them get reacquainted."

When the Cokers came to my house to check out Max, the two dogs got along well enough for the few minutes they were together, though Max didn't make any amorous moves. Of course, Gertie wasn't in heat then. I expect more aggression from him now.

I take off his leash.

Gertie steps toward Max.

I hold my breath.

Max cowers.

Gertie sniffs.

Max looks back at me, tilts his head, yelps.

Good grief. Some Don Juan. I smile at the Cokers and shrug. "It's his first time."

Sally giggles. "He's nervous."

Rod smirks and takes another drag. "What kind of stud dog gets performance anxiety?"

"Rod!" Sally cuts her gaze my direction. "Maybe he doesn't like an audience. Let's give them some space."

They follow me to the car. I get out Max's kennel, his water and food bowls, his favorite chew toy, which Rod eyes with undisguised scorn. Not a good idea, bringing the squeaky pink kitty, I realize, shooting a glance in Max's direction just in time to see him squat and water a sparse patch of snow.

Nice touch, Max. I hold my breath, hoping the Cokers won't turn around. Why can't he lift his leg? The big wuss. Doesn't he care that his reputation's at stake? Not to mention the stud fee?

I drop the kitty and the bowls, stalling for time. "Oops. Sorry to be so clumsy."

Sally picks up the toy. "How darling! Look, Rod."

He grunts, then pokes the half-smoked cig into the corner of his mouth and lifts the bowls from the ground. I take them from him, and Sally and I follow as he hauls the kennel onto the porch.

"Well, that's it, I guess." I whistle for Max. He prisses up onto the porch and sits at my feet. I stoop to look at him. "Mind your manners. Be good to Gertie."

As Rod mumbles his way down the steps and Sally coos for Gertie, I lean forward and whisper into Max's ear. "Prove Bert wrong, would you? Don't be a girly-dog. Show the world you can be as macho as the next guy."

He blinks at me then looks out into the yard where Gertie's humping Rod Coker's leg.

"Good gawd," the man snaps, shaking the dog off him.

Max lifts his gaze to mine. *This is the girl you've chosen for me?* his eyes seem to ask.

Poor dog. He doesn't want a date any more than I do. I'd call the whole thing off, but unfortunately this breeding thing isn't just a diversion anymore. If Sue Kiley really goes forward with a lawsuit, who knows what kind of legal fees I'll wrack up? The extra money will ease my mind.

I give Max a little shove to the rump. "Where's your sense of adventure, buddy? Go get her. You can do it."

But as I drive away and see Max in the rearview mirror, lying in the yard, his head between his paws, I'm not so sure he can.

I tell myself he'll warm up to her eventually.

Or maybe not. Maybe he needs a boost.

I could go back to the hospital and ask Mr. Rayburn the name of his Viagra connection. Better yet, I could read Max a few choice chapters of *Penelope's Passion*. Maybe the book will have the same effect on animals that it does on people.

The offices of Colby and Colby Attorneys are modest by Dallas standards. Robert Spinks, my divorce lawyer, assured me that the Colby brothers' lack of refinement in decor did not denote a lack of professional ability. According to Robert, Nathan Colby is the best, the one you want on your side if you end up in court. As I stand in the lobby staring at the empty chair behind the receptionist's desk and the dusty computer atop it, the big fish mounted on the wall, frozen midflop, I start to have serious doubts about Robert's judgment.

I slip out of my coat, fold it over one arm, then step closer to the entrance of the short adjoining hallway. There's an open door on the left. I see a long conference table inside surrounded by chairs. Farther down the hall is a second open door, across from it, a third.

"Hello?"

No answer. Rhythmic tapping drifts from door number two. Deep, throaty laughter from three, the squeak of a chair.

"Hello!" I call out, louder this time.

The laughter stops. A head pokes out of door number

three. Salt-and-pepper crew cut, wire-framed glasses. "Hey, there. I'm sorry." Nice smile. Sincere. A touch of small-town Texas in his drawl. "Be with you in a second. Let me end this call." The talking head disappears.

I take another step into the hallway, tap the sole of my snazzy new pumps against the carpet. My shoe fetish patient sold them to me at a drastic discount. They're perfect with my suit. I dressed up for the occasion. Or down, depending on your perspective. Nice and conservative. Serious professional. Don't want to look like the sort of loose, lecherous woman who'd lure old folks down the pathway to sin.

After a minute, the salt-and-pepper crew cut strolls out of his office, tightening his tie. "Sorry about that. Could I help you?"

"Are you Nathan Colby?" I hope so. His eyes are a sharp blue. Alert and intelligent.

"I'm Everett. Nate's brother. You here to see him?"

I glance at my watch. "I have an appointment at ten."

"Ah." He nods at door number two, beyond which the tapping ensues. "Follow me."

A man sits behind the desk, his back to the door, his boots propped and crossed on the credenza beneath the window he faces. The boots are scuffed hikers, not buffed cowboys like You-Can-Call-Me-Hank's. He wears jeans that look new, a pale blue dress shirt with sleeves rolled up to the elbows…and earphones. His fingers drum the flat surface of the laptop that's perched on his thighs.

Everett walks into the office and across to the edge of the desk. "Nate."

The man turns slightly, but the movement has nothing to

do with his brother's voice, which he obviously doesn't hear.
I see his face in profile. His eyes are closed. His head moves
along with the beat he drums on the laptop. Rubberneck-
ing, my dad would've called it. *"I can't get…"* he sings under
his breath, off-key.

"Nate!" Everett knocks on the desk. "Hello."

"…sa-tis-fac-tion…" tap, tap, tap *"no sa—"*

Everett pulls one earphone aside. *"Nate!"*

I expect a startled shout, boots falling from the credenza,
the laptop crashing to the floor. Instead, he simply opens one
eye. "Hey there, brother." The earphones come off. He yawns
and stretches then, easy and smooth, lowers his feet and
twists his chair around. "Well, now…" He nods at me. "Hello
there, ma'am."

A slow grin spreads across a long face carved in hard,
jutting angles. Only the grin is soft, full of sheepish charm,
a boy caught fishing when he should be in school.

Everett shakes his head and sighs as Nathan places the
laptop on one of the many paper stacks that clutter his desk.
"Your ten o'clock's here. Ms—?" He glances across at me.

"Dupree." I slip an arm from beneath my folded coat and
shake Everett's hand. "Cecilia."

"Glad to meet you, Cecilia." Everett nods at his brother who
walks around the desk to join us, tucking his shirt in. "Meet
Nathan." He cups a hand around the corner of his mouth and
whispers, "He thinks he's Mick Jagger. Humor him."

"Sorry I didn't hear you come in." Nathan Colby extends
his hand. "The place goes to pot when Jo's not here. Our
secretary. She's off on her honeymoon. Cancun."

I give the younger of the two men the once-over as I

shake his hand. His hair is longer than his brother's, over the ears and minus the salt. His drawl is lazier, deeper. No grooves at the corners of his eyes or mouth yet, only the hint of their approach. He doesn't wear glasses. No tie.

"I'll leave you to it," Everett says, heading for the door.

I want to yell, *Come back!* Robert made a mistake. He referred me to the wrong brother. He meant to say Everett, not Nathan. Middle-aged Everett of the professional attire and haircut. Fast-moving, professional Everett. Everett, whose appearance says "ambitious, savvy, mature." Everett of the wide gold band, third finger, left hand.

Nate's eyes are the same blue as Everett's and, surprisingly, as sharp, but the resemblance ends there.

He motions me into a chair then returns to his place behind the desk. "So… I read the papers Robert faxed over."

"I was served last week. Sue Kiley didn't waste any time. The media, either. There's already been a small article in the *Dallas Morning News.*" Uneasiness ruffles inside me, a premonition of danger ahead, an icy curve in the road. "At least my name wasn't mentioned." Yet.

He shuffles through a pile on the right corner of his desk, finds Robert's fax, glances over it. "Four plaintiffs. Looks like Miz Kiley isn't the only one who wants to sock it to you."

"Apparently there's no end to the number of people who want to blame me for their parents' resurrected hormones." I gesture at the paper. "I don't even know who two of them are."

Nate lays the fax on the desk. The chair squeaks as he leans back and laces his hands behind his head, elbows out. "You want to tell me what led up to this?"

I draw a deep breath and launch into the facts. Mother

and the reading group, the fall-off of attendance, the intro-
duction of *Penelope's Passion*. The sudden surge of amorous
incidents among Parkview's residents, the warning from
Doris Quinn's son and Frank Rayburn's daughter. Finally, I
finish with the Viagra incident and Frank's close call.

When I finish, Nate whistles. "That's quite a story." He
doesn't laugh, but his eyes do.

I sit straighter. "They don't have a case, right?"

"Of course they have a case." His expression becomes
more serious. Good move on his part since I refuse to hire
an attorney who considers my predicament a big joke. He
leans back farther, so far I'm afraid he might fall backward
through the window behind him. "Remember the restaurant
chain that got sued years back over serving the coffee too
hot?"

I nod. "McDonald's."

"They paid through the nose. It was all over the news."

"I remember."

"The right lawyer can make a case out of most anything.
I figure you know that."

I feel sick. I'm not sure if it's the bad news or the blue-
berry doughnut I ate in the car on the way over. "I guess I
was hoping you'd say it isn't so."

"It's so." The corner of his mouth curves up. "Sorry." He
lowers his hands from behind his head, lets the chair drop.
"The good news is, the right lawyer can also fight any case.
And with a little luck, win."

"Are you the right lawyer, Mr. Colby?"

"Nate." He grins that grin again, full of little boy charm.
"I think I am."

"And how are you in the luck department?"

"I get my fair share."

I bet you do.

He holds my gaze. "Of luck, that is."

Did the room just heat up by twenty degrees, or am I having my very first hot flash? The man's either flirting or trying to run me off. Must be the latter. What would a studly young lawyer like him want with a pastry-addicted, peri-menopausal girl like me? A girl who, at the moment, desperately needs to burp?

I fold my hands in my lap and force myself not to glance away from Nate's eyes. "I realize this case is a crap shoot, Mr. Colby."

"Nate."

"If you don't think it's worth your time, I understand."

"On the phone, you said the reading group is unanimously on your side? Even the parents of the people filing suit?"

"That's right. They feel that I'm not only being victimized, they are, too. They're eager to testify or give depositions or whatever else is needed."

"And they're all of sound mind, in your opinion?"

I start to answer in the affirmative, but then I think of our new member Paulie Perkins who blurts out his own lines of dialogue in response to Penelope's questions. And Nita Mae Newsome, who once in casual conversation, mentioned that she hadn't slept all night because she'd been worrying about what would happen to Penelope if the captain deserted her after the ship docked. I wince. "*Most* of the members are mentally sharp, yes."

"Well, I'd like to give it a go, then. It'll be a nice change from medical malpractice and car wrecks."

After a short discussion about fees and a payment plan, an awkward moment of silence follows. Awkward for me, anyway; Nate doesn't seem fazed. We stare across at each other. He smiles. I smile back and try to digest the doughnut in a quiet, ladylike manner. His eyes lower to my calves, and suddenly I wish I'd worn slimming, concealing black slacks instead of a beige skirt. I cross my legs, then wish I hadn't. Don't get me wrong, I'm flattered by his interest, but I feel like Sharon Stone in that infamous *Basic Instinct* scene where she's being interrogated. Not that the man would be turned on by my granny panties if he did see up my skirt, but still.... At least my shoes are good. Young shoes, not dowdy, not middle-aged like the panties.

Uncrossing my legs, I press my ankles together. Why does it matter what he thinks about the shoes? About my legs? The panties? My age? I lift my chin, glad there's no pimple on it today, mad at myself that I'm glad, that I even care. "So, what's next?"

"I have some documents to file. Lawsuits usually take their sweet time. I'll stay in touch, though. Let you know what's happening each step of the way."

He takes down my phone number, my address, a few other facts.

Sensing we're finished, I stand and slip on my coat, then reach beside the chair for my purse.

"Just out of curiosity," he asks, "what do you think about all these old folks getting cozy? From a therapist's view-point?"

"Seniors who engage in healthy sexual relationships tend to be happier and more active. They maintain better social skills. But I never encouraged their actions. I just read a novel to them. They made their own choices about their romantic relationships."

"And from a daughter's point of view? What if it were your mother involved in a relationship at this stage of her life?"

The question catches me off guard. "My mother's not alone." The words sound snappish, even to me. Opening my purse and avoiding his eyes, I dig inside for my keys. "She lives with my daughter and me. She has plenty of companionship, plenty to keep her busy."

I glance up, find humor again in his blue, blue eyes. I don't appreciate his amusement, don't like what it seems to imply. That I'm not fooling him. That he sees right through me. But what does he see? That I know what's best for my own mother? That I don't want her hurt again? That I can't stand seeing her with a man who isn't my dad?

I return my attention to my purse. *Where are those damn keys?* And where did that last thought come from? It's not that way at all. I'm not like the people suing me. I'm not thinking about me, I'm thinking about Mother. What if she begins to care too much for Oliver and ends up like Doris? Shattered, emotionally fragile, worried to death over the health of some old man? Or worse, what if she marries him?

From the corner of my eye I see Mr. Colby unfold his tall, rangy body from the chair. "Here they are," I say. The keys jingle as I reach across the desk to shake his hand. "Keep me informed."

"Sure thing. And don't worry."

"I'm not worried."

He tilts his head to the side, cocks a brow. "If that look on your face isn't worried I don't know what is." He glances at his watch. "We could grab an early lunch. You could ask me more questions. Ease your mind."

"It's eased, I assure you." He sees too much. If he didn't have Robert's endorsement, I'd change my mind about hiring him. I muster my most confident smile. To prove I'm not worried. To prove him wrong. Crazy, I know, since Nathan Colby's on my side. "Goodbye."

"Sure you won't join me for lunch?"

The burp escapes. *Classy, Cecilia. That'a way to make an impression.* Heat creeps up my face. "Thanks, but I'm not hungry."

"Obviously not." I can tell he's wrestling with a grin as he escorts me down the hallway. "I'll call you soon. In the meantime, don't you be putting ideas in any old geezers' minds. You might want to check out the Christian bookstore down on the next corner."

I open the door, then turn to glance back at him.

"I bet they sell romances." He loses the wrestling match. The grin wins. "The safe-sex kind. Kisses only."

Saturday morning, Erin, Mother and I head for the Galleria to finish our Christmas shopping. The mall is crammed with other procrastinators, all in a wild-eyed rush. Ah, the spirit of the season.

We agree to meet at one-thirty for lunch at a café on the upper floor of the mall, then Erin heads off in one direction, and Mother and I in another.

It's almost two before Erin, arms loaded with packages,

makes it to the café and goes through the line. Mother and I are already finished eating and are watching the mass of shoppers below.

"I found shoes to go with my concert dress." Taking another bite of roasted chicken, Erin pulls a box from beneath the table and removes the lid.

The shoes look painful, the heels high and spiked, the toes narrow. I'm crazy about them. For me, not her. I keep my mouth shut. I'm learning. It isn't easy.

"Very funky," I say, sipping my tea. "They're perfect."

Mother winces. "I'd hate to have to walk in them. There was a time I would've, though."

The concert's tomorrow afternoon. Erin's been in a good mood all day and yesterday, too. It's great to see her so enthused about something besides biker-boy. Not that I can complain too much about him. They don't really date much, he usually just comes over. A couple of times they've left with Suzanna and another kid in Suz's car. But they're always back early, before Erin's curfew.

"I can't wait to hear your solo," I say.

Erin picks at her food. "It's not really a solo. Just a short part of one piece where only I'm playing."

Mother takes off her glasses. "Hmmm. I thought that's what a solo was." She polishes the lenses with a handkerchief she pulls from her purse.

Erin shrugs. "Sort of, I guess."

I smile at her. "Well, I bet you'll do great. You've been practicing hard these past weeks."

Erin blushes and looks away.

"Well you *have* worked hard!" I've never known my

daughter to be so modest about her music. "Two and three nights a week is a lot. I feel like I've hardly seen you this month."

A kid with mohawked blue hair walks by. Nose ring. Tattoos by the dozen. He wears a T-shirt sporting a picture of some strung-out looking rocker on the front. "Thank God you're into orchestra instead of some punk band or something," I mutter under my breath. "I'm really proud of the choices you've made, honey."

I wait for Mother to back me up. She doesn't.

Erin picks at her chicken and doesn't look up.

Baffled, I set down my glass and lean back in my chair. "Are you excited about the concert or just ready to get it over with?"

She looks up and smiles. "I'm excited."

Good. Maybe she's through with the boy-crazy phase and ready to focus again on what's important. Her music. Her schoolwork. Scholarship applications.

"Noah's coming."

"What?"

"To the concert tomorrow. Noah's coming to hear me play."

"Oh." I sigh. So much for what's important.

"That's nice, Erin," Mother says. "I like him."

"You see too much of him," I say. Which isn't exactly true, but I can't help worrying about her having a steady boyfriend so young. "You should spend more time with girlfriends. Maybe see other boys from time to time."

Erin makes a face. "Don't start. A minute ago you said I was spending all my time practicing."

"It's just…." I fidget, desperate for the right words, words she'll hear. "You can't be too cautious when it comes to guys. How well do you even know him?"

"Well enough."

"What's his college major?"

She lifts her chin. "General Studies."

"General Studies isn't a major, it's a cop-out for someone with no direction, no ambition."

"He has ambition! He just took this year to decide what he wants to do."

"Which is?"

"Go to film school. He's applied for scholarships all over. He's waiting to hear."

She folds her arms and fidgets, as if she's upset, which makes me suspect that the scholarships are not to schools around here. I remind myself how it felt to be young and to care for someone, then watch them leave, and I feel a twinge of sympathy for her. But relief outweighs it.

Mother tucks her hanky back into her purse. "Noah seems to be a nice enough young man, Cecilia. He's very polite."

"So was Eddie Haskell and look at all he did when the grown-ups' backs were turned."

"Who is Eddie Haskell?" Erin asks.

"*Leave It To Beaver* Eddie? *'Good morning, Mrs. Cleaver.'*" I mimic in a sarcastic voice.

Mother laughs. "Oh, CiCi. You've become such a cynic. Why don't *you* spend some time with Noah when he comes over? Get to know him better. Maybe he'll surprise you. Maybe you'll like the boy."

My daughter beams at her Nana. "I bought him a Christmas present."

I cross my arms. "You didn't put it on my credit card, did you?"

She gives me the same irritated look that Maxwell did when I left him at Gertie's. "I paid for it."

"Where are you getting so much money all the sudden?" Erin blushes again.

Outside the door of the café, a girl calls her name.

Erin waves.

"You were awesome the other night!" the girl yells. "I can't wait—"

Erin knocks her soft drink to the floor as she pushes back her chair. Mother and I gasp, but the lid stays on. Erin leaves the cup where it fell and rushes over to the girl.

Watching the two of them talk, I pick up the cup. Erin keeps glancing over her shoulder at me. "Wonder what that's all about?"

"I wonder," Mother echoes. Something in her tone raises my suspicions that she just might know the answer, but isn't telling.

Erin's face is flushed when she returns to her chair.

"Who was she?" I ask.

"A girl from orchestra."

"I don't recognize her."

"She, um, plays violin. For some reason, she can't wait to hear my solo, either."

She picks up her fork, and pushes the food around on her plate.

"Okay, what's up?"

"Nothing's up." Erin pushes her plate to the center of the table.

Shifting my gaze, I say, "Mother? Do you know something?"

"Leave me out of this, Sugar. It's none of my business."

I narrow my eyes. Since when did she start butting out? "So…what were we talking about? Oh, the money for Noah's gift."

"You give me an allowance." Erin pulls the straw from her drink and starts chewing the end of it.

"And you always complain that it isn't enough to get by."

"So maybe I'm learning to budget. Just like you said I should."

Why am I so tense? She's old enough to be interested in a boy, to buy him a present. If I don't lighten up, I'll push her farther away from me. She's a normal teenaged girl.

Which answers my question of why I'm so tense.

Counting to ten, I relax my shoulders. "Well, that's good that you're budgeting. So, what did you get him?"

"I'd rather not say." She tosses the straw on her plate.

I can't help it; I scowl at her, make a noise of frustration.

Erin scowls right back at me. "You'll find out soon enough. I'd just rather Noah see it first, if it's okay with you."

And even if it isn't okay with me, her tone of voice implies.

"I wish you could come to the Parkview Christmas Pageant this evening and hear Oliver sing," Mother says. I know her well enough to recognize that she's trying to ease the tension by changing the subject.

"I wish I could too, Mother, but if Sue Kiley or any of the others suing me are there, it would be too awkward."

"I doubt they'll attend. I'm sure they feel the same way."

Erin looks at me slit-eyed, then shifts and smiles at her grandmother. "I'll be there, Nana."

Mother pats her hand. "That's sweet of you, Erin."

"Noah's going, too. He's taking me."

"Not on that cycle, he isn't." My shoulders tense up again. I push back my chair, gather the packages.

"*Whatever.* We'll take my car."

I stand. "I've had enough shopping for today. Let's go home. I need to call a plumber to come fix the disposal."

"Oliver said he'd fix it," Mother says as we start off in the direction of the mall's parking garage. "The leaky bathroom faucet, too." Without missing a beat, she changes the subject again. "If the two of you don't mind, I was considering inviting him to spend Christmas with us. Since Jack and Lydia and the kids will be here I'd like them to meet him."

My stomach dips. She wants the rest of the family to meet him? Not a good sign. I stop walking so abruptly that Erin and Mother almost run into me. People swarm around us. "Aren't you moving a little fast? Daddy's barely been gone a year."

Mother looks stricken, and I want to kick myself. Still, now that I've started, I can't seem to stop. "Where are *his* kids? Doesn't he want to spend the holiday with them?"

"His daughter lives in Colorado. She's an animal rights activist and a vegan. His son is a cattle rancher up in the Panhandle. As you might guess, they don't see eye-to-eye. The two haven't spoken in years. They rarely spend holidays with Oliver for fear the other will show up and make a scene."

"Sounds like a lovely family." One I have no desire to make part of mine.

"I like Oliver," Erin says. "I think we should invite him." They stare at me. Mother's eyes look hopeful, Erin's, rebellious. I'm outnumbered. "Whatever you want to do. The more the merrier, right Mother?"

Ho, ho, ho.

The Parkview pageant starts at six. Oliver picks Mother up early so they can practice. He tells her she's "as pretty as a Christmas package," then looks at her as if he'd like to unwrap her.

Just a friend? My foot. She's only fooling herself.

At five-twenty, Noah arrives on his cycle. Erin suggests they take her car, then rolls her eyes toward me. He acts as if he thinks the car is a good idea, which only irritates me more. I know an Eddie Haskell clone when I see one. Why can't he be difficult so Erin would understand why I don't trust him?

By five forty-five, I'm alone. Again. No Mother, no Erin, no Max. This isn't exactly the new beginning I envisioned when I received the divorce papers.

It's already dark out. I call every one of the Margarita Martyrs but only get machines. My friends have probably given up on me. I've been so preoccupied with work, Mother, Erin and now the lawsuit, that I haven't been in touch in a while.

I slip into my flannel pajama pants and a long-sleeved T-shirt, put a pair of wool socks on my feet. In the refrigerator I find leftover pasta salad, ham for sandwiches, nothing that appeals to me. I close the door and open the freezer. No more frozen dinners since Mom moved in. I reach for the carton of ice cream.

Out of nowhere, a vision of Nate Colby flashes before me. Amused blue eyes, one-sided smile, lazy drawl asking, *Finally hungry, ma'am? Or just using fat and sugar as a substitute for the good ol' roll in the hay you really need?*

Heat slaps my cheeks. I draw back my hand. Stupid of me to be irritated at the man. He's not even here. I only imagined him. It's me I should be mad at, for letting him get to me. Grabbing the carton, then a spoon from the drawer, I head for the den and my movie video collection.

Fifteen minutes into *Chocolat* and a quarter of the way through the carton of chocolate praline pecan, guilt gets the best of me. I should be at the pageant. When did I turn into such a wimp? I don't *want* to face any of the people who filed suit on me, but why should I hide? They're the ones being foolish, the ones who should lay low, not me. I'm supposed to be spending more time with Mother. And, honestly, I'd like to hear her on the piano accompanying Oliver's solo. And do I really want to miss The Frans' tap dance to *"Jingle Bell Rock"*? Jane Binkley's bell solo? Don Knotts as a reindeer, or Frank as Mr. Claus with Doris as his missus?

Tonight will probably be my last chance to see all the members of the reading group together. Unless, of course, the Parkview case goes to trial and they show up. Frank and Doris are moving out after the first of the year, thanks to their children. Frank's moving in with his daughter. Doris will lease an apartment at a new facility in Fort Worth, closer to her son. A few of the others are being forced to leave, too. And all because of a romance novel.

I sigh. No, not because of the novel; because of their kids' attitudes, their expectations about how people their age should behave.

I'll miss them. All of them. They've grown on me, become my friends. Something I never counted on when I started the reading group. Truth is, I considered them more of an imposition, a duty, than anything else.

Nathan Colby's question to me about Mother plays through my mind. I dig the spoon deeper into the carton, scooping out another bite of creamy, gooey comfort and denial.

I'm a therapist. I recognize my own shortcomings. Sure, I'd like to ignore or deny them, but right now I can't. When it comes to my mother and Oliver, my attitude and expectations are no different than those of the people suing me. I admit it. I also admit that their interest in one another is normal, natural, even healthy.

But she's *my mother.*

I allow myself one last bite. Dad could be a real pain in the butt sometimes, but I miss him. I want Mother to miss him, too. She was his yellow rose of Texas. The love of his life. He's not here to stand up for himself. Maybe that's why I feel that's my job now. Silly, I know.

Placing the lid on the carton, I check my watch. I'm missing the dinner, but the entertainment doesn't start until seven. If I hurry, I can make it.

Luckily I haven't taken off my makeup yet. I put on the black pantsuit I wished I'd worn to the law office, run a brush through my hair, grab a coat and head for the door.

Before I reach it, the phone rings.

"Ms. Dupree, it's Sally Coker."

"Oh, hi, Mrs. Coker." It's been a couple of days since we last talked. "Is Maxwell okay?"

"He—" She titters. "This is embarrassing, just a minute."

I hear muffled talking, like she has her hand over the mouthpiece, then, "This is Rod Coker." Gruff. Annoyed. "We're through with your dog. He can't get it up."

"Oh, I—"

"Or won't. I don't think he's interested."

"Maybe he—"

"Face it, lady. If your dog wore clothes, he'd be prancing around in purple sequins."

CHAPTER 15

To: Erin@friendmail.com
From: Noah@friendmail.com
Date: 12/18 Tuesday
Subject: news and other stuff
My Dearest Erin Elizabeth Dupree,
(i started out that way because it sounds more romantic.) i got the pics developed that i took at your grand-mother's Christmas pageant and at your concert. there's this one, and when i saw it, it was love at first sight. she has long brown hair, big brown eyes, a killer bod. you just wouldn't believe her. who would guess I'd fall in love with someone in the parlor of an old folks' home?

i finished my last final today. it went all right, i'm just glad to be done. when i got home a few minutes ago, there was a letter in the mail for me from Montana State University. they're giving me a scholarship if i transfer there in the fall. have I told you about that school? i visited last summer and it's awesome. you probably wouldn't think a state like Montana would have a great film school, but they do. a lot of celebrities have vacation homes around there. I heard Peter Fonda is an adjunct professor, or was at one time. anyway, they've filmed some great movies around there, too, like A River Runs Through It.

now for what I really want to say. the thing is, Erin, i'm excited and i'm not. i mean, this is my dream, but I don't want to leave you. MSU is something like almost 2000 miles from here. i'll miss you so much. but, I don't want to talk about this in an e-mail. i just wanted to tell you first, even before my parents. and the truth is, I was afraid to look in your eyes and say it in person.

change of subject. i wish you'd tell your mom about the band. you have to play with us at the beat on new year's eve, even if the gig isn't over until 3:00 a.m. we're only half-ass without you. Tonto and Reese feel the same. the crowd thinks you rock and so do we. but that's not the only reason i wish you'd tell your mom. i'm just afraid you're gonna get caught and then things will be really bad for you with her. and she'll like me even less. i'll talk to her with you. i'll tell her how i'd never let anything happen to you, that i don't let you out of my sight when we're at the club, and that i never would. if anything bad happened to you, i'd die.

call me after you eat dinner tonight, and i'll come bye. later, love noah

(p.s. don't worry—the girl in the picture was you, not that old lady who played the elf!)

I stare at the screen, too numb to move. Why? That's what I want to know. Why does life hand you something good, let it become important, then snatch it away?

A little zing of music announces an instant message. Suz's ID pops up on the screen.

Suzicue: you there?

Pinkflipflop: just got on.

Suzicue: what u doin?

Pinkflipflop: crying. noah e-mailed. said he fell in love with me at nana's pageant.

Suzicue: that's so sweet! why r u crying?
Pinkflipflop: he got a scholarship to msu. montana

Suzicue: ohmigod!

Pinkflipflop: yeah. he'll find someone else.

Suzicue: no worries. montana girls don't shave their legs or pits. they have to be hairy to stay warm.

Pinkflipflop: hahaha. now I'm laughing and crying.
Suzicue: they all have ugly toenails.
can't reach to paint em cuz of bulky fur parkas.

Pinkflipflop: whatever!

Suzicue: have the lowest teenage pregnancy rate in nation. guys don't want to do it in back seat of car for fear they'll freeze off u know whats.

Pinkflipflop: stop! stomach hurts!

Suzicue: k. i'll stop if u stop crying. he won't last a semester he'll miss you so much

Pinkflipflop: it's wrong for me to hope that.
should be happy for him.

Suzicue: maybe you should go to msu 2.

Pinkflipflop: ha! mom won't let me move across town.

Suzicue: can't imagine u with hairy pits anyway.

Pinkflipflop: i should just break up with him.

Suzicue: wow, you'd do that?

Pinkflipflop: it'll be easier to get it over with.
Suzicue: maybe. so what about the band?

Pinkflipflop: don't know. guess i'll have to quit.

Suzicue: not before new year's! u have to play.

Pinkflipflop: beat wants us too late. noah says come clean with mom. she'll never go for it. don't know how I lasted this long.

Suzicue: spend night at my house on new year's.

Pinkflipflop: what if she calls your mom?

Suzicue: parents will be at party till wee hours.

Pinkflipflop: what if she calls and nobody answers?

Suzicue: we'll think of something. cateye should dress retro with u in body paint and outfit we bought including katie's fake ta-tas. think of them as part of costume.

Pinkflipflop: whatever.

Somehow or another, Suz got the idea that she's the band's manager. We all play along. It makes her happy.

Suzicue: i'll do your makeup and hair. it'll be fun.

I seriously doubt it. Nothing sounds fun anymore. Makeup, hair and ta-tas are the least of my worries. Who cares? After New Year's Eve, I won't have Noah anymore. Nothing else matters.

Pinkflipflop: gotta feed max.

Suzicue: thought he was away making puppies?

Pinkflipflop: he couldn't do it.

Suzicue: do what?

Pinkflipflop: you know, IT.
Suzicue: shut up!

Pinkflipflop: seriously. dad cracked up when i told. said max is light in the loafers.

Suzicue: omigod! hehehehe. light on his paws u mean.

Pinkflipflop: hahaha. mom took max to vet.
he's depressed not gay. mom thinks he's upset about family stuff. u know dad leaving, nana moving in.

Suzicue: your mom's a therapist, can't she help him?
Pinkflipflop: says she didn't take doggie depression course. I think she's depressed 2. she's gorging on dessert like we're having a sugar shortage. some family, huh? dog needs therapy and so does mom the therapist. she only hangs out with old people, my dad only hangs with young bimbos. nana's lovesick and

Suzicue: nana's in luv?

Pinkflipflop: she's all flirty whenever Oliver's around moody when he leaves. weird seeing her with some 1 besides grandpop.

The truth is, though, I'm glad she's not hiding out anymore. Before she moved in with us, whenever Mom or I would talk to Nana and ask what she'd been up to, it was always reading, or watching TV or trying a new recipe. She never spent time with friends or went anywhere. Which must've been totally boring, if you ask me. Even for an old person.

Now it's Mom who's hiding. She's closed the door on life

outside of our house or her office. Like she's afraid of what might happen if she ventures out. Not that I want her to start dating or anything. As weird as it is to see Nana with someone besides Grandpop, it would be even weirder to see Mom with someone besides Dad. That's not really fair, though. Dad has a girlfriend. I guess Mom's allowed, too. She could at least do stuff with her friends. The Margarita Martyrs haven't even been around lately.

Suzicue: b glad your family's not boring like mine.

Pinkflipflop: nope they aren't that. max is howling now.

Suzicue: see u and sorry about noah.

Pinkflipflop: me 2.

CHAPTER 16

From The Desk of
Belle Lamont

Dear Harry,
Merry Christmas! Though I missed you, we had a wonderful day. Jack and Lydia and the kids are here. It's so good to see them. We don't do so nearly enough since they moved. The children have grown. Except for the earrings, nose stud and tattoo, Jack junior looks just like you.

You won't believe the news! Cecilia's being sued over that book I told you about. Can you imagine? What a big ol' silly mess. She doesn't know it, but the entire reading group has been meeting here during the day while she's at work. We're putting our heads together to come up with ideas to help her case, or at least help pay her legal fees. Doris and Frank, whose children are lead plaintiffs in the suit, suggested everyone finagle money from their kids in the name of charity, then give it to CiCi for her defense. That would serve them right. Ellen Miles suggested a bake sale, as well. And The Frans are getting together a petition. More ideas are in the works. I'll keep you informed.

Oh, Harry…another year over, a new one ahead. That and a dear friend's near-death Viagra accident have me thinking about my life. If I could've stopped time in one place and lived there forever, when would I choose? The summers of my childhood? How good it would be to see Momma and Daddy again. To run through the fields on our farm with my Callie, Will and Claire, my legs lean and strong, baked brown by the sun. No worries to speak of. I'd always feel safe, knowing my parents were there to take care of me.

But then there'd be no you, no Jack or Cecilia. So maybe I'd choose when our children were little, before they started school, when we lived in our tiny white house on the corner of Tenth and Vine. The one with the faulty plumbing that always made the bathroom smell like rotten eggs, and that clanky furnace we decided only worked on odd-numbered days of the month.

I often recall the winter it snowed past the windows and you made that sled out of an apple crate and old skis. We bundled the kids up and took them to the steepest hill in the park, then all piled on and rode it down, again and again, until one ski fell off and everyone toppled over. Cecilia got a mouthful of snow and cried so hard her eyes swelled. You and Jack teased her so mercilessly that she rode it again just to prove she wasn't afraid.

I could've clobbered you, Harry. Sometimes you were too hard on her. Trying to toughen her up, you'd tell me. Well, she's tough now, Harry. You succeeded. She's tough on herself and everyone around her at times. She won't admit that she's hurting or reach out to me or anyone else for a shoulder to cry on. I tell myself that she'll get over this and show her soft side again. She always forgave you, didn't she?

I'm sorry. I don't mean to cast blame. You were a good father, you just expected so much. Still, despite your mule headedness, rotten egg smells and a clanky furnace, our children's early years were a happy part of my life. I was content. We'd waited an eternity, it seemed, to finally be blessed with children, and after it happened, I never took that blessing for granted. Even with the stress of more bills than money, hectic days of stubbed toes and runny noses and no social life, I could stay in that time forever and be satisfied.

But then I'd miss seeing our children grow up, all the times they'd struggle over something and succeed, the fun of having teenagers in and out of the house at all hours of the day and night, all of them laughing and so full of life. Of course, I haven't forgotten that it wasn't always fun and excitement. We had plenty of sleepless nights. Worry. Tears. Even disaster. But I wouldn't have traded it. Just as I wouldn't trade our years together after we'd raised them. Alone again, just the two of us. Rediscovering each other. Traveling. Grandchildren.

So I suppose it wouldn't do to stop time. Each stage had joy and heartache and so many surprises. I love every memory, though I admit that, while we were making those memories, there were moments I wanted to run away and leave no forwarding address.

When you died, Harry, I thought that time had stopped for me, too. Stopped in a place I didn't want to be. A place of no joy, no more surprises, only heartache. But I was wrong. Tonight I discovered that, if I allow it to be so, even this stage of my life can be rich and full.

Oliver kissed me. Remember, I told you about him? Oliver the old fart, as CiCi calls him? Well, the old fart kissed me, and it was wonderful.

So, there you have it. Maybe I'm wrong to tell you, but that's that.

I'm so torn. Happy and ashamed. Thrilled and guilt-ridden. Most of all, angry. Angry at you for making me feel so confused. I tell myself that if our destinies were reversed, if I were gone and you were here, I'd want you to keep making memories, not just exist on the ones from the past. Just because a person is old and widowed, why should they be expected to sit on the sidelines, only existing, not living. Why, Harry? Tell me. Is that what you want for me? If not, then why do I feel I am betraying you by caring for Oliver?

I want one last gift from you. A sign. Something to assure me you understand and accept whatever I decide to do with the rest of my life.

I love you, my husband. Ornery as you sometimes were, I always did, and I always will. Caring for someone else, too, will not change that.

As always, your yellow rose,
Belle

CHAPTER 17

Cecilia Dupree
Day Planner
Friday, 01/5

1. 9:00 a.m.—First Weight Wackers meeting.
2. 10:30—patient follow-up/Roger & Cindy Hoyt.
3. 1:30—1st meeting w/Smythe's teenaged daughter, Halee (drug problem).

At noon, I close the Hoyt's file, remove my reading glasses, and head for the fridge in the office kitchen for my fat-free, sugar-free, carb-free, taste-free shake, compliments of my new Weight Wackers diet plan. I'm popping the top on the can when Willa, my secretary, steps in, her purse over her shoulder.

"Sure you don't want to grab a burger with me?"

"Why would I want juicy beef, hot melted swiss and crispy fried potatoes when I can have this?" I lift the can.

"Bless your heart. Tried that one. Lost five pounds, gained back eight." Willa, who I would swear purposely gains weight so she can test each new fad diet that comes along, eyes me with sympathy. "New Year's resolution?"

I nod and point at my butt. "I'm tired of looking like a pear."

She scowls. "Girl, don't give me that. You're tiny."

"Okay, so I'm a tiny pear. A pear's still a pear. Small at the top, bigger at the bottom."

She shakes her head. "All right, then. Enjoy."

I take a sip. "Yum."

Back at my desk, the Hoyt file beckons. They're making progress. Roger fired his secretary, Bitsy or Bootsy or Betsy, whatever her name is. Cindy takes classes to sell real estate now, so her entire world no longer revolves around her husband. They claim I've helped them save their marriage. If that's true, I'm glad. Still, I wonder why I couldn't save my own marriage.

The phone rings. Since Willa's gone to lunch, I pick it up. "Cecilia Dupree."

"CiCi, it's Bill Burdette over at Parkview. Do you have a television in your office?"

"A TV? Sure. Why?"

"Turn it on to *The Scoop*."

"What's up?"

"Just do it."

I start to inform him that I don't take orders from anyone, least of all him, but curiosity gets the best of me. With the cordless phone pressed to my ear, I walk to the entertainment center across from my desk. "You don't strike me as someone who'd watch tabloid TV, Bill."

"I don't. My secretary does. She said they mentioned something about the case."

"Our case?" Opening the cabinet doors, I flip the television on.

"Yep. After the commercial they're supposed to—shhh. Here…it's on again."

A perky blonde wearing too much makeup appears on screen. "And now the stories our reporters are hard at work on to bring to you in the weeks ahead. First, from deep in the heart of Texas, we have reporter Steven Motley with news of a retirement village sex scandal. Steve—"

The scene shifts. Dread sucks the air from my lungs. A shivering man holds a microphone. He stands beside the sign at the entrance to the Parkview Manor grounds. Cars whiz past on the highway beside him.

"Son of a bitch," Bill hisses.

"Hi, Mary Ann," the reporter says into the microphone, "Recently I spoke with Dale Renfro, a prior Parkview Manor employee…"

"Son of a bitch!" Bill explodes. "That asshole."

"Who is he?"

"Our maintenance guy. He quit two weeks ago."

"…an eighty-year-old gentleman ended up in the hospital," the reporter continues. "According to Mr. Renfro, this Dallas retirement community became a haven for hanky-panky after the facility brought in Dallas therapist Cecilia Dupree to host group readings of sexually explicit material to the senior citizens residing here."

"We'll definitely look forward to more on that," the blonde says with a wink, a chuckle and a rise of her brows. "And now over to Lyle Peters in Minnesota who's covering—"

I switch off the TV, close my eyes, clasp one hand over my mouth.

"No wonder that slimy weasel quit." Bill has murder in his voice. "I'd bet my last dollar he's selling this story. There's no telling who the bastard's talked to."

I lower my hand. "What do we do?"

"Watch our backs and screen calls. The media will be after us next. Get ready."

In the pit of my stomach, the diet shake starts to gurgle. I sit on the edge of my desk. "You really think so?"

"Count on it. I've already had one call. The guy wanted to film a seniors-gone-wild video here at the Village."

Not so long ago, I might've laughed at the prospect of such a movie. Not today.

Bill and I promise to keep one another informed if the vultures start circling, then say our goodbyes.

I decide to call Nathan Colby about all this. It's been more than a couple of weeks since we've spoken. Before I can look up his number, the phone rings again.

"Cecilia Dupree."

"Hey."

"Bert?"

"Yeah. I was afraid you might be at lunch."

I glance at my half-finished shake. "I am."

"Sorry to interrupt. I wanted to talk to you before I call Erin."

"Is something wrong?"

"No, everything's great. Fantastic, actually. I'm getting married."

"Oh." I deflate like a punctured bicycle tire. Lovestruck.

That's how he sounds. Like a man who's head over heels. I remember when he sounded that way about me. About us. I remember how sweet he looked and the guilt I felt because I didn't share his feelings, and because he didn't even realize it yet. "Wow. Congratulations."

His laugh is self-conscious. "Thanks. Her name is Natalie."

The college coed and coffee-shop counter girl. "The redhead."

Irritation creeps into his voice. "No, not the redhead. Erin's met Natalie. They seemed to get along."

Right. Like a cat and a canary. "Erin told me about her." How old did she say? Twenty-four? Twenty-five? How nice. The older sister our daughter's always wanted. They can have pillow fights. Trade clothes. Paint each others toenails. "I hope you're both very happy. I wish you the best." And I should, I guess. Wish him the best, that is. I really do hope this time his bride marries him for the right reasons and will love him from the start, not wait until it's too late.

"We'll be moving to Amarillo."

"Oh." Another puncture. "Why Amarillo?"

"The coffee shop where Natalie works? They're branching out. They've offered her the management position. And since I can work anywhere…"

"I see."

Silence. Then, "CiCi, I just, well, I want you to know—"

"You don't have to explain—"

"I regret a lot of things."

A sigh seeps past my lips. "I know that, Bert. So do I."

"I made mistakes, and I wish…I want you to know that I did love you."

"Don't, Bert. Please."

He coughs. "I just wonder…" Another cough. "How do you think Erin will take the news?"

"I guess you'll find out soon enough."

"I don't want to upset her."

Since when did our daughter's feelings become a priority to him? Not when he came on to our cute, young neighbor. Not when he so easily gave up on our family and marriage, or when he stopped calling Erin more than every other week or so. "She's dealt with worse and survived, Bert. She'll survive this, too."

And so will I.

I continue to try to reach my attorney, but only get a machine.

Work is my salvation, a fact my one-thirty appointment backs up. Sixteen-year-old Halee Smythe's drug experimentation takes my mind off *The Scoop* segment and makes all my other problems seem insignificant in comparison. At least for a while.

At four-thirty, I show up at the attorney's office unannounced, hoping Nate can work me in. I want to hear his take on the television segment. Surely the negative publicity will hurt the case. Or maybe I'm just the pessimist Bert often accused me of being.

Inside Colby and Colby, I go through the same routine as before.

"Hello?"

This time, Nate comes out into the hallway instead of his brother. He wears a suit, and wears it well. Hormones that have been missing in action for so long I'd thought them dead, show up waving flags.

"Well, hi there," Nate says. His eyes are tired, his smile is anything but. Lazy, yes, but in a flirtatious way. Could that be true? Could it be possible he's flirting with me? That he really was the last time I was here, too? Silly or not, I'm flattered to think it might be possible.

He blows out a work-weary breath as he runs a hand through his hair.

I catch myself wanting to do the same thing; run my fingers through his too long, wavy brown hair, to feel the heat of his scalp on my skin. To just touch him, period. How long has it been since I've touched a man? Since a man touched me? Going without has caught up to me, I guess. Here's this virtual stranger, and just because he's all male, just because his eyes seem filled with promises of forbidden fun, because his arms look strong and inviting, I have this overwhelming urge to throw myself into them.

Shocked, I step back. "I hope you don't mind, I, um…" Oh, God. I burst into tears.

He frowns, then moves toward me.

Turning my head away, I raise a hand to stop him. "I'm sorry. I don't even know why I'm crying." Which is true. The lawsuit and sudden publicity? Bert's engagement to a blushing debutante? Mother and Erin moving on without me? That I haven't had sex in so long I could probably classify as a virgin again? Maybe all of the above. I should be ashamed, I know. At least I don't have a child in crisis. At least I have work I love. A good book to curl up with at night.

I cry harder.

Finally, I shudder and sniff. "I'll quit. I promise. Just give me a second."

"Don't worry about it. I'm used to tears. I have three sisters. When I was growing up, we had more crying jags around our house than a hospital nursery."

Sputtering a laugh, I look up at him.

He nods toward his office and I follow him in. From a CD player on Nate's credenza, Led Zeppelin sings about climbing a stairway to Heaven. I imagine that's what sex with him would be like. Climbing straight to Heaven.

Oh, help. My knees are shaking.

Nate turns off the music then hands a box of tissues to me as I slink into a chair. I take one and blow so hard into it my nose honks, which should probably embarrass me, but the man's already heard me burp, so what the heck? Miss Manners I'm not, and he knows it.

Facing me, he leans against the desk, crosses one ankle over the other, loosens his tie, then takes it off. "Tough day?"

Shaking my head "yes," I honk again into the tissue.

"I can relate." His eyes are kind. No more mocking glint, no hint of salacious thoughts. Damn, I blew it. Probably a good thing.

"You too, huh?" I dab my wet cheeks.

Nate lets out a long breath. "Missed my morning racquet-ball game 'cause I had to be in court."

"Wow, that is tough." I don't even attempt to keep the sarcasm out of my voice.

He points over his shoulder at his desk, which is even messier than the last time I saw it. "Jo's gonna have my hide when she gets back from maternity leave and sees all this."

"Maternity leave? I thought she was on her honeymoon just before Christmas?"

"She was. The baby came early."

"I'll say."

"The kid couldn't have had worse timing. Everett and I are swamped."

I tilt my head. "*You're* not about to start bawling, are you?"

"Not unless it'd make you feel better."

I laugh, and my tension melts like wax beneath a flame.

For a minute, he doesn't say anything, just squints and studies me. "So, you wanna tell me what stirred up those tears?"

"The part you can help me with, yes. The rest I'll have to work out myself."

As I fill him in on the *Scoop* segment, he reaches for a fishing fly rod that's propped against his computer and winds the reel, listening. "Sure didn't take 'em as long as I thought."

"You expected this?"

"I figured the national media might catch wind of the story. A sex scandal in an old folks' home is too good to pass up."

"Please. It isn't a sex scandal."

"They'll make it into one, I can pretty much promise you that." He starts to work on a knot in the fishing line. "Sex stories make for good ratings, and this one has an interesting twist."

"The publicity's going to hurt the case, isn't it?"

"Maybe, maybe not. Guess we'll just have to wait and see about that. Either way, we'll deal with it."

"How? Bill seems to think reporters will be breaking down our doors soon."

"Well, ma'am…" Nate props the fishing pole against the

wall. "You just give 'em your best smile and say your attorney advised you not to talk about the case. I'll be the bad boy."

I'd *love* him to be the bad boy. Bad with me. Very, very bad. Pathetic? Maybe, but that's what I think when I look into his eyes and his mouth quirks up at one corner. I just wish he wouldn't call me ma'am. Ma'am is a middle-aged woman, which to him I guess I am. I peg him at thirty-one, thirty-two at the most. A decade behind me. Who do I think I am? Demi Moore? Obviously I'm reading too much into the way he looks at me. He could be my younger brother. My very sexy, very much younger brother. Problem is, my body's reacting to him in a way that's not the least bit sisterly.

My cell phone rings, fizzling all fantasies. I see that it's mother, and excuse myself to answer the call.

"Hi, Sugar. Oliver called this morning and said everyone's worried about you. So I invited some of the reading group members to dinner tonight. Can you make it home by six-thirty?"

I glance at my watch. "Sure. I'm just about to leave the attorney's office."

"Oh, good. Invite Mr. Colby. It would be the perfect time for him to meet us and us him."

I cut my gaze toward Nate. "I don't know if that's a good idea," I say, my voice low.

"Why not? I made my special pot roast."

I chew my lip a moment, then lower the phone. "How do you feel about pot roast?" I ask Nate.

Nate's crazy about pot roast. Carrots, too. And potatoes and brown gravy and homemade rolls. All of which Mother spent the afternoon preparing and none of which is allowed on my Weight Wackers diet plan. Since, with this group, anything's up for discussion, and I don't especially want my extra pounds to end up the topic of the night, I nibble Mother's meal rather than eat the prepackaged food I bought this morning.

Erin nibbles, too. Pushes her food around with her fork and offers a polite response whenever someone addresses her. After about fifteen minutes, she excuses herself, takes her plate to the kitchen, lets Max in, then heads off with him toward her bedroom. Which isn't unusual. What worries me are her downcast eyes, her pinched voice and drawn-in posture. Bert must've called and told her his news. I'll talk to her after everyone leaves.

Iris Shelby, now Mrs. Herbert O'Dell, refills her plate for the second time. Her generously padded physique reminds me of my own grandmother, her cushiony hugs, how good it felt to snuggle against the pillow of her bosom and listen to her read to me when I was a kid. Food obviously isn't Iris's only passion. After a month of marriage, she still looks at Herbert with moon eyes.

Nate lifts the breadbasket and offers it to her. "What brought you to Parkview Manor, Iris?"

She takes the basket from him. "I lost my first husband four years ago. We owned a home, and I had a mind to stay in it since the mortgage was paid up." With great care, Iris butters a roll. "For close to a year, I puttered around in that big ol' house. I wasn't scared by myself, just lonely."

Nate nods his understanding. "So you moved."

"It took a peeping Tom to get me to budge."

Jane Binkley's eyes light up, then narrow. *"Really…"* She leans forward. "Why don't I ever get the good calls?"

Mother flattens a palm to her chest. "My heavens, Iris, you must've been scared out of your wits."

"Scared and shocked silly." Iris dips her roll into her potatoes and gravy. "I was climbing into bed one night when the phone rings and this deep quiet voice says, 'I've been watching you. I've seen you naked in the shower.'"

"Bastard," Mary Fran mutters.

Francis snorts and nods.

"Mercy," Stan McDougal says, his eyes lighting up as he exchanges a suggestive look with Jane.

"Wow, Iris," I say. "I can't imagine."

"Neither could I." Iris's brows arch. "He saw me naked and he still wanted to call? When I asked him that, the sucker hung right up."

Silence drapes the table. Then I snicker and Nate starts laughing.

When Iris tilts her head back and joins us, the veil lifts and everyone else laughs, too.

Iris looks pleased with herself. "Well, I got a little spooked, I guess. The very next day I started looking for a retirement community. A place where I'd be surrounded by people in my same situation. A place without a window in the bathroom." She turns to her new husband. "And then I met Herbert."

As he lifts her hand and kisses it, Herbert's puppy dog eyes smile back at his wife. I notice they don't look so sad anymore. "Took me a while to get up my nerve to ask Iris out. CiCi's reading group helped break the ice."

Nate leans back and squints at Herbert. "How so?"

"See, I'd never thought to join because it just seemed so high-brow and boring, folks sitting around shooting the breeze about made-up stories. Then that old boy over there," he nods and grins at Oliver, "he tells me about this new book the group's ready to start. *Penelope's Passion.*" Herbert slaps his thigh and wiggles his brow. "Hey, now! This sounds more up my alley. A little adventure, a little hoochie-koochie. When I find out Iris is in the group, that cinches it for me. I talked to CiCi one afternoon after we adjourned. Told her about my worries. She called me later that night to continue the conversation and set my mind right. The rest is history."

Recalling that conversation, I feel proud, despite myself. Herbert was so nervous, so insecure and unsure, so lonely. Look at him now. Happy. In love. Confident. If I had a part in making that happen, I'm thrilled. And confused. Why wouldn't I want those same things for my mother?

Smiling at me, Nate lifts his glass. "A toast to Iris and Herbert." Iced-tea glasses and coffee cups come together above the center of the table. "And to living life to the fullest."

I sense Nate's eyes still on me, but I'm too busy watching Mother and Oliver to return his look. Their fingers brush, and they stare at one another with such tenderness my heartbeat speeds up and all the muscles in my body spring to attention, on alert for impending disaster.

"And to CiCi and *Penelope's Passion,*" Stanley McDougal booms, his deep voice at odds with his scrawny, stoop-shouldered body.

"Here, here!" the group cheers in unison.

My gaze stays glued to Mother and Oliver. Their gazes stay glued to each other.

The party breaks up soon after the peach pie is served. (I allow myself one bite. No ice cream.) I walk Nate out to his car, an old white Porsche, obviously restored by loving hands. After a glance in the window, I look up at him. "Wow. You're full of surprises. I expected you'd drive a SUV." Or ride a white stallion.

"You like it?"

"Yeah, I do." I skim my palm across the glossy paint. "The old ones are classy, aren't they?"

"The very definition of class," Nate answers when Stanley McDougal toots his horn and pulls his truck out of the driveway with Jane sitting next to him, center seat.

I realize Nate's not only referring to the Porsche, and I like him all the more because of it.

"You think I should call Bill Burdette and tell him to guard the gazebo?"

Nate chuckles. "That's quite a group of friends you've got there."

Watching Stanley's taillights shrink into the darkness, I shiver and smile. "I started out thinking I was doing something to help them stave off boredom and stay active, but it ended up the other way around. They're the highlight of my week. Or were. We don't meet anymore."

"I think you did more for them than you realize. It's clear they're all a lot happier since they got together. And better off. They seem pretty darn grateful to you for giving them the nudge they needed to go after what they wanted in the first place."

"You mean a little hoochie-koochie, as Herbert said?"

Nate's laugh is uninhibited. Just hearing it makes me feel good all over. "He makes sense, CiCi. By starting that reading group and bringing a book they could actually have fun with, you helped break the ice. It got 'em to really talking instead of just saying 'hi' in the hallways. That's a good thing."

"Please tell me you can convince a jury of that."

"You worry too much."

"And I'm starting to think you don't worry at all. About anything."

He shrugs. "Why waste the energy? It won't affect the outcome. Only action'll do that." With a jerk of his head, he motions me toward the car. "Come on, I'll take you for a ride."

I bite my lower lip, hug myself, glance over my shoulder at the house. "I'd better not."

"What? Afraid I'll go too fast for you?"

Terrified, I think, sensing we're talking about more than a drive in his car. But I don't want to admit I'm chicken, so I drop my arms and stand straighter, my pulse thumping loud in my ears. "Me? No way. Speed's my middle name."

"Okay, then." He reaches out a hand to me. "Let's hit the road."

When Nate drops me home again, Oliver's restored Studebaker still occupies the driveway. I feel too good to stew about it.

Nate did drive too fast. We went out of the city to a stretch of back road seldom traveled, then he cut loose.

For once, so did I.

The chilled wind blew out all the tension I've stored up

inside of me these past months and carried it away through the car's open windows. (Nate insisted we keep them down, despite the weather.)

Invigorated, I step from the Porsche and lean down to look at Nate through the window. "Thanks. That was fun. Freezing, but fun."

He tips a nonexistent hat. "My pleasure, Speed. See you at my office next Friday at five."

"Did we schedule an appointment?"

"Don't tell me you forgot already."

"Refresh my memory. Why are we meeting?"

"I'll think of some reason before then." He winks and takes off, leaving me standing in the cold looking after him. And laughing, which is such a relief.

Now, as I enter the house, Mother's delighted shrieks drift to me from the kitchen. Oliver is singing, if you can call it that. It's a rap tune, I think. I listen closer. Truth is, he's not half-bad.

I walk through the dark living room to the kitchen door and peek in. His arms are out in front of him forming a circle, holding an invisible partner, and his hips grind slowly left then right then forward to the beat of the song.

My mouth drops open.

Across the room, Mother is doubled over, clasping her stomach. "Ollie! Quit! That's terrible."

The singing stops. The dancing doesn't. "This is how the youngsters do it, Belle. See? Dirty dancing, they call it. I've been paying attention. I've got it down." He does a shuffle across the tile floor and grabs her. "Here, I'll show you."

Oh, no you don't, old fool. I start to barge in and interrupt them, then stop when his hands settle at her waist and she raises her arms to encircle his neck. Mother's laughter quiets and they sway gently; she smiles up at him, he smiles down. Such intimacy in the look they share, so much revealed in their sudden stretch of silence.

My eyes fill; so does my heart. With tangled emotions I can't unravel. I press one hand to my chest, step backward into the darkness of the living room where they can't see me.

Beneath my palm, the beat of my heart slowly steadies.

What's happening to my mother is a miracle...a gift. Difficult as it is for me to see her with another man, I know that Oliver is good for her. I know and, for the first time, feel a bittersweet twinge of pure joy for my mother.

Not long ago, I watched her heart break.

Now I'm watching it mend.

CHAPTER 18

To: Erin@friendmail.com
From: Noah@friendmail.com
Date: Friday 01/05
Subject: us

Erin,

why won't you answer my calls? i know you have caller id on your cell. would you listen to me? what you said last night about me finding someone else when i go away to school is bullshit. and it will piss me off if you think i will because i am not even interested in anyone else but you. OK? OK! and that is final. i love you and only you. it will be hard being apart, but we can last. i don't care what anybody says. we're not 'most people.'

i'm wearing the necklace you gave me for Christmas. i sleep in it and shower in it and everything. if you don't talk to me soon, i'll go crazy. i don't think i can stand it. new year's eve was the best night of my life. i love you so much erin. i need a kiss from you, to know you're ok. call me. i love you, noah

When my bedroom door creaks open, I close my eyes and pretend I'm asleep. I knew I should've locked it. Mom still thinks I'm twelve, that if the door's not locked, she can just walk in without knocking.

I smell her perfume; the same scent she's worn always. Not too flowery or exotic or mysterious. Sort of crisp and fresh and no-nonsense. Like her. It makes me remember a thousand hugs, days of playing dress-up when I was little. Mom would let me wear her shoes, her perfume, her jewelry. She'd fix my hair and make up my face.

The bed shifts from her weight as she settles beside me. Her fingers brush hair from my cheek, which is wet from about a million tears.

"Erin?"

A sob shudders out of me. My shoulders shake.

"Sweetie, what's wrong?" She strokes my head.

I open my eyes, roll onto my back and scoot up in the bed. I open my arms and so does she. For a long time, she holds me and lets me cry. We don't say anything, just rock back and forth.

"I'm so sorry, Erin."

"You knew?"

"Yes."

"How?"

"He called me this afternoon."

Leaning back and wiping my eyes, I frown at her. I can't believe Noah would call Mom about our breakup. "What did he say?"

"That he didn't want you to be upset."

I kick off the covers and climb out of bed. "Well, what

did he expect? I mean, I'm happy for him and everything. It's just—" I sob. "I'll miss him so much."

"Oh, Sweetie. This isn't going to change the way he feels about you. You can still see him. You can go visit whenever you want."

What? I stop pacing and stare at her. This must be a dream. "You wouldn't freak out?"

Mom looks confused. "Why would I freak out? I understand that you need to spend time with him. You love him and he loves you. I know that. I wouldn't want it any other way."

Wow. I am totally not believing this. Is my mother on drugs, or what? "Thanks, Mom. You're awesome." I circle the bed, sit and throw my arms around her neck. "Thanks for understanding. I didn't even think you liked Noah."

"Noah?" She breaks free of my hug.

"Yeah. I'm surprised you'd let me go see him without throwing a fit." I laugh. "Not that I'm complaining. I mean, it's about time. I *am* almost eighteen."

"Erin…what are you talking about?"

"Visiting Noah in Montana. What are *you* talking about?"

"Montana?"

"When he goes away to school there in the fall. I thought you said he called?"

Mom places a hand across her forehead and pinches her temples. "Shit."

"*Mom*. What is going on?" I knew this was too easy, too surreal. She was being way too nice.

"I was talking about your father, Erin. You visiting him and Natalie after they get married and move to Amarillo."

"Dad's marrying Natalie and moving?" She nods and I

burst into tears again. I pick up a pillow and throw it across the room. *"Fuck."*

"Erin! That sort of language won't help anything."

Never mind that she just said "shit." I pick up the other pillow and throw it, too. "You don't know how it feels. You had your dad your whole life. He acted like a real father. Not some stupid—" The words choke me. I bite my lip, lower my chin to my chest and stare at the mattress as tears roll down my cheeks.

"Maybe not. But I do know how it feels to love someone and have them leave." She dips her head down to see my face. "Noah got one of those scholarships, didn't he?"

I nod. "But it's different than you and Dad. I mean, we're young." Right after the stupid words leave my mouth, I wish I hadn't said them. I know how much the divorce hurt her.

"Believe it or not, Erin, I was young once, too, and in love with someone other than your dad. He left. And it hurt so much I thought I'd die. I still remember how that feels."

I can't believe what I'm hearing, or how sad Mom sounds for me.

She lifts my chin and wipes at my cheeks with her fingertips. "It's not that I don't like Noah. It's just that I guess I'm more like Grandpop than I want to admit. He never thought any guy was good enough for me, and I feel the same way about you. Because I love you so much."

"I love you, too." I lay my head on her shoulder. When I was little and something was wrong, just being this close to her always made me feel better. Some things don't change, I guess. "I know you've been upset about Dad for a while,"

I say. "I'm really mad at him for lots of reasons but mostly for making you so sad. If I knew how to make things right again—"

Mom squeezes my hand. "I know. Just be you. That's all I need you to do." She stands. "How about some hot tea? Maybe it will help you sleep."

Sniffing, I smile up at her. "Now you sound like Nana."

"I'll take that as a compliment." She turns.

"Mom?"

Pausing in the doorway, she glances over her shoulder at me.

"So…you're still cool with me visiting Noah in Montana whenever I want, right?"

She crosses her arms, tilts her head and smirks. "Nice try, Sweetie. Nice try."

CHAPTER 19

Cecilia Dupree
Day Planner
Monday, 01/15

1. 7 a.m.—Weight Wackers weigh-in.
2. 8-noon—Leave open to study for continuing education course.
3. 3 p.m.—Pt. Appt.—Joy Cowles (divorcing).

At eight o'clock, I leave the Weight Wackers diet and exercise center after my workout. Showered and dressed for the office, I walk through the parking lot with my tote bag over one shoulder and my hands burrowed into my coat pockets, on the lookout for anyone watching me. Several days ago, a guy with a camera snapped my picture as I stepped from my car on this very lot. My nerves have been haywire ever since.

Willa's on the phone when I enter the office. She points to the receiver and widens her eyes at me. "I'll certainly give Ms. Dupree the message. Yes, sir, I wrote down the number.

We'll be in touch." She hangs up. "Girl, you will never guess who that was."

I set my briefcase beside her desk and frisk my palms together to warm them. "I won't even try then. Who?"

"*20/20*. They want to interview you about the Parkview Manor sex scandal."

"How many times do I have to say this? It isn't a sex scandal. It—"

She stops me with an upheld hand. "I'm just calling it what everyone else is."

"Everyone else?" Unbuttoning my coat, I sink into the chair across from her desk.

Willa lifts a second pink slip of paper with another phone number scribbled across it. "*People* called, too."

A tremor ripples through me. It isn't excitement. "You're kidding me."

"Nope. And it gets worse." After opening her center desk drawer, Willa pulls out a magazine then holds it up. *News-flash*. She passes the tabloid across the desk to me. "Page six. I marked it."

The article talks about the "scandal" but is predominantly about me. The therapist who gives others advice on how to live their lives successfully while her own spirals out of control. And there are pictures.

Me in my car in the Weight Wackers parking lot, scarfing a doughnut before my workout. Bert and his bimbo fiancée kissing in front of his condo. Mother and Oliver dancing at a nightclub, the only two gray heads in a room of gyrating teens and twenty-somethings. A blurry Erin dressed in a skimpy outfit, body painted à la Goldie Hawn in her *Laugh*

In days. The breasts are too large to be hers, though I swear I see nipples poking through the clingy fabric of her top.

I start to shake. "Where did they get these?" I meet Willa's sympathetic dark gaze. "They've invaded my privacy…my family's. I'm going to murder somebody, I swear to God, Willa, I am."

Tossing the magazine on the desk, I stand, grab my briefcase and start for the door.

Willa stands up so fast that her chair, which is on rolling casters, bangs into the wall behind her. "Hold it, CiCi. Calm down." Her phone rings. "Don't you go do something stupid you'll regret. Gulp down some air while I take this call." Her eyes never leave me as she lifts the receiver to her ear. "Cecilia Dupree's office." She pauses. "Let me check." Placing a hand over the mouthpiece, she whispers, "Your ex. Are you here?"

I take the phone. "Hi Bert." He's yelling. "Yes, I saw…no, *you* listen… *I* didn't take the pictures. I'm as pissed off as you are. I—no, Erin hasn't had a boob job…I don't know, I can't be with her every second of the day and night. I guess I could bar all the doors and windows in the house and hide the key."

Drawing a breath, I let him rant uninterrupted for a minute, then I start yelling, too. "Well, poor little Natalie. I'm so sorry she's humiliated. I'm sure it's not the first time, and I doubt it'll be the last since she's marrying you." I slam the receiver down and grab my briefcase again.

Willa comes around the desk, takes my arm and herds me into my office. "Sit down. Give yourself a minute, then call your attorney and see what he says about this." I slip off my coat. She hangs it on the rack in the corner. "Girl, I'm telling you, you won't do yourself any favors by killing Erin or that photographer outside."

Slouched in my chair, I blink at her. "What photographer?"

"You didn't see that bozo lurking in the bushes out front? He's been there ever since I came in this morning."

I shake my head and blow out a breath. "What a mess." Propping an elbow on the desk, I cover my face. "Erin…"

"Don't be too hard on her. Kids her age all do stupid things. I sure did. Just didn't get caught on camera, thank you, Jesus."

"It's me I'm mad at, not Erin. What kind of mother doesn't know what's going on with her own daughter?" I look up at Willa. "Where have I been?"

"Don't be too hard on yourself, either." She smiles, her teeth flashing white against her caramel skin. "I'll get you some coffee."

"Thanks. Put a shot in it, would you? There's some Southern Comfort in the top kitchen cabinet."

"You sure? It's eight-thirty in the morning."

"I promise I'll get an earlier start on the drinking tomorrow."

"Girl, if tomorrow's anything like today, I'll join you."

The Colby brothers' secretary finally made it back from maternity leave. She answers when I call for Nate, and in her raspy smoker's voice, informs me cheerfully that he's out of the office for most of the day on a mediation.

"Figures," I say. "Men are never around when you need 'em."

She laughs and agrees, then promises Nate will return my call.

At noon, fearing a run-in with photographers or reporters if I leave, I order lunch to be delivered and hide in my office. I watch *The Scoop* on television. Somehow I just know there will be a tidbit about the case, and I'm right. Their "Update" segment practically repeats the article in *Newsflash,* complete with identical photographs, making me suspect that the same people own the program and the tabloid.

The phone rings at twelve-thirty. Willa's out for lunch and I don't want to answer, so I let the machine pick up. It's my three o'clock appointment calling to cancel.

I spend the next couple of hours doing paperwork, then leave before three to drive to Erin's school. There's no orchestra practice today, and I want to be waiting when she comes out so I can warn her about the photos, if she doesn't already know.

When I spot Suzanna's Honda Civic in the high school parking lot, I pull to the curb across the street. Suzanna gave Erin a ride this morning since Erin had a flat tire. I wait, my gaze on the door I think they'll exit.

Sure enough, they emerge side by side, surrounded by a swarm of other students. I grab *Newsflash* from the seat beside me and hurry across the parking lot to meet them.

"Erin!" By the time I reach her, I'm out of breath.

She stops walking, her books clutched to her chest. "Mom? What are you doing here?"

I don't want to make the hike back through the now-crowded parking lot to my car and drag out Erin's worry, so I turn to Suzanna and nod at her vehicle. "Could we have a minute alone inside?"

"Oh." She tucks her long blond hair behind one ear and looks from me to Erin and back. "Sure." Placing her books on the hood, she digs through her purse and produces a set of keys. She unlocks the Civic then leans against it. "I'll just wait here."

The inside of Suzanna's car smells like a mix of stale corn chips and perfume. I settle behind the wheel eyeing my daughter, who sits on the passenger side. Her face is pale, her eyes dark and wide.

"Is Nana okay?"

"Nana's fine. It's nothing like that." I swallow my sudden nervousness. "The publicity about the lawsuit has gotten out of hand, Erin. I wanted to warn you before anyone says something to you about it. It's been all over television today." I hand her the tabloid, already open to page six.

Her breath draws in so quick and sharp, I hear it. She doesn't look up from the pictures.

"I'm sorry, Sweetie. To have your privacy invaded and displayed like this…it's unfair. I'm just so mad I could—" I blow out a breath. "I'm worried, too. About you. Where was that picture taken? Why were you dressed like that?"

"It doesn't matter, Mom." She glances up at me then quickly down again. "I don't go there anymore. Don't worry about it."

"But I am worried."

"It's not a big deal."

"Not a big deal?" I point at her breasts in the photo and struggle to stay calm. "You're right. They aren't big—they're enormous! Don't you realize how you look, dressed like that?"

She turns and stares out her window. "Why do you have to make a federal case out of everything? Who cares how I dress?"

I lose the struggle. "Me, that's who. I want you to tell me right this minute what's going on with you."

"Or what?" Her sharp glare pierces me. "You'll ground me? I might as well be already my curfew's so early. You'll forbid me to see Noah? Well, we broke up, remember? And he never felt comfortable coming around anyway. You made him feel unwelcome, no matter how nice he was to you. What's left? No moving out in the fall? You already struck that down. Taking away my keys? My phone? Fine. Go ahead. I have friends, Mom. You're not the only person in my life. They'll come get me if I ask them to, and you can't stop me from leaving." She tosses the tabloid at me and opens her door.

"Erin, wait."

"Why don't you get your own life, Mom, and stop trying to run mine?" She gets out. The door slams.

Too numb to move, I grasp the steering wheel, my knuckles bone-white. Outside, Suzanna stares in at me, her mouth forming a circle as round as her eyes. After a minute, I force myself to open the door, to step out. With a choked voice, I thank Suzanna. Erin stands beside her friend, her back to me. I want to say something to her, too, but what? I feel like a twisted dishrag, every word, every good feeling and ounce of hope wrung out of me. Nothing's left.

Turning away, I walk to my car and drive home.

Nate's Porsche sits in my driveway. I find him with Mother at the kitchen table, laughing, mugs of something hot and steamy in front of them. Their laughter fizzles the moment they see my face.

Mother scoots back her chair. "There you are."

"When I called your office," Nate says, "your secretary said you'd gone home for the day. She told me what's going on and said you were pretty upset, so I dropped by on the off chance—"

"I'm sorry." I toss my copy of *Newsflash* on the table between them. "I just…" Turning, I start from the room. "I can't talk right now."

In the living room, I sit on the floor and lean against the couch. Max climbs into my lap and licks my cheek. Closing my eyes, I bury my face in his soft, sleek neck. I feel the throb of his heart against my hand. The calm, faithful beat of it steadies me.

After a few minutes, I look up to find Mother and Nate standing over me. "Oh, Sugar." Mother wads up the tabloid. "This is nothing but a big ol' bunch of trash. What they say about you is untrue. You're a wonderful therapist. You've helped so many people."

"That doesn't bother me as much as having our privacy invaded. Yours and Erin's. Even Bert's."

I stare into Max's sad eyes. "Let's not talk about this now. It makes me too crazy."

Nate squats beside me. "I have an idea that might make you feel better. Will you come with me?"

I shake my head. "Thanks but, right now, I don't think anything can change how I feel."

"Sitting around here mulling over your troubles certainly won't," Mother says.

Nate offers his hand. "When I want to pound someone's head in, this always does the trick. Keeps me out of jail, too."

Doubtful, I blink at him. "What?"

He winks. "Trust me."

Relaxing my shoulders, I hold the bowling ball out in front of me, bend my knees slightly, focus.

"Okay," Nate calls from where he sits at the scorekeeper's table behind me. "See that center pin? Imagine it's the *Newsflash* photographer. And the one to the right of him? That's the reporter from *The Scoop.* You see them?"

I squint. "Yeah, I do. The plaintiffs who filed suit on me are there, too." An evil laugh bubbles up from my chest. "Doris Quinn's son is on his knees begging. Sue Kiley's trying to hide behind the ten pin."

"You going to take pity on 'em?"

"Are you joking? Like they took pity on me?"

"Good girl. Give 'em hell."

I count to three then take off. My arm pulls back, swings forward, the ball leaves my hand and hits the polished wooden lane with a smooth and satisfying *thump.* It seems to gather speed as it moves up the center and crashes into the pins, scattering all ten of them.

I squeal and jump, pump the air with my fist. "All right!"

"Beautiful." Nate claps as, dancing a jig, I make my way toward him.

I pause to bow. "Who'd have thought I'd have a knack for this? I haven't bowled since Erin was little, and then I mainly helped her."

Nate hands me my beer when I stop beside him, then

clinks his bottle against mine. Earlier, he informed me that bowling without beer was like fishing without bait. "Feel better?" He stands to take his turn.

"As a matter of fact, I do."

"Works every time."

"You do this a lot?"

He gets up and holds both palms over the air blower to dry them, then hefts a glossy black ball. "Like I said, it keeps me out of jail."

Two games later, we drink another beer in the adjoining bar. In the corner on a tiny stage, a cowboy strums a guitar and sings of unrequited love. He's far too good for this smoky dive. His voice sounds pure and is filled with such longing the melody pulses like heartache.

When the song ends and our bottles sit empty, we bundle into our coats and head outside to Nate's Porsche. He opens my door for me. "You did great in there. Both games were close."

I climb in. "Next time I'll beat you."

A minute later, we're on our way. I thank him for the evening and apologize for my earlier negative frame of mind. "I've had a difficult few months. A difficult year, really. Too much change in my life, I guess."

"You don't like change?"

"I'm not good at it."

Since he's an attorney, I expect him to interrogate me. He doesn't. But I find I want to tell him everything anyway. If he has this effect on witnesses, it explains why he's so good at his job.

"My dad died a little over a year ago. Mother sold their

house in Cleburne and moved to Parkview Manor to be closer to us. Not long after, my husband and I separated. Then Mother moved in. She wasn't happy at Parkview and I was worried about her failing eyesight. I thought she needed me."

All at once I realize my true motive for moving Mother in, and the admission slips right out of me. "Really, I needed her. Bert was gone. Erin started to declare her independence and wasn't home as much. The house felt so empty." *I felt empty.* "Now Oliver and Mother have fallen in love and she's preoccupied, too." I glance across at him and feel myself blush. "I didn't mean to go on and on. God, I sound pathetic."

"No." His eyes hold sympathy. "That's not only a lot of change, it's a lot of loss. You've had a tough time. Change opens new doors, though." He shrugs. "Might lead to good things."

"I'm too scared to find out what's on the other side."

When we pull into the driveway, Noah's cycle is parked out front of the house. I shake my head. "He doesn't give up." Nate frowns and I point to the cycle. "Erin's boyfriend. She broke up with him."

"Smart kid, that boy. Your daughter's a good-looking girl. Just like her mother." He leans across to kiss me. When I turn my head, he hesitates, then kisses my cheek. "Erin's boyfriend isn't the only one who doesn't give up easy," he mutters.

His mouth hovers close to my ear, and his quiet, deep voice vibrates through me, raising goose bumps on my skin, bringing all my long-suppressed needs to the surface where they hum and shimmer and ache like that love song the cowboy crooned in the bowling alley bar. And I'm tempted.

So tempted. And so afraid. To move my head just a fraction, to let his lips touch mine.

"Isn't this unethical?" I ask, my voice hardly more than a whisper.

His breath warms my cheek. "What?"

"An attorney on the verge of kissing his client." I risk facing him and smile. "His client on the verge of kissing him back."

"I'm not sure. Maybe."

Oh, help. I'm dizzy. "I don't want to get you disbarred."

"I promise that's not going to happen. And even if it did, I'm dead sure kissing you would be worth giving up the practice of law." He leans closer.

I start to go for it, then waver and scoot nearer to my door. Even if I weren't his client, kissing Nate would be wrong. I'm not ready to get involved. Not with him or anyone.

I offer my hand. "How about a handshake, instead? Just in case a kiss would be breaking some lawyer oath you took and don't remember."

Nate leans back, shrugs. "Sure," he says, "whatever you want." The smile in his eyes tells me he's well aware that it wouldn't take much coaxing to change my mind.

He reaches for my hand, but instead of taking it, his fingertips brush mine. So soft, that touch, yet it makes the muscles in my stomach tighten. He slides his fingers up my palm and when our thumbs lock, he clasps my hand gently, strokes the pad of his thumb over the top of mine. And all the time he does this, he stares into my eyes, looking very sure of himself. Which he should be, since I'm melting; if I don't get out of this car in the next few seconds nothing will remain of me but a puddle on the floorboard. No doubt about it.

I grab the door handle, pull it, climb out of the car. "Good night, Nate." My knees almost buckle as I bend down to look in at him.

"I'll see you at Friday's appointment. Five o'clock. Don't miss this one."

That again. "What's with you and imaginary Friday afternoon appointments? We don't need to meet. You said yourself the suit's in waiting mode."

He holds my gaze so long I don't feel the chill in the air anymore. "Listen to your attorney, ma'am. He'll keep you out of trouble."

"Or get me into it."

"That depends on your definition of trouble."

"I'm looking at it."

"I hear some things in life are worth it." His cheek twitches. "Trouble, that is."

CHAPTER 20

To: Erin@friendmail.com
From: Noah@friendmail.com
Date: 01/20 Saturday
Subject: hi
Erin,
thanks for letting me come over the other night. have
you decided if you'll play with us? i know you love
Cateye. whatever happens between you and me, you're
still part of the band. just show up by eleven. we'll be
there. i promise not to push you about anything else.
love, noah

Suz and I get to The Beat at ten forty-five. We take a quick
walk around the club, squeezing through the crowd, saying
hello to people we recognize. Noah's e-mail isn't the only
reason I decided to come tonight. Ever since I saw those
pictures in Newsflash I've been freaked out about being
followed. And not only by reporters, by Nana and Mr.
Winston. I'm sure that picture of them was taken at The

Beat. I can't believe I didn't have a clue. If anyone's following me tonight, I plan to catch them in action.

Suz tugs my arm and leans close to my ear so I can hear her over the noise. "Come on. I'm dying of thirst and you need to get on stage. Besides, no one's watching you."

"Not yet. Or maybe they're just hiding. Obviously they're good at it."

"You are so paranoid."

"And you wouldn't be? You saw the pictures. I'm completely humiliated! In more ways than one."

Her face squinches up. "I think it's funny."

"You only think it's funny because you aren't the one getting teased."

"I'm sorry," she says, but keeps on laughing. "I promise while you're playing I'll keep an eye out."

Noah, Tonto and Reese are tuning up when I get on stage. "Hey, girlie!" Tonto nods at me and smiles. "Glad you could make it.

"Relieved, too," Reese adds. "The crowd complains when you don't play with us."

Noah stays quiet, but his expression tells me exactly how happy he is that I'm here. His eyes say I'm the only person in the place who matters, the only person in the world. Which makes it really hard for me to stay cool toward him. Not that I'm mad or anything; I'm not. I just want to stop caring about him, so it won't hurt so much when he leaves for good.

The entire time we play, I search the crowd, but it's hard to see faces since we're in the spotlight, and they're in the dark. The dance floor is a sea of swaying bodies, heads bobbing like buoys.

At midnight, we take a break. Suz has soft drinks waiting for us at her table. While she flirts with Tonto, I gulp my Coke, then take off to pee. A long line stretches from the door of the women's restroom. At the head of it, I spot someone who doesn't fit in with this crowd.

"Do you mind?" I'm half angry, half nervous as I weave my way through the line. "Sorry. I'm in the band. I have to hurry." A few people grumble, but most seem to understand as I push toward the bathroom.

Once inside, I glance beneath each of the four stalls, pausing on black polyester slacks scrunched around ankles above a pair of flat shoes. Black leather lace-up *Naturalizers.* Cushiony soles. Shoes made for comfort, not fashion. Easy on the bunions.

Facing the stall, I lean against the sink across from it, my arms crossed. A girl comes out of stall number three and glares at me since I'm blocking the only unoccupied sink. She starts to say something, but I press my finger to my lips and point at the shoes.

The girl's forehead wrinkles and she gives me a have-you-gone-insane? look. But I guess she wants to see what happens, because she stands beside me, her eyes on stall four. Humming starts behind it. A church hymn. I cover my mouth and smile. Sure, I'm pissed, but I can't be *too* mad.

The feet shuffle. The polyester pants unscrunch. The toilet flushes. After a couple of seconds, the stall door opens and Nana steps out. Her magnified eyes pop wider when she sees me. "Oh, Erin. Hello, Sugar." Her eyelids flutter like moth wings and she fidgets with her blouse, fanning it away from her chest. "It's hot in here. I've never heard the band sound better. You and the boys are really rocking."

The girl beside me snickers as Nana nods at the sink. "Excuse me. I'd better wash up."

I don't move. "What are you doing here, Nana?"

"Why, dancing, Sugar. What else?"

As if. "We don't play the kind of music people your age dance to."

She looks all offended. "Says who? Since when, Erin Dupree, did you become an expert on people *my age?*"

"*Nana.*"

"I'll have you know, Oliver and I come here often and we have the time of our lives. And I can't speak for my own dancing, but that old man puts some of those young dudes out there to shame."

Laughter erupts. All at once I realize the restroom is packed with people. Heads poke through the open door. Everyone watches Nana and me.

I grab my grandmother's hand. "Come on."

"But I didn't wash up." She glances back at the sink. "Neither did you."

I pull her through the giggling crowd. Oliver stands outside the door, sweating like a rock star. A really old balding one. "Well, hello there, Miss Erin." He chuckles. "I was starting to worry about your grandma she'd been gone so long."

"How are you, Mr. Winston?"

"Exhausted." He lifts a foot. "My dogs are howling. How about a slow tune in the next set?"

"Sure," I say. He's so funny, it's hard to stay annoyed.

"Cateye's in top form tonight. The crowd's hopping like cold water on a hot griddle."

"Thanks, Mr. Winston." I nod toward my table. "Come meet the band."

As we work our way through the crowd, I'm totally shocked to hear kids call out to my grandmother and Oliver like they're old friends.

"Hey, Belle. Ollie," a guy wearing a ball cap yells.

Nana waves. "Trey! You shaved your beard. You look so handsome."

A girl rubs the guy's cheek. "The kissing's better, too."

Oliver chuckles. "Now, didn't I tell you she'd think so, Trey?"

I'm not believing this. I turn to Nana. "Who are they?"

"Our friends Trey and Megan."

"Where'd you meet them?"

"Why, here, Sugar."

When we reach the table, everyone stops talking and looks up. Suz says, "Oh." Noah's mouth drops open. I make introductions. "You guys keep Mr. Winston company while Nana and I go outside to the car to talk."

The guys pull out my empty chair for him, and Suz tosses me her keys. Oliver launches into a story as Nana and I head for the exit.

At the door, a two-hundred-fifty-pound tattooed bouncer in leather, stops us. "How ya doin, Belle?"

"Fine, Bongo," Nana gushes. "And you?"

He rubs his temples. "My ears are ringing again. I got another headache."

Nana plants fists on her hips. "You didn't buy those earplugs like I told you to, now did you?"

Bongo looks all sheepish. "No, ma'am."

"You'd better, young man. There's no such thing as an eardrum transplant, and working around all this loud music night in, night out, is bound to ruin your hearing if you don't do something."

He opens the door for us and grins. "You're right, Belle. I'll buy some tomorrow. I promise."

As we walk outside, I don't know what to say, so I don't say anything. Once inside Suzanna's car, I turn on the ignition and crank up the heater.

"Now, I know you're not happy with me, Erin, but—"

"How long have you been following me?"

"Since the second night I watched you climb out your bedroom window."

My stomach does a somersault. No wonder everyone here knows her. My grandmother's a regular. I feel defensive, but ashamed, too. I know she must've been worried about me. And tired of following me around to make sure I'm okay.

"This is not a safe place for girls your age to come to alone. Especially if no one knows where you are."

"Nana…things have changed since you were seventeen."

"Yes, they have. The world's even more dangerous now. I couldn't just sit back and hope for the best while you stayed out until the wee hours. If anything happened to you, I'd never forgive myself."

"I know that." My throat aches, like a pebble's stuck in it. "You didn't tell Mom?"

"No." Folding her hands in her lap, Nana lifts her chin. "That's probably a mistake on my part. But I don't want to be the one to tell her, Erin. I want you to."

"I can't."

"I know your mother seems unreasonable at times."

I huff a laugh.

Nana surprises me by laughing, too. "Her mind's as closed and locked tight as a safe at the bank, isn't it? Especially when it comes to allowing you to grow up." She stops laughing and gets all serious. "Your mother went through some things when she was hardly older than you. She wants to spare you the same hurts she suffered."

"Was it a guy?"

"That's not for me to tell. Go to her. Ask her your questions. Tell her how you feel. I'm sure the two of you can find some middle ground. Just try not to lose your temper while you're doing it."

"Tell *her* that."

"I have, and I will again." Nana heaves a sigh. "I understand your need for more freedom, it's just your method of getting it I don't like. I hate that you haven't spoken to your mother since those photographs hit the news. That's not good for either of you. You need each other. I know things haven't been easy for you since the divorce, but they haven't been easy for her, either."

Outside my window, cars speed past on the street, like it's early instead of after midnight. Where are they going? Are the people inside them as confused as me? Are their lives as big a mess? "I'll talk to Mom," I say. "I promise. Just give me some time. It won't be easy."

"Until you do," Nana points a finger at me, her voice teasing but firm, "I'll have my eye on you, young lady."

I laugh. "You just don't want to give up the dancing and

the music. You like it. I can tell. Just don't break a hip or some-thing."

"Don't worry about that. My hips are well-padded." Nana smiles. "You, your mother and I are more alike than you might think."

"I've never heard you lose your temper like we do."

"When I was your age…well that's a story for another time." With a nod at the building she says, "Better get back inside. Your fans are waiting, and I've got my second wind."

As we start toward the entrance to The Beat, I feel lighter than I have in weeks, like I'm walking on air without the big burden of my lie weighing me down. But then I think of the promise I just made, and the air turns to quicksand. Nana expects me to do the impossible.

Talk to Mom.

CHAPTER 21

*From The Desk of
Belle Lamont*

Dear Harry,

I've been under the weather today with a stuffy nose. Well deserved, I suppose, for staying out so late and in such cool weather.

Harry, I'll just speak my mind and be done with it.

Oliver Winston asked me to marry him. I haven't given him an answer yet. But I won't lie to you; I want to say "yes."

What's wrong with me? How can I feel like I do? Happy with another man? Excited about a new life? A life without you in it? I think of our years together, how full and rich they were, and I tell myself that should be enough. That I'm selfish to want more when we had so much.

I'm ashamed to admit that, when I'm with Oliver, for a time I can almost forget the pain of losing you. I feel alive again. Is that wrong? Am I betraying you by loving him?

I do love him, Harry. I'm finally happy again. It's been so long.

At Christmas, I asked that you give me your blessing to move on, that, somehow, you let me know you accept my decisions, *whatever they might be. I've watched and waited, and you've yet to give me a sign. Please don't make me wait forever. Time is passing, and I'm not a young woman. Until then, please know I'll love you forever.*

As always, your yellow rose,
Belle

CHAPTER 22

Cecilia Dupree
Day Planner
Tuesday, 01/23

1. 8:30—Ask Willa today's schedule—forgot to write down.
2. Resume training Max.
3. Ask Erin out for Tex-Mex tonight, just the two of us.

Mrs. Stein is sweeping her front porch when I go out to get the morning paper. "CiCi!" she calls. "I'm so glad to see you." She props the broom against the house, scoops up Pom Pom, then starts across the yard in her slippers and long flowery caftan robe.

Oh boy. I grab the paper and force a smile. One good thing about starting my day with Mrs. Stein, the hours ahead can only improve. "How are you?"

"Fine, hon." She purses her poofy lips. Strange. I'm sure she's always been thin-lipped. No, make that lipless.

Mrs. Stein must notice me staring because she purses her mouth and turns her head left, then right. "Well, what do you think? I had them done last week. I've always wanted Cupid's bow lips."

Poor Mrs. Stein. Her lips look more like Cupid's buttocks than Cupid's bow. "Wow," I say. "They're incredible."

Pom Pom licks the topic of conversation, making me shudder and Mrs. Stein squeal. She ruffles the puff of curly hair atop the poodle's head and says in a high-pitched tone, "Pom Pom likes them, too!"

After a moment, her expression shifts to one of concern. She places a hand on my wrist. "How are you holding up?"

"I—"

"I don't blame you for hiding out." Her brows aren't penciled on yet, so I can't be sure, but I think one hikes.

"Well, actually—"

"How in the world did you get yourself in such a situation?" She scans the block, as if the neighbors might hear my dirty little secret. "The things the media's saying…how humiliated you must be. I can't imagine."

"Mrs.—"

"I don't understand it. Neither does Henry Bocock. You remember Henry. The patient I sent you? Strapping bear of a man? Rugged? Nice jewelry?"

She means You-Can-Call-Me-Hank, but since it's against the rules for me to acknowledge seeing someone, even though she referred him, I only blink and smile.

Leaning closer, Mrs. Stein gives me a woman-to-woman grin. "I do so love a man with a little hair on his chest, don't you?"

A little? The man was Teen Wolf grown up.

"Well, just so you'll know, Henry said that after only one meeting, he's certain you're too much of a lady to be involved in something so sordid, and I agree."

"I appreciate your support, Mrs. Stein. Mr. Bocock's, too. I hope you'll tell him."

"You can do that yourself. He plans to make another appointment."

Lovely.

"So, CiCi." Her eyes blink sympathy as artificial as her nipped and tucked face. "I'm here for you, hon. Tell me what started all this nonsense."

"It's a long story."

"I'm not busy. Come on over for coffee. I have a fresh pot on."

"Another time, maybe." I glance at my watch. "I have to get to the office. But thanks." I make my escape.

Willa's on the phone when I arrive. Since I never book anything prior to nine, I know I'm not late for an appointment, but I've been so scattered lately, and I hate not knowing what's ahead in my day. I grab a diet shake from the kitchen fridge, then head for my office, mouthing for Willa to join me when she finishes on the phone.

After a couple of minutes, she comes in. "Good morning, boss." She eyes my breakfast. "What? No coffee and Southern Comfort?"

"Not yet. Check in with me again in a couple of hours. Do I have a nine o'clock?"

"Not anymore. The toe sucker just cancelled." When I scowl, she says, "You know, girl. The foot-fetish guy?"

I laugh. "Darn. He always keeps me posted on the best shoe sales. Why'd he cancel?"

"Didn't say." The phone rings. Willa stretches across my desk and grabs it. After a short conversation, she hangs up. "That was Mrs. Smythe, your two o'clock. She and her daughter Halee can't make it this afternoon." Worry creases her forehead. "Or any other Tuesday, apparently. She canceled their standing appointment."

My stomach stops growling; I'm suddenly too filled with anxiety to be hungry. "Did she say why?"

"She mentioned the scandal."

That word again.

"Said she heard about it on *LIVE With Regis and Kelly* yesterday."

"*Regis and Kelly?*"

"Don't you know?" Willa plants a hand on her hip. "You're famous, girl. They talked about everything on the program yesterday. Parkview. That poor old guy taking too much Viagra. You and that book."

"I don't want fame, I want patients. Get me Mrs. Smythe's number, would you? I want to call her back."

When Mrs. Smythe answers, I ask her straight out if she's dissatisfied with the progress Halee's made since we started meeting.

"This is difficult for me to say to you, Ms. Dupree. Maybe I'm wrong to judge, but with all I'm hearing on television and seeing in the papers and in magazines, I've lost trust in your advice. Face it, your daughter's as big a mess as mine."

She's dead wrong about that, but no way am I going to beg this woman or anyone else to continue using me as a therapist. Don't get me wrong, I want to, at least a part of me does. For the sake of my career, my mortgage and Erin's college fund, I want to plead and reason and grapple until Mrs. Smythe takes pity on me. Instead, I grasp on to the threadbare remains of my dignity, wish her well, and hang up.

The second the receiver is down, the phone rings again. Willa looks as antsy as I feel when she picks up. "Cecilia Dupree's office...yes, sir...I'm sorry to hear that. Would you like to reschedule on a different date?" She looks away from me. "I see... No, I understand."

Willa lowers the receiver to the cradle and her butt to the edge of my desk. "Tomorrow's ten o'clock just cancelled." Her troubled gaze meets mine. "Lord, girl, what's going on?"

"They're pulling out because of all the negative publicity."

"Surely they know you better."

"Can you blame them? My marriage fell apart, my mother is acting like a teenager, my seventeen-year-old daughter sneaks around behind my back and lies to me, my dog needs Prozac and I can't stop stuffing my face."

Shoving the diet shake aside, I open the bottom desk drawer, revealing my secret stash of Reese's Chocolate Peanut Butter Cups. "If I can't solve my own problems, why should anyone believe I could help them solve theirs?"

After dinner alone yet again, Max and I sit in front of the TV and channel surf. Mom and Oliver went out to eat and to a movie. Erin opted for fast food with Suzanna over Tex-Mex with me. I'm just glad she's stopped the silent treatment.

We still haven't talked things out, and I know I should insist she either confess her sins or be grounded the rest of her life, but I've decided to ease up. Bide my time. She's had a lot to deal with lately; we both have. I can't force her to talk to me. Nor can I watch her every second of the day and night, like I informed Bert. And I refuse to bar the windows.

I pause on *Extreme Makeover* and watch until the first commercial.

"Tonight at ten," a familiar local newscaster announces, "join us for all the latest on the Parkview Manor sex scandal…."

All the latest? There's more I don't know? I turn off the set.

Picking up a magazine that came in the mail today, I flip through pages of ads for cosmetics, articles about facial peels, lip enhancements, Botox injections. Soon the world will be full of Mrs. Stein clones. A scary thought.

I read a couple of paragraphs about the Botox, then go look in the mirror, scrutinizing my laugh lines, the deepening frown groove between my brows. Maybe if I didn't go overboard, a quick trip to the plastic surgeon would be okay. A little touch-up couldn't hurt, could it? Especially if my current trend continues and the only men who interest me are so young they've never seen or even heard of an eight-track tape.

Sick of myself, I leave the mirror and head for my closet for warm clothes. A walk, that's what I need. What I *don't* need is to look twenty-something again. I was a confused wreck back then. Forty-one is a much happier place. At least it would be if Bert hadn't screwed up. Or, more accurately, if he hadn't screwed the Butterfield girl.

Bundled up in a coat, earmuffs and gloves, I leash Max and head out. It's been a while since we walked and it shows on both of us. I decide on our usual route, down to the end of our street, turn left to the park, circle it, then return to our street and head back to the house.

A chill nips the air, but it's more invigorating than uncomfortable. Max must disagree. He's sluggish as we run through the training manual routine. After once around the park, I decide to walk a couple more blocks rather than head home, hoping to perk him up. When I try to pass by our street, though, Max puts on the brakes and glues his butt to the sidewalk.

I tug his leash. "Come on, boy. We're adding some variety to our routine."

He tugs back, looks at our street, then back to me.

"Don't be such a fuddy-duddy. I swear, I must be rubbing off on you." I tug again and, when he doesn't budge, I walk over to him and squat so that we're eye-to-eye. "Look buster, I'm the boss here, and I say move it. Understand?"

He lays a slobbery dog kiss on my cheek.

I stand. "Look at us, Max. Out of shape, lethargic." *Scared to death of all these changes in our lives.* "It's time we stop moping around and get back on track. What do you say? Come on. Let's do it."

Again, I tug the leash. No deal.

"Fine then. Be that way. I thought I could at least count on *you* not to make my life difficult." I drop the leash and start walking the direction I want to go. "Run home if that's what you want to do," I yell as I walk away with my back to him.

Max barks, so I look over my shoulder at him while I

continue to walk. He's still perched right where I left him. "Sit there until your butt goes numb. See if I care."

I turn in time to see the curb, too late to stop my next step off of it. Stumbling, I cry out. My right ankle twists as I fall.

Max comes running, dragging his leash behind him. He circles me in a prancing panic, barking and licking my face. I try to stand, but it hurts so much that I sink to the ground and squeeze my eyes shut tight to stop the tears.

Pushing to my hands and knees, I crawl to the corner and grab hold of the Stop sign pole. I pull myself up onto my left foot, take a breath, try my weight on the right one. I jerk my hurt foot up again. "Ow, ow, ow!"

Max barks and stares at me.

"Sure, now you're sorry." Holding tight to the pole, I bend and grab his leash. I hop three steps on my left foot, put my right foot down to rebalance, wince and squeal, pick it up, hop three more steps. Headlights turn the corner and approach. A welcome sight, though I feel like an idiot.

Nate's Porsche pulls to a stop alongside me. He rolls down the window and I hop over and lean against the trunk. "What happened?" He gets out and helps me around to the passenger side. Max jumps into the floorboard at my feet.

"I twisted my ankle."

Nate goes back around and slides behind the wheel. "Want to tell me about it?"

"Not really." Crossing my arms, I stare out the window and sulk. "So, you just happened to be cruising my neighborhood?"

"Haven't heard from you lately. I called your office. Willa said you went home early again."

"No reason to stay. All my patients are bailing thanks to my sudden sorry reputation."

For several seconds, he doesn't say anything, then, "I tried your house. The phone's been busy all afternoon and evening."

"It's off the hook. Too many calls wanting my side of the story."

He takes off in the direction of home. "I want to talk to you about the case." When I shoot him a skeptical glare he says, "No, really. I have an idea." He pulls into my driveway. "Are your mother and Erin home?"

"No. Some people in this family actually have a social life."

"My, we're in a cheery mood, aren't we?"

"Sorry. Mother's out with Oliver. Erin's studying at Suzanna's."

I'm close to tears as Nate helps me into the house with Max at his heels. It's not just the ankle. Everything in my life feels out of my control. What happened to the together woman I was two years ago? I'm tired of this gloomy cloud hanging over my head, tired of getting pelted with grapefruit-sized hailstones.

Nate checks out my swelling ankle and decides no bones are broken. I direct him to the bathroom cabinet for an ice pack and an Ace bandage.

When I'm settled on the sofa, my ankle wrapped, iced down and propped on a pillow on the ottoman in front of me, Nate sits at my side.

"I've been talking to Everett about your case."

"Your brother?"

"Yeah."

"What does he say?"

"He'd like to represent you."

"But that's your job."

"The ethics, remember? It's clear you're not comfortable mixing business with pleasure. And when I think about it rationally, I know you're right."

"Nate…" He smells like shaving cream. God, I love that scent on a man. I want to bury my nose in his neck and take deep breaths. "I thought we agreed to keep our personal relationship at a handshake level?"

"CiCi…" Nate scoots closer, hooks a strand of hair behind my ear. "As much as I want this case, I want you more. Everett and I aren't legally partners. We're sole proprietors. There isn't anything unethical about getting involved with your brother's client. And Everett's a great attorney." He grins. "Almost as brilliant as me."

He keeps talking. I listen, but my mind returns again and again to three little words. "You want me?" If he doesn't say yes, I'll be forced to eat an entire carton of double-chunk chocolate.

Nate shuts up and grins wider. "That's what I said. So… what do *you* say?"

I place my hand at the back of his neck, bring his face close to mine. "I say, you're fired."

CHAPTER 23

When the alarm goes off at seven, I cover my head with a pillow and swing blindly at the radio to stop the buzzer. Why get up? Yesterday, all my appointments for today cancelled. Other than my three o'clock, that is. You–Can–Call–Me–Hank. What a guy. The only patient I have left, and he doesn't even really want therapy, or need it. What he wants, and thinks he needs, is a sparkly woman on his arm to match his sparkly gold neck chain.

With the buzzer silenced, I burrow deeper into the covers and clear my mind. Or try to. Music flows into my room through the ceiling vent. Erin's alarm. I press the pillow tighter against my head.

A memory of Bert surfaces. The two of us in this very bed when we had the old mattress, muffling our laughter while trying out every position we can think of that won't make the springs squeak so Erin won't hear us through the vent.

Groaning, I throw the pillow aside and sit up. No more thinking about Bert and the old days. Get over it. Be a big girl and move on. Quit being a victim. That's what I'd tell a patient. Not so bluntly, but the message would be the same.

The phone rings as I limp into the bathroom on my sore ankle. I decide to let Mother or Erin pick up. I've just stuck my toothbrush into my mouth when someone knocks at the door.

"Mom, it's for you."

I poke my head out the door. "Who is it?" I ask, the brush still in my mouth.

"Nathan Colby," she whispers, extending the cordless phone.

I stare at it and continue brushing.

Erin frowns. "Where's Nana?"

"Isn't she cooking breakfast?" I say around the brush.

"No, and she isn't in her room. The bed's made."

"Go look out front. Maybe she went to get the paper and ran into Mrs. Stein."

Glaring, Erin jabs the phone at me. "*Mom,* I'm going to be late. Here."

Choice time.

Three nights ago after I fired Nate, we ended up in my bedroom. Wouldn't you know it? Erin picked that night as the first one in months to be home by eight. The slam of her car door interrupted us before any clothes came off. I'm thankful for that. And not. Thankful, because getting in over my head with him so soon, before we really thought it through, would've been a mistake. Not thankful, because right or wrong, I *wanted* to make that hot, sweaty, irresistible mistake.

Turning, I spit into the sink, rinse my mouth, then face Erin again. She fidgets, huffs, rolls her eyes. I take the phone and close the bathroom door.

"Hello, Nate."

"Okay, what's the deal? Am I that bad of a kisser?"

I recall the feel of his mouth on mine and a hot wave of want almost makes me stagger. I lean against the sink. "You're the best kisser I've ever kissed."

"You sure? Because if I'm not, we can practice until I get it right."

I smile. "In that case, you're terrible."

He chuckles. "How's the ankle?"

"Better. Still a little tender, though."

"Why haven't you answered my calls?"

I stare into the mirror at my less than radiant complexion, spot a gray hair at my temple, fumble around in my top drawer until I locate the tweezers. I put on my reading glasses, lean closer to the mirror and see that the hair is pale blond, not gray. A ridiculous surge of relief shoots through me. "How old do you think I am, Nate?"

"I don't know. Thirty-seven? Thirty-eight?"

"Try forty-one. And you're…what? Thirty?"

"Thirty-three. So, what are you saying? I'm not experienced enough for you?"

Erin knocks on my door again. "Mom, open up. Look at this."

"Just a minute," I say to Nate, then open the door. She hands me a note with Mother's handwriting scrawled across it, then shrugs and leaves.

Ran an errand with Oliver. Nothing to worry about. Home soon. Left warm sweet rolls in the oven for your breakfast.

Nothing to worry about? Ha! Please tell me they didn't elope.

Still staring at my mother's perfect script, I say into the phone, "Sorry about that."

"Anything wrong?"

"Mother's AWOL. She left a note saying not to worry. So I won't." Yeah, right. "Where were we?"

"You said I'm not experienced enough for you."

"I didn't say that." I slip the reading glasses off of my nose and frown at them. "I was about to say I'm too old for you. You probably never even saw *Footloose* or danced to the Bee Gees. You probably have perfect up-close vision. What could we possibly have in common?"

"Lust?"

I bite the inside of my cheek. "Seriously. You're a young, interesting, sexy, unencumbered guy. You've got it together. You could have any hot babe you want. Why me?"

"Because—"

"I'm middle-aged, boring, chubby. A divorced single mother. My life is a mess right now."

"Boring? The Parkview Manor madam? You're kidding me, right?"

"Very funny."

"And you're not chubby, you're curvy. I like curvy." When I start to interrupt, he continues, "I don't care if you're forty-one."

I close my eyes. "My ex is making a fool of himself with a girl seventeen years his junior. I don't want to follow in his footsteps."

"I'm eight years behind you, CiCi, not seventeen. So what are you really afraid of?"

Of risking my heart again. Of screwing up. Of getting hurt. I could go on.

"I'm not afraid of anything."

"Good. Have dinner with me tonight. It's Friday. No work in the morning. We could go to a movie, too."

A real date. I squeeze my eyes shut tighter. "I can't."

"Tomorrow night, then."

I chew the earpiece of my glasses. "I'll think about it."

"I'll call you in the morning. Answer the damn phone. If you don't, I'll just come over. There's no hiding from me. I know where you live."

An uneasy laugh ripples out of me. "I'll answer. I promise."

At eight-thirty Mother's still not home. I call Willa to tell her I won't be in until Hank Bocock's appointment this afternoon. I plan to spend the morning worrying while painting the sunroom daffodil-yellow.

The moment Willa picks up, I hear a television in the background. "Do you have your feet on my desk?" I ask in lieu of a greeting, knowing she's in my office.

"Girl, you are not going to believe what's happening around here. The phone was ringing when I walked in a half hour ago and it hasn't stopped since."

My heart does a swan dive to the pit of my stomach. "More cancellations?"

"What do you mean? You didn't have any appointments left to cancel."

"Didn't?"

"Now you're booked solid through Wednesday of next week. Not a one of them under the age of seventy." Willa hoots. "They've been reading about you and the scandal, hearing about you on television. They all say the same thing, CiCi. That they're behind you."

"I can't believe this."

"I'm telling you, these people are thrilled about what you started at Parkview. They say no one ever takes their matters of the heart seriously. One old gentleman's driving all the way from Oklahoma City just to bend your ear."

I sink into a kitchen chair, lift a sweet roll from the pan Erin left on the table, take a bite and wash it down with my diet shake. "So, what? Now I'm the geriatrics' Dr. Ruth?"

Willa laughs. "Is that so bad? I think—oh…sweet Jesus… oh, my…" She shrieks.

"What? What's going on?"

"Get to a television set and turn it on channel four. Hurry! They just cut in with a live report."

Still holding the phone, I run into the den and switch on the set. I flip to four. It must be a job requirement that female news reporters be blond, I think, as the perky, young bombshell appears on screen, microphone in hand.

"I'm standing in front of the accounting office of Donald Quinn, a Dallas C.P.A. and one of the plaintiffs in the lawsuit against Parkview Manor Retirement Village and licensed therapist Cecilia Dupree."

The camera pans out, and there, standing beside the reporter, are Mother and Oliver. Behind them, elderly pick-eters bear signs and pace back and forth in front of the office door. Among the crowd I see The Frans. Mary Fran's sign reads, Senior Citizens Should Not Be Censored. Francis's sign, End Senior Oppression.

"I have with me," the reporter continues, "Belle Lamont and Oliver Winston, members of the Parkview Manor reading group and the organizers of this rally." She turns to

Mother. "Mrs. Lamont, your daughter, Cecilia Dupree, is being sued along with the retirement village for exposing the Parkview reading group to soft pornography and, as a result of that exposure, inciting some of the members to engage in rash, potentially harmful acts. What do you and your group hope to accomplish here today?"

Mother clears her throat as she faces the camera. "I want Mr. Quinn and the other plaintiffs to realize how silly they're being. My daughter has devoted her life to helping people. She didn't hurt us, she brought us together, gave us something else fun to look forward to each week. It's true that one of our members had a medical emergency, but it wasn't Cecilia's fault, or Parkview's, either." Mother lifts her chin. "I'm very proud of my daughter. *Penelope's Passion* is not pornography. It's an adventure. A lovely romance."

Willa and I groan at the same time as the reporter lifts the book and the camera zooms in on Penelope's naked back and the captain's hand touching it. "A lovely romance with quite a bit of sex," the perky blonde responds in a bedroom voice.

The camera shifts to Mother, who doesn't flinch. "Since when did sex become a four-letter word?"

Willa shouts, "You go girl."

I cover my mouth and laugh. I guess I never took a long enough look at my mother to see how truly gutsy she is. She always says I'm like her and don't realize it. Right now, I hope it's true, that her strength lives inside me. Lurking. Waiting for me to find it.

The camera moves to Oliver who points to the words on his sign, We're Old, Not Dead, then at the picketers behind him. "We aren't kids. Not a one of us is senile. We don't need our grown children to shelter us." He looks directly into the camera, directly at me. "We may be a little worse for wear on the outside, but inside…" he taps his fingers against his chest, right over his heart, "inside, we're no different than we've ever been. At least Cecilia Dupree seems to be figuring that out, if no one else is."

Willa's sigh travels across the line. "That sweet old man."

My eyes fill. "Sweet old conniver's more like it. Damn him. He's going to end up making me love him."

Mother and Oliver step back and Doris Quinn steps forward. The camera zeroes in on her sign—Seniors Need Love Too. When the scene widens again, Doris waves a hand at the building and twitters, "This office belongs to my son. If you're watching, Donnie, I just want to say that it's time for you to give up this ridiculous lawsuit. Quit being a bully. Straighten up and act right, for heaven's sake. Make your mother proud."

The live report moves to a male reporter on the sidewalk in front of a house he identifies as Sue Kiley's residence. A similar rally is in progress there, led by Sue's father, Frank Rayburn, now fully recovered from his Viagra incident, his blue Paul Newman eyes sharp and gorgeous as ever. The sign he waves at the camera says, Free To Read, Free To Love, Free Parkview & CiCi. I watch until the report ends, then turn off the set.

"Wow," Willa says.

"My thoughts exactly."

"Those folks are something else. Your mother's one feisty lady. She's got gumption. You must be proud of her."

"I am." So proud I could pop.

★ ★ ★

No painting for me this morning. Instead, I pace, channel surf and wait for Mother. I consider driving to Donald Quinn's office to see her, but the thought of a possible face-off with reporters keeps me locked in the house. Okay, I know what you're thinking. Where's that gumption I supposedly inherited from my mother? Nowhere to be found at the moment, that's for sure.

Midmorning, I flip to *LIVE With Regis and Kelly,* and my heart beats in double time when I hear Regis speak my name. It seems that since their earlier program where they discussed the "Dallas retirement village scandal and therapist Cecilia Dupree, who allegedly instigated it," senior citizens from all over the country called in to voice their support for me and what I "started."

When my phone rings, I check the caller ID, see that it's Willa and pick up.

"You're on *Regis and Kelly,* again."

"I'm watching. I got in on the middle of it, at the part about all the calls coming in. What else have they said?"

"Seems book groups of retirees all over the country are reading *Penelope's Passion.* Kelly suggested they invite you on the show, girl. Maybe the author, too. And Bill Burdette."

"Me? On television?" Somehow I always imagined celebrity would excite me, not make me sick to my stomach. "That's not going to happen. I'd be a wreck."

"That's not all," Willa continues. "Sela Summers? The lady who wrote the book?"

"What about her?"

"She called a minute ago. She wants you to call back.

Penelope's Passion just went into a third printing. It's selling like crazy because of you. Ms. Summers wants to thank you."

"Since I've made her rich and famous, did she offer to pay my legal fees?"

"Shoot. Who are you fooling? The only payment Nate Colby's gonna want from you is—"

"Funny, Willa. Anyway, I fired him."

"You did what?"

"Long story. Relax. I hired his brother."

"Is he as cute?"

Before I can answer, the front door slams and Mother and Oliver walk in, both pink-cheeked, animated and talking nonstop.

"Gotta go. Mother's home."

"Give her a high-five from me."

"Will do."

"Oh, and CiCi? I booked the rest of next week and through Tuesday of the next. All new patients."

"Any of *these* under seventy?"

"Only one." She chuckles. "He's sixty-nine."

CHAPTER 24

The next day, Saturday, is rare and wonderful. Erin is home, Mother's home, I'm home. No one has anywhere to be until this evening when we all have dates, although my feet are getting colder by the second at the thought of mine.

Calls from television shows wanting my interview have come in nonstop the past twenty-four hours. I take the phone off the hook, and we spend the morning washing and drying loads of laundry while watching a couple of movies; Erin's favorite, *Finding Nemo,* then an old dramatic tear-jerker Mother and I both love, *Imitation of Life.*

When we break for lunch, Erin fills Mother and me in on everything from school, to Suz's latest crush, to Noah's plans for college. I have a feeling she's headed toward something touchy and important, but she never arrives. After we finish eating, I slip off and call Nate to cancel our dinner date and am relieved that his machine picks up. I leave a message.

Back in the den, Mother puts her Glenn Miller album on the ancient turntable I never got rid of, cranks up the volume, then the three of us fold all the clean clothes we dumped center floor earlier. Not once does Erin complain, which surprises and pleases me. She seems content to pass the day with us. Yesterday on the six o'clock news, she saw a replay of the protest rally outside Donald Quinn's accounting office, and she's as proud of her nana as I am.

When "In The Mood" starts to play, Mother drops a towel and grabs my hand. We jitterbug like she taught me when I was a girl, hands waving, feet slapping the carpet to the beat of the song. Erin laughs and shrieks, then finally joins in. Nothing else matters as we dance together, my mother, my daughter and me. Nothing intrudes. No problems. No fears. No differences, age or otherwise. There is only our laughter, the pulse of our feet, the energy flowing between and around us.

Later, they leave with Oliver and Noah, and I'm still so alive with the joy of the day that I almost reconsider and call Nate to say I've changed my mind. But I tell myself this is all I want in my life now, enough to fulfill me for the time being. My family under one roof, the three of us learning to relate to one another as grown women, not merely mother and daughter, grandmother and granddaughter.

I admit, I'm the one who's had the toughest time adjusting. Even tonight, when Mother left with Oliver and Noah led Erin out the door, a twinge of worry and resentment and, yes, jealousy too, crept up to try and tug me down from my high. They'll break your heart, I wanted to warn them. They'll turn your life upside down, let it crash and then leave you alone to pick up the pieces. One way or another. Death, divorce, dreams. Something will take them away. Erin, I know, will have to learn that the hard way, there'll be no convincing her. But Mother's been through it once already. It's hard to see her set the stage for another broken heart.

I'm painting the sunroom, looking lovely in daffodil-yellow-splattered sweats and wool socks, hair in a ponytail, no makeup when, at eight, the doorbell rings. It's Nate. Surprise, surprise. He holds a sack in one hand, two bottles in the other.

"If I can't tempt you with myself," he says, "I thought maybe a little merlot and Chinese might do the trick."

I cross my arms.

He smacks his lips and lifts the sack. "Beef with oyster sauce and mushrooms. Yum, yum. Spring rolls. Fried rice, too."

Hunger gnaws at my stomach. A hunger not only for food, but also for his company. Sighing, I step back to let him through.

I grab a couple of wineglasses from the kitchen cabinet and scrounge up an opener. Nate whistles in the next room. A Paul Simon song. Listening closer, I recognize the tune. Something about making love with a woman named Cecilia up in a bedroom. How subtle. Laughing to myself, I join him in the den where I put one of Mother's Frank Sinatra albums on the turntable to shut him up. We sit side by side on the floor and eat off the coffee table.

"One of your neighbors must be having a party. I had to park down the street," Nate says between chews.

"Mrs. Stein next door. She's upset that I didn't come. She wanted to introduce me to her lesbian niece, Cleo something-or-other. Since I've refused every setup she's tried to arrange with men, I guess she's decided I'm gay."

Nate grunts and keeps on eating. "Everett said he scheduled depositions for the week after next."

Sipping the wine, I nod. "He called this afternoon and we coordinated the date."

I wish we didn't have to discuss the lawsuit and risk spoiling the meal. The beef tastes so tender and delicious; I want to concentrate on that, on Old Blue Eyes crooning on the stereo, the spice-scented air, the nice hum of awareness skimming just beneath my skin, caused by the wine and Nate's nearness. If we have to talk, I'd rather talk about him. Since we've met, my problems have taken center stage. It occurs to me I know next to nothing about his life. Just that he's a lawyer. That he has a brother. He enjoys fishing. And he likes older things; sports cars, rock and roll. Me.

"After that news segment yesterday, it wouldn't surprise me if the plaintiffs dropped the suit," Nate says, refilling our goblets. "Doris Quinn seemed madder than a wet hen at her son for starting the thing in the first place. Nothing like a mother's wrath to set a son straight."

We clink our glasses together. "You saw?"

He nods. "Belle and Oliver were great. They all were."

Pushing my empty container aside, I shake my head and laugh. "Who would've thought reading a romance novel would cause such a stir? You wouldn't believe the calls I'm getting at the office. Every senior citizen in the greater Southwest seems to want an appointment with me. Suddenly I'm Masters and Johnson for the Geritol crowd."

"Good for you. They obviously need your services. You took a bad situation and turned it to your advantage. And theirs."

"I'm not sure I had anything to do with it. The whole thing just happened. And I'm not sure how I feel about it, either. I've pretty much focused my practice on troubled teens, troubled families and troubled marriages up until now."

Nate reaches for the opener and goes to work on the second bottle. "Well, maybe it's time for a change."

"I told you, I'm not good at that." Groaning, I take a long drink. "How much change can a person stand? In the space of less than two years, my husband started going down on women half his age, my stud bulldog's so depressed he can't get it up, my mother's moved in and my daughter wants to move out." I lift my glass for a refill. "Oh, and on top of all that, my dad died and my mother's in love again. Now you're telling me my career focus should change, too?"

"You said yourself the members of the reading group were the highlight of your week. That they did as much good for you as you did for them."

"That's true, but…I don't know." I start laughing and can't stop.

He watches me, a look of delighted surprise in his eyes.

"I'm sorry. I think I'm a little drunk." I try to compose myself, but it's no use. "I'm sorry," I say again, giddy for no particular reason. "It's just, I mean…me? A senior sex therapist?"

"I'm sure they have other issues to discuss with you besides sex." Nate takes the wineglass from me and sets it on the coffee table. "Now, I, on the other hand…" He slides his fingers into my hair, against my scalp, and kisses me. The awareness beneath my skin stops humming and sings along with Frank.

As I push Nate to the carpet and kiss him back, the music crescendos.

The bed is spinning when I wake in the middle of the night. I blink to look at the clock. The numbers glow green in the darkness—4:12 a.m.

Moaning, I close my eyes. They hurt. So does my head. I can't move my body. It feels like a weight presses me into the mattress.

I lift my right hand to cover my gurgling stomach and touch something else. A weight *is* pressing me into the mattress. I pat my palm against it. A leg. A hairy leg.

My eyes pop open again as I raise my left hand to my breasts.

Oh, God. I'm naked. I'm going to throw up.

I slide my right hand up the hairy thigh…up…up… pause…jerk it away.

Oh, God. He's naked, too. I'm going to have a coronary. *He. Nate.*

It all comes back to me. The wine. The laughter. The kissing. More wine. More laughter. More kissing. And finally, no wine. No laughter. Only kissing and…

Oh, God. We did it. Tell me I dreamed it, then let me go back to sleep.

I lie perfectly still; my eyes don't even blink. The only thing moving in my entire body is my heart. Boy does it move. Like a tap dancer on speed. Images flash through my mind. Everything.

Oh… It was fun. Fun and thrilling and sexy and…

A sneeze sounds somewhere else in the house.

Erin? Mother?

In a panic, I squeeze from under Nate's leg. My head pounds, but my heart pounds harder. I shake his shoulder.

"Wake up!" I plead.

He stirs. A satisfied sound rumbles up from deep in his chest, sending a shiver down my spine. When he reaches for me, I bolt from the bed and scramble around in the dark, searching the floor for my clothes, desperate that they be here in the bedroom instead of in the den where Mother or Erin might've seen them.

Out of nowhere, a scene appears and plays through my mind. Nate undressing me, piece-by-piece, clothes flying over his shoulder, landing on the rocker in the corner.

I run to the rocker. Sure enough.

After struggling into the sweatpants, I tug the sweatshirt over my head and run back to my bed.

"Nate! Please!" I shake him again. "You have to get out of here."

He bolts straight up. *"What?"*

I cover his mouth. "We fell asleep. You have to go before Mother or Erin catch you here."

We don't speak as we move around in the darkness. I wasn't as tidy as Nate when I undressed him. The clothes landed everywhere. His shirt on the dresser. Pants at the foot of the bed. One sock on the nightstand, another in the corner. Underwear? No underwear. I'm sure he wore them. I vividly remember taking *them* off. Boxer briefs. Gray. Snug.

Oh, boy.

I drop to my hands and knees, reach beneath one side of the bed, then crawl around to the other. Nate trips over me, falls against the wall with a loud thud.

"Shhhh!" I rise to my knees. He seems okay. Closing my eyes, I tilt back my head and take several deep breaths. When I open my eyes again, the first thing I see is the shadow of the ceiling fan and something hanging from one blade. I stand and reach up. Nate's briefs. How did that happen?

Nate sits at the edge of my bed and dresses while I pace. Seconds later, as we leave the bedroom, I say a silent thanks to Mrs. Stein next door for having a party. With Nate parked down the street, surely Mother and Erin didn't notice his car.

We tiptoe down the hall toward the entryway. Halfway there, I hear a noise behind us and pause. Dizzy with dread, I look over my shoulder.

Oliver is at Mother's bedroom, his back to us, closing her door. His shirt is untucked, and he reaches to remedy that as he turns. His startled eyes meet mine, but before either of us can react, Erin's bedroom door opens and Noah, sleepy-eyed and rumpled, backs out on tiptoe.

My heart does a quick slide to the floor, hits it, then bounces back up to my throat. "What in the *hell* do you think you're doing?" I glance from Noah to Oliver and back again, every cell in my body poised for battle. "Both of you! Do you know what time it is?" Anger burns through my body like a shot of whiskey. I shake from the force of it.

Neither of them move; it's as if they're frozen in place. Suddenly, Mother and Erin are in the hallway, too. I see them through a red haze. All of them.

Erin's face is white and wary. When I start toward Noah, she steps in front of him. "Mom. Don't."

That's all it takes. I lose it. "Get out of here!" I scream at her boyfriend. To his credit, Noah moves Erin aside and faces me. "Get out of my daughter's bedroom and out of this house. Do you understand?"

"Yes, ma'am. I—"

"If I ever see your face here again, I'll—" I pause for a

breath, feel Nathan's hand on my arm, shake it off. "I'll have you thrown in jail. Don't think I won't. She's a minor, did you know that? She's a minor, and I could get you into a lot of trouble, young man."

Now Erin's screaming back at me, crying and screaming words that don't penetrate the roar of anger and fear and worry in my head. And then there's Mother, her arm around Erin, tears in her eyes, saying, "Don't do this, Cecilia," and Oliver behind her, his hands on her shoulders, and behind me, Nathan's on mine.

The roar subsides enough that I finally hear Erin.

"We fell asleep," she screams. "We were watching a movie."

"You expect me to believe that?" I scan her clothing. "Look at you." She wears a T-shirt, no bra, baggy flannel drawstring sleep pants.

Erin crosses her arms. "Believe what you want. I don't care anymore."

"How can I believe you, Erin, when photos show up in a tabloid of you dressed like a slut, out at some bar, and you refuse to even talk to me about it?"

Mother tightens the belt of her robe and shakes her head at Erin. "Oh, Sugar. You didn't tell her?"

I go still. Mother knew? They kept this from me together? I can't say anything, can only stare at them both, feeling like I might explode into a million tiny pieces and splatter the walls.

"Okay." Erin bites her lip, pushes hair from her eyes. "You want to know? I'm in a band." She glances at Noah. He looks like he might pass out. "It's called Cateye, and I've been sneaking out a couple of nights a week to play at a club called

The Beat. They pay us, Mom, and I'm saving the money so I can move out of here in the fall when I go to college. So I can get away from you and finally have a life."

So she can get away from me. A fist in the stomach would've felt like a kiss compared to those words. "You're not eighteen. How do you get into a club?"

"I have a fake ID."

I narrow my eyes at Noah.

"He didn't get it for me, Mom. Judd did. Do you want me to call him so you can yell at him, too? No guy is ever going to be good enough for me, is he? You told me that once. I should've known you really meant it. You'll never let me go. Never. You just want me to stay here and hide, scared of everything, suspicious of everyone, bitter and mad at the world. Like you."

"We used to talk." I choke back tears, my voice quiet now. "What happened?"

"You stopped hearing me, Mom."

Nate rubs my shoulders as I take deep breaths to steady myself. "I just want to know one thing. Did the two of you use protection?"

"See? You're not hearing me now." Erin looks up at the ceiling. "We fell asleep watching a movie."

"Answer me, Erin. Did you use protection?"

"We would've if we'd done anything. How about you two?" She pokes a finger at Nate and me. "Did *you* use protection?"

I feel Nate tense, and shame washes over me. What was I thinking? I *wasn't* thinking. "We're not talking about me. We're talking about you."

Mother steps between us. "Now Erin, Cecilia—"

"You knew about this, didn't you? You knew Erin was sneaking out of the house."

Mother shifts a nervous glance Oliver's way, then meets my gaze. "We've been following her, making sure she's not in any trouble. I—"

"You had no right to keep this from me. She's my daughter—"

"I was wrong, I know that now. I urged Erin to tell you, Sugar. But I guess I should've given her an ultimatum to either tell you, or I would. You just made it so difficult for her with your overprotective—"

"Don't you *sugar* me. So, I'm overprotective? Maybe if you'd been a little more overprotective of me when I was her age, things would've been different. Maybe—"

"CiCi…" Oliver clears his throat. "I'll ask that you not talk to your Mother with that tone."

I turn on him, glaring. "You're not my father. I'll talk to her however I want." Returning my attention to Mother, I say, "You and Erin have been conspiring against me, haven't you? What are you trying to be, Mother? Her friend instead of her grandmother? Look at you and that horny old man…acting like a couple of teenagers. What kind of example is that?"

Everyone glances from me to Nate and back. My knees go weak. So. I get it. I'm a bad example, too. They're right. One night. I slip up once, and look what happens.

I draw a breath. "At least I didn't stand back like you did and watch without saying a word while my seventeen-year-old daughter, your *granddaughter,* let her raging hormones overrule her good sense."

"Shut up!" Erin screams. "Leave her alone! I told you we didn't do anything." When Nate steps forward, she points at him and adds, "And you aren't *my* father, so you keep out of this."

The hallway goes quiet except for the sound of staggered breathing and tears. Mother's the first to break the silence.

"I've made mistakes, I admit that." When I start to interrupt, she lifts a hand. "I'll have my say. I'm seventy-five years old, and I've earned the right to speak my mind. I've been quiet too long, hinting and encouraging and hoping for the best for you, Cecilia. For you and for Erin. Well, I'm through beating around the bush." She blinks again and again, her eyes tired and misty. "I've learned some things over the years, through trial and error. Oh, yes, CiCi, we made lots of errors, your father and I. I'm well aware of that. We weren't perfect. But blind as I am, I see some things more clearly now that I'm an old woman. And here's what I see."

She links her fingers with mine. I don't pull away, just stare at her knuckles, the protruding blue veins on the back of her hand, her long, thin fingers. Fingers exactly like mine.

"You've allowed Bert's escapades and your own regrets to make you close-minded and cynical. Terrified of life. That attitude, my darling, will sabotage not only your relationships with the people you already love," she glances at Nate, "if you let it continue, it will sabotage any chance of a new relationship with a man, as well. Don't you see that? Don't you understand that you're hurting yourself? Hurting Erin?"

I can't speak; I can only stare at our joined hands.

"You've been unwilling to accept Oliver in my life or Noah in Erin's because you're afraid. Isn't that true?"

I tuck my lower lip between my teeth, look up and into

my mother's gentle eyes. I am afraid. Afraid of losing them, of being alone. Afraid they'll get hurt. And that I will, too. Again.

"Mother…I haven't been fair to you. I'm sorry," I say quietly. "It's just so hard to see you with a man who isn't Daddy. And I can't stand the thought of you caring so much for Oliver then losing him, too, some day."

She squeezes my fingers as I turn to Erin. "I'm scared to death you'll repeat my mistakes, that you'll fall in love too soon, before you're ready. That he'll be the wrong person, and you'll end up shattered, like I was."

Tears stream down my daughter's face. Her brows pull together, and her eyes are filled with so many questions. When we're alone, I'll have to tell her about Craig, the boy I loved before her father. And maybe, too, about the baby we lost. That's a decision I'll have to make soon.

"So I guess that in my attempt to protect you, I've gone overboard with restrictions. But it backfired. It forced you to take foolish risks to get what you want and need. What you deserve. The chance to grow up." I take a breath. "But we need some middle ground, Erin. You can't just run wild, doing whatever you please, no matter what."

Erin nods.

"We can get through this, Cecilia," Mother says. "All of us. Together."

I want to. So much. I don't want to be the woman my mother described. I'm tired of being unhappy. Closed off. I don't want to push my family away. I need them now more than ever.

A sob escapes me as Erin steps toward us. She takes her

grandmother's free hand in one of hers, then mine in her other. We form a circle. And I have hope. With their help, I can move on. And let them do the same.

After Oliver and Nathan leave, Mother makes coffee. Then, despite Erin's horrified protests and Noah's cringing embarrassment, the four of us sit down to discuss the responsibilities and risks involved in having sex at any age, but especially as teenagers. Maybe they aren't sleeping together, as Erin has implied, but I still have my doubts. Either way, it won't hurt for them to listen to the facts for an hour, instead of their hormones.

Stars still wink in a navy blue sky when Noah leaves on his cycle. Shivering, I stand on the front porch and watch him drive away. I've realized in the past hour that he's a nice kid; I should've known that all along. Should've trusted that my smart daughter wouldn't care so deeply for anyone who didn't have a good heart.

Despite the cold, I don't go in for a while. I hug myself and watch the horizon. When morning dawns, so does the truth, and I accept it. My daughter is growing up and must be allowed her own mistakes and triumphs. My mother has found true love again. Their lives are changing and so is mine. I think of my evolving counseling practice, of what happened last night with Nate, and smile.

For the first time, excitement trickles through me as I wonder about my future, the next chapter of my life. Some of it won't be written by my hand; I know that. But most of the blank pages are for me to fill.

However I choose.

CHAPTER 25

I have plenty of time to reflect during my flight to New York City, but I'm too nervous and excited to take advantage of it. So I just sit back and endure the bumpy ride.

Bill Burdette, on the advice of his legal counsel, declined an interview. Everett left the decision up to me. He thought telling my side of the story couldn't hurt, and Nate agreed.

So, here I am.

LIVE With Regis and Kelly put me up for the night at the Omni Hotel. At 8:00 p.m., I meet Sela Summers, author of *Penelope's Passion,* in the lobby, and we go to dinner at Tavern on the Green. We've become phone friends over the past three weeks, and I find I like her even more in person. She's smart and ambitious, yet friendly, funny and down-to-earth, too. Sela's giddy over her newfound success, and thanks me with every other breath. Last week, she sent each member of the Parkview Reading group a copy of her new release, *Irma's Indiscretion*.

The next morning, a limo picks us up and takes us to the studio. After that, everything's a blur of excitement until, finally, Sela and I walk onstage serenaded by music.

Regis is funny and warm and witty, while Kelly is gorgeous, enthusiastic and funny, too. Soon I'm at ease, or at least as calm as I'm going to get while on national television. Anyway, I'm relaxed enough to enjoy the conversation with Sela about her book.

I expect jokes about the sex at Parkview, and sure enough, they soon begin.

"Can you *blame* the residents?" Regis asks. "What would *you* choose? Shuffleboard or steamy sex in a gazebo overlooking a *pond?*"

"But the temp that day in Dallas was close to freezing!" Kelly shivers. "Talk about shrinkage!"

The audience roars.

"They had to do it *someplace* cold to stay *awake,*" Regis says. When Kelly slaps his arm, he continues, "Come on! The couple were in their *eighties,* for crying out loud! They need their rest."

I take my cue from Sela who, when teased about the sex in her book, laughed, then set the record straight.

"Like Sela's novels, what happened at Parkview was about relationships, not sex. It had everything to do with human needs, no matter a person's age."

I tell them how Mother came to live with Erin and me after Bert and I separated. How we are three women at three different stages of life with three different sets of issues and points of view. How, despite all that, I've discovered in our hearts, where it counts, we're as much the same as we're different on the surface.

"Through my mother and my daughter, I've come to understand that it doesn't matter if you're young, middle-aged or older, people are alike at the core. Everyone has dreams, fears and desires. Everyone needs love, laughter and acceptance. None of that stops just because children grow up and leave, hair turns gray or faces wrinkle."

Heads nod in agreement all around.

"Life is full of risks, and love is one of them. But, at seventeen or seventy-five, it's a risk worth taking, don't you think? People should be allowed to live until they die, not just exist."

The audience claps. So do Regis and Kelly and Sela.

I feel vindicated.

Sela puts an arm around my shoulders. "I just wish the grown children who filed the lawsuit against you and Parkview Manor would realize the same truth about their own parents. If a steamy novel, be it mine or someone else's, added romance to their lives, that's great!" She relates a quick story about her own mother starting to date after being a widow for the past two years.

Kelly mentions hearing that my counseling practice nosedived when the so-called scandal hit the news, and I explain that, though I did lose prior clients, I gained new ones, that senior citizens from all over the Dallas metroplex and beyond have been making appointments.

I face the camera and take a deep breath. No one knows the decision I've made. Not Nate, not Mother, not Willa, Erin or any of my friends. I didn't know it myself until right this second. "In fact," I say, "I'm shifting the focus of my practice away from marriage and family therapy. From now on, I plan to address the needs and concerns of senior citizens exclusively."

A week later, it snows. Fat, wet flakes fall during the night, and Mom, Erin and I awake on a Saturday morning in early

February to a sight seldom seen in Dallas: the city blanketed in pristine white.

As we drive to Cleburne in the afternoon to attend a wedding shower for the daughter of a family friend, we discuss my new weekly radio show, *Sex and the Senior,* which will air in selected markets starting in the fall. I'll take calls and answer questions on issues affecting senior citizens. After my appearance on *LIVE With Regis and Kelly,* I received offers of every kind. The radio program worked out best for me since I can do it from a Dallas station and still maintain my practice.

Sue Kiley, Donald Quinn and the other plaintiffs dropped the lawsuit against Parkview Manor and me. Though no one ever said, and I didn't ask, I can only assume they saw me on television, too.

We arrive in Cleburne early. I ask Mother, who sits across from me, if she'd like to drive by the old house. At first she says "no," then changes her mind. She's been quiet most of the drive, listening to Erin and me talk, not adding much to the conversation. As we turn into the old neighborhood where I grew up, where she lived with Daddy for so many years, I find out why.

"Did I tell you Oliver asked me to marry him?" Her words are spoken casually, but I notice her head trembles, that her hands are restless in her lap.

For weeks, I've dreaded hearing this news. But I don't feel the resistance I expected, the need to stand up for my father, the fear of this major adjustment ahead in my mother's life. And mine. I imagine her living the rest of her years with Oliver. Somehow, it seems right.

I turn to her with a little laugh of surprise, then look back at the road. "No, you didn't tell us that." Emotion wells up in me. I smile at her. "Oh, Mom…"

"Nana!" Erin squeezes between the bucket seats and gives her grandmother a hug. "When's the wedding?"

Mother blushes and blinks. "I haven't given him an answer yet."

The uncertainty in her voice alarms me. Is this thing with Oliver just an attempt to help her through her grief over Daddy? "Maybe it's too soon, Mother. It's only been a little more than a year since Daddy died."

She shakes her head. "It isn't too soon, Sugar. I'm ready."

I turn the corner onto our old street. "So, you love him?"

"Of course I do."

"Well, what are you waiting for, then? If it's my blessing, you have it." I take one hand from the wheel and cover hers on the seat between us.

"Mine, too," Erin echoes.

Mother's eyes mist. "I know this isn't easy for either of you. If I marry Oliver, things will be different for all of us, I won't pretend otherwise."

"What do you mean, Nana?"

"Well, holidays for one. It won't be only our traditions anymore. I'll have to embrace his, too, of course. And his children, as difficult as they sound, they'll be a part of my family, too. Then there's—"

"Mother…" I squeeze her hand. "Everything's already different. Life changes all the time. We can either adapt, or we can be unhappy. I've spent way too long nursing misery. From now on, I plan to adapt. But if you're not sure about Oliver, then please, please, don't marry him."

"Oh, I'm sure about him." She looks down at her lap. "It's myself I question. Am I wrong to love him? I feel as if I'm betraying your father."

"If you are, then so am I. I care for Oliver, too. Not that I didn't fight it." I laugh. "The sneak. He has a way of working his way into your heart, like it or not."

She laughs with me as I pull to the curb in front of the house. Still, I sense she's not convinced.

"You're not wrong, Mother. You have to go on. We all do."

"So," Erin says when the silence stretches too long, "When are you gonna say 'yes'?"

Mother sighs. "I wish I knew. It's your grandfather I'm waiting on. I talk to him, you know. All the time. Through letters. I asked him for—"

"Nana, look!"

Mother gasps as we glance in the direction Erin points.

At the side of the house sits the only one of Daddy's rose bushes the new owners didn't pull up. Barren from neglect the last time we were here, it's now covered in snow. And in the center of the frosty white bush, as lush and beautiful as if it were spring, blooms one perfect yellow rose.

"Harry..." Mother whispers, and I turn to see tears streaming down her cheeks. She opens the van door and climbs out.

Through our own tears, Erin and I watch her walk across the snow-covered lawn toward the bush, then bend forward to smell my father's last flower.

CHAPTER 26

From The Desk of
Belle Lamont

Dear Harry,
    Thank you.
    From the first moment we met, I loved you, and I never stopped. I will always remember our wonderful years together. I will never forget you.
    Goodbye, my love.
    As always, your yellow rose,
    Belle

To: Noah@friendmail.com
From: Erin@friendmail.com
Date: 08/20 Friday
Subject: Miss you and other stuff
Noah,

It was great to hear your voice last night. Thanks for letting me know you and your parents made the drive safely to Montana. I'm glad you miss me as much as I miss you. And that you love me. I MISS YOU!! How is MSU? How is your dorm? Have you met your roommate? I hope he's okay. I'm glad I have Suz. I would be so nervous to move in with a stranger.

I am e-mailing you from my dorm room! Suz has clothes everywhere already. We are gonna be tripping over each other, but I'm excited! I MISS YOU! If I wasn't so psyched about school starting, I don't know what I'd do.

I wish you could've been at Nana's wedding! It was beautiful! Not stuffy and dull like Dad's to Nat the brat. Nana looked so pretty in her cream-colored suit. Oliver looked handsome and proud. Mom gave Nana away. Or, as Nana said, walked her "into the next season of her life." Isn't that sweet? When it was over, and she and Oliver started down the aisle, some old guy shouted, "that-a-boy, Luther!" Everybody cracked up. Oh, and the funniest part—a few kids Nana and Oliver met at The Beat were there. Reese, Tonto and I played at the reception. (WE MISSED YOU!) Nana and Oliver can really dance! I've never laughed so hard. Anyway, they are in Hawaii now on their honeymoon. When they get back, they'll rent a little condo close to our house. I can't wait until they see the surprise Mom and I have waiting for them. It's a really awesome brass bed. Mom paid a fortune for it but she said Nana's always wanted one, and she deserves it.

Guess what? Maxwell is gonna be a daddy. The mother is our neighbor's poodle, Pom Pom. Mrs. Stein isn't too happy. She thinks Maxwell is a "brute" and not good enough for her precious, prissy poodle. She says Max "took advantage" of Pom Pom. As if. Pom Pom dug the hole and came over to Max. The hoochie. Mom thinks it's hilarious because Mrs. Stein has been trying to fix Mom up since the day Dad left and, instead, the dogs got together. Anyway, we wondered what had perked Max up, and now we know.

Well, tonight is my first night away from home. Mom cried when she left me here, but I think she'll be okay. She's really busy with her work and her new radio show starts soon. She and the Margarita Martyrs have started walking in the evenings and she's lost most of the weight she put on when she was stuffing her face 24/7. Oh, and she and Nate are still on. That dating-other-people-for-a-while-just-to-make-sure thing she suggested to him lasted about five minutes. They're together all the time. It's still weird for me to see her with another guy besides Dad, but Nate's nice and he doesn't try to act like my dad's stand-in. I'd rather see her with him than someone else.

So...have you met any girls? Do they have hairy armpits and legs? Never mind! Suz told me to ask that! Still, I secretly hope they are as hairy as King Kong. And as big, too. <grin>

Well, gotta go. Next time I write, I'll have gone to class and, hopefully, met some people. I'll tell you about everything. Write or call me soon and tell me everything that's going on with you. I MISSY OU!!!!!!!!!!!!!!!!!!!!!!!!!!!!!!!!!!!!!!

Love and miss you bunches,
Erin

CHAPTER 28

Cecilia Dupree
Day Planner
Monday, 08/23

1. 8 a.m.—First Sex & The Senior radio show.
2. 9:30 a.m.—New pt. appt—Maevis Carlyle (struggling w/staying active).
3. 11:00—pt. appt—George Godfrey (grief counseling over wife's death).
4. Noon—lunch @ home (salad). Check on Pom Pom. Decline date w/Mrs. Stein's husband's cousin's son. Excuse: incest (we're now related through granddogs).
5. 2:00—Parkview Reading Group. Start new Sela Summers novel, Daphne's Desire. (save copy for Mother and Oliver.)
6. 4:00—pt. follow-up—Iris & Stanley McDougal (marriage counseling over Iris's continued phone relationship w/obscene caller).
7. 6:00—Walk w/Martyrs, then put away Erin's baby photos & stop crying.

8.   8:00—Dinner w/Nate. Accept invite to weekend
     in Cozumel next month. These conditions:
     (a) pressure about the scuba (maybe, maybe not);
     (b) iffy on bikini for me (no promises);
     (c) definitely no Speedo for him (Pu-leese!);
     (d) no wine (well, maybe a little);
     (e) separate rooms (extremely negotiable).

Visit the shop on Blossom Street again!
A GOOD YARN *by Debbie Macomber*
will be available in February 2007.

It's a year later, and Lydia's shop is thriving.
Visit old friends Alix, Jacqueline and Carol,
spend time with Margaret and Brad, watch Lydia's
relationships unfold and meet new friends
you'll come to love.

Turn the page for an excerpt from the first chapter...

One

"Making a sock by hand creates a connection to history; we are offered a glimpse into the lives of knitters who made socks using the same skills and techniques we continue to use today."
—Nancy Bush is the author of Folk Socks (1994), Folk Knitting in Estonia (1999) and Knitting on the Road, Socks for the Traveling Knitter, (2001), all published by Interweave Press

Knitting saved my life. It saw me through two lengthy bouts of cancer, a particularly terrifying kind that formed tumors inside my brain and tormented me with indescribable headaches. I experienced pain I could never have imagined before. Cancer destroyed my teen years and my twenties, but I was *determined* to survive.

I'd just turned sixteen the first time I was diagnosed, and I learned to knit while undergoing chemotherapy. A woman with breast cancer, who had the chemo chair next to mine, used to knit and she's the one who taught me. The chemo was dreadful—not quite as bad as the headaches, but close. Because of knitting, I was able to endure those endless hours of weakness and severe nausea. With two needles and a skein of yarn, I felt I could face whatever I had to. My hair fell out in clumps, but I could weave yarn around a needle and create a stitch; I could follow a pattern and finish a project. I couldn't hold down more than a few bites at a time, but I could knit. I clung to that small sense of accomplishment, treasured it.

Knitting was my salvation—knitting and my father.

After he died, I realized I had a choice: what to do with the rest of my life. I wanted to honor my father in whatever I chose, and that meant I was prepared to take some risks.

I opened a yarn store on Blossom Street in Seattle. That might not seem earth-shattering to anyone else, but for me, it was a leap of faith equal to Noah's building the ark without a rain cloud in sight. I had an inheritance from my grandparents and gambled every cent on starting my own business. Me, who's never held down a job for more than a few weeks. Me, who knew next to nothing about finances, profit-and-loss statements or business plans. I sank every dime I had into what I *did* know, and that was yarn and knitters. Naturally, there were a few problems. At the time, Blossom Street was undergoing a major renovation—in fact, the architect's wife, Jacqueline Donovan, was one of the women in my first knitting class. Jacqueline, Carol and Alix, my original students, remain three of my closest friends to this day.

I didn't get the support you might expect from my family. Mom, bless her, tried to be encouraging, but she was in shock after losing Dad. She still is. Most days, she wanders around hopelessly in a fog of grief and loss. When I mentioned my plan, she didn't discourage me, but she wasn't actually cheering me on, either.

My older sister, Margaret, on the other hand, had no qualms about drowning me in tales of doom and gloom. The day I opened my doors for business, she marched in with a spate of dire forecasts. The economy was down, she told me; people were hanging onto their money. I'd be lucky to stay afloat for six weeks. Ten minutes of listening to her ominous predictions, and I was ready to rip up the lease and close my door—until I realized this was my first official day on the job and I had yet to sell a single skein of yarn.

As you might've guessed, Margaret and I have a complicated relationship. Don't get me wrong; I love my sister.

But Margaret, to put it mildly, isn't the warm, spontaneous type. I didn't understand how much she cared until I had a third cancer scare just a few months after I opened A Good Yarn. *Scare* doesn't come close to describing my feelings when Dr. Wilson ordered those frightening, familiar tests. It was as if my entire world had come to a sudden halt. The truth is, I don't think I could've endured the struggle yet again. I'd already decided that if the cancer *had* returned, I would refuse treatment.

My come-what-may attitude disturbed Margaret, who wouldn't accept my fatalism. Talk of death unsettled her, the way it does most people, but when you've been around death and dying as much as I have, it's as natural as turning off the lights. I don't look forward to dying, but I'm not afraid of it either. Thankfully, the tests came back negative and I'm thriving, right along with my yarn store. The only reason I mention it now is that it was during those few weeks that I discovered how deeply my sister loves me. In the last seventeen years, I've only seen her cry twice—when Dad died and when Dr. Wilson gave me a clean bill of health.

Once I returned to work full-time, Margaret bullied and cajoled me into contacting Brad Goetz again. Brad, who drives the UPS truck that makes deliveries to A Good Yarn, is the man I'd started seeing last year. He's divorced and has custody of his eight-year-old son, Cody. It would be an understatement to say Brad is good-looking; the fact is, he's drop-dead gorgeous. The first day he came into the store, wheeling several cartons of yarn, it was all I could do to keep the drool from dripping down my chin. I got so flustered I could hardly sign for the delivery. He asked me out three times before I finally agreed to meet him for drinks. Given my experience, male-female relationships fluster me and I was sure I'd be completely out of my element dating Brad. I would never have found the courage to say yes if not for Margaret, who harassed me into it.

I always say that A Good Yarn is my affirmation of life, but according to my sister I was afraid to really live, afraid to venture outside the tiny comfortable world I'd created inside my yarn store. She was right and I knew it, but still I resisted. The truth is, it'd been so many years since I'd spent any amount of time with a man other than my father or my physician that I had the social finesse of a dandelion. But Margaret wouldn't listen to a single excuse, and soon Brad and I were having drinks together, followed by dinners, picnics with Cody and ball games. I've come to love Brad's son as much as I do my two nieces, Julia and Hailey.

These days Brad and I see quite a bit of each other. We're cautious—okay, I'm the one who's taking things slow, but Brad's fine with that. He was burned once when his ex-wife walked out, claiming she needed to "find herself." There's Cody to consider, too. The boy has a close relationship with Brad, and while Cody loves me too, I don't want to disrupt that special bond between father and son. So far, everything is going well, and we're talking more and more about a future together. Brad and Cody are so much a part of my life now that I couldn't imagine being without them.